£ 3.49

F (42)

CW01085846

Fleur

Enjoy the journey!

With love

Anna-Marie

xx

Anna-Maria Athanasiou is a wife and mother of two, who after many years of creating fantasy stories in her head decided to take the plunge and put one of them onto paper. She wanted to write a story people could relate to and consequently feel an empathy with her characters. A story that would touch the reader and ultimately make them fall in love. *Waiting for Summer* is her first novel.

WAITING FOR SUMMER

BOOK ONE

Dedication

For the three men in my life. Marios, George and Michael.
I was recently told that I was the luckiest woman in the
world because I have three men that loved me.
I *am* the luckiest woman in the world, because I love *them;*
totally, completely and unconditionally.

Anna-Maria Athanasiou

WAITING FOR SUMMER

BOOK ONE

AUSTIN MACAULEY
PUBLISHERS LTD.

Copyright © Anna-Maria Athanasiou

The right of Anna-Maria Athanasiou to be identified as author of this work has been asserted by her in accordance with section 77 and 78 of the Copyright, Designs and Patents Act 1988.

All rights reserved. No part of this publication may be reproduced, stored in a retrieval system, or transmitted in any form or by any means, electronic, mechanical, photocopying, recording, or otherwise, without the prior permission of the publishers.

Any person who commits any unauthorized act in relation to this publication may be liable to criminal prosecution and civil claims for damages.

A CIP catalogue record for this title is available from the British Library.

ISBN 978 1 84963 503 5

www.austinmacauley.com

First Published (2013)
Austin Macauley Publishers Ltd.
25 Canada Square
Canary Wharf
London
E14 5LB

Printed and Bound in Great Britain

Acknowledgments

I have been extraordinarily lucky over the past two years to have had the continued support of my family and friends. I could not have finished *Waiting for Summer* without their encouragement. A huge thank you to the three loves of my life, Marios, George and Michael who put up with my mood swings and my craziness as I bashed away and allowed 'standards' to drop! Who were all as excited as I was and helped me 'technically'. There were times when they were not best pleased with my obsession, but thankfully they endured it.

An enormous thank you to all at **Austin Macauley Publishers**. Especially to Hayley, Annette and Robert, who gave me and *Waiting for Summer* the opportunity to be published, a dream that came true for me. To Vinh, thank you so much for putting up with my continuing harassment and the rest of the production team who had to deal with all my toing and froing.

I will be forever grateful to my Aunty Maria for her animated words and thoughts. My friend Emma whose simple 'more please' kept me going, they were both the first sounding boards for my writing, their encouragement spurred me on. My cousin Christina miles away, who even though she was passing through a difficult time, still managed to encourage me. My cousins Lee, Kamini and Eva whose expertise I truly value.

A big thank you to my Aunt Liz who made me laugh with her interesting comments, (you know which ones) and Irina my sister-in-law, we shed a number of tears together over this.

To my friends Laura and Janneka for their perspective, and to Jackie and Sarah, their continuing and colourful feedback brought a smile to my face and a giggle to my lips. To Lucy, whose unbelievable enthusiasm for my story had me grinning from ear to ear for days, I'm incredibly grateful. Thank you Sue in Australia, whom I have never met, for taking the time and effort and giving me your unbiased opinion. A big thanks to Lilianna, you know why, and to my techno man Savvas, who saved my life!

Jaine, mon amie, Jaine who after over twenty years tracked me down and reconnected with me. My college buddy whose selfless encouragement and support made me think that *Waiting for Summer* could be published, without her I would never have taken the plunge, I will always be indebted to you.

To my parents who have always believed only the best of me, when I'm really not worthy. My Mum's words of wisdom and my Dad's unlimited and constant help and their unconditional and endless love. And finally to my brother Antony, who railroaded me totally and completely into doing things I was incredibly uncomfortable doing. You pushed me to take the risk and thankfully, by some miracle, it paid off. Thank you.

PART ONE

AUTUMN

A wind has blown the rain away, and blown the sky away and all the leaves away, and the trees stand. I think I, too, have known autumn too long.

E. E. Cummings

CHAPTER 1

CHANGING TIME

S ylvie was up at around six as usual; no matter what time she slept, it was at six o'clock on the dot that her eyes opened.

It didn't matter that she always wore her eye mask to obliterate any kind of light, be it sunlight or the TV Chris had forgotten to put on the timer, again. He couldn't sleep without it on, it drove her insane but after twenty two years she had resigned to his many idiosyncrasies. It was the last Sunday in October and it was still warm. That was the best part of moving to Cyprus; autumn and winter in England were unbearable, dull, wet, cold and miserable. The sun shone eleven months of the year here. When Chris and Sylvie had lived in England, the standard question every morning was, 'What's the weather like?' Once they had moved, the question was still asked every morning until one day Chris asked that same question and was greeted with:

"Chris, sweetie. For six months you've asked me the same question every day, and every day I tell you it's sunny and warm. Don't you get it yet? It's sunny every day!"

Sylvie stepped into the bathroom and examined her face as she brushed her teeth. She splashed cold water over it so as to shock her sleep wrinkles away. It was no good though, they were still there as she patted her face dry. She felt her age in the morning. That was the thing that no one prepared you for once you passed your forties. You may look better as your face repositioned itself as the morning moved on, but that first look in the mirror made the years you could rub out with creams and concealer creep back on your face for the morning. She knew she looked good for her age, at least six or seven years younger. But there was no escaping inevitable crow's feet and blotchiness. She pulled her chestnut hair into a loose pony tail, slipped on her thin dressing gown as she looked at Chris sprawled out on their bed. His long limbs splayed over his and her side of the bed, the sheet barely covering his naked body. He was in really good shape again, he'd been exercising over the last six months and it showed. Sylvie crept down the stairs leaving Chris sound asleep in bed.

This was the best time of day for her. No one was up and she had time to collect her thoughts, or just daydream before everyone bombarded her with requests, or chit chat. She glanced at the clock in the kitchen as she flicked on the kettle. Six fifteen. She strolled over to where her phone was and checked for messages when she noticed the time. Five fifteen? That couldn't be right. Of course – the clocks went back last night! Sylvie hated that job, resetting the clocks. Their house was strewn with clocks. There were four in the kitchen alone; microwave, oven, wall clock, and central heating and water timer. Luckily her phone change automatically. She put the tea in the pot and let it brew while she started tracking down all the clocks around the house. *So much for gathering my thoughts!* she thought. *At least I get an extra hour alone.*

It took about twenty minutes to find them all. Sylvie looked in every room to double check when she remembered Chris's watch. He usually left it in the hall along with his mobile on the charger. She picked it up and looked at it, six forty three. The Omega watch was the first present she'd ever bought him while they were married. She'd bought him hundreds of presents over their twenty two years together, but always with money he had earned. This was the first she had bought with *her* money, and it had felt fantastic.

He had been absolutely flabbergasted. He was used to the customary, clothes, underwear, aftershave under the Christmas tree, but that particular year he was totally taken back by the small beautifully wrapped box. His face had absolutely beamed. That had been the best present she'd ever had. His phone luckily automatically changed the time, thank goodness for technology!

The sun filtered in through the window, sending a beautiful array of coloured light through the crystals that Sylvie had hung in the windows around the sitting room and kitchen. She poured her tea and settled into the settee, tucking her feet under her like she always did.

She loved this time of day. Their house had a panoramic view of the sea and the city stretching twenty kilometres across. You could see the boats coming in or leaving the port and the morning sea mist rising defusing the sun's gaze. The sea looked so calm and still, there really was nothing more therapeutic than just staring out over the city as it was waking up and then to the beach spreading out towards the sea.

The time passed, and Sylvie walked back to the kitchen to make her second cup of tea. Then she remembered Chris had his car phone, which was an old model. She knew she had better change the time on that too; he'd never get round to it and to be honest he didn't know how to do it! She grabbed the keys and made her way to the garage.

The Mercedes that Chris drove was an older model, but he loved it; he wasn't one for flashy state of the art technology. He'd had the car five years and it had already been another five years old when he had bought it. It was very much like him; charming, well kept, classic... with a very powerful engine!

Sylvie scrabbled with the phone, which was plugged into the car. While she was there she also decided to adjust the car's clock too, so she started up the engine. As she reset the phone a message bleeped through. *That was strange*, she thought: *at six forty five in the morning, on the car phone?*

Without thinking, she opened up in the Inbox.

It happened within a split second, the realisation, the pit in her stomach. Her whole body ran cold and her ears were burning.

'Xxxxxx'

The message read. The number wasn't familiar, or saved. Shaking Sylvie scrolled back to see the time it was sent: five to twelve yesterday. Chris had been out with a colleague, Julian. He was home by eleven thirty, which granted was early for him. She then scrolled the Inbox and there to her horror were over thirty messages from the same number.

> 'When can you get away babes x'
> 'Hope you weren't bored x'
> 'Miss you, need you, want you xxxx'
> 'Not as much as me! Xxx,

And so they went on. At first she wanted to delete them, to make them disappear, her heart was racing. Had he sent replies from this phone? Her finger hovered over the key which would open 'sent'. There they were, again over thirty of them.

> 'I'm in a meeting will be there in 1 hr. x'
> 'Family lunch'
> 'Can't wait xxx'
> 'I'm so turned on!'

Sylvie ran out of the car and just made it to the kitchen sink to throw up.

"Are you alright, Mam?" came the gentle voice of Marcy the housekeeper. Shit! It must have been after seven already and everyone would be around.

"I'm fine Marcy, just an upset stomach."

"You must have really strained yourself Mam; your eyes are running terribly."

"Yes, I just need to sort out the car and I'll be back in a second, could you please make me a ginger tea to settle my stomach?" She gripped the side of the sink to steady herself.

Slowly walking back to the car she was thankful that Marcy only popped in on Sundays to drop off groceries. Carefully Sylvie put back the phone exactly as it was but leaving the correct time. She sat for a moment to get herself together before walking back to the kitchen.

Marcy was pouring the tea with a concerned look on her face. "You're sure you're okay Mam? Your tea's ready, sit down a moment."

"Oh I'm fine Marcy, just an upset stomach from those wretched migraines I keep getting. Thanks for the tea. You really didn't need to come this morning, I'm sure Petros and you have plans."

And so the banter went on for the next fifteen minutes. What were they doing today? How was her daughter settling in at college? Had Petros managed to save the lemon trees at the top of the garden? Any kind of small talk to distract her from the pounding in her chest.

Thankfully Petros, Marcy's husband for the last seven years came in ready to go to his village for the day, leaving Sylvie sat at the kitchen table with a promise to bring back whatever was ripe from his family's orchard.

Marcy had been a godsend to Sylvie. She had come to work for them almost twenty years ago when Sylvie had fallen pregnant with their second child. She had come to Cyprus as a housemaid from Columbia and had left her two year-old daughter behind. Once Sylvie had realised that she was more than a housemaid and was able to run the house exactly the way that Sylvie herself ran it, she insisted her daughter should also come to live with them. Marcy's husband had died in a car accident so this arrangement was everything Marcy could ever have wanted. Her daughter Teresa was then educated locally and Marcy could work without being far away from her. Though Marcy was very much part of the family she insisted on addressing Sylvie as 'Mam' and Chris as 'Sir', which had never sat well with either of them. However, over the twenty years they had got used to it.

Marcy had consequently met Petros, Sylvie's garden contractor while working for her. Their relationship grew over two years. It was so heart warming to witness a man whose wife had left him because he could not have children fall in love with a woman who had lost her husband and struggled to raise her daughter. They were truly meant to be. Call it fate,

Karma or divine intervention, Petros and Marcy, along with Teresa, had found each other.

The sun streamed through the French doors and Sylvie's tears dripped into her tea. What was she going to do? She couldn't go through this again. She couldn't believe it was happening to her. She opened up the doors leading out to the garden, shrugged off her dressing gown and walked to the edge of the swimming pool. The sunlight was bouncing off the water's surface, making it glisten and, without a second thought, she plunged into it.

CHAPTER 2

SUNDAY LUNCH

"Sylvie? What the hell are you doing! It's freezing in there. Come on, get out. Let me get you a towel."

Chris had come down to the kitchen to grab a coffee and seen her in the pool. Throughout the summer, Sylvie swam every morning. However, the pool hadn't been connected up to the solar heating yet, now that it was getting cooler, so the pool was cold. He reached out his hand to help her out of the pool and hauled her out.

"Jesus, Sylvie, you'll catch your death. You're shaking all over." He wrapped her in a towel he'd retrieved from the pool house and started rubbing her. She stood there like a child watching him.

"There that's better. You didn't even have your costume on. I really need to sort out the heater for the pool, remind me tomorrow. Let's get you inside and get you out of those wet clothes."

The whole time, Sylvie just looked at him. How could he be so caring and loving, and yet be cheating on her? He was holding her tightly and she could feel the heat from his arms through the towel. He had managed to acquire a deep, dark tan this summer, which was unusual. He usually avoided the beach or the pool, but this summer had been different. His recent re-interest in the gym had knocked years off him. No one would have guessed he was in his late forties. Sylvie looked into his dark eyes.

"I'm fine," she replied weakly.

He looked at her for the first time. "Are you alright, darling? What were you thinking?" He was genuinely concerned and reluctantly let her go.

"Really I'm fine, I had a bad headache and thought if I cooled off it might subside. Let me go change."

She had to get out of there; her voice was breaking and he would know something was wrong. She ran up to their room and jumped into the shower, allowing the heat of the water warm up her frozen skin. Chris followed her upstairs out of concern, which was something she really didn't want, so she stayed in a little longer than normal so that she could pull herself together.

"Do you want company?" Chris was in the bathroom sat on the closed toilet seat, and Sylvie started to panic. Normally a morning sex session in the shower would have been just up her street. Her hands were still shaking as she messed with the shampoo bottle.

"The best remedy for a headache is exercise, you know." He was teasing her as he usually did.

"Morning!" the familiar voice chimed from the hallway. It was Markus, their youngest son. He had just walked in. With the shock of the phone messages, Sylvie had forgotten he was coming home on leave this morning. As usual, he'd barged into their room without thinking. "Please don't tell me you're at it in the shower. I'll be scarred for life!"

"Don't be silly, sweetie! I'm in the shower and Dad's just keeping me company. I won't be a mo. I hope you didn't drag your muddy boots through the house…again!" Sylvie called to him from the bathroom. At least she'd be able to be distracted with Markus in the house today and it had gotten her out of a very awkward situation with Chris.

"Bang goes that idea, then. Maybe later?" Chris whispered, then reached into the shower and squeezed her bottom. Sylvie flinched, but he didn't notice.

Thankfully they'd both gone downstairs before she'd got out of the shower which gave her time to get dressed and collect her thoughts. There was nothing she could do right now. She didn't want a confrontation with Markus in the house. She'd just have to put her best acting face on and grin and bear it.

Alex, their eldest son, was also due back this week for a short break from university too, so she'd have to hold it all together until Tuesday when he left. That would mean eight days of faking it, keeping it together and going through the motions. She could feel the anxiety cramps starting. She reached into the medicine cabinet and gulped down some antacid. How would she manage that? At least she'd have cooled down by then. Maybe gain some perspective. Maybe even find out it wasn't what she thought it was. She flicked on the hair dryer and gently massaged her head to dry her hair. *Fat chance!* She thought.

She padded downstairs to find Chris and Markus drinking coffee and talking about his week. She went straight over to hug and kiss him.

"Hi sweetie, how's it been this week?" He'd been in since July and after basic training he'd been transferred to a camp around fifteen miles away. He was out most Sundays.

"Same old stuff, Mum – guarding, running, hiking. You know, army stuff. I do get bored though." Markus was an athletic boy and had always been very active, so he wasn't put out that he had to do just over a year national service. He was tall, six foot two, and slim. He was very artistic and originally had wanted to study fine art. However he realised it wasn't a degree he could use so much in later life and decided to follow in his elder brother's footsteps and study architecture.

"The time will fly past. It'll over before you know it." Sylvie started making herself some more tea as she spoke. "What shall we do for lunch today? Any ideas?" She hoped that Markus wanted to eat out, or at least see some friends so that she wasn't forced to play 'happy families'. Her hands were still shaking but luckily no one had noticed.

"I need a hot shower first. I brought my dirty clothes too so they need washing. I'd like to go down by the marina you know. Stathis's place. We haven't been down there in ages." Chris and Sylvie always did something special for him when he came out. They would always choose what he'd prefer and normally he'd want to invite a friend along. "I thought I'd ask Greg to come, is that ok?"

"Whatever you want Markus. I'll meet you both down there. I'm off to meet Zach for a coffee down town. I may get them to come along too. I'll ring Stathis and book it for one thirty. Is that alright?" Chris leant over to kiss Sylvie bye, he picked up his keys, watch and phone and started for the door. "Is this the right time Sylvie?" he looked at his watch and then at the kitchen clock.

"Yes. I've changed all the clocks and watches. Your mobile adjusts automatically because it's a new one." She stopped and thought very carefully before she added, "I changed the clock in the car too." She watched as he nodded, still looking at his watch as he put it on. He ran his fingers nervously through his slightly greying hair and then turned his head slightly, as though he was going to ask something, but then he thought better of it and headed for the garage.

"He still can't change the clock in the car Mum?" Markus remarked in disbelief. Sylvie smiled a half smile and shook her head. Had it crossed his mind about his phone? If he saw the correct time on it he would know that she had done it. At least it would make him worry a bit. Keep him guessing as to whether she'd seen the messages or not. What would he do? Ask her outright? That was never going to happen. Let him sweat it out a bit. The next eight days would be hard enough for her, why shouldn't he suffer too?

Sylvie walked over to the docking station and pressed the remote so the radio came on. Sylvie loved to listen to music. She always had some on, whether it was the radio or her iPod; she hated the quiet, especially while she was cooking or working. She would often dance around the room ,to the horror of her children. They'd got used to it now but she was sure they didn't approve.

"So when's Alex back?" He was swinging on the chair as he spoke, his young face calm and carefree. He watched his Mum mumble along to a song.

"Wednesday, he gets in around five in the afternoon." Alex was away at university studying. He was a very gentle boy who was greatly missed by all of them. He had a very calming effect on all his family. He had always been more mature than his years and as he had become older he had turned into a very quietly confident man. He had been a strong influence on Markus and he missed him terribly. Alex's frequent visits back home were for his benefit.

There had never been any rivalry between the boys. Markus looked up to Alex and always consulted him on most issues. Alex always gave him the best objective advice he could. They were very different and what may have been right for Alex did not always apply to Markus. He was very careful to point this out. Alex admired Markus's drive and competitiveness.

Even though Alex was good in his field he had a more relaxed manner, Markus had always needed to be the best or, at least, he pushed himself as far as he could to get to his goal. Both Chris and Sylvie were thrilled that they had chosen architecture as this would mean that they would be able to be part of their expanding company.

Sylvie and Markus spent the next couple of hours catching up before they headed down to the marina. Markus's friend Greg was already waiting for them with Chris along with Lilianna and Zach.

Zach was Chris's oldest friend and partner. They had known each other from school and while Chris had left to go study, Zach had stayed to help his father run his small builders merchants business. Once Chris was back and had set up his developing company he'd asked him to join him as the business was growing rapidly. Zach had been Chris's right hand man since. Lilianna was his fiancé at the time and so the four of them had become very close. Their lives were always intertwined, be it business or personal.

Sylvie was glad to see them. It would make the lunch less stressful. Lilianna would no doubt talk non-stop and take her mind off things. She saw them sat on the terrace. Lilianna's slight figure and her blonde bob swinging has she talked animatedly. Zach was leaning back in his usual relaxed manner, his dark complexion in complete contrast to Lilianna's. Her heart started pounding as she approached the table. Thankfully they would definitely diffuse any tension that she was feeling. Sylvie said her hello's and sat next to Lilianna.

"Hi sweetie. How are you?" Lilianna smiled at Sylvie, genuinely pleased to see her.

"Ok, you?" They hugged and kissed each other.

"Great, the gallery called. The painting's ready, so you can pick it up in the morning. In fact, if you don't mind, we can meet for coffee and we'll go together. What do you say?" Sylvie was having a painting framed by a friend of Lilianna's. She'd just finished an interior design job and the painting was the finishing touch.

"That's sounds like a great idea."

"What's a great idea?" Chris overheard.

"I've got to drop something off at Julian's tomorrow, so we're meeting for coffee first." Sylvie could hardly look at him, but he didn't seem to notice.

"Oh, I forgot to tell you. He told me last night how thrilled he was with everything. He said he's going to recommend you to everyone. Honestly Sylvie, he's really pleased. He'll bring you loads of business, he's very well connected."

"Who's well connected?" It was Stathis, the restaurant owner. He was a friend of Chris and Zach's. He owned a couple of restaurants and two nightclubs. All had been built or remodelled by Chris.

"Stathis, how are you? We're talking about Julian the architect. Sylvie just decorated his offices." Chris was up and shaking his hand. Stathis beamed over to Sylvie. He had classic good looks, like a movie star in the fifties and he oozed charm.

"Really... that's great. Chris is right, he's very well connected. He will bring loads of work your way. I want you to come down to my new club that I'm opening. You always get a feel for the place. Better get in early before you get swamped, eh! What do you say Chris?" He looked expectantly at Chris.

"You know Sylvie's always there at the start of all my projects. I wouldn't have it any other way." He leant over and took her hand. "She's the best thing that ever happened to me.

I can't imagine what I'd do without her." He picked up her hand and kissed it, making Sylvie blush and feel even more uncomfortable.

"I know, Chris... What she saw in you I'll never understand!" He joked back at him. "Bring her next Monday, when we go and have a look at it. You've been bang on about every one of my places, Sylvie; I really would appreciate your input."

Sylvie had always liked Stathis, he was a real gentleman, and almost had an aristocratic air about him. His businesses had always been his priority, but he had recently married and had managed to balance family life too. "Of course I'll come. I'd love to see the place."

"She might charge you now though for her opinion." Chris warned Stathis with a smile, "She's got her own business to think about now!" Chris laughed.

"Well I'd rather work with Sylvie than you any day." Sylvie felt her face flush slightly feeling uncomfortable with all the attention. She shied away from it, but Chris always wanted to shine the spotlight on her, it was something she still found hard to accept.

The conversation continued as it usually did with Zach, Stathis and Chris ribbing each other about how old they were getting. The times they had at school and catching up on what was going on in mutual friends' lives.

Sylvie and Lilianna listened while they chatted as she watched on Sylvie started to feel nauseous. She knew it was the stress and she got up to head for the restrooms as her stomach cramped. Lilianna, seeing her lose her colour, accompanied her while the men carried on talking thankfully oblivious. Sylvie made it to the sink just before she started to retch.

"Jeez Sylvie, are you alright?" Sylvie nodded as she rinsed her mouth out then popped an antacid. "If I didn't know you better, I'd think you were pregnant!" Lilianna chuckled.

Sylvie shot her a murderous look and Lilianna made a mock sorrowful face. Lilianna had unwittingly hit a nerve. Sylvie had come to that age in her life where she knew that any more children were out of the question. Even if she wanted to, at the age of forty three she couldn't and she felt a slight tinge of sorrow. Chris had insisted on a vasectomy a year after Markus was born. He really didn't want any more children.

He loved his boys tremendously, but they had put a strain on their marriage and the thought of more didn't appeal to him at all. Sylvie had always wanted four children. She had three older brothers and loved being part of a large family. Chris was an only child and wasn't used to 'sharing', so Sylvie had reluctantly agreed.

When they had decided to start a family it had happened instantaneously. Sylvie always joked that Chris only needed to look at her and she fell pregnant. Sylvie now wondered whether he'd opted for a vasectomy for other reasons other than not getting only her pregnant. That thought nagged at her now in the light of her recent discovery.

Sylvie pulled herself together and they headed back out to the terrace of the restaurant. Before long it was time to set off home. Sylvie loved it at the marina. She watched the boats and yachts bobbing in the bay. The marina had only recently been finished and had brought new life to the old port district. There was a huge array of shops and cafes along with very smart restaurants. The best part was that you could walk around and look at the boats. As it got later the boat owners brought their yachts back into dock and the whole marina was alive with activity.

"They look so majestic, don't they?" Sylvie turned to Lilianna as she spoke. Everyone was getting up and saying their goodbyes. "What a fabulous feeling of freedom, to be able to sail away whenever you want." Right now that's exactly what she would have wanted to do. Anything but have to deal with what was going on in her life.

Chris was by her side, he put his arm around her. It felt good to have him touch her.

"Julian's son just bought one. Maybe I could get him to take you out on it." She turned to him as he spoke. He was watching her with his dark eyes. He squeezed her and kissed her forehead tenderly as they set off to their car. This was going to be much harder than she had ever imagined.

CHAPTER 3

THE PAINTING

Sunday had been a real test. Sylvie's anxiety cramps had gotten worse as she carried on her charade for the sake of appearances. She needed to be sure of what was really going on. She couldn't accuse Chris without being absolutely sure.

This morning she wanted to be up and out of the house before Chris had even woken up. She didn't want to spend any more time with him than necessary. Markus had left late last night, so she hadn't needed to be there for him either. She quickly showered and dried her hair after her morning swim, being as careful as possible not to wake him. Sylvie scanned her wardrobe trying to choose something to wear.

Her eyes fell on her red wraparound dress that she knew Chris liked. Well – maybe she should fight fire with fire, she thought. Pulling out her red silky bra and the thong that she had bought a few weeks back, she snipped off the labels and wriggled into them, then slipped on her dress and her red sling-backs. She stood back to check herself in the mirror. Maybe it was a little too low-cut for a morning coffee.

"Hey you're up early." Chris stood in the entrance of her dressing room.

"Oh you're up. Yes I'm meeting Lilianna for a coffee then picking up that painting for Julian's office." Chris narrowed his eyes and nodded, his eyes travelling slowly over her body making her feel a little nervous.

"You look lovely in that dress." His eyes darkened.

"Not too much?" Sylvie asked innocently.

Chris squinted and twisted his mouth. "I'll change if it is," she added, seeing his reaction.

Chris immediately corrected his expression. "No, don't. I like you in that dress."

"Okay, I'd better get going." She leaned to give him a peck on the lips as she always did, but he pulled her closer and kissed her harder, taking her by surprise.

"You sure you can't stay a little bit longer?" his voice was husky.

"Sorry, I'm already running late." She pulled herself back and Chris reluctantly let her go. Sylvie exited her bedroom as fast as she could. Her head was spinning and her body quivering. Shit, he could still turn her insides upside down!

Chris was leaving for Athens on one of his many business trips in a week's time. It had occurred to her that maybe Chris wasn't going alone. In fact the more she thought about it, the more it seemed likely. She would need to find out.

The meeting they'd arranged with Stathis had been unfortunate, but she couldn't very well change it without revealing to Chris that she knew about his so-called business trip. She'd have to find time before he left to confront him.

She drove down to her usual coffee shop where Lilianna was waiting for her. They met up at least three times a week. Today was a little different as she was going with Sylvie to an art gallery to collect the painting that would finish off her first interior design job for Julian. She'd put on her red fitted dress in an attempt to cheer herself up; she loved the colour. It reminded her of strawberries, warmth and love. Sylvie sighed inwardly. She really was an incurable romantic.

Julian was an architect friend and colleague of Chris's. He had asked Sylvie to redesign his offices after seeing what she had done for Chris. The painting was in a gallery owned by a friend of Lilianna's.

Lilianna was sitting at their usual table waiting for her. She had already ordered their drinks.

"Morning sweetie." Sylvie hugged and kissed her oldest friend.

"Morning." Lilianna was always so pleased to see Sylvie. "Wow, you look lovely in that dress."

Sylvie flushed shyly and muttered her thanks. "It's not too slutty is it?"

"Slutty? Sylvie honey, you could never look slutty, not even in a micro mini and a boob tube, not that you'd ever wear them." She laughed.

They had been each other's crutches throughout their married lives. Lilianna was one of the few people Sylvie felt at total ease with. She was her surrogate sister without the rivalry. They were very different in character but they shared very similar views. Their approach may have differed but their goals were the same.

Lilianna was a straight talker. She said it how it was. She was very black and white. In contrast, Sylvie was very much the diplomat. She hated hurting anyone's feelings and avoided confrontations and would do her damnedest to find a middle ground. Lilianna did have a soft side though. Children loved her. Both Alex and Markus adored her. Chris had always cared for her too, but was a little wary of her as she would often call him on anything. Zach was the softest and gentlest person and they complimented each other perfectly.

Sylvie had been with her when she had miscarried her first child and helped her back to recovery. Lilianna had taken it very badly, as they had had difficulty conceiving. When she did eventually fall pregnant again, Sylvie had insisted she come stay with her as she needed constant and complete bed rest. This formed an extremely close bond between them. They now had two girls; Electra, who was fifteen, and Melita, eighteen, whom Sylvie was Godmother to. To this day, Lilianna still felt indebted to Sylvie.

"The gallery opens at nine, so once we've had coffee we can go and collect the painting." Lilianna dunked her biscotti in her coffee as she talked.

"You really needn't have bothered to come into town for this today. I could have got it on my own."

"Nonsense, any excuse for a coffee! Julian's going to love that painting. It's perfect." Her pale blue eyes sparkled as she spoke.

They chatted incessantly until it was time to go and then set off to the gallery. Sylvie contemplated telling her about what she suspected, but was concerned that if she was wrong she would have worried her dearest friend over nothing. She also felt that maybe if she said it out loud, it might actually be true! She knew Lilianna would force her to find out quickly rather than sit on it for a week. She also knew she would succeed, and Sylvie wasn't ready to find out just yet. What was that saying? *'Ignorance is bliss.'* Well, not exactly bliss!

The painting was only small, but it was perfect for Julian's finished office. It was a painting of the library in the old part of town and it had been painted by a young local artist. The building was old, so the artist had painted it as though it were a black and white sepia photo. Julian loved the buildings in the old town, so Sylvie was thrilled when she had spotted it displayed at an art cafe. Luckily, Lilianna had known the gallery's owner. He'd framed it for them and Sylvie was going to take it round to Julian's office this morning.

"Are you going to come with me?" Sylvie asked as they were leaving the gallery.

"Sorry, I can't I've too much on this morning, I'm sure he'll be thrilled with it though. Tell him I'll pass by and see it in situ. I have a sneaky feeling he'd rather see you on your own anyway." A knowing smile crept across her flawless pale complexion.

"Whatever do you mean?" Sylvie looked at her with a puzzled expression.

"You know he's soft on you, don't you? Oh my....you didn't realise?"

"Sure he likes me but, soft on me? I think that's a little strong."

"Big time!"

"I'm about twenty years too old for his taste, for starters." Sylvie replied haughtily. "Chris is always going on about how he has really young girlfriends." Sylvie shook her head in disbelief.

Lilianna smiled at her naïve friend. She was totally oblivious to how attractive she was. She hugged her friend.

"Not that he'd do anything, he thinks too highly of Chris and you. But given half the chance." She winked and with that she kissed Sylvie bye and left her thoughtfully packing the package carefully into her car.

Sylvie had built a close relationship with Julian over the last few months and she enjoyed his company immensely, but she was sure Lilianna had read far too much into it. He was Chris's friend, for goodness sake. Sylvie shook her head again trying to dispel the thought Lilianna had planted. She started up her car and checked her lipstick in the wind mirror. He was a good looking man though, very successful too, she thought and a small part of her felt flattered. She smiled to herself. *Not quite washed up, then!*

Julian's offices weren't far from Chris's. He occupied four floors of a very smart modern building, which naturally he had designed. Sylvie pulled into the parking area at the side of the building. She pulled out the painting and headed towards his offices.

OVERLOOKING THE CAR PARK was Julian's office. It had a large veranda where he often sat. Today however Nick, his son, was leaning over the glass balcony smoking his cigarette while waiting for him to finish his meeting. Nick was Julian's eldest child of three; he also had twin daughters. Nick was a remarkable looking man. He had his father's piercing blue eyes that were hooding by thick, dark lashes that any woman would have given her right arm for. His hair was light brown with natural blonde flecks caused by the sun. His face was chiselled and tanned with a strong jawline. Handsome didn't really cover it. He watched as Sylvie's car pulled up and the attractive brunette eased herself out. She opened the boot of her car. Nick watched her every move as she carefully pulled a package out as he rubbed the stubble on his chin.

She struggled to close the boot as she held the package and her bag. He couldn't quite see her at first as the wind blew her hair over her face. As she turned to head for the entrance the wind gently moved her hair off her face and Nick could see her perfectly. He was stunned by her incredible features. He couldn't work out her age. She looked to be in her mid-thirties. She had a honey coloured complexion with huge dark eyes and she smiled the whole time as she walked. Her hair fell softly behind her as she walked with a slight swing showing off her curves perfectly as her dress skimmed her hips. She was what his mother referred to as a 'real woman'.

The wind gusted around her, causing her skirt to billow revealing perfectly toned legs and a flash of her red underwear. Awkwardly she pushed down her dress while gripping on to the package and her bag as she struggled to walk to the entrance. She looked around nervously to ensure she hadn't been seen. Relieved she'd been saved the embarrassment, she chuckled to herself and Nick grinned as he saw her mouth something to herself. It looked like she'd said 'Thank fuck for that', but he wasn't sure. He laughed to himself as she recomposed herself and walked quickly to the door.

Sylvie entered and spoke to the receptionist. Nick walked back into his father's office and watched Sylvie through the blinds that covered the window overlooking the reception area as she chatted. Now that he could see her closer he could see that her eyes were unbelievably expressive and she had a playfulness about her that instantly drew you in. The receptionist explained that Julian was in a meeting. So she left the package and headed back to the elevator. All the while she was smiling as if she was the only person in on a private joke.

Within a couple of minutes Julian came out of the meeting and noticed the package. The receptionist explained that Sylvie had just left. He hurriedly opened the package to reveal the beautiful painting. He ran to the elevator in order to catch her but it had already descended. He hurriedly pressed the call button then thought better of it had sprinted down the stairs. Sylvie was just getting to her car as Julian reached the entrance to the building. Nick witnessing his father's reaction moved back to the balcony and quietly observed from above.

"Sylvie! Wait!" Julian shouted from the entrance. Sylvie jumped and turned with a huge smile on her face.

"My God, you made me jump out of my skin!" she laughed. He had managed to run up next to her.

"The painting. It's absolutely perfect, Sylvie, really beautiful. I love that old building. Won't you please come up?" He had his hand on her arm.

"Really I can't, I just wanted you to have it. Maybe some other time. Lilianna says she wants to come and see it now it's all finished."

"You're both welcome anytime." He kissed her on the cheek then hugged her. Julian opened the car door for her and she got in. "Thanks for dropping it by."

"It was my pleasure." She widened her smile then waved as she pulled away, leaving Julian staring after her.

Nick watched intensely from the veranda. He was intrigued by her. At first he thought maybe she was a girlfriend of his father's. But she was ten years too old for him, he only dated young girls, and secondly he had kept a respectful distance from her. Maybe she was a client? Whoever she was, Nick wanted to know more about her.

Julian walked into his office with the painting under his arm. He had a huge smile on his face as he rubbed his chin smoothing over his designer stubble.

"Hi Nick, sorry. Have you been waiting long?" He was so glad to see his son. They'd made the arrangement to meet today as Nick had bought a new yacht and wanted to take his Dad down to see it.

"That's okay Dad." He went over and hugged him. "Nice painting! Is that a gift?"

"Yes, well sort of. My interior decorator bought it for me. She thought it went well with the rest of the place. What you think?" He held up the painting for Nick to see.

"I'd say it's pretty damn perfect. She did a great job with the offices too. Is that who you were talking to in the car park?" His eyes narrowed slightly as he spoke.

"Oh you saw her, yes that's Sylvie. Actually this is the first job she's done for me."

"Where did you hear of her?" He tried to sound casual. Maybe this would shed some light on who she was.

"I work with her husband Chris. Sapphire Developers? I think you've met him. We've done a lot of work together. She did a great job on his offices so I asked her to do mine. She's mainly done houses and shops before."

"Oh I see. Yes, I think I do remember him. I think I've met him here a few weeks back." Nick recalled meeting Chris once at his father's office. He remembered him because he had told him that he got seasick just looking at boats. Something he had in common with his father.

So within a few minutes he'd learned that Sylvie was just a work colleague of his and also married. That figured. He went back out to the veranda and lit up a cigarette. Regardless of the information he still couldn't get her smile out of his head.

Julian came out to join him.

"So you ready to show me your new boat?" He beamed with pride at his son.

"Yacht, dad. I'm not fishing in it!" Nick scolded.

CHAPTER 4

WHEN SYLVIE MET CHRIS

Sylvie sat looking out over at the view that she almost took for granted. The sun was still strong even though it was late October. She'd spent a lot of time just sitting these past couple of days, staring at the sea.

The feelings of hurt she had been experiencing had not subsided. In fact it had morphed into a total chaotic mix of many different emotions. From anger to bewilderment and then to utter devastating, all consuming, heart wrenching pain. It had been two days since her discovery and she still wasn't sure what to do with the information. Her main question was why? Why had this happened? She really couldn't comprehend it, and this was why she couldn't forgive it. Had she felt even slightly, that she was also to blame then maybe she could.

What made everything worse was that Chris had been very attentive. He almost seemed to have reverted to how he had been when they first were together. It made it harder to be angry with him. In an attempt to get some sort of perspective, Sylvie pulled out her old photo albums. Maybe if she saw how they were when they first met she could forgive him. She loved him, she knew that, but did she love him enough anymore? Someone very wise had once said that sometimes the hardest thing to do is to do nothing. That would be hard. Hard to pretend, and hard to live with. She wandered over to her iPod and put Eros Ramazzotti album on and smiled as his distinctive voice crooned out 'Adesso tou'. She started leafing through her albums and the memories of how they met came flooding back.

SYLVIE HAD LIVED IN a house split into small, self-contained studios. Her student days were pretty much the same as most students. Socialising, last minute dead- lines and cramming for exams. The only difference for Sylvie was that, in the house she lived in, all the occupants were male. She had no interest in them romantically; they were her buddies, mates, pals and nothing more. This however was not how her fellow housemates felt about her! They had one by one tried to break through the 'friend zone', and all had failed miserably. It wasn't that they were not attractive, they were. It was just that Sylvie was more focused on getting on with her degree without complications. She'd had her fair share of complications before she came to study and she'd vowed she wasn't going to have her heart broken again!

SHE'D SPENT HER GAP year working in Corfu in a tourist office. On the beach in front of a family run hotel was a water sports centre run by a twenty year-old local. Andreas had been everything an eighteen girl could wish for. He was far too handsome, had a body to die for, owned his own speedboat and had a wicked sense of humour. The beach's personal blond God. All the local girls were in love with him, but he tended to pick on young holiday makers who were over for a good time and then were off after two weeks of sun, sea, sand and sex! Sylvie would go down to the beach every day after work when she finished at two and sit on the hotel's terrace reading her book and taking in the sea.

She'd become friends with the hotel owner's wife and she would often sit with her and pass the afternoon. Over the weekends Sylvie would help out at the hotel's bar in the evening.

Andreas would be at the beach every day teaching water skiing, paragliding and windsurfing. Sylvie would watch a string of women try their hardest to grab his attention and he was more than willing to fulfil his role as the holiday romance to the odd few. Sylvie was always polite to him. In fact her office recommended his services, so on occasion she'd need to make arrangements with him directly.

When Andreas didn't have lessons scheduled he'd sit in the hotel terrace too. As the weeks progressed Andreas would sit with Sylvie and chat and they got to know each other. It turned out he was only working there for a year until he went to University to do his degree. As their friendship grew he offered to teach Sylvie how to water ski and drive his boat as a thank you for recommending him to the tourists visiting her office.

As the weeks moved on Andreas stopped preying on female tourists and spending more time with Sylvie, just as friends. On one particular Saturday night he was at the hotel bar where Sylvie was helping out and they arranged to spend Sylvie's day off on his speed boat getting her ready for her test. Andreas normally got up late and so he asked Sylvie to come and wake him up. Sylvie agreed but in the cold light of day she wasn't comfortable going round to his apartment, so she chickened out and decided to wait for him at the hotel.

Andreas woke at around midday and was horrified that he'd slept in so late and was disappointed he hadn't been woken up by Sylvie. He quickly dressed and sped down to the hotel finding Sylvie reading on the terrace.

When he asked why she hadn't woken him, she shrugged and said: "I didn't feel right coming up to your apartment."

He was floored by her honesty. He knew any other girl would have come over and that inevitably he would have bedded her. He realised that Sylvie was different and almost felt embarrassed that he'd been so disrespectful.

Sylvie passed her test on Andreas's twenty first birthday a week or so after, so the hotel owner and his wife held an impromptu party for them both. Andreas got progressively merrier and a number of girls kept draping themselves over him as the party got into full swing. Sylvie watched feeling her first pang of jealousy. She'd been used to Andreas being with her over the past few weeks and now seeing him with all these women she realised she'd started to have feelings for him. She had no experience with men before and felt totally out of her depth.

The evening wore on and the hotel bar was heaving. Andreas kept coming over and talking to her but then he'd be dragged off by some hotty to dance. When it got to midnight

Sylvie said her goodbyes and headed for home, leaving the party without saying Goodnight to Andreas.

Sylvie had only walked a little way when Andreas came running up behind her.

"Hey, you didn't even say goodbye." He looked genuinely hurt.

"You were busy." Sylvie tried hard to keep the bitterness out of her voice as she continued to walk. Andreas narrowed his eyes at her.

"Stop walking, Sylvie!" She stopped abruptly and stared at him. "You're jealous?" he whispered in disbelief.

"Andreas, go back to your party. I'll see you tomorrow."

"I don't want to be there unless you're with me." He edged closer to her so they were inches apart.

"Just go Andreas." Her voice was raspy and he took her chin and lifted her head so he could see her expression in the dark. Her eyes were wide and he cocked his head to one side obviously confused. She sighed and took a deep breath.

"Sylvie?"

She gently jerked her chin free. "Goodnight Andreas. Your friends will be missing you."

He stood looking at her unsure of what to do or say and Sylvie turned away from him to continue her walk home. A split second passed and Andreas grasped her arm and pulled her hard against him his eyes burning he put his hand up to her cheek and stroked it. Then making his intentions clear he gently held her face between his hands and kissed her softly. Sylvie felt herself succumb instantly and she responded allowing her hands to move to his arms. Andreas pulled back to look at her.

"I thought…" Andreas looked so confused.

"You thought what?" He shook his head and pulled her close so his lips were nearly touching hers as he looked deep into her eyes.

"I thought you weren't interested……I only ever wanted you, Sylvie. Just you."

The remainder of her time on the island of Corfu was spent with Andreas. They had nine months together and when it came for them to leave, they had both taken it very hard. Andreas left for the U.S on a scholarship and Sylvie had gone back to the U.K to start her degree. They had tried to keep in touch but in the end the distance proved too hard. So Sylvie resolved not to get involved with anyone as she was still nursing her broken heart.

EVENTUALLY HER ROOMMATES HAD got the message and they were content with having her as their friend.

It had become their ritual at around ten in the evening on Saturday night, the seven housemates would cajole Sylvie into a mad dash for last orders at the local pub. On average they stayed in and had house parties, mainly to save money but once a week they would venture off campus and go to the Blue Pig Inn. It was *the* place to be. Sylvie, nine times out of ten didn't go, as she either went home to her family at the weekends and on the odd occasion she stayed, she knew it would mean them crawling to the very dodgy nightclub further down.

This night she was feeling pretty good as she had stayed on campus to finish all her assignments and felt she deserved a night out. A chance to glam up a bit instead of living in jeans, pullovers and sneakers! There was also the added advantage that most of the housemates had girlfriends or dates, so there was minimum pressure on her.

"Jesus Sylvie, you look great!" Dave fleetingly thought about blowing off his date seeing Sylvie in her skin tight blue dress and six inch heels. Sylvie threw on her biker jacket, picked up her bag and followed him out the door.

"Thanks Dave, thought I'd make an effort, where are the rest of them?"

"Waiting in the hallway, wait until they see you!" As they reached the last stairs and they came into view of the rest, the wolf whistles and heckling started.

"I'll go back up if you don't stop, for Christ sake it's only a dress!" Sylvie was pleased her Mediterranean colouring didn't give away how totally embarrassed she really was.

They arrived to a heaving Blue Pig Inn. Luckily the rest of their group had secured some seating. In all there were fifteen of them, and luckily the few girls in the group were also friends of Sylvie's. They ordered drinks and settled in on their one night off campus.

Across from where they were sitting was Chris. He had come over from his campus to meet up with some friends he hadn't seen for a while. This place wasn't particularly where he would normally go but his friends went there regularly. He had spotted Sylvie the second she had walked through the door. His eyes never left her. He was trying to work out if she was with anyone, not that that would have stopped him, but he wanted to know who he was up against. He realised very quickly she was with none of the men that were in her group. She was chatting away to everyone and not cosying up to anyone in particular.

"Are you okay Chris?" asked Steve, Chris's friend, looking over to see what was distracting him.

"Do you know any of that group over there?"

Steve strained over to see where exactly Chris meant. "Dave is in my accounting class, the others I see around…"

"Great! I want to get over there…there's someone…"

"Yeah, yeah I get it, the brunette in blue. I saw you clock her as she came in. I'm not sure about her she's very reserved, hardly goes out actually."

The truth was Sylvie had posed a bit of a mystery to most of her year and fellow students on campus. She was very polite, came to on campus events, always left early and was never linked to anyone. She studied hard but was in no way a geek or a bore. She was also not a party animal. She was very much a 'look but don't touch' kind of girl.

Steve and his friends walked over to the crowd and started talking to Dave who was taking a tray of drinks to the table. Chris offered to help him and began passing the drinks around. There wasn't a woman in the bar that had not already noticed Chris. He was tall, just over six foot, with dark hair and olive skin. He had an athletic body without being overly muscular and a chiselled face that belonged to some Giorgio Armani model, not an engineer. He was confident with a touch of arrogance, and somehow he managed to portray a hint of vulnerability.

Chris picked up each drink and started passing it to every doe-eyed girl – white wine, vodka and orange, gin and tonic – and each girl looked and stared at him without even realising how ridiculously obvious they were.

Sylvie was engrossed in conversation with Dave's new girlfriend about whether she should change her course before the term ended. She stopped mid-sentence when someone tapped her on her shoulder.

"White wine, or Chivas on the rocks?"

"White wine's mine," said Dave's girlfriend, blushing unashamedly.

"So you're Chivas on the rocks then... Great choice!" He held her gaze long enough for it to matter, but not too long to make it awkward.

"No I'm Sylvie actually... thanks."

His eyes were steadfast and a smile flirted around his mouth. "Chris, pleased to meet you. I was told you were the Chivas!"

"Ah yes that's Dave, everyone is defined by their drink, an interesting concept..."

At this point Dave had retrieved his girlfriend, Steve was chatting to a pretty blonde he vaguely knew and the rest of the party was conspicuously trying to listen in on what the distant Sylvie and the new stranger were talking about.

"Very....so how does this concept work?"

"Hmm? Straight spirits usually mean no nonsense, but you'd need to ask him, it's his theory." His eyes hadn't wandered for a second; Sylvie couldn't tell if he'd even blinked.

"Honestly? I just love whisky... I'm pretty fussy though."

"The only way to be, cheers." And with that the two of them talked all night about many subjects including their love of blended and single malts.

Sylvie knew from the minute Chris tapped her on the shoulder she was in big trouble. She really didn't want to get involved with anyone. She wanted to focus, no complications and no distractions. Her plan was to graduate and start on her career, something her mother had instilled in her.

She could hear her now. "Women need an education and a career prospect. Men can find work anytime!" It was her mantra.

Graphic design was what she needed to focus on. There would be time for 'distractions' later. She was already working part time as an intern in an advertising agency which had offices worldwide and had expressed interest in her on a permanent basis. Chris was a very charming, ridiculously handsome man who was only going to create chaos; she knew she would be drawn in. He was just too dangerous for her.

His gaze never faltered, he had eyes for no one else, something Sylvie had never encountered. Was he truly so interested in her? As the bar got ready to close, the group started to make arrangements to move to the nightclub further down. Sylvie was not ready to move on so she made some excuse to the rest of her friends, while Chris, Steve and their friends were getting rides to the club. It was better this way. He hadn't made a move or asked to take her on to the club. She was sure that he couldn't have been that interested in her and that their only common interest was a good whisky. She managed to slip away before he'd even realised it.

Over the next two months Sylvie carried on with her course and immersed herself in work. She occasionally thought of Chris and his incredible eyes, but from what her friends had said he was a regular at the Blue Pig Inn. In fact every time her girlfriends went down on Saturday he was there. They had all tried in every way possible to get him to ask them out but he never did. He was very friendly to them and her house mates but that was it.

THE BEGINNING OF DECEMBER came and Sylvie decided to stay the weekend to complete her projects before she was due to go back home for the holidays. There was also a party organised at the Grand Hotel, the Christmas Ball. All her friends were going as a group and, truth be told, Sylvie was looking forward to letting her hair down. She'd really worked hard to complete everything before the holidays as her family were going to Athens for Christmas.

Dave and Jeremy, Sylvie's housemates, had arranged the limos to take the fifteen of them all to the hotel. Everyone was dressed in their tuxedos and evening gowns. Sylvie pulled out all the stops and wore a red backless floor length dress which showed off her every curve.

They all arrived at the ballroom and found the seating plan. The room was beautifully set out with dim lighting and millions of fairy lights around the columns and ceiling. Everyone had to walk down the grand staircase to the tables which were on different levels around the dance floor. Sylvie and her friends found their way to their tables and took their seats.

"Chivas on the rocks?"

His voice was instantly recognisable. It may have been a couple of months, but Sylvie was taken aback as to how much the sound of his voice affected her.

Sylvie swung round and was met by those unmistakable, dark, hooded eyes and the most radiant smile. He was holding two glasses.

"Oh my God! What a surprise!" She was totally caught off guard and desperately trying to compose herself. He was even more handsome than she remembered him. *Shit, shit, shit!* She really was in trouble.

He pulled her out of her seat and gently steered her to the bar area. He placed the drinks on the bar. They were both totally oblivious to the fact that their friends were staring at them, puzzled as to why they needed so much privacy.

"I'm so sorry to pull you away like that, but I really didn't want to take any more chances!"

"You've totally lost me. I really don't understand what's…" Sylvie looked at him trying to fathom out what his face was saying, he looked a little nervous, stressed even.

"For the last two months I have been going to the Blue Pig Inn and meeting up with your friends in the hope that you will *finally* come there. Steve my friend has, as a result of my nagging him to go, started seeing one of your classmates, Jayne…"

"Yes! That's right, she really likes him. He seems so…" Sylvie still was none the wiser, but maybe Steve and Jayne were the reason for this intense heart to heart.

"Sorry to interrupt but I really need to say this," he took a gulp of his drink and fixed her with those dark eyes. "From that night that I met you I haven't been able to get you out of my mind. I cannot believe that I never got your number. I didn't want to ask your friends as I thought they may realise I was only spending time with them to get information on you. When I realised that you'd be here tonight I arranged with Steve to also come so that I could finally tell you face to face. I know it's come out a little abrupt, but I didn't want you to disappear again!"

Sylvie was totally lost for words. She gently eased herself onto the bar stool and took a sip of her drink

"I really don't know what to say… … . " her heart was racing. He really was going to make things very complicated. Two months of putting up with her friends throwing themselves at him, that must have been something to watch. "Well I'd better give you my number then. I don't want you stalking my friends for another two months!"

The relief washed over him, he regained his composure. This had been hard for him. He had had to let down his guard in his desperation not to lose this small window of opportunity.

This was a new experience for him, being vulnerable, but he was fascinated by her, she was like none of the other girls he had met. She was confident without being forceful. She was extraordinarily beautiful without realising it and she was honest, without any pretence or hidden agenda.

"I'm not usually this rude. I pulled you away from your friends… I would normally take things a little slow, be a little more smooth and be less obvious," he picked up his glass again and swirled the ice around nervously.

Sylvie picked up her glass and Chris looked up at her. She knew she was done for as he fixed her with his incredible eyes. She felt her heart lurch and the butterflies in her stomach rise up into her chest. All her well-laid plans flew out of the window just with that one look.

From that night they were inseparable.

CHAPTER 5

LILIANNA AND SYLVIE GO TO JULIAN'S

"**H**ey, what are you doing? Are those our old pictures?"

Sylvie's thoughts were abruptly interrupted. Chris had walked in from the office as Sylvie was leafing through the albums. His sudden presence made her jump. He'd loosened his tie and rolled up his sleeves, showing off his toned arms.

"You're home early! Yes, I was just looking at them." She started to tidy them up.

"Which ones were you looking at?" He moved over to where she was sitting and sat next to her. "That's the night of the Christmas Ball isn't it? Feeling a little nostalgic? Old photos and Eros playing?" He cocked his head to the side and smiled warmly. "My goodness, there's Steve. I wonder what he's up to, and that's Dave who had a crush on you. Come to think of it they all had a crush on you. Jeez, I feel old!"

"Why did you get these out?" He pulled the album closer as he spoke.

"I don't really know. I just felt like looking at old photos." Sylvie started to feel a little uncomfortable. She shifted in her seat. She really didn't want to get into the real reason she was looking at the albums. Chris had taken the album from her and was looking at the pictures.

"You know you've hardly changed a bit." He turned to look at her. "You were absolutely stunning that night. Your housemates must have really hated me." He grinned to himself.

"You're still stunning." He turned and looked at her as he stroked her hair and moved down to her cheek. Sylvie stiffened slightly and turned to look at him. His eyes bore into hers and he pulled her close to him. He kissed her softly at first, but as

Sylvie softened he kissed her more passionately. Sylvie knew she was done for, she knew exactly where this going and she wanted this. His touch still made her tremble after all these years. She had never loved anyone as much as Chris. She couldn't think of anything, only that she wanted him. She needed to feel that he felt the same way. He pushed the albums onto the floor and gently eased her backwards as he kicked off his shoes. Sylvie reached up and started unbuttoning his shirt after removing his tie. He reached down and pulled off her top and slid his hand up her skirt. Sylvie moaned. Chris kissed her neck and followed her collarbone with his lips.

"After all this time you still turn me on," he took off his shirt as Sylvie stood up to unzip her skirt. Chris pulled her to him and kissed her as she let her skirt drop. She stood in front of him as he stared at her from the couch. He reached to her and pulled her hips to lips and trailed soft kisses across the line of her panties. Sylvie held his head as her head reeled backwards.

She felt the same as she felt the first night they had made love. There was the same electricity, the same passion and the same need. She willingly fell to him as he pulled her down.

"God you're so beautiful." He murmured in her ear. "After all this time."

He expertly unhooked her bra and threw it to the floor. He cupped her breast and Sylvie moaned. Something stirred deeper in her and she wanted to show him, show him that she was the only one for him. Sylvie grabbed his firm shoulders and rolled him to the floor, sending the albums flying. Chris looked up in wonder at her, stunned at her sudden forcefulness. She straddled him as she unbuttoned and expertly unzipped his trousers. Rising slightly she pulled them down.

"Oh Sylvie." Chris moaned as she kissed his chest moving down to his hips as she slowly slipped his boxers down. He raised himself on his elbows to watch, his legs tensing under her touch as she pulled off his socks. While still kneeling between his legs she removed her panties and slowly crawled up his body, kissing and nipping as she moved.

"Fuck, Sylvie," he groaned as he flopped back onto the floor. He was overwhelmed by her sudden assertiveness. Sylvie revelled in his total surrender. This was the only way she could fight back. Make him see what he would lose. Chris reached down to pull her to him but before he could Sylvie took him in her mouth and he fell back down to the floor writhing.

"Holy fuck, Sylvie!" His eyes clenched shut as she continued to suck and move around him. She moved up and down slowly at first then feeling that he was weakening under her touch she started to move faster.

"Ah," he moaned until he couldn't take it anymore and this time he reached down to her and pulled her up to his mouth to kiss her. She positioned herself over him and let him sink deep into her.

"You're incredible, Sylvie," he marvelled at her as they moved in perfect unison up and down and she closed her eyes feeling the power she had over him as she grasped his hands, the power he had over her. Sylvie opened her eyes and held on to his shoulders as he seized her hips, lifting her and then pushing deep into her. She watched as he started to tighten and his face slackened. In that moment seeing him undone by her, they both found their release together as one and Chris pulled her to him, clinging to her as he cried out.

They lay in each other's arms between the couch and the coffee table amongst the albums. Sylvie felt so peaceful and safe in his arms. He stroked her arm gently with his fingers and periodically kissed her forehead.

"This is one of the advantages of having the house to ourselves again!" Chris chuckled. "None of that creeping around anymore."

Sylvie smiled to herself. "I know, I could never relax when they were in the house, especially as we never had locks on the doors." She eased herself up.

"Hey, where are you going?" he reached for her leg and gently grabbed it.

"I was thirsty, you want anything?" Sylvie looked out of the window as the sun was going down. The whole room took on an orange glow. Twilight the best time of day in this room, she thought wistfully." I was going to get some water."

"Sure. Do you want to go out to dinner, just you and me, tonight? We haven't done that in ages," he pulled himself up onto his elbow and admired her as she walked back from the kitchen with the water.

"Sure, that'll be really nice." They usually went out with business clients. Sylvie hardly ever had Chris to herself. She started feeling a little uneasy. This whole week Chris had been home early, she had tried to avoid him. She didn't want him to know anything was wrong but at the same time she knew that he was trying hard to be attentive and he was most definitely succeeding. He was either feeling guilty or he was trying to pull a smoke screen. Either way Sylvie was enjoying every second, however unsettling it was. Maybe it was over with whoever it was.

It was seven in the evening which meant that they should really be getting ready to go out. Chris gathered his strewn clothes and started up the stairs. Sylvie went into the bathroom to run her bath.

They never made it to dinner. They ate bread and cheese washed down with Chivas while in the tub. As Sylvie drifted off to sleep as she rested her head on his chest, her last thoughts were that there really couldn't be anyone else in his life.

THE NEXT MORNING SYLVIE was up and out of the house before Chris had woken. She'd left him a note telling him that she and Lilianna had made arrangements to go up to Julian's office after they had been furniture scouting for a new client. Lilianna often accompanied her on shopping trips, Sylvie liked to bounce ideas off her.

They'd ended up in an upholsterer trying to find the right fabric for the dining chairs.

"I really can't decide whether fabric is the right way to go. Maybe leather." Sylvie was looking at the swatches.

"Take the swatches with you and bring them back in a couple of days when you've seen them up against the rest of the room." The assistant was very helpful, Sylvie had brought plenty of work their way and so nothing was ever any trouble. She couldn't concentrate, her thoughts kept going back to last night. It had been a while since Chris had had the energy or time to be able to spend a whole evening with her. He'd switched off his phone and had been totally engrossed in her. He had wanted to know about her work, what she was up to today. She had enjoyed every second, but it still had thrown her.

"You're right, I'll bring them back on Friday." Sylvie looked at her watch. It was twelve already and they needed to get up to Julian's.

"Sylvie? You look a little distracted, are you alright? You don't normally take this long to make a decision." Lilianna was looking at her with a smile. "Are you in, love?" she laughed at her own joke.

"Just had a late night," blushed Sylvie.

"Oh, I get it Chris home early eh......no need to say any more." Lilianna carried on laughing as she saw her friend squirm embarrassedly. Lilianna was forever teasing her.

"Shut up and let's get to Julian's before he leaves for lunch."

"So Chris has still got it in him then? To make you daydream like a schoolgirl. He's probably charging up his batteries before he goes to Athens." She carried on ribbing her friend.

"You're terrible, Lilianna." Sylvie giggled back.

They got in the car and sped off to Julian's.

Lilianna parked up next to Julian's flashy charcoal grey sports car.

"Well, he's either compensating for something he's lacking, or he's having a long midlife crisis," they both giggled. "What car *is* that?" Lilianna strained to look.

It was true Julian was a bit of a walking cliché. He was an attractive man who had divorced twenty years ago. Since then he had only had fleeting relationships with women in their twenties. He worked hard and had become very successful. His cars were always flashy, he lived in a penthouse and basically enjoyed his bachelor status. He didn't take himself seriously, which was one of his endearing features. Neither did he pretend to be anything he wasn't. He was considered a real catch, if anyone could actually get him to commit.

"Maserati."

Lilianna raised her eyebrows in surprise. "How do you know so much about cars?"

"I live with three men obsessed with them. It was bound to rub off on me!" She giggled.

He was waiting for them in his office when they arrived. He immediately, dropped what he was doing, removing his glasses and placing them on his desk. His eyes perfectly matched his sky blue opened necked shirt and he had the remnants of a tan still. Even though his hair was light brown with grey, it didn't seem to age him.

"I thought you'd changed your mind," he beamed, immediately getting up from his desk. His comment was directed to Sylvie.

"I'm sorry we're late, we got delayed at the upholsterers." Julian was taking her outstretched hand and gently kissed her cheek. He turned to Lilianna and kissed her too in an effort not to differentiate between the two.

"Wow the view from here is great!" Lilianna walked to the window. She turned and spotted the painting on the wall. "Oh, Julian the painting looks fabulous. Great job Sylvie, really." She was genuinely proud of her friend.

"I know; the whole place looks a lot more together, doesn't it? I'm afraid it was a mismatch before Sylvie worked her magic. It's a lot more organised too. Let me show you the boardroom." He couldn't hide his enthusiasm.

Julian spent an hour giving Lilianna the grand tour of his offices all the while Sylvie watched as he explained how she had transformed his rather dated working environment. He pinpointed every detail down to the door handles and hinges. Sylvie couldn't believe he had actually taken note of all the things she had laboriously pointed out to him. Most people pretended to be interested out of politeness, and then promptly erased them from their mind. Julian had really taken notice.

Sylvie put it down to him being an architect, details mattered. He joked and teased her as he showed Lilianna around, saying that it was a terrible hardship having her rearranging his work space, but at least the results were worth it. His eyes kept flitting back to Sylvie a little more than necessary.

"Thanks so much for showing me round Julian. I loved seeing it all. You're a walking advert for Sylvie," Lilianna was being her usual unsubtle self. Luckily only she and Sylvie knew what she was insinuating.

"Yes well, we'd better let you get back to work, I'm sure we've taken up enough of your time," said Sylvie, feeling as though maybe they had overstayed their welcome.

"Well I was actually going for lunch; I'd love for you to join me."

"That's really kind, but really it's not necessary," Sylvie started to feel even more uncomfortable.

"Nonsense, I insist. Shall we call Chris and Zach maybe they could join us?" Instantly Sylvie felt a little less awkward.

Julian went into his office to make the calls and left Sylvie and Lilianna in the reception area.

"Well, well…" Lilianna grinned. "I told you he was soft on you."

"I don't know what you mean; he spent the last hour talking to you!"

"Oh yes, so he did. He spent the last hour talking to me about you! You really are stupid for someone so clever, Sylvie." She shook her head still smiling.

"What does it matter anyway? I'm not interested, I'm married." Sylvie started heating up as she waved her wedding and engagement ring at her.

"I didn't say you had to do anything about it. It's just nice to know, don't you think? I know you love Chris and you'd never do anything, but it is nice to know that you've still got it." She was smiling her cheeky smile. "Sometimes, Sylvie, you are too good for your own good. Enjoy it while you can! Keep Chris on his toes. Make him sweat a bit. I tell you what, he's so sure of you it might do him good to worry a bit."

Sylvie looked at her friend. It was as if she knew something, or was it that she could sense something. They often talked freely about their personal life, but this was unprompted. She knew Lilianna didn't know about the other woman. If she did, she would have told her; that was how Lilianna was. So was this just a coincidence? Sure Julian was an attractive man that most women, young and old would jump at. But as far as she was concerned he was Chris's friend and that's all Sylvie saw.

"Well I always said he had impeccable taste!" Sylvie joked; she really couldn't deal with anything right now but maybe she should loosen up bit.

"Looks like it's just us three, they're both tied up. But at least I got their permission to wine and dine their wives! Shall we go?"

Julian had chosen a very smart restaurant in the heart of the old town which was known for its fresh seafood. They settled themselves into their booth at the restaurant as the waiter brought over the menus. Sylvie was feeling a lot less uncomfortable as she knew Chris was aware of her whereabouts. It made her feel less guilty. What she felt guilty about she wasn't quite sure, but nevertheless, after her conversation with Lilianna, she was determined to enjoy herself. Well at least she had a chaperone.

The time flew by as Lilianna quizzed Julian on his life. She had a knack for being direct without seeming nosey. She discovered that he had been married and had three children and son, Nick, and twin daughters, Elenora and Vicki. He was very close to them all and had very good relationship with his ex-wife Maggie. His son Nick had his own business in the marina. Elenora was an art teacher and engaged to be married next April. Vicki was a lawyer in a large firm. He'd made his money over in the Arab states in the eighties but decided to base his family in Cyprus. After the Kuwait problem in the early nineties he'd decided to work solely on the island.

"You'd both really like Maggie. She was a lot more mature than me when we were married. I was selfish and had a lot of growing up to do. We met at college and married straight away. She loved the idea of being a wife and mother. I wanted that too but not as quickly as it came. Before I knew it I was a father of three. Maggie saw that I was feeling trapped so she suggested we separate until I could deal with it. Pathetic really."

He was being genuine; It was obviously hard for him to admit his shortcomings. "I'd just finished building the house they live in now. After ten years of marriage I moved out. Nick was eight and the girls were five. Maggie managed brilliantly without me, better than when I was with her. So after a while we decided it was better to divorce, especially for the kids. We didn't want to confuse them anymore.

"She never once stopped me seeing them. Whenever I wanted to see them I would just turn up. She's very special, not many women would put up with that. Her theory was we were a family and with family you accept the good and the bad. The fact we lived apart was, how did she phrase it? 'Just a unique quality to our dynamic.' Very liberal eh? Well, we were brought up in the sixties!" He looked up at Sylvie as he spoke and his expression was almost apologetic.

"I think it takes all sorts. And sometimes what's right for one person is totally wrong for another. I think you're very lucky to have found what works for you. People spend a lifetime trying to find a balance or even just some peace. You seem to have found it though. It's obvious you love all your family very much."

Sylvie realised that Julian was not quite the man she had thought he was. His family were obviously a huge part of him. He was also not afraid to admit his mistakes. Something else Sylvie didn't come across very often.

"You should meet her. She'd love you both. If you'll excuse me for a moment," he got up from the table and walked towards the rest rooms.

"It would seem to me there's a lot more to Julian than we thought ,eh." Lilianna spoke softly with a bemused expression.

"His ex-wife sounds like a saint. No wonder he's screwing all these young bimbos, who could measure up to that?" mused Sylvie

Sylvie looked over to where Julian had gone. As he emerged, an extremely attractive young girl had cornered him. She was perfectly dressed with an unbelievable figure, though she seemed to be wearing far too much make up for the time of day. Her long blonde hair cascaded down her back. It looked like he knew her as she threw herself around his neck. He glanced over to their table and Sylvie saw that he was embarrassed, so she turned away so as not to make him feel worse.

"A little too much face on that makeup!" Lilianna whispered trying to stifle her laugh.

"Pack it in!" hissed Sylvie.

He politely spoke to her and she forced a card into his hand. He said his goodbyes and returned to the table.

"A client of yours?" Lilianna asked with a hint of sarcasm.

"Err no, her father is, was should I say." His embarrassment was hard to disguise.

"Well it's getting late; Julian, it was a lovely lunch, but I think we've taken up far too much of your day," Sylvie was already up and ready to leave before Lilianna quizzed him on *that* relationship too.

"The pleasure was all mine. Those husbands of yours had better keep an eye on you two. They don't know how lucky they are!" He kissed both of them goodbye and they left leaving him looking at the business card the young woman had thrust into his hand.

"He's a difficult one to work out. I was beginning to overlook his obvious 'middle aged crisis acting out' side to his personality. And then little 'Miss Bouncy Tits' shatters it again. He's a player and that's that." Lilianna almost sounded disappointed.

"I don't know. He's been the perfect gentleman to me throughout the refurbishment. Granted you found out more in the last two hours than I have in the last two months. I think there's more to him than his bonking his way through all the young talent in town. Well we had a great lunch and with any luck he'll recommend me to loads of new clients." Sylvie jumped into the car as Lilianna looked at her friend in amazement.

"I swear to God Sylvie, is that where your mind is, business!"

"I've just started out Lilianna!" laughed Sylvie, "And I need all the business I can get, so yes, that's all Julian is. Business."

CHAPTER 6

DYNAMIC FAMILY

Julian sat for a few more moments, looking at the business card Ellie had put in his hand. After enjoying the company of two intelligent, attractive women, he felt pretty sad and pathetic. Not to mention embarrassed. Ellie had been an old flame he had earlier that year which had run its course and fizzled out. She was opening her own beauty salon, all financed by 'Daddy', and she wanted him to come and see it. Julian knew she was only using it as an excuse to start up with him again. It had been fun while it had lasted, but as usual Julian had become bored once the initial excitement had worn off. She was in her early twenties, had an extremely high sex drive and had been one of his most uncomplicated liaisons. But other than that she had nothing of interest to offer him. She was a very attractive girl. Tight and bouncy. But that was it.

Julian paid the bill and made his way to the car. He craved some intelligent company. Someone who was at least on the same wavelength as him. Maggie was the only woman he had ever had that kind of affinity with. All his other relationships were driven by sexual attraction alone. It was true Julian had had a string of meaningless, short lived relationships with young attractive women. He just couldn't seem to find the right person with whom he could fill what was lacking from his personal life. There were not many women who could put up with the close relationship he had with Maggie. So he settled for shallow affairs with minimum complications. The only other woman he'd ever had some form of relationship with was Sylvie. He knew it was only business and that she was married to his friend. But over the last couple of months he had grown close to her.

At first they had been polite and businesslike. Sylvie was quite reserved in many ways. It took her a while to warm up to people. She was always very hospitable and good at small talk, but she always kept a distance. It was as if she didn't want anyone to get too close. As time had progressed Julian had seen Sylvie relax and become more open. She had never asked about his personal life. This was, he presumed, because she already knew everything, or she didn't want to seem nosy.

Their conversations always started about work then moved on to views and thoughts on current events, food, travel and many other unrelated topics that Julian had never been able to share with any of his girlfriends. As the time had passed they had formed a bond that Julian couldn't quite explain. They had closeness without any sexual undertones. That wasn't to say that he didn't find her attractive, he did, but he would never have crossed that line. He had the utmost respect for Sylvie and she had never given him any reason to think she saw him as anything other than a business associate and now a friend. Had she not been married to his good friend, things may have been very different. That thought made him feel a lot more uncomfortable than he'd like to admit.

That being said, today's lunch had confirmed the fact that he was going to miss her a lot now his offices were finished.

It was three o'clock as Julian started his car. As he started off out of the car park his phone began to ring. It was Maggie.

"Hello Mags."

"Julian. How are you?" she had such a calm voice that Julian felt instantly better.

"I'm okay, what are you up to?"

"We came down to see Nick's yacht. He's taking it out for the first time today. Can you make it? He won't go out unless you're here too."

"You mean you're down at the marina now? Me too. I'll come straight there then." That was just what he needed, to meet up with his family. He realised he was lucky to have them. Sylvie was right; they did bring him peace.

Julian pulled into the parking area of the marina and made his way down to where Nick had his yacht moored. He spotted

Maggie first in her floaty sundress. He called out to her and she turned around with a huge smile on her face and waved, her long wavy light brown hair blown about by the breeze. Elenora squealed and ran down the quay to meet her Dad.

"Oh my God Dad it's amazing isn't it? It's so big inside. Nick keeps trying to tell us all about its features and all the technical stuff. Like I care or even understand. It's just so plush and luxurious. I thought it was going to be like those boats we went on in Greece. Remember? Those day trips, with the blue paint peeling off and metal stairs everywhere. I can't believe it's so lovely. Vicki's messing with the loo, like a big kid. Come on, he's going to take it out for us."

Elenora was running back up the jetty as Julian walked up behind her. He couldn't believe she was getting married next spring. That really made him feel old. She was a lot like her mother, always positive and enthusiastic. Today she looked like a teenager again in her jeans and T-shirt. Her light brown hair flecked with blonde streaks in a ponytail jumping about all excited.

"So you decided you'd brave another visit, Dad?" Nick was wiping his hands on a cloth as he came up from below deck. His T-shirt had oil stains on it and his hair was dishevelled from sweat. "It looks better now it's been cleaned up." He put down the cloth and helped his father onto the deck. Julian hugged and kissed him. His son had made a huge success of his short career and this yacht was living proof.

"I wasn't going to take her out unless you were here too. I promise we won't go far. Mum bought some sea sick pills and ginger biscuits for your stomach!" Nick joked. He knew his father was making a huge sacrifice. "Let me just wash myself a bit." He went back below deck as Julian surveyed his sons work.

"Nick it looks fabulous. I see you haven't changed the name then." He called down to him.

"I thought it was a good positive name, *Silver Lining*. Mum thought so too." Nick called up from the galley.

"Definitely a good name. Come on then Nick sweetheart, I've got the champagne for you to open! Vicki, leave the toilet and come up, Dad's here!"

Maggie was over by Julian's side and he kissed her on the cheek. "So glad you came. We were going to wait until five to call you. I thought you may have been busy. Nick wouldn't go unless you came. Vicki made me ring you earlier."

"I'm glad you did. You couldn't have timed it better. I was just round the corner."

"Dad, I knew you'd come straight away!" Vicki threw her arms around her Dad. She was slightly shorter than Elenora, and petite with blonde shoulder length hair that she normally wore in a low bun for work. Today though she had let it down, which made her look relaxed and less business like. "It's got everything. Three bedrooms and a kitchen. No, no that's not right; Nick's been teaching me the correct terminology. It's a six berth, with a fully fitted galley. It's got two bathrooms, loo everything. He's even got TVs."

"I know darling, I saw it on Monday. It's pretty amazing."

Within a few minutes they were all on the Quayside, Nick holding the bottle of champagne flanked by Maggie, Julian, Elenora and Vicki. Vicki pulled out her camera and started taking pictures.

"You have to make a speech Nick." Vicki smiled. "It's tradition."

Nick pulled a face. He looked round at the people he loved and took a deep breath.

"Since the age of eight I have dreamed of nothing else than having my own yacht. Today after twenty years I finally have the most important people in my life here to witness my dream come true. To the *Silver Lining*, and all who sail in her."

He turned and expertly opened the bottle over the bow of his yacht. He turned to look at his family as they loudly clapped and cheered. Maggie was the first to hug and kiss Nick, and then each of them took their turn. Nick jumped up to start the engine, while Vicki untied the ropes. One by one they got on to the deck. Nick expertly manoeuvred the *Silver Lining* out of the dock and into open sea. Julian watched him, full of pride, as he hugged his daughters.

SYLVIE STOOD IMPATIENTLY WAITING at the arrivals gate scanning for Alex. Luckily he always travelled light on these short visits, so he would be out quite fast. She couldn't wait to see him. It had only been a month, but it seemed so much longer. She hated the fact he was away, though she tried her damnedest not to let on. Whenever she was stressed or upset she always wanted her boys around her.

They had an uncanny way of making her forget whatever was troubling her.

Within five minutes she spotted him beaming at her as he passed through the electric doors. He was tall, like his father, with the same Mediterranean colouring, but he had a larger frame, his features were less angular and his eyes were kinder. She ran round to the opening and threw her arms around him. Luckily he had passed the age where open displays of affection embarrassed him and he reciprocated the hug and kiss without a second thought.

"Oh my goodness how I've missed you, how was the flight?" They moved out of the arrivals lounge and walked to their car. Sylvie had her arm linked in his.

"Not too bad; sat chatting with some holidaymakers all the way. How're Dad and Markus? I hope he's swung a couple of days off while I'm here."

Alex's main concern was always Markus. Throughout their childhood Markus had been very demanding on Alex's time. As they had grown Markus had become more independent and their relationship took on a different dynamic. They were very close, which pleased their parents. Chris had no other siblings and Sylvie's were so far away, she often felt very alone. Both parents had instilled in their children that their relationship was very precious. When all was said and done no one would understand you better than your own family. You had lived through the same experiences which bonded you in a way no one else could really understand or appreciate.

"He's coming out on Saturday morning and going back Monday morning, so two whole days! We'll probably have a barbeque on Sunday and get Thea Miria to come too. She's dying to see you!"

Thea Miria was Chris's aunt. His parents had died when the children were young and Thea Miria had taken on the role of grandparent. She had never married and so had no children of her own. Sylvie adored her. She was a little eccentric and lived alone with four cats. She had been a school teacher, teaching in the local elementary school until she retired. To this day she kept in touch with a huge number of her pupils.

They caught up on the way home on everything that had happened over the past month. Sylvie was so glad Alex was home. He managed to make things seem back to normal. She reminded her of Chris when they had first met. They looked very similar, but Alex was a lot calmer and a less ambitious. He always seemed content.

As they pulled into the house, Chris's car was already in the garage. He was home even earlier today. It was probably because Alex was coming home.

"Dad's home early," Alex commented, he knew his father's hours, so it seemed strange that he was home.

"Well he knew you were coming, so he probably arranged it that way."

Chris was already changed into his casuals sitting in the lounge flicking through the TV channels. As soon as he heard them come in he was out of his seat and straight over to Alex.

"God it's good to see you son. We've missed you. It's going to be a great weekend with Marcus out and you home. The house will feel full again." He held his son tightly before releasing him.

"I've only been away a month!' Alex shook his head and laughed.

Chris caught Sylvie's gaze for a split second before she turned away to wipe the tears she was unable to control.

CHAPTER 7

BUSINESS AS USUAL

Chris sat at his desk, going through some paper work he'd avoided doing. He hated this part of his business and wherever possible he delegated it to anyone he could. He much preferred to be out wherever his company was building. As he put the last piece of paper down, there was a knock at his door. Dina, his assistant entered. She had worked with Chris for over five years now.

"You remember that Julian's coming over in half an hour? I reminded you this morning." Dina smiled. "He's coming over to discuss Stathis's new club. He's got the plans from the council. Zach will be here in a minute. Irene called him to remind him."

Between Dina and Irene they both managed to keep the partners in some sort of order. After Sylvie left, both Zach and Chris had realised that they needed someone permanent to organise them, so they hired Irene, a middle aged secretary who was extremely efficient and fiercely loyal. As the workload increased and Sapphire Developers grew Sylvie suggested that Chris employ another assistant to help him out with the technical side of the work, and leave Irene to manage the office and work as Zach's secretary.

Sylvie had found Dina working in an estate agent's office and suggested she come for an interview. She was an ambitious girl who was confident and surprisingly assertive. Sylvie knew she would be able to manage Chris and hopefully take some of the workload that he was finding harder to get round to.

"I got caught up in these wretched papers and forgot. We'll probably need to order in lunch then." Chris ran his fingers through his hair as he always did when he was stressed or thoughtful.

Dina leaned over to his desk and picked up all the papers. "Already organised. Did you check them all through?" She raised her eyebrows at him, almost in disbelief.

"Yes I did. Took forever!" He looked up at her with his hooded eyes as he leaned on his chin. "What did you organise for lunch?"

"Chinese."

"Great, you're the best. What would I ever do without you?"

Dina smiled as she smoothly walked out of his office.

Within twenty minutes both Julian and Zach had arrived and they were set up in the board room.

"Look, the building itself is sound. It was built fifty odd years ago, but apart from a little earthquake damaged structurally its good." Zach was going over the surveyor's report. Julian had opened up the plans on the large table. Stathis had managed to acquire an old police station in the old town which had now been relocated to a brand new station built on the outskirts. Its location was perfect for a club. Chris leaned in to look at the plan from all the angles.

"Stathis isn't sure if he wants to knock out the interior yet or whether he wants to use the original design as a feature. It's going to need extending round the back and it'll need extending at the entrance. The roof will need replacing and remodelling. What do you think, Julian?" Julian had opened up his laptop and was scanning through some of his old work to try and find something that he felt would give them a better idea.

"It's a great building. I'd be reluctant to knock everything out. I did a renovation on an old building a couple of years back and I've got some visuals of the extensions, so you can get an idea." The three of them carried on with their meeting bouncing ideas off each other.

Over the past year the three of them had built a close working relationship. Julian had mostly worked on offices and apartments. But since been introduced to Chris he had branched out into different areas, which he was finding a lot more enjoyable. Chris trusted Julian's judgement and respected his input. He also had a great work ethic and had never let him down. A quality Chris valued more than anything. He needed to be able to trust his colleagues. After all it would be his name that would be affected.

"Well we seemed to have got quite a few ideas together. Julian can you get some visuals together to show Stathis when Chris gets back from Athens? When are you going to see the place?"

"We arranged to go on Monday morning, just before I head out. I'm going to take Sylvie there too. She'll be able to come up with a few ideas too." Chris got up and stretched. "God I'm knackered. I've got to dash off I've a couple of things to do before I get home. Alex is back, so I want to spend some time with him."

"That's okay; Julian and I can sort out the next meeting, you get off. How long's he back for?"

"Until Tuesday. I'm thinking of throwing a barbeque on Sunday. Will you be able to come?"

"I'm sure Lilianna and Sylvie have already arranged everything." Zach laughed. Chris and he were usually the last to be informed of any social event.

"Are you free on Sunday, Julian? Or have you some hot young blonde lined up!" Chris sniggered.

Julian had become used to the constant ribbing of his choice of companions from Chris. "Actually I will be free on Sunday." Julian replied, surprising them both.

"Great so I'll see you Sunday around one." And with that he put on his jacket and headed for the door. Dina was at her desk. "I'm off. If you need me for anything urgent call me on my mobile."

"Leaving so early?" Dina looked puzzled.

"Yes, Sylvie's been a little… off. So I need to spend some time with her. Plus Alex is home for a few days. And with the trip next week… I really need to go." He was almost whispering. She looked at him with a concerned expression.

"You remember that I won't be here tomorrow? I asked Maria to cover me for anything important. But I think everything's in order. I sorted out your tickets. I put them in your desk drawer. All the plans and documents will be… well they'll already be in Athens." She looked at Chris with a knowing smile. To everyone in and around the office it sounded like an assistant and boss going over work details. But had they looked and listened more closely, every word that was spoken was a lot more loaded. It was as if they were having an entirely different conversation.

"Well then, have a nice few days off, Dina."

"Oh I'm counting on it," she replied arching her eyebrows. Chris shook his head slightly at her reply.

Chris made his way to his car and started the engine. He sat for a moment thinking and running his fingers through his hair. He checked the time then turned on his car phone. Within a couple of seconds it rang. Without even looking at the number he knew who it was.

"Hi darling. Miss me already?"

SYLVIE PARKED UP HER car outside her upholsterers so that she could drop off the samples she'd borrowed. She decided on bringing them earlier as a trip into town on Friday would be murder. As she turned to release her seat belt her eye caught sight of Chris coming out of a small jeweller carrying a small bag. She ducked down so that he couldn't see her and adjusted her wing mirror so as to see what he was doing. He'd parked a little further up the road. He got into his car and drove off.

Sylvie sat there for a moment trying to make sense of what she had seen. This wasn't their usual jeweller. They had a close friend who Chris and Sylvie only bought from. Even if it was a special item, he would ask his friend to organise it. So why was he buying jewellery from another shop? Sylvie knew exactly why. So that she wouldn't find out what or for whom he was buying for. He couldn't very well go and buy something for his mistress from the very place he bought for his wife. This city was far too small and it would get back to her somehow.

She slowly pulled herself up and undid her seat belt. Her hands were shaking again and her stomach cramped. She knew she would have to find out, but there was no way she would humiliate herself by going into the shop. She just hoped that he would take the bag home. Sylvie got out of the car and picked up the samples. Her hands were clammy and her stomach lurched as she tried hard to keep her composure. She hurriedly got to the door of the upholsterer and pushed into it.

The journey home was a blur. Her hands were still trembling as she pulled into the garage. Chris was already home. She felt sick and was trying hard to control her urge to vomit. This was going to be even more difficult. Thank goodness Alex was home. She'd be able to prattle on to him about anything just to not break down. She sat a little while longer in her car taking deep breaths to control her gag reflexes before she made her way into the house.

Marcy had luckily prepared dinner which only needed putting in the oven. Sylvie put in the casserole and quietly slipped into the hallway where she could hear Chris and Alex in the lounge watching some action film. She looked around trying to work out where he might have put the bag.

"Is that you, Sylvie?" Chris called to her.

"Yes, I won't be a mo. Just trying to get dinner together." She hoped she sounded normal. She felt her voice start to break.

She made her way back to the kitchen when she spotted Chris's car keys. She picked them up and went back into the garage. He'd probably left it in the car. He wouldn't have had enough time to hide it. She quietly opened the car and looked on the seat. Nothing. Maybe it was in the boot. She walked to the back and opened it. It was empty. It was only small, so it could fit in a pocket maybe or even the glove compartment. Sylvie got back into the car and opened the glove compartment.

Bingo! There it was. A slim box wrapped in gold paper. There was a tag hanging from the bow. Sylvie's trembling hand reached to pick up the box. She took a deep breath and turned over the tag. It was blank. He'd obviously not had time to write it yet. She'd hoped that she at least have a name to go on. She quickly put the box back and returned to the kitchen. How was she ever going to find out? She went over to the drinks cabinet and poured herself a large whisky.

"Rough day, Mum? You look like you've seen a ghost, are you okay?" Alex had come in as she'd poured her drink. Sylvie took a large gulp and turned to Alex with her best fake smile.

"Oh you know, same shit, different day." Her comment took Alex by surprise. His mother was usually very upbeat, but he had noticed she wasn't her usual self. "What have you been up to?"

"Chilling out really. Went and got some DVDs for us to watch tonight. Dad and I have started on one now."

"Oh that's sounds great. Dinner won't be ready for a couple of hours; shall I put some nibbles together?"

"Sure, I'm a bit peckish."

"You go and watch your film; I'll bring something out and ask Dad what he wants to drink."

Alex sauntered back to the film which left Sylvie enough time to calm down, before she had to face Chris. She busied herself putting a platter of cheese, hams and salad together all the while sipping her drink. She refilled her glass and popped in another couple of ice cubes and eventually plucked up enough alcohol-induced courage to go in and face Chris. He was slouched on the sofa and Alex has sprawled out on an armchair.

"That looks fabulous, Sylvie. Oh great, and you got me a drink." He pulled himself up and took her drink from her. She placed the platter down and as she bent Chris put his hand around her waist and gently pulled her down next to him.

"It's been ages for us to have a movie night. I forgot the last time we did this. Aren't you drinking?" Chris pulled Sylvie closer to him as he sipped her drink. She could feel herself stiffening.

"I'll get it for you Mum, you stay put. I need a beer anyway." Alex looked skywards and smiled as he watched his parents on the sofa. His father really was oblivious sometimes.

"Are you alright, love? You look a little tired." He brushed Sylvie's hair back off her face and kissed her forehead. She closed her eyes and tried hard not to grit her teeth.

"I am. I had a lot of running around to do today. Nothing a stiff drink won't solve."

Alex brought back a fresh drink as well as his own. He couldn't quite put his finger on it but he felt that something wasn't right. His father was being very attentive to his mother, which wasn't unusual; he'd always been very tactile.

This was different, though. He was being genuinely caring, as if his mother was fragile or ill. Sylvie had never been fragile and, as far as he knew, she wasn't ill. She did look very preoccupied and he'd caught her looking into the distance, almost in a trance. He was just glad that they had each other. He watched them as his father took her hand and held it as they watched the film.

"I thought we should have a barbeque on Sunday. We should ask Zach and Lilianna round, what do you think darling?" He picked up her hand and kissed it.

"Sure, that sounds like a great idea." Sylvie replied as she stared into her glass. He hadn't a clue that she'd already arranged it.

CHAPTER 8

SYLVIE GOES TO THE OFFICE

Sylvie had just about held the charade together. It had been all of five days since she had discovered the messages, but it had felt like an eternity. She noticed that Chris had spent an abnormal amount of time home, going in later and coming home earlier. He would normally put in a nine hour day, but try and be home for lunch. That was their tradition, having their main meal at lunch. However, this week he had missed lunch and come home around seven. And last night at five! Which begged the question – had he realised she knew?

Since she had read the messages Sylvie had refused to check his mobile again. However, she was the contract holder of all their phones and so had access to the phone records. She could check when and who he called and who he texted.

Convinced that whoever had sent the messages was also going with him to Athens, she was determined to uncover the woman's identity. The easiest thing would be to call their company's travel agent and check who the tickets were for. But Sylvie didn't want anyone else to know. Chris was well known and she didn't want unnecessary gossip.

Once Chris had left for work and Alex had gone to meet up with some friends, she logged into the phone company's phone records and started scanning them. The number appeared regularly every evening around seven in the evening an occasionally around eleven at night. So he called once he was out of the office every night.....and probably just before he came home from late evening dinners and meetings. Sylvie's hands were shaking. Many of the calls he made were first to her then he would immediately call home. Covering his tracks, getting an alibi together so as not to create suspicion.

"Sylvie darling, I'm off to check the site at Pissouri, I'll be back at eight thirty," was a typical line. "Sylvie, we've got a problem with a supplier, I'm popping round to his office to see if we can straighten out the delay."

And of course, Sylvie would be her usual, understanding self. Her husband was under enormous strain. Dinners were ruined, plans cancelled all without any confrontation because Chris was working hard for his family. She felt a total fool. It wasn't the affair as much as the lies. They came so easy. What was worse was that on the very odd occasion Sylvie called him, she hated to disturb him while in meetings or even at work unless it was something urgent.

She'd often ask, "Where are you, sweetie?"

He would never actually answer, it would always be, "I won't be long."

If Sylvie pushed the question he would then reply, "On my way home, traffic's crazy!"

There was no name saved on the mobile, so Sylvie had nothing to go on. She didn't want to call it; she knew her voice would give her away. She could hardly control her hands at her moment!

Then she had a brainwave; what if it was someone she knew, maybe a customer of his or a supplier that would mean that their number would be logged in the company's directory? Thankfully Sylvie had processed all these details and their staff had continued the system Sylvie herself had devised.

The company's data system was accessible from their office computer at home, so Sylvie closed off her laptop and logged into the company's database. She typed in the phone number in the customer's file and it came up blank. Again she tried the supplier's files and again it was blank, no match found.

She was so sure it was someone she knew; if it was a random woman she would have made things harder for him, calling him at home, calling his mobile, bothering him on weekends. After all she'd been there before. No she was someone who knew them well enough not rock the boat, someone who maybe had as much to lose as he did. A friend?

She couldn't go there, it was too humiliating, too frightening! She felt her stomach cramps start and the urge to throw up.

Sylvie had their entire friends' and family's details all logged in on a file. Apprehensively she typed in the number and closed her eyes. Once she'd opened them, the relief flowed through every nerve in her trembling body!

'No match,' the computer wrote. Thank God it wasn't any of their friends, she was almost appeased! And then it dawned on her. Who would have as much to lose as Chris? An employee. That pit in her stomach came back with such force that she could hardly breathe. Sylvie returned to the company's files and typed in the number.

Dina Psaras – secretary.

What a cliché. His secretary! He couldn't be serious. She was a thirty-three-year-old, single, reasonably educated, attractive woman that Sylvie had not only interviewed for Chris, but had recommended. She'd had experience in a real estate office and was looking to get into developing. This was the only way she could work up to project managing, she'd told her. She was ambitious and thought that learning the ropes this way would be ideal. *That and of course screwing my husband!* If she squealed she'd be out of a job, an unbelievable one at that!

So, were they leaving together for Athens? Wouldn't everyone at the office notice them both off, unless it was common knowledge? No, she couldn't believe that their employees would be so two faced. Faced with being fired though, who would blame them? If their boss is screwing around, what business was it of theirs?

It was eleven and there was really nothing pressing, so Sylvie got herself together, put on a knockout cobalt blue clingy dress and killer heels and drove to Chris's office on the pretence that she needed the itinerary of the flight. Of course Dina organised all work-related travel.

CHRIS'S OFFICES OCCUPIED THE three top floors of a sea front building Chris had built ten years ago. Sylvie had done all the interior design and had updated it eighteen months ago.

She had absolutely loved working beside Chris. He had given her free reign to do whatever she thought best and it had been one of the best times in their married life. Working side by side, they reconnected.

Like the majority of couples Chris and Sylvie had had their share of ups and downs, on the roller coaster ride that is married life. When the children came along Sylvie's role was more mother than wife, and Chris ploughed on with the traditional role of breadwinner and provider. They slowly drifted, until the children were in school, meaning that Sylvie got some of her life back.

It had been hard to get involved in a working environment but Sylvie had pushed herself into Chris's world at the time he was branching out on his own. Together they had set up the developing company and brought in only close friends. While Chris was out project managing Sylvie did the rest. They asked Chris's best friend, Zach, to come and work for them. Chris was swamped and so was Sylvie. Zach had known the family for over thirty years and was the only person, other than Sylvie, that Chris trusted.

The company grew fast in the boom of developing at the turn of the new millennium, and before they knew it, they were occupying three floors of a seafront property. Their staff grew and projects were extended to Greece and the Islands. Though they weren't based there, they travelled often and employed consultants to project-manage. This was one of the trips Chris was going on. He sometimes went over weekends and took Sylvie or Zach with him, but sometimes he went alone, like this trip.

Chris's and Zach's offices were on the top floor. Sylvie had a key to the main door. She was aiming to disarm Chris along with Dina. Previously she would have rung to check firstly that he was in and secondly that he wasn't busy. Now she wanted the element of surprise. Their reaction would confirm what she already suspected.

The lift opened at the top floor and into Dina's work area. When Sylvie had designed the interior, she had wanted this area to give a sense of calm and tranquillity, predominately because Chris was always stressed or pressured. The tones were earthy, with light wood and creamy textures. The sofas were the softest, silkiest leather that had worn in and looked better with age. The walls were the colour of a creamy coffee which complimented the caramel veined marble flooring. Cream orchids were displayed in matching planters and the whole reception area was warmly lit with recess lighting and an ultra-modern chandelier. The art displayed on the wall were of black and white sketches of world famous buildings around the world.

Dina was not at her desk, so no element of surprise there! Maria one of the office girls from accounting was in her place a sweet girl, around twenty three fresh out of university.

"Morning Mrs Sylvie, how are you? Is Mr Chris expecting you?" She was very relaxed, not nervous at all. She obviously didn't know.

"No, I just was in the area and thought I pop in. I need the itinerary for Chris's trip to Athens on Monday. Is Dina in? She'll have everything I need." Sylvie hoped her voice sounded as relaxed and calm as hers was. She didn't want to give anything away. The thumping in her chest has unbearable. Was she really ready for this confrontation?

"Dina's off today, but she left everything on her desk. Here it is. Shall I take a copy for you?"

"That would be great, I seem to have misplaced it." *Damn it!* Thought Sylvie. *Why was she off; should I ask why, or is that too obvious? Obvious to whom.....for God's sake, Maria doesn't know that Dina's my husband's strumpet!*

"Is Dina sick?" Sylvie asked with enough concern in her voice to ensure a full answer.

"Not that I know of, I think she just wanted a long weekend and with Mr Chris being away 'til Wednesday I think it was perfect timing for her."

"Yes, perfect timing." Sylvie replied trying to keep the sarcasm out of her voice.

The lift doors opened and in strolled Chris. The look on his face said it all. It had been a long time to see Chris caught off guard and then recover within a split second. *Yes...years of practice.*

"What a lovely surprise! What are you doing here?" There was that famous Chris charm. He slipped his arm around her waist and kissed her gently on her lips. Would he have done that had Dina been sat there instead of sweet Maria?

"I misplaced the itinerary for Monday, so as I was in the area I thought I'd pop in." *Keep it together, keep it breezy!* She pushed herself "Dina's off then? Haven't seen her for ages, Maria said she's having a long weekend. That's nice for her, she needs a break. You're not exactly an easy boss, eh Maria?" Where had she found the strength to prattle on like that, she really needed to get out of there before she broke down.

"Oh he's not that bad." Maria giggled.

"Maybe I should take a leaf out of her book and take a long weekend off too, maybe I could come with you on this trip." Chris's face hardened, just for a second and then the recovery, expertly executed.

"It's only a phone call darling. If you want I can call Harry to arrange it." His tone had just enough conviction to be believable but his hands were fidgeting. Sylvie pressed the lift call button.

"Maybe next time. Well I'd better leave you to get back to whatever you were doing. See you at home sweetie; I'm making seafood pasta for lunch."

"Oh that's great... Sylvie?" his face was puzzled, but relieved. It was almost a pained expression.

"Yes, Chris?"

"You look fantastic." Was there a touch of remorse in his eyes? Guilt, even?

"Thanks." And the doors shut.

Sylvie made it to her car before the tears that were pricking her eyes in the lift journey downwards spilt over and streamed down her face. How she got home and into the house she couldn't recollect. It was as if she was on autopilot. She reached the kitchen just in time as the contents of her stomach emptied into the sink.

CHAPTER 9

BARBECUE

The last week had felt like a month. Sylvie was tired. She had hardly slept with the constant thoughts that kept coming into her head.

Markus had returned on Saturday, which had meant the house was buzzing. Alex and he had been in and out of the house all day. They'd been up late jamming in the den, playing old songs that Sylvie loved. It reminded her of happier times when Teresa, Electra and Melita would be round and they'd pretend they were some famous band. Alex strutting around with his guitar, Markus bashing away at the drums, Teresa playing keyboards and Electra and Melita belting out vocals, from Beetles songs to Queen.

Alex, Markus, Teresa, Electra and Melita had all grown up together and it was rare these days for them to be in one place as the older ones were away studying and Markus was in the army. Over the years they had become very close. They had spent endless summers all camped out in the den, swimming and playing water volley. Their house was always full and Sylvie felt a little bereft now that her boys had grown. Today would be a reminder of those fun and very noisy times. It was the best distraction Sylvie could have had. It would be lovely having them altogether under one roof again.

Chris had stayed home since Friday. He just popped out to get some supplies for today. Sylvie was sure that he had only volunteered so that he could call Dina. The boys had offered to go too, but he told them he could manage.

The guest list had grown to ten. This included Zach, Lilianna and their girls, Thea Miria and Chris had asked Julian too. Under normal circumstances, Sylvie would have been happy to have a house full. But her nerves were in tatters and she felt she might cave. Marcy had offered to help out, though it was her day off. She had noticed that Sylvie was not her usual self and tactfully suggested she should be there. Sylvie had insisted that she could only if Petros and Teresa had come also, bringing the total to thirteen.

Thea Miria was the first to arrive. She was in her middle sixties and had an almost regal air about her. She had her hair in a modern bob though she had left it to naturally turn all white. She was dressed in a pair of khaki slacks and a cream blouse and was carrying one of her magnificent apple pies. Sylvie cared for her enormously.

"Oh Thea that pie looks fabulous! I'm so glad you came, we haven't seen you in ages." Thea Miria had put down the pie and was hugging Sylvie.

"It's still hot. I wouldn't miss one of your Sunday barbecues. Let me look at you." She stepped back, as if she was admiring a painting, still holding Sylvie's hands. "Is my nephew working you too hard? You've lost weight. Still as pretty as picture though." She said it as a joke, but there was concern in her voice.

"You say that every time, I'm fine. Just a little tired. I run my own business too you know."

"You do too much and that nephew of mine runs you ragged, I know. He's just like his father, God rest his soul." She spoke louder so that Chris could hear. "Why do you think I never got married? Didn't want anyone ordering me around!" she laughed.

"Who would put up with you!" Chris called as he came into the kitchen, laughing. He went over to his aunt and kissed her. "Dad said all the boys were scared of you."

"Including him," Thea Miria added. This was their usual banter.

"You two are terrible, honestly." Sylvie shook her head.

"So what have you been doing to our Sylvie to make her look so tired?" She gently tapped his cheek.

"She's working hard on her business, not my fault!" He replied, putting his hands up in surrender. Sylvie looked down for a split second and let her smile slip.

"Hmm, well you look after her. Work or not, she's looking peaky." Thea Miria slipped her arm around Sylvie's waist. "Let's have a drink. Chris, fix us a couple of drinks while Sylvie shows me the garden. I'll have an ice cold vodka." she turned and winked at Sylvie. Thea Miria could put anyone in their place and work out exactly what was going on without you even realising it.

"So, are you going to tell me what's really going on? I love Chris like my own son, but I know he can be a little distracted, or self-involved. That's who he is. But he must be bloody blind if he can't see you're not your usual self."

They walked in silence then Sylvie stopped at the lavender bush and picked a couple of flowers off it and turned to her. She tried hard not to let the tears she was blinking back spill over. She couldn't tell her what was going on, but Thea Miria was no fool. She would have to be as honest as she could without actually saying what was going on.

"It's a little complicated at the moment, but I'm trying to work things out. When I'm ready, I'll tell you, but I really can't right now." She was fiddling with the flowers.

"Say no more. I'm here for you, whenever you need to unload. Let's get those drinks! I think you need it." She turned and looked at the garden and said, "I love autumn. All the citrus trees laden with fruit, and the first rain. Everything comes back to life after the hot, dry summer." She'd understood Sylvie perfectly and was trying to distract her with idle chit chat before they got back to the house.

Soon all the guests had arrived and Chris, Zach, Alex and Marcus were busy cooking the various cuts of meat. As usual there was the debate on how best to cook the food, it was the ritual at their family barbecues. Sylvie, Lilianna and Marcy busied themselves in the kitchen, while Melita and Electra set the table.

Thea Miria was entertaining Julian. This was his first official 'family event' so he was feeling very honoured.

Sylvie was taking out the salads and placing them on the table as Petros and Teresa brought out the last of the chairs.

"Sylvie, your home is really beautiful. Thea Miria took me round for the grand tour." Julian was handing Thea Miria a drink.

Sylvie cringed a little. "Thanks, it's a work in progress. About a twelve years in progress!"

"All the time I've known Sylvie, she's always rearranging, repainting, redesigning or something. She's very talented." Thea Miria beamed obviously proud of her.

"I know. She did out my offices," agreed Julian.

"Meat's nearly ready darling," Chris had come over to where Sylvie was.

"I was just telling your aunt about Sylvie redecorating my offices."

"She did a great job Thea."

"Of course she did, it's about time she got paid for it," she winked at Sylvie.

"You know Chris she should do Stathis' club. She practically gives the ideas away to us and then we pass them on to his designer. She should do it herself. What do you think?" He looked over to Sylvie.

"I don't know. A club is a little bit different to offices and houses." Sylvie wasn't sure she was up to that.

"Nonsense, Sylvie dear. You could do it with your eyes closed." Thea Miria chimed in.

"It would mean you'd be working with me a lot, darling. If you're up for it I can run it by Stathis tomorrow at our meeting. You're going to be there anyway, he asked you to come." Chris was trying to read her. She looked a little apprehensive.

"I don't know. It's definitely a challenge. But aren't there regulations on clubs. I'm not familiar with them. Noise levels, lighting, fire and I'm sure many more." If it meant she was working with Chris again, it might be what they needed. Sylvie started to feel excited. For her personally, it was a huge step. It would definitely put her in a different league.

"I can help you with that. Chris has all the right connections too. Sylvie you should do it. I'm telling you, it'll be great exposure for you." Julian's tone was persuasive and he seemed to be more excited at the idea as he thought out the logistics. "What's holding you back Sylvie?" Julian asked a little more softly.

Sylvie looked back at him trying to read where he was going and why he was so insistent. She remembered what Lilianna had said about how he was sweet on her. Was that what it was? Well maybe it would keep Chris on his toes, spending more time with Julian.

"It'll be a long project. At least five months on and off. That's quite a commitment. I've never done such a big job." Sylvie directed the reply to Chris. She knew that if he wasn't on board with it, it would be harder to convince Stathis.

"Like Julian said, he'll be able to help you out whenever you need it. In fact to begin with you'll be working with him. Once the plans are done, that's when Zach and I take over. If you're worried about the commitment and other clients, don't be. You'll have gaps to fit them in. If you really want to do it, I know Stathis will want you to."

"Well, if he's really is okay with it and I mean really. Don't pressure him. I know he's our friend, but I don't want him to feel you've backed him into a corner. I would actually love to do it!" a smile crept across Sylvie's face and she could feel the buzz of excitement. She only hoped Stathis would agree. She'd be working with Chris again. It would be like it was in the beginning. And with the boys doing their own thing it would be even easier. Chris put his arm around her and pulled her close.

"You've got that sparkle in your eyes again," he said as he kissed her forehead.

Lilianna came out with the last of the food and placed on the table.

"Zach, what do you say to Sylvie doing the interior of Stathis new club?" Chris called over.

"Sounds like a very good idea to me. It'll be nice having her around again. It'll be like old times, eh Sylvie? Whose brilliant idea was that?" he looked over to Sylvie and winked at her.

"Oh no, I can't take the credit for that. It was Julian's idea."
Sylvie motioned with her head.

"Stathis said he'd bring you a lot of business. I bet he
didn't think it would be him!" Zach laughed.

Lilianna caught Sylvie's eye and raised her eyebrow, only
slightly, and gave a knowing smile. Only Sylvie understood
what she meant. But the gesture wasn't lost on Thea Miria.
Sylvie busied herself with the table as Alex and Markus
brought the cooked food to the table. Julian had a wistful
expression on his face, as though he was secretly pleased with
himself.

"Enough work talk, let's eat before it gets cold. Let me get
the wine and drinks." Sylvie hurried into the kitchen and
collected a couple of bottles. Then she piled the rest of the
drinks on a tray to take out.

"Here, let me help you with those." Julian had just come
into the kitchen. "I hope I didn't push you into that." He had a
smirk on his face, but he was genuinely concerned.

"Maybe a little bit," Sylvie handed him the tray. "But that's
okay sometimes I need a push. I'm a little out of practice." He
smiled at her.

"I'll bear that in mind for the future." She knew they were
both talking about work, but it felt like they were talking about
something entirely different. She felt herself start to blush so
she turned away to get the wine. "It'll be fun working together
again."

"Yes, but this time I might be more difficult. You won't be
a client so I don't need to be so accommodating!" She laughed
at him. She needed to lighten the mood. She was worried that
he might take her comments the wrong way. "Better get those
drinks out, they must be parched." He turned and left the
kitchen.

Sylvie started to open the wine. This was going to be
interesting. Sylvie was beginning to think Lilianna was right. It
wasn't that she was interested in Julian. Yes he was an
attractive man, actually he was very attractive. He was also
charming and she really enjoyed being around him. But for
some reason she couldn't see him as anything other than a

friend. All that aside, if it was true, if he did like her, she couldn't deny she was flattered. Sylvie pulled the cork out of the second bottle and started to take them outside. At least she'd be close to Chris again and she'd be doing something she really loved, even if it was a bit daunting.

"There you are! I was going to come and get you." Thea Miria was sitting at one end of the table and she patted the seat next to her. Julian was sitting on the other side of her. "Come and sit down." She grabbed the wine bottles and poured Sylvie a glass. She raised her glass and said, "Cheers, ya mas! To family and good friends. May we always be together!"

Everyone raised their glasses and clinked them together. Sylvie looked around the table at all the people she loved and thought to herself that there was no way Chris would want this to be torn apart. She looked at him as he joked with their boys and knew she couldn't be the one to break this up. They would work it out and for the first time in a week she felt a sense of calm.

Once lunch was over, the table was cleared for dessert and coffee. Alex, Markus, Melita, Electra and Teresa set up a card table and were engrossed in a game of poker. The rest of the guests were sitting around drinking brandy and reminiscing, with Thea Miria taking centre stage. While she was finishing off one of her famous stories about Chris's father and her childhood, Julian's phone rang.

"So sorry, I need to take this." He excused himself and went into the house. Chris got up to excuse himself until Julian returned. He looked a little nervous as he almost ran inside.

"Shall I make some more coffee?" Sylvie asked, as she gathered up the dessert plates. Marcy and Petros had already left. She walked into the kitchen where she thought she could hear Julian talking in guest toilet. She flicked on the kettle and went to see if Chris was alright. As she passed the guest toilet she heard Chris's distinct laugh. She stopped dead in her tracks.

"You're incorrigible! In less than twenty four hours I'll be there. So you'll pick me up from the airport?   I know, I've missed you too… Yes, four days is a long time. I'll make it up to you. Okay got to go…Me too."

Sylvie ran back to the kitchen; her hands were shaking as she poured the boiling water into the Cafétier. She heard the flush of the toilet and then his footsteps. She kept her back to the door so that he wouldn't see her and she held her breath as he walked passed her to the garden.

She couldn't believe he'd been so careless. Anyone could have heard him. He really must have wanted to speak to her. He must have *needed* to speak to her. Sylvie couldn't take it in. Within the space of seconds, her feeling of calm was re shattered. Was it *so* important to speak to her now? Now, when all his family and friends were here?

That meant that she was on his mind. She was on his mind when he was with her and the boys. He was thinking of her while they were talking about old times, laughing and joking, remembering their times together. He'd had his arm around her on the outside settee and all the while he was waiting for his chance to sneak off to talk to *her*! He wasn't even giving them his hundred per cent attention. She wondered how long he'd waited to find the right time to slope off.

She leant over the sink as she felt herself start to retch. She took deep breaths to control it and then straightened up. She slowly started to calm her stomach down but she was angry, really angry now. She shook her head and steadied herself by holding the sink.

He must have been standing there a while before Sylvie noticed.

"Are you alright, Sylvie? You were shaking your head." Julian was standing by the door. She quickly turned. He'd startled her. "Sorry; I didn't mean to make you jump."

"I'm fine. Would you like some more coffee? I've just made a fresh pot." He looked at her closely and noticed her hands were shaking. Not wanting to make her feel uncomfortable, he came over to her and took the tray.

"Sure, that sounds great. I'll take the tray, you bring the coffee." He smiled at her, hoping it would put her at ease.

"Thanks Julian, I'll be out in a mo." He left her realising she needed a minute alone. She heard Chris ask Julian where she was. He was obviously worried that she might have heard.

Once he'd left, Sylvie put her face in her hands. Well, that was all the confirmation she needed. Whatever happened, once Markus had left in the morning and before Chris left for Athens she was going to have to confront him. Until now she was prepared to forgive him, but he had crossed the line. He'd put *her* above his family, above everything and he was willing to risk getting caught in a house full of his closest friends and family. She pulled herself together and set out towards the garden. Alex had come over to collect some coffee for himself and Electra.

"That was Maggie on the phone. My ex. She's decided to redecorate a couple of rooms before our daughter's wedding next spring. She wanted to know if I knew anyone to help her out. I suggested you Sylvie. Is that okay?"

Sylvie nearly dropped the coffee pot.

"Really? Well… if you… I don't know what to say." It was all getting a bit too much, her eyes were welling up. She wasn't used to the attention and especially now, at this moment.

"Say yes. As long as he doesn't start charging commission!" Zach joked. "Julian's your biggest promoter. Your business will be outshining ours soon."

Sylvie looked over to Chris. It was dark and the outside lights weren't very strong, but she could make out his expression. His face was hard set and he was running his hands through his hair, as he always did when he was stressed or worried. Then she looked over to Lilianna who was pouring the coffee and pretending she wasn't listening. She handed her a cup and looked up through her eyelashes with an impish smile.

"Well, yes then." Sylvie blinked her tears back and sat down between Chris and Thea Miria. *Screw you!* She thought. *Two can play at this game!*

"I'll set up a meeting for the two of you and let you know. You'll love Maggie. I'm so pleased you'll get to meet her."

Julian sat back down next to Zach. Chris reached over and picked up Sylvie's hand and brought it to his lips. He kissed it ever so tenderly. Sylvie felt herself stiffen. Alex looked over at his parents and then let his eyes flit over to Julian. He walked back to the card game with a pensive look on his face. He wasn't sure what it was but he felt the reason that things were a little different at home had something to do with Julian. He glanced back over to where they were sitting.

"You okay, Alex?" Markus nudged him. "You've got that look in your eyes."

"What look?" Electra studied his face.

"Alex has this bad-ass look. He gets it when he's gonna lose it," joked Markus. Alex glared at Markus. "Ask Teresa." He stifled a smile as Electra turned to Teresa who was shaking her head and mouth 'later' to Electra.

"Shut up, Markus, and deal!" hissed Alex.

Markus tried hard to keep a straight face then in an attempt to lighten the rather tense atmosphere he turned to Electra. "Hey, do you know what they call a French kiss in France?" Electra looked at him puzzled shaking her head. She hated French.

"I haven't a clue."

Markus smirked. "They just call it a kiss!" He let out a belly laugh as everyone round the table groaned.

"That's *so* bad!" Melita cringed. Alex grinned at him. *Mission accomplished!*

"Two jobs in one day! That's pretty good. You're getting to be very popular." Chris said quietly, so only Sylvie heard.

But she knew the excess attention to her was unnerving him. For once in her married life she really didn't care. There was a time that she would have shied away from the attention, or purposely dispersed it. Not today though. The tables needed to be turned. Maybe she wasn't such a sure thing after all. She turned to look at him with a renewed confidence. Chris was taken by surprise and his expression turned anxious.

Thea Miria leant over to her, squeezed her hand and whispered.

"He's like a child. Once he sees that someone else is interested, he'll want you even more."

CHAPTER 10

THE CONFRONTATION

S ylvie and Chris were meeting up with Stathis in the morning, as arranged.

After last night Sylvie had avoided any alone time with Chris for fear of confronting him. She busied herself tidying up after everyone had left. Chris had gone to bed and was sound asleep when Sylvie eventually went upstairs.

They were going down to the location for them to go over their plans for the reconstruction. Chris would always bring her in at the beginning of each new job to bounce ideas off her. Sylvie loved this part, seeing and being at the start of a project. Using her imagination. Looking at a derelict site and visualising the end result. This time was totally different for two reasons.

Firstly, Sylvie might actually be an integral part of this project and secondly, Sylvie knew that Chris was leaving for Athens to meet Dina that afternoon. They had scheduled this meeting with Stathis last week, so Sylvie didn't want to cancel it. Stathis was a good friend and it really wasn't his fault his club construction coincided with her and Chris's marital problems!

By the time Sylvie got there Chris had already arrived.

"Hi darling! Stathis is inside, he's so stressed out he needs to open in six months and he just can't see it happening. I told him we'd manage, but you know Stathis, he needs to panic... He loves the rush."

He looked as handsome as ever in his dark jeans and red polo shirt extenuating his toned chest. Crap! Thought Sylvie. She knew she was still in love with him. That's what was making this so hard. *Keep calm*, she encouraged herself.

"The place is a bit of a wreck inside but luckily the supporting walls and exterior construction are sound, so they will only need cosmetic work. Inside needs gutting though, come and have a look."

Chris took her hand and led her through the main door. It was true, the inside was like a war zone. The station had been abandoned for a couple of years and vandals had set fires in there and defaced it, but Sylvie could see instantly that it had the makings of a very unique club.

"Well, what do you think?" Stathis was sitting on an old desk. Of all Chris's friends Stathis was the only one Sylvie had ever been attracted to. He was tall and athletic, like Chris. He was also handsome, but he was less confident and though attractive, he never used it, he wasn't a flirt; in fact, he was very much a gentleman. He had a unique charm and an incredible memory. He knew all his clientele by name and always knew what they liked.

He'd had a string of casual girlfriends throughout the time Sylvie had known him, and had recently married. He had realised that at the end of the day family was what he needed. Olga, his wife, was twenty years younger than him. She was very sweet and kind but lacked any ambition. Stathis was the total opposite; dynamic, he needed to be stimulated, hence his obsession with his business.

This would be his third nightclub. He already had two café/restaurants and he never seemed to tire. They had had two children in very quick succession which had meant Olga was preoccupied with childcare, leaving Stathis to throw himself into this new venture.

Chris and Sylvie were involved with the construction of all his establishments. They had always worked very closely on every business, but this one seemed different.

"It's a great building Stathis, very open. I love the high ceiling and the different levels. You should use that for a 'chill out' section." Sylvie pointed to an area that looked like offices on the second floor. Then she turned around and looked at the opposite wall. "That part there should be V.I.P." She motioned with her head.

She scanned the different levels as she spoke, her mind working overtime as she summoned up mental pictures of what she felt would work. Chris stood propped up against a crumbling doorway as he watched Sylvie, his eyes fixed on her and he swelled with pride.

"The bar should be split into two on the ground level. Have you thought of a name yet?" continued Sylvie. It really was a great building, and Sylvie allowed herself to get a little excited at the idea of her actually decorating it. For a moment the thoughts of Chris, Dina and her troubled marriage were shoved into an empty corner of her mind.

"That's why I love you, Sylvie. Unbelievable, ten minutes ago Stathis was pulling his hair out saying that he thought the place was too open for a club, and in thirty seconds you've just made him realise it's the best thing about this building!" Chris strode across to where she was standing and put his arms around Sylvie and kissed her so passionately on the lips she pulled away, unbelievably embarrassed in front of Stathis.

"I always told you you'd married the best girl. There's not a man I know that wouldn't disagree. How the hell do you put up with him, eh, Sylvie? He's one lucky bastard!"

Chris looked at Sylvie, his eyes filled with passion. What the hell was he playing at? It's true he never made her feel unloved or undesirable, so why was he sneaking off? Sylvie pulled herself together. Maybe she'd been mistaken after all. She stood for a moment running through the evidence. The texts, the phone call and his sudden interest in the gym. Was it her overactive imagination, paranoia? His actions were making her doubt her instinct. She'd been here before and she refused to be made a fool of. Only one way to find out….Her errant thoughts were interrupted by Stathis.

"I'm not sure about the name. I wanted something simple. I've been messing around with a couple of ideas. 'The Station' possibly." Stathis was looking round. "Jesus we'll have to get rid of those horrible bars, they freak me out!"

"Remembering sins of the past, eh Stathis!" Chris was teasing Stathis; he had once got arrested for being drunk and disorderly as a teenager and spent a night in this very station.

"You could call it Celle, it's cell in Italian. That's pretty simple."

"Celle? Hmm…I like that, it's appropriate without being obvious." As he got up to hug her, his phone rang. He frowned at it and shrugged as he answered it. "Yes, tell them I'll be there in ten minutes," he put his phone down and turned to Chris. "Have to dash off mate, some suppliers are getting worried and I set up a meeting at my office, they arrived early. So you think we can open end of March?"

"I don't see why not. The external construction which would need planning permission isn't tricky. The interior's bad but doable. I'll get some visuals to you by Friday, come to the office and I'll have a virtual plan for you."

He hugged and kissed Sylvie, then sped out the door. Chris turned to Sylvie with his wide smile,

"Quite a project, eh darling? Takes me back to the first club Stathis opened. Thank God the outside's decent; these older buildings at least were built well. I didn't have a chance to ask him about you yet. But I will on Friday. Zach and Julian will be there too. So he'll get the full assault. Are you alright darling? You're very quiet, is something wrong?" His eyes were searching hers as he spoke.

Sylvie's heart was racing again. She knew this was her only chance to confront him. In an hour he'd have to leave for his flight and she wanted him to know that she was aware of his arrangements.

"Are you going alone on this trip?" Sylvie asked tentatively, still hoping that she was wrong, even though her instincts were more than a hundred percent sure. A last bid to give him a chance to back out.

"Yes darling, Zach didn't need to come this time. I just need to clear a few things up with the…" Before he could finish, Sylvie realised he was prepared to carry on the charade. She wriggled out of his arms and stepped back away from him.

"Chris. I may be stupid sometimes, but I'm not an idiot." She was surprisingly calm.

"I don't understand, I never said you were either. What is it, Sylvie?" He seemed to be a little baffled, but his next reaction would be crucial.

"I know about Dina." Sylvie held his eyes for as long as she could, he cracked first and looked down at his hands. That was all the confirmation she needed.

"I take it that your lack of denial means it is true. I have your flight bag in my car, and I packed a few extra clothes for you. I would prefer you it if you didn't come back to our home when you've finished in Athens…" He was about to interrupt, but Sylvie put her hand up.

"Please let me finish. I realise that this must have been going on for some time. While I was prepared to work through your last slip up, there is no way I can forgive you this time. I feel totally and utterly betrayed. You let someone into our lives and you have broken me, broken us. You allowed someone else into what I believed was unique and untouchable. I only hope she's worth it…" The tears spilled over her trembling cheeks as she turned away in a feeble attempt to hide them.

"Sylvie, it isn't anything, really. It's just…" His face was ashen and full of panic.

Sylvie swung around to face him again her tears trickled steadily down her cheeks. "'It isn't anything'! To you maybe. My God Chris, that's worse, at least let it mean something to be worth all this pain. You risked us for something that isn't *anything*. That means that what we have, or had, is also nothing if you were prepared to lose it. You have hurt me on so many levels I cannot begin to express, but I will not allow this to happen again. The last time I can say we were equally to blame. We were following different paths, things were tough and we drifted apart. Since then we have both grown and we both, I thought, were happy. Obviously not." Sylvie wiped away the remnants of her tears with the back of her hands.

"I never wanted to hurt you Sylvie, really, she means nothing to me, and she's just …." He was trying to be delicate and find the right words so as not to hurt her any more.

"She's just what, Chris? Are you sparing my feelings… She's just younger than me, sexier than me, better in bed than me, more intelligent than me, more attractive than me… What, Chris, *what*?" she shouted, unable to control her anger.

She clenched her teeth together, taking a deep breath. "You are such a cliché; your fucking secretary, really? And what's really hysterical is that I found her for you, Jesus! If it wasn't so tragic it would be funny."

She shook her head sharply trying to shake the thought out of her head. "I don't really care anymore what she is to you, or why, or how. If it was a fumble in the office you'd get over it, but it's been going on for the best part of six months, I'm sure. You obviously didn't want to give it up and everyone in the office seems to be quite oblivious, so you've hidden it well. That's probably because of Zach and the fact she'd have to lose her job if word got out. If what we had was worth anything to you, you would have stopped it. I'm not so naïve to think that you're the ever faithful husband, but a one night stand is way different to six month relationship."

Sylvie was trying her hardest to be rational; she was even making it easy for him. She should have made him confess his feelings, actually say the words out loud and watch him fumble some reason or apology, but she didn't need it. She knew him very well and she wanted him to know how well.

"Maybe you thought you could have it both ways. The devoted and respected wife at home and the mistress; Jesus, I thought you had more brains than that! You know how much fun and easier it would be if I only had to think about making myself sexy and beautiful all day and make secret dates with a lover. Not having to deal with real life.

"But I don't. I don't have that luxury. I have to get up every day and run myself ragged organising your fucking life, the kids, the house and run my own, be it a small and insignificant, business. It must be great to be able to escape to a woman who just has your interest at heart and doesn't need to bore you with, what bills need paying, problems with the kids, family problems and God knows what else. Are you really so insecure that you need the attention of another person to make you feel better about yourself?"

Part One – Autumn

Chris stood rigid in front of her, his hand fidgeting. He was looking at her with his strong dark eyes, yet he seemed almost childlike. Sylvie drew strength from his obvious shame.

"Did you ever think that I might also have had opportunities to have an affair? Believe me, I've had the opportunity, and with men you would never expect; but you know what, I never did. I never could, you have always meant too much to me, obviously that does not apply to you!"

"Darling, I really don't know what to say... How to make this right. Believe me when I tell you that I love you, I have always loved you and this is just me being stupid. She really means nothing to me, I was flattered by her attention... I know it sounds ridiculous and childish but truly that is all it is. Sylvie? It's always been just you and me..."

He was coming towards her, reaching out to her and she felt herself begin to waver. Then she squeezed her eyes tightly together and gritted her teeth, remembering the pit in her stomach that morning when she read those messages, then hearing him secretly talk sweetly to her on the phone. How could he have done that to her make her feel so worthless?

She stepped backwards and held her hands up. "Stay away from me, Chris! You're not going to sweet talk your way out of this." She was beginning to get angry again and was trying desperately trying to calm herself down. *Yes, angry was good!*

"I'm not sweet talking, I'm being honest. Please let's talk about it Sylvie, work it out. I can't bear seeing you this way. It's always been just you and me..." His voice was soft and tender and his eyes were genuine, but it was too late for Sylvie, she couldn't forgive him this time, she'd never be able to live with herself.

"There's nothing to talk about Chris, there is no you and me anymore. I'll never be enough for you, I realise that now." She almost whispered the last line and in that moment of clarity she realised he would do it again someday. She was determined to keep it together.

"Whatever I do, however I am, I'll never be enough. You meant the world to me. No-one has ever come close." Sylvie rubbed her wedding and engagement ring nervously. Then, gathering herself up, she added: "You need to get going; you'll miss your flight. I'll pack your belongings while you're away and you can come and get them when you've found somewhere to stay. I'd like to say have a good trip, but I think that's a given, so I'll just say have a safe trip instead." With that she walked calmly passed him towards the car park.

He stood stock still as he began to comprehend what she was saying, then he turned and quickly ran out to where Sylvie was lifting out his suitcase from her car. "Sylvie, what are doing? What are you saying... That's it... It's over? Twenty years of marriage ended... You can't..." He was totally caught off guard; he didn't know what to say, what to do.

"It was twenty two years, and I didn't Chris, you did. You decided to end it when you put Dina over me and everything we had. This is not my decision; you made it six months ago. I cannot live through this scenario again; my heart has been broken once and I won't let it happen again.

"You have no idea what it's like to have your trust taken from you. I never made you feel that way; you knew I would never do that to you. You were always sure of me, until now. Well now I'm done!" Sylvie's raised her voice as she spoke the words and her eyes started brimming again. Everything she had said was true, and she felt every word. She knew she was hurting him, that she had turned his life upside down too. Sylvie still loved him but she just couldn't live through the doubt anymore. She sat herself down in the driver's seat and started the engine.

Chris ran round to her side. "Sylvie please... Don't leave like this. I won't go to Athens... I'll stay. Let's work things out. I'll sack her and I'll never see her again. Just don't go like this."

"I love you, I always have. But I just can't do this anymore. We'll talk when you get back." He leaned in to kiss her but Sylvie turned so that his lips just caught her tear stained cheek. She pulled away and left Chris standing alone in the parking area of the derelict police station. As she checked her rear view mirror, she could see he had his face in his hands and her heart stopped for a split second. He had managed to shatter it into a million pieces a second time.

Sylvie sped off until she was sure she was far enough away from him. The pain in her stomach was excruciating and she could feel the bile rising. She pulled over and gripped the wheel in an attempt to calm down and tried hard to control her stomach. She reached into her bag and popped two antacid tablets. She turned up her radio and pulled back out again and headed home. She could hear her phone ringing and she knew it was Chris. She pulled it out of her bag and silenced it.

CHAPTER 11

THE PHONE CALL

S ylvie went over the last telephone conversation she'd had with Chris. He'd promised that he was ending it with Dina and that once he was back home things would change. He would get Dina to leave the company and he pleaded with her to forgive him.

She poured herself a drink and sat on the sofa. Alex had flown back to the U.K. that morning which had been very hard. Sylvie had cried uncontrollably at the airport.

"Mum, I'll be back in December, for goodness sake any one would think I was leaving for good!" But the truth was she really missed her boys when they were gone and with all this that was going on she really wanted them close to her. Thank God they were oblivious. Markus had gone back to the army on Sunday night, at least she saw him once a week when he had leave. It was going to be hard telling them.

"Call me the minute you arrive, don't forget."

She cried the whole journey home. Chris had called her to check he'd got off alright.

"Sylvie?"

"Hi," she kept her tone cool.

"Hi darling. Did Alex get off okay?"

"Yes, his plane left on time. He's going to call when he lands."

"How are you?" His tone was gentle and guarded.

"What do you mean?" He wasn't going to get off that easy!

"Well with Alex leaving and well me… I'm going to break it off. I'll get her to resign. She'll be out of our lives, I mean it. I was a total fool. I don't know what I was thinking. I don't know what I'd do if you didn't forgive me. I'll never do anything to hurt you again, I promise! You know you mean everything to me." He was genuine, she knew he loved her, but that wasn't enough anymore. She wanted to trust him. She wanted to know that she came first, but she knew that was never going to happen. She'd known it for a very long time. "Sylvie?"

"I take it you spent the night with her, so what's changed?" her voice was cold and hard.

"No I didn't. I made some excuse…" Chris tried to explain but Sylvie cut him off.

"I don't give a flying fuck what you said or did with her. The fact still remains that she is there with you. Like I said, nothing's changed."

"It's not like that, please understand I need to break it off with her as carefully as possible. Sweetheart, aren't we going to talk?"

"Don't you 'sweetheart' me! Sell it to someone who doesn't know you!"

"Sylvie I love you, you know that don't you?"

"That doesn't seem to be enough though. There's nothing to talk about anymore. I told you the last time, you only get to break my heart once. You don't get a second chance. I thought I made that clear. I'll text you when Alex has landed. Goodbye Chris." She put down the phone.

She couldn't believe she was here again. She'd just started to feel that all was right in her world. Both her children were moving on with their lives. Alex was in his second year at university and was doing extremely well. Markus was completing his national service and was accepted at the same university when he finished. Chris's company was going from strength to strength and her own interior design business was growing steadily. As a family they were very united and close. But that never seemed to be enough for Chris.

AFTER MARKUS WAS BORN things had been very hectic. Sylvie had two small children to look after as well as help Chris with his business and run the house. Marcy had obviously helped enormously but Sylvie wanted to be a full time mother. Chris agreed that it was impossible for her to do both, so Chris asked Zach to help him out on the day to day running of Sapphire Developers. The company was small and Sylvie was still involved but not full time.

It became harder and harder to maintain a closeness to Chris as he worked very long hours. Their relationship took a back seat as the children kept Sylvie occupied and Chris built his business. Sylvie tried to keep in touch with his world but it proved to be very difficult. Sylvie realised if she didn't try harder she would lose him. He was a man that needed constant attention, he wanted her to be part of his world and he did his best to keep her always in the picture. Her opinion was paramount to him and other than Zach, he trusted no one else more.

Looking back Sylvie knew that his first affair was inevitable. She knew she had no chance of competing against a young girl who only had time for Chris. He'd met Penny at the gym that he went to. She was also a regular. She was a young twenty year old who had finished college and was working in a men's boutique until something better came along. Chris was in his late twenties then and had a lot on his plate. A wife two kids and a new business, she offered him light relief and undivided attention. They were in the second month of their affair when Penny started being more demanding. She wanted more time with him, not just three times a week after gym. She wanted weekends, to go out to places not just back to her flat.

Chris quickly realised she was becoming a liability and needed to break it off. She was merely a distraction, a bit of fun. She wasn't worth risking his family for. Penny was not so easy to discard though. The breakup was not easy. She was distraught and made Chris feel guilty for using her. He consequently stopped going to the gym.

The phone calls started at home. The first few Sylvie picked up during the day. As soon as she answered the caller would hang up. Sylvie thought nothing of it. Then they became more frequent and during the evening. Sylvie started to get worried and mentioned it to Chris. He looked worried too but for an entirely different reason. He told Sylvie to ignore them and he'd speak to the police about it.

The first thing he did was track down Penny. He went to the boutique where she worked and pleaded with her to stop. She threatened to tell Sylvie about the affair. He realised then that he'd have to come clean. If Penny knew that Sylvie knew, she'd have to stop as she had no leverage. As a last attempt he asked her to leave him alone. He tried to be gentle with her but she grew hysterical explaining that she was in love with him and that this wasn't just a bit of fun for her. He explained that he didn't mean to lead her on but he believed that she had understood the nature of their relationship. He apologised and left.

By the time he'd got home it was already too late. Penny had called Sylvie and told her everything. He walked in on Sylvie crying in the kitchen. She'd asked Marcy to take the children out to the park as she didn't want anyone to see her like this.

He went straight over to her in a feeble attempt to comfort her, but she pushed him off and got to her feet.

"Don't even bother to justify yourself. You didn't even have the guts or decency to tell me yourself. I had to hear it from *her*. I hope she's worth it." Tears were streaming down her face.

"Oh Sylvie. I really didn't want you to find out this way. I was coming home to tell you, try to explain that I'd been a complete idiot but…."

"Well she beat you to it. What? Did she threaten to tell me and that's why you were coming home… to confess? If she'd have kept quiet would you still be seeing her? Is what we have so insignificant that you'd let anyone come between us?"

"Sylvie I broke it off over a week ago, but she wouldn't let it go."

"That's supposed to make me feel better is it? That you did me the honour of breaking it off. I hope I didn't inconvenience you in any way! It must have been terrible for you!" She couldn't keep the sarcasm out of her voice. He tried to get close to her. "Don't touch me! Don't come near me. I'm the idiot, how could I not see the signs? While I've been home running round the kids and trying to make your life as stress free as possible you've been 'working out' with some schoolgirl. I can't believe you could do this, to me, to us!"

"Sylvie, it's been hard on me too you know. I'm trying to run a business, keep ourselves above water. You're always tired, or tied up with the kids. I hardly see you and when I do either the kids are crying or waking up or being put to sleep. We spend no time together. We're just going through the motions. I know it's hard on you but it's hard on me too."

Sylvie sat down and looked at Chris she could see he was hurt too. It wasn't entirely all his fault, she *was* always preoccupied. She was finding it hard to juggle everything. It didn't help the hurt she felt though. She knew what kind of man she was marrying. He was high maintenance. He'd always been dependent on her and since the children had come he had taken second place in her life. She knew she would need to change the way she was to keep him and he would need to be a lot more understanding.

"Couldn't you just have talked to me? Tell me how you were feeling? We are supposed to be a team."

"Tell you what? That I miss you, that want to spend time with you? You know that don't you? I've never spent a day away from you from the day we met. I know the kids are a handful and that the hours I work are shitty, but I haven't seen you naked in what seems like forever. Jesus I miss you."

He walked over to her and put his arms around her. "Don't you get it? I never wanted anyone but you. You get me, you know my very core. You and the kids are why I work those shitty hours. Who else would I be doing it for? I love you and I'm in love with you. You're the only one I ever needed. From the moment I set eyes on you." With that he kissed her passionately. Of course she was done for. She had never loved anyone as much as she loved Chris. But he had betrayed her trust. While she was prepared to forgive him she knew she could never forget. He had hurt her so very deeply. He would never be allowed to do that again.

Over the next few weeks they worked through the affair. It had been hard. Penny never totally went away. She would periodically call the house. Or call his mobile crying that she couldn't be without him. He always told Sylvie. He never kept anything from her. He was determined to prove to her that she could trust him again. Penny started coming to the office, which made things even more difficult. Zach, who had known nothing of the affair, had had to be told. Chris couldn't believe how badly she had taken it. He didn't want to be cruel to her but it would seem that the soft approach was not working. So he led her into his office one morning and called Zach in as a witness.

"Penny, this has to stop. If you continue I will be given no choice but to get the police involved. I won't as long as you stop harassing me and my family. I'm sorry I hurt you, as I've told you, it wasn't intentional. But I'm afraid you've left me little choice." She looked at him with tears in her eyes and without a word she left. Chris looked at Zach. "I hope she got the message."

Zach raised his eyebrows. "I hope so too."

They didn't hear anything from Penny for the next couple of days. Then on the third night after the talk there was a phone call around eight in the evening. Sylvie was putting the boys to bed while Chris was in the shower.

"Hello?"

"Hi Sylvie, it's Zach. Is Chris there?" Zach was normally chatty when he called this time though his voice sounded strained.

"He's in the shower, shall I get him to call you when he's done… Oh hang on a minute he's just got out." She handed him the phone with a puzzled look on her face.

"Hello? Oh hi Zach, what's up?" As Zach spoke to Chris Sylvie saw Chris's face go into shock. "Oh no! I…Oh God! I can't believe it. Jesus, how did you find out? Yes of course. Now? Yes please, come and pick me up." He turned to Sylvie. She was still looking at him with a puzzled expression. "It's Penny; she took an overdose. Zach's coming to pick me up. I need to make a statement at the police station."

"Oh my God!" Sylvie put her hand to her face. "Why do you need to make a statement?"

"She's dead, Sylvie. When they found her she had my card in her hand. They called the office. Zach was still there. He's also called our lawyers."

"You mean they're implicating you?" whispered Sylvie. Her blood ran cold.

"No, no it's just that they need to know my relationship with her. I need to come clean. They've ruled it as a suicide. It's just procedure. What a mess, I never wanted her to... Her poor parents. I'm so sorry, Sylvie. I can't believe I've put you through all this. I don't deserve you, really I don't."

He hurriedly pulled on some sweat pants and a T-shirt. He walked over to her as she stood in shock and put his arms around her. She was very still unable to comprehend what had happened, was this nightmare never going to end? He kissed the top of her head. "Are you okay?"

She nodded weakly. The doorbell rang so they both went downstairs. Zach was at the door.

"How you holding up?" His question was directed to Sylvie. She shook her head ever so slightly.

"I'm just so shocked." She turned to Chris, his face was almost grey. He seemed to have aged.

"It shouldn't take long." Sylvie closed the door behind them as they walked to Zach's car. She went straight to the drinks cabinet and poured herself a drink.

Sixteen years on and she felt she was back there again, sat on the couch, looking into her glass. The feeling of dread was permanently in her stomach. She couldn't forgive him. It was going to be hard on everyone but she couldn't spend the rest of her life waiting or wondering if it was going to happen again. It had taken her sixteen years to rebuild her trust in him. Last time she could see that they were both at fault. That didn't mean she condoned his actions. After all she had been just as lonely as he was and never felt the need to find someone else. She forgave him nevertheless.

This time it was different. She had been there for him. Their children were grown, she had more free time and her focus was on him and her. They spent a lot more time together. But over the last six months she had seen a difference in him.

He'd become more preoccupied with work and his hours increased. He'd stopped going on their evening walk. It was their time to chat about their day and reconnect. He sometimes missed their lunches and of late he travelled a lot more alone and over weekends.

Now, looking back, Sylvie saw that the changes were small and subtle and that was probably why she hadn't realised. She was also building up her own business, which Chris had encouraged her to start. So she was also a little distracted. Whatever his reasons she felt they were totally unjustified. It was clear that he had thought he could get away with it and had chosen someone who had as much to lose as him.

IT WAS DARK AND Sylvie looked out through the window at the new moon as it reflected onto the pool. The garden had an eerie darkness about it, making Sylvie shiver. Her hands were freezing. She must have been sitting there a while. There were no lights on in the house and she realised she was sitting in the dark. The radio was on and its light glowed brightly. She got up and turned on the lights.

She looked around at all the pictures around the room and suddenly felt very alone. This is how it would be. This is how she would feel once Chris had left. Her heart lurched and the thought filled her with dread.

She was startled by the urgent buzzing of the doorbell. She glanced at the clock. It was seven fifty. She rushed to the intercom wondering who would be coming round at this time.

"Hello?'

"It's Zach." She buzzed him in and went to the front door to let him in.

The second she saw his face she knew something was wrong.

"Zach?" her heart was pounding.

"Sylvie, darling, sit down." She moved backwards, realising that it was something serious, and sat on the chaise in the hallway.

"Zach, what is it? You're freaking me out!"

He took a deep breath and knelt down to her. "It's Chris. He's had a heart attack. They called me from Athens. I'm really sorry Sylvie, but he's......" he couldn't say the words. It was too hard for him to say.

"No," she whispered as her hands flew up to her face.

Sylvie's face crumpled and Zach took her in his arms as they both wept uncontrollably.

PART TWO

WINTER

"Are the days of winter sunshine just as sad for you, too? When it is misty, in the evenings, and I am out walking by myself, it seems to me that the rain is falling through my heart and causing it to crumble into ruins"

— Gustave Flaubert, November

CHAPTER 1

NEW M.D.

Zach walked into Chris's office where Sylvie was staring out at the sea. It had been a week since the funeral and today was the first day Sapphire Developers had re opened after Chris's sudden death. She was wearing black which was a colour Sylvie had never worn much. She much preferred lighter, brighter colours. It sadden him to see her in mourning, Chris would never have expected her to.

"Sylvie?"

She carried on staring at the sea, almost in a trance. "Yes Zach, are the papers ready?"

"Yes…but that's not why I came in. Dina's handed in her resignation to me. Just now actually. Of course she'll need to work her notice….."

Zach was edgy. He didn't know how Sylvie would react. He hadn't wanted to her to come at all and had tried to persuade Sylvie to have lawyers bring the papers to the house, but Sylvie insisted she show her face at the company. She said that it was important for the staff to see her as soon as possible. It would make it less awkward later. His face was gaunt. He was finding it hard being in this office without his best friend. He was finding all of this hard, period.

"Pay her a full month's salary plus any holidays she was due. Tell her you'll put together a reference for her too but I want her out of here by close of business today." Her gaze didn't leave the window.

"Of course Sylvie, whatever you say. I think it's for the best. Are you ready for the lawyers? Shall I send them in?" He was increasingly concerned that Sylvie was remarkably calm. She had only seen Dina at the funeral and as luck would have it she had somehow missed her today.

"Yes I'm ready but please, once you've got Dina's papers together and her salary, can you bring them to me?" She had turned round to face Zach. "I'd like to be the one to give them to her." There it was. He knew it had all been too easy. He sighed deeply.

"Sylvie love, do you think that's a good idea? You are very upset at the moment, maybe it's best I deal with all this…" He really didn't want a scene, he realised she had a lot to get off her chest but maybe now wasn't the right time.

"Zach, I know you think I'm going to cause a scene but I'm not. I wouldn't give her the satisfaction. I need to do this for me, please don't make me have to explain. Trust me, I haven't got the energy." She was still very calm, which made Zach all the more wary.

"Okay, I'll send in the lawyers so we can sign everything over to you. I'll get the other stuff organised within the hour."

She felt sorry for him. He'd had a lot to deal with, far more than he'd signed up for. Chris would have been very proud of him. He had always leant on Chris. He had never been the risk taker or taken part in any of the decision making. He was happy to follow whatever Chris decided or did. These last ten days had probably been the hardest of his life. He walked out of the office and within a couple of minutes the company's lawyers walked in.

It took roughly an hour and a half to transfer 'Sapphire Developments' to Sylvie. She was now the Managing Director and major shareholder of her late husband's company. A company she had helped create. She had already had twenty four per cent but now with Chris's fifty one per cent she was controlling shareholder. Zach had the remaining twenty five.

It was after midday when they eventually left Chris's office and Sylvie sat alone again gazing out the window. There were clouds bubbling and it looked like it might rain. There was a gentle knock at the door.

It was Maria, the girl from accounting. She did the running around for Dina and Irene, Zach's assistant. Maria was a pleasant girl whom they had taken on straight from college and who had worked up from filing. She'd recently got engaged.

Sylvie remembered because their engagement party had fallen on Sylvie's and Chris's wedding anniversary.

"I made you a cup of tea. I thought you might need it." She smiled at Sylvie and put it down on the coaster along with a plate of biscuits. She was a very confident girl and Sylvie had always liked her.

"That's really thoughtful of you. Thanks Maria."

She was about to leave the office when she turned around and said, "We really appreciate you coming in to see us, Mrs Sylvie, it must be very hard for you."

Sylvie really didn't know what to say, it was a little unexpected. Most of the staff had just offered their condolences, but avoided any conversation with her. Who could blame them? They had also lost their boss too. For all his other faults Chris was a very good boss. He took a personal interest in all his staff and had helped many of them. From arranging bank loans, to paying doctor's fees. He'd even paid for a honeymoon for one of his foremen. None of their staff had ever left their company, except for today. Maria turned to leave.

"Maria?"

"Yes, Mrs Sylvie?"

"Would you like to come and work for me?"

"I'm sorry, I don't understand."

"Well it would seem that I will be taking over here, and I'm going to need an assistant."

"Wouldn't Dina be your assistant then?" Maria looked a little confused.

"I'm afraid that she will not be working for us after today, so I'll be needing someone to show me what goes on around here. You do all the running around for Irene and Dina don't you?"

"Well yes, I suppose I do," she answered shyly.

"Then it's settled. That's if you want the job." Maria's face was a mixture of surprise and elation.

"Yes; I'd love to work for you, Mrs Sylvie!"

"On one condition."

"Of course, anything."

"I'm just Sylvie." Sylvie walked over to Maria and shook her hand, "I'll let them know in human resources. Just keep it quiet until Dina leaves, it wouldn't be proper."

"Thanks M… Sylvie. Really thanks ever so much," and with that she hugged Sylvie and backed out of the office beaming. From the very next day Maria was Sylvie's right hand man.

Sylvie opened the drawers in Chris's desk, trying to find some paper to write down all the details for human resources, when she came across a long box wrapped in gold paper with a gift tag. The same box she'd found in Chris's glove compartment nearly two weeks ago. This time the gift tag had been filled in.

'To my darling Dina. Love Chris X'

Her hands started shaking. Even today there had to be something, something else to be rubbed in her face. Without a second thought she ripped open the wrapping and opened the black velvet box.

It was the most beautiful emerald bracelet. Sylvie stared at it for a moment. Chris always had good taste; she had boxes of jewellery he'd bought for her over the years, every one of them stunning . She held it up to the light and the emeralds sparkled casting reflections around the room. She fixed it back in the box and pressed the gift tag inside. He'd obviously forgotten to take it with him to Athens or had second thoughts after their confrontation before he left.

Zach walked into the office holding a couple of envelopes. He took one look at her and realised something was wrong.

"Sylvie? What is it?" he looked down at the box and his face drained of colour. "Oh my… What the… Give it to me, I'll deal with this." He was agitated and his face flushed. But before he could get to it, Sylvie snapped the box shut.

"Don't touch it Zach, you are not here to clean up *all* his mess." Sylvie's eyes glared at him.

"Sylvie you have enough to handle, let me please," he knew he was fighting a losing battle. One look at her face told him to back off.

"Are those her salary and references?" she snapped.

"Yes… but I can do this." Zach was literally pleading.

"Zach, let me do this my way. I won't do anything stupid." She held out her hand, waiting for him to give them up, and he reluctantly handed over the envelopes. "Call her up and please leave."

"I'll be right outside, okay?" Sylvie nodded and walked over to the window looking down at her wedding ring and engagement ring. Her hands looked pale without her red nail varnish, she thought fleetingly, then turned to look at the sea.

CHAPTER 2

FAREWELL DINA

There was a quiet knock at the door. Sylvie took a deep breath stood up from her chair and smoothed down her skirt.

"Come in."

The door open and in walked Dina. Her hair was scraped back into a ponytail, which made her look hard. She had hardly any make up on and she looked as though she'd been crying. Her black dress clung to her slim figure. She gently closed the door behind her and walked towards Sylvie's desk. Her eyes were downcast.

"Sit down, Dina." Sylvie tried not to show any emotion.

She looked at her and realised that Dina was very nervous. She was fiddling with her hands. In all the time Sylvie had known Dina she had never seen this side of her. She was a very confident woman. In fact that was what had made Sylvie hire her. Chris needed someone who could take the pressure and who wasn't afraid to stand up for herself. He was a very demanding boss and so who ever worked with him needed to be able to handle that. As it happened, Dina 'handled' Chris very well.

"Zach tells me that you handed in your resignation today. I suggested that it might be better for everyone if you left today, rather than work your full month's notice."

Dina looked sharply up at Sylvie. But Sylvie had already walked over to the window. She took a deep breath. "I have your full month's salary along with any holiday pay you were due. Zach also prepared an excellent reference which I'm sure will help you find another position."

Dina's look changed from nervous to shocked. "Thank you, I really didn't expect... That is, I wouldn't have expected a reference."

Sylvie could hear the disbelief in her voice, but she didn't want to see it, so she kept looking out of the window. They hadn't had eye contact yet. Sylvie knew she wouldn't be able to hold it together if she saw how distraught Dina obviously was. Sylvie actually felt sorry for her. If she had genuine feelings for Chris, at the end of the day, she had lost him too.

Sylvie had prepared a number of speeches in her head that she had wanted to say to Dina. But now, standing in his office, they all seemed inappropriate. Dina wasn't being defiant; in fact, she had been very discreet. Zach had insisted that no one knew anything about what actually went on and she had been in total agreement. She didn't want to suffer any embarrassment, Sylvie and her children included. She'd also wanted to protect Chris's name.

"You have always worked very hard for our company; it would be unfair of us not to acknowledge that." Sylvie walked over to the desk and picked up the envelopes. She held them out for Dina to take and their eyes locked. Sylvie felt herself grit her teeth as she looked at her tired green eyes. She was determined to stay gracious, "Good luck, Dina."

Dina took the envelopes and put them in her bag. Sylvie turned back to the window and prayed she'd leave before the tears that were pricking her eyes spilled over.

"He loved you very much, Sylvie. I know it's inappropriate of me to say it, but the fact is it's true. He would never leave you; I asked him to, many times. He made it clear to me that I was just a distraction, that you were the only one he loved and if I didn't like it I could stop seeing him."

She paused, stifling a sob. "I chose not to. I didn't mean to hurt you, I really didn't. But the truth is, I loved him. He was breaking it off with me when... when it happened." Tears were rolling down her gaunt cheeks. "I really appreciate that you didn't fire me. If I had been you... I would have." She turned to leave, but before she got to the door, Sylvie turned from the window.

"He left you something."

Dina swung round. Sylvie walked back to the desk and picked up the velvet box. Dina cautiously walked back to the desk. "I found it in his desk." She handed it her and Dina reluctantly took it. She stood there for a second and Sylvie realised she wanted to open it but had thought better of it.

"Open it." It was a demand rather than a request.

"That's okay. I've taken up enough of your time. Thank you." She wiped her tears with the back of her hand. The atmosphere in the room changed and Dina was feeling increasingly uncomfortable. Putting the box into her bag she turned and walked to the door. Sylvie lowered herself into her chair as Dina opened the door.

"He obviously chose it to go with your eyes."

Dina turned to Sylvie and smiled slightly. She realised now why Chris had never wanted to leave Sylvie. He had needed her. Sylvie was strong, stronger than him. She had never needed him. Today Dina had witnessed that incredible strength. She walked out of Chris's office for the last time and closed the door behind her.

Within a minute, Zach was in the office. He stood in the doorway assessing what must have happened. Sylvie sat, her back to him. He walked in and shut the door.

"Sylvie? Are you alright?" As soon as he spoke the words, he could see she was obviously not. He walked over to the chair and saw she had buried her face in her hands. Zach was right by her side. He knelt down to her level and took her in his arms while she continued to sob uncontrollably. She shook so violently Zach pulled her off the chair to the ground where they both sat with their backs against the desk, his arms still holding her. He was so overcome with her grief he couldn't find the words to console her.

He sat there in silence and let her cry. He couldn't believe his best friend could make her feel this way. He loved Chris like a brother, but if he'd been here right now he would have killed him himself. They sat there for at least twenty minutes. Slowly Sylvie's sobs began to subside.

"I'm okay now Zach, sorry about that."

"Was it very bad?"

"I wanted to say so much to her, you know. Really vent my frustration, but when I saw her… She looked broken too. She must have loved him to put up with his shit. She behaved like… Well, like a lady. She really could have made everyone's life hell, Chris's especially, but she didn't. When all said and done, you have to give her that. I gave her the bracelet. He bought it for her, after all. What was I going to do with it?"

"My God Sylvie, you really didn't need to go through this today." He was squeezing her. "I loved Chris, but he fucked up royally this time. And he left us to sort it all out."

Sylvie could hear the disappointment in his voice. Zach and Chris were completely different in that way. Zach was steady and dependable whereas Chris has always been impulsive and a risk taker. But then again that had actually been his appeal, dangerous, he pulled you in. That was why Sylvie had loved him.

The intercom buzzed and Zach peeled himself away from Sylvie to answer it.

"Yes? I really don't want any interruptions, Irene." He very rarely lost his cool but he really had all he could take today.

"I'm sorry, Zach, but Lilianna's here. She's waiting downstairs."

"Ok; give me ten minutes, Irene, and then send her up."

He turned to Sylvie "I still haven't told Lilianna anything about Dina like we agreed, she knows nothing. I kept my promise Sylvie. Hard as it is, especially today!" Zach was the most loyal person Sylvie had ever known. He was prepared to keep Chris's reputation at all costs, even if it meant his wife was not to know the truth.

"I think the less people know, the better. Not that Lilianna would ever say. But I don't want her thinking badly of him… She might not be as understanding. Is that alright, Zach?"

He understood exactly what she meant. Lilianna was the best thing that had happened to Zach, but he knew that had it been him in Athens with Dina, Lilianna would have killed them both! "Whatever you say, Sylvie. Come on, sweetheart, get up off the floor. She's been very worried about you coming in today. Are you ready? Or shall I give you a few minutes?"

"No, I'm fine. Just get Maria to make us some tea. I didn't get to drink the last one she made me. Oh, and by the way, I made her my new assistant. Is that okay?"

"Fine by me. Forget the fucking tea though, we need a real drink!"

He left the office and came back within a couple of minutes with three glasses, a bottle of Chivas and ice. Lilianna was right behind him, her face full of concern. She'd also tried to persuade Sylvie to stay home and wanted to be here to support her in any way she could.

"Jesus Christ Sylvie, you look like shit!"

Sylvie burst out laughing. Zach rolled his eyes. "Now don't hold back; say what you feel, Lilianna." Sylvie shook her head. Trust *sledge hammer* Lilianna!

They had been through pretty much everything together. Lilianna was the complete opposite to Sylvie; she didn't suffer fools gladly and had very little patience. She always said it how it was and never sugar coated anything. Most people found her a little abrupt, but Sylvie loved her.

Lilianna was straight over to her with her arms outstretched.

"That's better," she hugged her tightly and kissed the top of her head the way a mother would to her child. "Need to keep it real love eh?" They moved over to the couches where Zach was pouring whisky into the glasses.

"Here you are Sylvie," Zach passed round the glasses and was about to lift his up for a toast then stopped. Thinking it wasn't really appropriate. Sylvie smiled at him reading his mind.

"Well cheers," Sylvie lifted her glass. "To the future."

"To you Sylvie, the new Managing Director." Lilianna winked at her.

"To you Sylvie," Zach smiled at her. He took a gulp and then said "Does that mean I have to call you boss now?"

"Oh Sylvie make him do it, go on, please make him do it!" Lilianna joked; she was always the best ice breaker.

CHAPTER 3

THE SUITCASE

The rain was thrashing down as Sylvie pulled into the garage. It was getting harder every day to see Chris's car parked up. Alex and Markus refused to drive it, so it had stayed in the exact position for the last two weeks as Chris had left it.

Sylvie turned off her engine and sat in silence. She needed to be composed after the day she had had. Seeing Dina for the first time and having to deal with her had taken its toll on her today. She felt better for closing down that chapter of this horrifying episode in her life. Never the less, Sylvie felt very drained. Her anger was subsiding, but she was still tremendously hurt. What made it worse was that she couldn't show how hurt she really was to anyone.

Everyone misunderstood her emotions as those of a mourning widow, but there was so much more going on inside her. Chris had betrayed her and that hurt. She also had so many unanswered questions that she could never fully know the answer to. Was he really going to break it off? Or was that just to pacify her. And why, why oh why had he done it again? Was it her? Was she so difficult to stay faithful to? She was thankful for Zach. At least he knew and, to some extent, understood her. But it had been very hard on him too and she felt bad always dumping on him.

She knew both Alex and Markus were waiting for her inside. She was pretty sure that they had rung Zach or Lilianna to see how today had gone, so as not to ask too many questions when she arrived home. Zach would have told them all the details. At least she would be spared that.

Zach had spared her so much over the last ten days she really didn't know how he had been able to do it. Throughout their whole professional and personal relationship she had never seen this side of Zach. He had found an incredible strength to deal with a whole number of delicate and emotional situations. Situations that he really had nothing to do with or any idea of let alone any control over. Never the less, he had handled everything sensitively and had taken control of each situation with the greatest consideration to everyone.

His first test was when Dina called him from Athens.

"ZACH?"

"Dina? I thought you were away." Zach was puzzled as to why Dina would be ringing him while she was on holiday.

"Zach… There's been a terrible…" Her voice was very tight and quiet.

"Dina, what is it? Where are you?" Zach grew increasingly worried. It wasn't normal that she would be ringing him.

"Zach, I'm in Athens. I came here… with Chris," she paused hoping she wouldn't have to spell it out. She could almost hear Zach trying to fathom out what she had just said.

"You mean you're together?" He was almost whispering as he replied in disbelief. He was praying he'd misunderstood. He rubbed his face and took a deep breath. "Dina, are you saying what I think you're saying? Because I really… well. I really don't know what to say." He'd lowered himself into his chair and was thankful no one was home to see him or hear this conversation.

"Zach… I'm so sorry, but that's not why I'm calling. We were having an argument, he was trying to break it off… I got hysterical… And he was trying to calm me down… I carried on shouting at him and then he just… collapsed." She spoke in fits and starts in between sobs.

"Where is he? Is he alright?" Zach's voice began to waver. He was trying to make sense of everything.

"Zach, he had a heart attack." She stopped, hoping again that she wouldn't have to spell it out. "Zach?"

Zach couldn't answer. He knew what was coming and he didn't want to hear it. He didn't want to believe it. His eyes started brimming and his hands trembled.

"Zach, Chris died." She sobbed uncontrollably as she said the words.

There was silence on the end of the phone. He closed his eyes as the tears rolled down his face. Then he mustered up some courage and spoke. "Dina, where is the... where is he now?"

"The hotel arranged for the body to be taken to the hospital. They asked me if they should contact the next of kin, but I told them I would. I didn't want them to tell Sylvie about... you know. That's why I called you."

"Dina, can you pack up all his things? You're going to have to do that. Get yourself packed too. Give me the name of the hotel manager and I'll arrange with him what we need to do. You need to get back here as soon as possible. I don't want Sylvie finding out. She's going to have enough to deal with."

"Zach...She already knows," Dina whispered.

"What!"

"They had a fight yesterday and she told him she knew. That's why he was breaking up with me. It's a mess, Zach, a real mess. What are we going to do? I can't believe he's gone." She carried on sobbing.

Zach tried to comfort her before he hung up. But it was hard for him. Apart from his own grief, he also had to deal with the pain he knew Sylvie would be going through.

Zach realised this was only the beginning and the hardest part was yet to come. He was going to have to tell Sylvie. He was going to have to break the news to her and he just didn't know how. He picked up his keys and headed for the door.

The next two days passed in a blur for Zach. He went into autopilot and arranged for Chris's body to be shipped back home. He had a number of good friends who helped him with the arrangements. Originally he was to fly out to do it himself, but he realised it was more important that he stay with Sylvie, Alex and Markus. He needed to be there for them. After all, it was just a body coming back. Here, he had to deal with the living and their pain.

Lilianna, Zach and Sylvie went together to break the news to Markus at his camp. If Zach had thought it was hard telling

Sylvie, nothing could prepare him for how Markus reacted. The officer in charge had given them the privacy of his office for them to use. Once Markus entered the room, he took one look at his mother and Zach and realised something was wrong.

He fell to his knees and held his head. Sylvie and Zach were immediately next to him, holding him as he cried violently. Lilianna tried her hardest to be calm and strong for all of them, but was unable to and gently rubbed Sylvie's and Zach's backs as they held on to Markus as he rocked backwards and forwards repeatedly muttering the word 'no'.

Sylvie insisted she rang Alex once they got home. He was totally devastated and Sylvie could hear the heartache in his voice, but he kept as calm as he could as he spoke to Zach about all the arrangements. He then asked to speak to Markus. He was his main concern. He knew how badly this would have affected him. They spoke for over thirty minutes. Sylvie could hear Alex's calm voice giving Markus encouragement as Markus nodded and mumbled his replies as the tears continually poured down his grief-stricken face. Alex was on the next flight out.

Zach shut down the offices until the funeral was over and also a week's mourning period was given to all the staff. While Zach dealt with all the legal implications, Lilianna helped Sylvie with the funeral arrangements. Marcy and Petros worked around the clock to keep everything as normal as possible.

THE NEXT TEST FOR Zach was when the airline brought Chris's suitcase to the house. Zach was downstairs in the kitchen with Marcy and Petros when it arrived. Luckily Lilianna had been round and taken the boys out of the house for a change of scenery. Sylvie heard the doorbell go and came downstairs to see who it was. Zach had tried to move the case to the office before she came down, but he wasn't fast enough.

"Zach, bring it upstairs," Sylvie said calmly.

Zach could tell by her expression it was no use arguing. "We can sort this out later. It's really not that important, Sylvie, love." He smiled at her weakly, knowing it was futile.

"Just bring it up Zach, please." Reluctantly he carried it upstairs as Marcy and Petros watched on in dismay.

Zach put it on the bed and Sylvie opened the combination lock. She unzipped it and flung open the lid. It had hardly been touched. His things were pretty much how Sylvie had packed them, except for Chris's leather jacket that he'd been wearing. Zach and Sylvie hadn't spoken about Dina up until then. Zach had thought it was better. She had enough to cope with.

"Did she pack it?" She asked as she lifted out the jacket. Zach clenched his teeth. He didn't know what to say. He didn't want to lie, but he also didn't want to hurt her anymore.

"It's okay, you can tell me. I know you must know everything. I just don't want any more lies Zach." He signed deeply and shook his head.

"Yes she did. But you're wrong about me knowing everything. I only found out when I got her call." Sylvie's head shot around to face him in disbelief. "Do you think I would have allowed him to carry on with anyone and not stop it? After everything we've been through. After last time? Sylvie, you're like a sister to me. I could never allow anyone to hurt you, Chris or anyone."

"I thought you knew," she whispered. Sylvie felt relief for the first time in what seemed like a life time. Her faith and trust restored.

"I knew nothing, I swear." Zach's eyes were rimmed with black circles from lack of sleep and from the tears he had shed in private. She stood by the bed and started fiddling with her rings.

"I confronted him on Monday, at Stathis's place. He'd been seeing her for I think the best part of six months. He'd lied to me so many times and I hadn't even realised. It's such a cliché, his secretary. All I could think about was what I had gone through the last time. I couldn't live with that again. I blamed myself last time, but this time I knew it wasn't me. He said she meant nothing to him. As if that would make me feel better. As if that was some sort of comfort for me. I don't know what he wanted from me. I gave him everything. Everything I had to give and more. I put my life on hold, I put him first, but it wasn't enough. He said she was just a distraction. He was flattered that a young, good looking woman found him attractive." She shook her head.

"He betrayed me on so many levels, Zach, and I'm just so angry that he left me, left me to have to deal with all of this. I don't know how to. My emotions are so raw. I can't fathom out what I'm feeling."

She paused for a moment before carrying on her revelation. "I asked him to leave. I told him I'd have his bags packed before he got back. That we were through. He pleaded with me to forgive him, but I couldn't, not again. He said he would break it off with her. As if that also was going to make it alright. If I hadn't caught him out, would he have kept it going… the lies? How could he do this to me again?"

She had sat on the bed with her head in her hands as the tears started trickling down her tired face. Zach had all the while been standing by the bed looking at the suitcase, looking at his dearest friend's possessions as Sylvie had been rambling.

"I loved him so much, Zach. I was happy to do anything for him. He took me for granted and that was fine by me, but this. I know I didn't deserve this. All I can think about, the only image I have in my head is that his mistress was the last person he spoke to. Not me, not the boys not you. *Her*!"

Sylvie reached into the suitcase and started pulling his things out and throwing them onto the floor. Her voice was shaking as she screamed. "She saw him last, touched him last, held him last. Hers was the last face he saw, not mine!"

She carried on throwing his clothes on the floor. Zach watched in horror, frozen. He felt her pain and he knew she had to get it out, so he didn't stop her.

"And now that he's gone, I've got to pick up the pieces. Sort out his mess. Carry on as if we were fine. As if we were blissfully happy. Continue the lie, the charade. When all the while I want to scream and shout. I'm so angry, with him and her. I don't know if he was going to leave her, I only have his promise that he was. How can I know? He'd been lying to me all this time. I can't tell anyone what I feel, because I would hurt them. The boys, my family, his family. Only you know what really went on, you me and *her*!" Sylvie sat back on the bed and sobbed. Zach sat gently beside her and put his arms around her.

"What am I going to do? How am I going to handle this? Argh! Everyone's consoling me and saying what a great man he was. And he was, but all I want to do is scream and say. You don't know the half of it! Is that awful, is that terrible of me?" She sniffed, wiping her eyes on the back of her hand.

"You do whatever you want, Sylvie. Whatever suits you and whatever feels right." He held her until her sobs subsided. As Sylvie got up to wash her face she thought hard about the repercussions of this getting out. Her feelings aside she had to think of her family. They were so much more important than her crazed emotions. She knew in time that would pass, so she needed to get a grip so that her actions now wouldn't be anything she might regret later.

"I don't want the boys to know. I really don't want the image of their father ruined. If you didn't know anything, then I'm pretty sure no one else did. The only other person who knows is..." She couldn't say her name.

"She won't breathe a word. I guarantee it. Leave her to me." He wiped his eyes for what seemed to be the hundredth time, and got up. "I will tell no one unless you tell me I can Sylvie, I promise. He doesn't deserve this, after everything he's put you through. Even now you're standing by him."

It had been hard for Zach to hear all these things about Chris. He didn't want to know. He also wanted to remember him in the idealistic way everyone else would remember him. He owed everything he was to Chris. He knew that his whole working life. Now it seemed Chris had forced him into a very unfamiliar role. One he wasn't sure he could fulfil. All he knew was that he had to do whatever he could to help Sylvie. Even if it meant listening about a side of Chris he really didn't know.

Sylvie never knew whether Dina left of her own free will or whether Zach suggested that it might be better for all involved. To be honest she didn't care. At least she wouldn't need to see her again.

CHAPTER 4

THE FUNERAL

The funeral took place two days after Chris's body arrived. It gave a chance for the arrangements to be made. Sylvie insisted that her family did not attend the funeral. It was a long journey for her elderly parents and to be honest she couldn't face having people in the house. She wanted quiet. Zach and Lilianna had a pretty much stayed with her throughout the two days leading up to the funeral. They hadn't left her alone and Lilianna had stayed with Sylvie and the boys.

On the morning of the funeral the weather had cleared up and the sun was shining once more. It really did seem unfitting for the sun to be shining on such a day. Sylvie had found it very hard to sleep and had spent most of the night sitting on her chaise with a blanket looking out of the window into the night. She'd managed to drift off in the early hours of the morning but woke at six as she always did. Her eyes were bloodshot and there were dark circles under them. She looked herself in the bathroom mirror, not recognising herself. She then looked down at the sink. There on the left hand side was Chris's tooth brush. Further to the left were his shaving things and aftershaves. Sylvie brushed her teeth and watched her tears splash into the sink. She washed her face and went back through to the bedroom.

Marcy's gentle knock gave Sylvie a start.

"Come in," she croaked. Marcy walked in with a tray. She'd made tea and some toast and placed it on the bed.

"Morning Mam, I brought you your tea. I thought you might want to be alone this morning." Marcy had an uncanny perception. She looked at the bed. "You shouldn't have made your bed Mam. I can handle these things…"

Her eye fell on the chaise with the blanket. "Oh... Didn't sleep, again? You really need to get some sleep. And in a bed not on a couch." She was over to the chaise, tidying up the blanket.

"Thanks Marcy. I just can't sleep, I can't." The tears rolled down her sallow face. Marcy was over in a shot to put her arms around her.

"There, there. You must be exhausted. Maybe you need a pill to help you. Let's sit you down." She guided her to the chaise.

"I can't sleep in that bed, Marcy. All I can smell is Chris," she sobbed. "I d-don't want the s-smell to g-go. What am I going to do, Marcy? How w-will I get through today?" Marcy was holding her as she continued to cry. "His things in the bathroom. The smell of his aftershave, I just keep expecting him to walk in the room. I'm not ready to say goodbye. I just can't let go, not yet." It took a few minutes for Sylvie to calm down again. "I'm sorry, Marcy. I just needed to tell someone. It's these small, silly things that I'm finding hard to handle."

"Mam. When you're ready we'll do whatever you can face, not before. I'll get Petros to bring that blow up mattress in here and we'll put it on the floor for now. You don't need to sleep in your bed. But at least it's better than that couch. No one will need to know. We won't move or touch a thing in here until you say so." She kissed the top of her head. "And don't apologise to me, I'm here for you, silly things and all."

"Thanks Marcy, I don't know what I'd do without you." Marcy got up and smiled at her. Her heart broke to see her this way. Someone who was always so happy and strong. She was glad that she was here to help. To pay her back for the endless kindness she had always shown her and her family over the years.

"Now drink and eat something. We've got a tough day ahead."

There was a huge turnout. Chris was very well known and respected and there were many of their customers, suppliers and business associates as well as family and friends. Sylvie had wanted it to be a little less overwhelming but it would seem that the choice was not hers to be made. What she did insist on was that only family and very close friends came to the house afterwards.

Sylvie hardly spoke to anyone at the funeral. She held on to her boys and only gave them her undivided attention. It was them she really worried about, them and Thea Miria. She had buried three members of her family in the last ten years and Alex and Markus were her only living relatives now.

The four of them were left alone for a while to say their goodbyes at the grave side as the rest of the mourners made their way to their cars. Only Zach stood back from them, more for support. He had already said his goodbyes at the funeral home alone the night before. He had gone there hoping to find some kind of peace. He was still reeling over the revelations he had heard from Sylvie and was disappointed in himself for not having picked up on it. He was with him every day, but yet he hadn't realised what was going on. He blamed himself. If he had known, he'd have stopped it. He would have made him give her up and he'd still be here. Sylvie wouldn't be a widow and Alex and Markus would have their father. The only thing he felt was guilt. He'd let them all down.

At the house everyone was trying their hardest not to be emotional. Thea Miria was sat solemnly on the sofa nursing her drink. Sylvie sat down gently next to her and took hold of her hand.

"You're the only family I have left." It was a statement rather than an observation. "You have always been special to me, Sylvie. Like the daughter I never had. I cannot begin to tell you how sorry I am, for the boys. It's just not right. There's me, with no one, no one dependant on me. I've had a good life, a full life. And yet Chris is the one to go. How can that be eh?"

Sylvie squeezed her hand. She had taken it very badly.

"Thea, don't say that. No one knows what's coming, what the future holds."

"I should be comforting you, being strong for you. But if I'm being honest, I'm finding it very hard to be strong. I can't make sense of it. Poor Chris, dying alone in a strange place. Thank goodness there was the hotel cleaner in the room when it happened. Otherwise, who knows how long he would have been there? Tragic. Alone, all alone." She was shaking her head. It was the story Zach and Sylvie had created. They had to think of a feasible scenario, so they said he had suffered a heart attack in his room and a hotel maid had been there to call for help.

Zach was looking at Sylvie as she comforted Chris's only living relative. She looked up at him and gave him a knowing smile. She knew she had made the right decision keeping the truth from everyone. How could she hurt this dear sweet woman? It would have achieved nothing other than heartbreak. It was bad enough she and Zach had suffered that. It was a small sacrifice in comparison, to put her feelings aside.

By six o'clock, most people had left. Marcy and Petros were being helped by Alex, Marcus, Electra, Melita and Teresa with the clearing up. Sylvie was sitting on the terrace with Lilianna, Zach and Julian.

"How are you holding up?" Lilianna was holding her hand.

"I'm just tired, sweetie. Mentally, physically. I can't sleep. Too many thoughts."

"I'd better go. Sylvie, whatever you need, I mean anything you call me. Anytime." Julian got up and hugged her gently. "I know Zach has your back but I want you to know that you can count on me too." Zach got up to show him out but not before Julian said his goodbyes to Alex and Markus. They walked steadily out to the driveway.

"You've had a lot to deal with, these past few days. How are you doing?" Julian was by his car as he spoke to Zach.

"Just taking it day by day. Hour by hour, actually." Zach sighed as he answered.

"What I said to Sylvie goes for you too. You need any help with anything I'm here for you. This is a lot to take on. I know you feel like all the responsibility falls on your shoulders. The business, Sylvie and the boys. So let me help where I can. After all ,you lost your friend too. We both did." Zach's eyes began to well up, he dried them quickly.

Julian changed the subject, realising Zach was starting to feel uncomfortable. "When will you be opening the offices again?"

"A week on Monday," croaked Zach.

"Okay then, I'll be calling you." He reached over and hugged Zach. "You take care of yourself." And with that he got into his car and drove off.

Julian looked into his rear view mirror as he left the driveway. He could see Zach still standing there. He really felt for him. He knew that Chris had always been the man in charge and their working relationship had worked that way. Zach was happy to follow his lead. That wasn't to say that Zach had little say in the company, on the contrary. Zach had plenty of input and he put in many hours to build their company. He was what Julian called 'the legs' of the company. If something needed doing it was Zach who got it done. Chris may have had the ideas and the contacts. He also took the risks and did all the negotiating too, but once a project was started it was Zach that actually got it done. How was he going to fulfil both roles now he really didn't know?

Julian thoughts drifted to Sylvie. How was she going to react to her husband's death? Sylvie had always been such a vibrant person. He hoped that wouldn't disappear. She had her two boys to think of. They would always take priority over anything else. He was worried that she may close herself off and that would be such a shame. He knew he would need to help Zach, but he felt that he needed to help Sylvie more. He'd got to know Sylvie and he could see she was enjoying her work. It had given her a sense of purpose. Julian hoped that in time she would be able to restart that process again and he would be there to encourage her.

His car phone started to ring. Julian smiled as he recognised the number.

"Hi Mags. How are you?"

"I'm fine, I was worried about you. How was it? Was it bad? I can only imagine how horrible it must have been." Maggie was worried about him. He'd taken Chris's death badly.

"All considered, it wasn't as bad as it could have been. The boys are pretty shaken up and Sylvie is obviously devastated, but she's holding it together."

"Well of course she is. She has to for her children. How about you? How are you?"

"I can't take it in. Last Sunday we were all together at the house, making plans and talking about future projects. And five days later I'm at the house at his funeral. It's surreal. I really can't get my head round it. I think it's really going to hit home when I have to go to his offices. I really am not looking forward to that."

It was true, Julian had been affected by Chris's death. After all, they had over the last year spent a lot of time together in work and outside of it as well. But he was still shell shocked. It hadn't sunk in yet.

"It's tragic, really tragic. That poor woman. How on earth is she going to cope? You know you'll need to help her out. He was your friend Julian. It's only right."

He knew she was right, but the thought of watching Sylvie falling to pieces was not an image he wanted to witness. Not because he didn't have the stomach for it, more because he didn't have a strong enough heart for it.

"I know Mags, I know."

"You really don't sound so good Julian." There was concern in her voice.

"I think I need a change of scenery, get my mind off it. I'll pop in and see Nick if he's in. Maybe go out for a drink. Today was pretty intense; I need some light relief."

"Good idea. He's on the *Silver Lining*, I spoke to him earlier."

Julian hung up and headed towards the marina.

SYLVIE MADE HER WAY up to her bedroom. She was light headed from a combination of lack of sleep, not eating and crying. She edged open the door as if she was dreading what she might find there. To her surprise she saw the air mattress set up at the far side of the room near the window. How had Marcy and Petros found the time today? Sylvie kicked off her shoes and quickly changed. She slid herself into the fresh sheets and felt her whole body melt into the bed. It wasn't long before Sylvie had fallen into a deep, deep sleep.

CHAPTER 5

LIGHT RELIEF?

It was dark by the time Julian reached the marina. He parked up his car and strolled over to where Nick had moored his yacht. He looked at the name as he approached the bow, *Silver Lining.* Where was the silver lining on this cloud, he wondered?

"Hello, is anybody home?" Julian called.

"Dad? What are you doing down here?" Nick came up from below deck.

"I was in the area and wondered if you fancied going out." Julian decided not to tell Nick of his ordeal today. He knew he'd end up having to talk about it and he really didn't want to. It would be hard enough in the weeks that followed.

"Sure I was just going to fix something to eat, but I'm up for going out. Have you just finished from a meeting?" Nick was looking at his Dad's dark suit and tie. More formal than he usually dressed.

"Err… yes." Julian took off his tie and slipped off his jacket. "I'll leave them in the car. Where shall we go?"

"Somewhere close, what about Stathis's place?" Nick knew he was a friend of his Dads.

"Actually I thought we could do Chinese." Julian didn't want to fall on Stathis tonight. He'd been at the funeral too and was in a very bad way. Chris had been a very close friend to him too and he was also shell-shocked. He'd sat in Sylvie's house numbly, unable to speak without crying.

"Great, I'll just lock up and meet you at the car." Nick looked closely at his father. He looked tired and drawn. "You okay Dad, you look a bit tired?"

"It's been a rough few days, that's all. You know what? Maybe we should go to that pub and eat there. We could play pool. We haven't done that in ages."

"Sounds like a plan. I haven't thrashed you at pool in a while!" Nick joked.

"I let you win Nick," laughed Julian.

"You haven't let me win since I was fifteen, Dad!" replied Nick.

They reached the pub and ordered their food. Nick brought their drinks over to the table and sat down opposite Julian. He could see his father was a little preoccupied. He lit up a cigarette and waited for the usual lecture about smoking. To his surprise Julian didn't say a word. Now he knew something was wrong.

"Dad, are you alright?"

"Yes, I'm fine. Tell me what you've been up to. How's the bo… I mean yacht. Have you been out on it?" He hoped Nick had a lot to tell him.

"I have, I took it out and sailed to the other side of the island. I really want to go a lot further, but I haven't got the time. The shop's keeping me busy and I'm going to have to go over to the south of France to look at a couple of yachts for this big Russian client I have."

"Wow Nick, that's good news! When are you going?" Julian was bowled over. Nick had really done well. It was just the news Julian needed to hear.

"Sunday. It should take a week, ten days tops. I just hope my buyer goes for it. It's a hell of a lot of money and my commission will be enough for me not to worry about my expenses for a year." The waitress arrived with their food and seemed to be a little too attentive than necessary.

Julian smiled to himself. Whenever they went anywhere together Nick always got special attention from the opposite sex. What made it funny was that Nick was totally unaware of the effect he had on women.

"South of France, eh? Are you going alone?" Julian was fishing and Nick knew where the conversation was going.

"Yes Dad, I'm going alone. Please don't start on the twenty questions about my personal life again. You should be happy you only have the one wedding to pay for at the moment!"

"I'm only asking." Julian held up his hands. "It's just that I haven't seen you with anyone for a long time and you seem to be so focused on your work. I worry you don't have a social life. Life's not just work, Nick. Believe me, I know. I've seen people be so preoccupied with their work that they lose sight of what's really important or realise it too late. Or just...." He couldn't find the right words. After today, seeing Sylvie and her family reeling at their loss, things were put into perspective. Chris had always worked too hard. He was always chasing the next deal.

"I have a social life Dad, I go out, don't worry. I'm just not ready. Or rather I haven't met someone who's right for me."

"I didn't mean that Nick. I meant just have some fun. You need to enjoy yourself too. Before you know it, time passes by and you'll be wondering what happened."

"Dad, I'm not you. I can't just flit from one meaningless affair to another." Nick stopped worrying that maybe he was being a little harsh on his father. He looked at him, gauging his reaction before he continued. "I'm not judging you. That's who you are. You're happy to be that way. I can't. When I meet someone I see them as the whole deal. I want to see myself with them for the long haul, or at least with the possibility of that happening."

It was true; in many ways Nick may have been similar to his father, but where relationships were concerned they were worlds apart. Nick was intense and an all or nothing person. Something Julian sometimes found hard to understand. But he was genuinely worried about Nick.

"You're still young, Nick. Live a little. At your age I had three children to worry about. There's plenty of time for settling down. Not that I'd want it any other way. I was lucky your mum was so mature."

He paused, realising from his expression that Nick really didn't want to get into it anymore. "Anyway, I wouldn't be paying for your wedding. That's the bride's parent's job!"

joked Julian. He saw Nick instantly relax. Nick pushed his plate to one side and reached for his cigarettes. "And you should pack that disgusting habit too!" Nick smiled and shook his head. He was back!

"You took your time to have a go! I don't think we've ever had a conversation where you've not started with 'It's a disgusting habit', or, 'Haven't you packed it in yet?'"

"Well, I like to be consistent. Now put them down so I can teach you a lesson at pool." They both got up from the table and made their way to the games room.

"Enough about me. How's your private life?" Nick really wanted to change the subject. He loved his dad. But he really didn't understand how he could spend time with vacant young women that were obviously only interested in his money. Not that he wasn't a good looking man, he was, but he wished he would settle down with someone more appropriate.

"Oh you know, same as always, Ellie tried to get back in touch a few days ago. But I really can't be bothered."

"Was she the beautician?" Nick found it hard to keep track.

"Yes, that's right."

"Didn't she know Vicki and Elenora?" remembered Nick.

"Alright, alright, you made your point. Yes they were at school together. Not the best situation. Maybe we should change the subject."

Nick was enjoying seeing his father squirm. What Julian failed to remember was that, as he was getting older, so were his children. So the chances of them knowing his girlfriends increased. He'd either have to date older women or change city!

"Okay then what about work? Any new projects?" Nick was still laughing.

"Enjoy making fun of me, eh? And there's me being concerned for your personal life while you mock mine." He was smiling as he picked up the cue and rubbed chalk on it. "As a matter of fact, I've got a rather different project coming up. I'm designing a new nightclub."

"Really? That is new for you. Where?" Nick was genuinely impressed. His father had only done apartments, house and offices up until now.

"It's Stathis's new club. He took over the old police station and I'm involved in the remodel of it. He's hoping to have it open by March." Julian stopped and thought for a minute. In the light of recent events Julian realised that that project may not actually continue. Or at least be postponed. Nick was racking up the balls and hadn't noticed that his father was deep in thought.

"What a brilliant idea. That spot is really ideal. When do you start? Dad?" Nick's voice disrupted Julian's thoughts.

"Sorry, what did you say?"

"When do you start?"

"Well we're supposed to start next week, but I think it'll be a month or so before we actually start. Some unforeseen circumstances. Hopefully things will work out."

"Heads you break, Dad." Nick flipped a coin and revealed it under his hand. "Tails. Sorry Dad, I'll break."

"Sorry if I came on a bit strong back there. I just worry about you. I just want you to be happy. It's just that I know I've screwed stuff up in the past and I don't want you to shut me out."

"I know Dad. But really I'm fine. I am. I love my work and it's going really well. As for, well my personal life. I haven't found anyone that's right."

"You're just too fussy. There isn't a perfect woman, you know?" Laughed Julian.

"Maybe not. She just needs to be perfect for me though." Nick replied. Julian looked at his son, realising that he was absolutely right.

CHAPTER 6

GUILT

Nothing had prepared Sylvie for the next few days that followed the funeral. It had been the best night's sleep she had had since the night she had found out about Chris, but waking up erased that deep sense of calm. She looked around the bedroom and her stomach churned and her heart began to ache. How was she ever going to get used to this? The truth was she didn't want to get used to it.

Downstairs, Marcy was making breakfast for Alex and Markus. She loved them being home just as much as Sylvie. It gave her the chance to pamper them and the house seemed full again. However, the mood this visit was obviously not the same as Sylvie walked into the sombre kitchen. Her boys were up instantly and by her side giving her a hug and kiss. She smiled weakly then walked over to the radio which was playing at a low volume and turned it off. Marcy looked over to the boys as they shifted in their seats.

"How did you both sleep?" she asked them, knowing that their answer would be a watered down version of the truth.

"Not bad, we were in bed by ten and got up about eight. How about you?" Alex replied for both of them.

"Much better last night." She glanced at Marcy and smiled. 'Thank you,' she mouthed to her. Marcy acknowledged her with a nod and a smile. "What are you eating?"

"Marcy made us French toast, have some Mum, she made enough to feed an army." Markus was trying hard to be upbeat. He knew that if his mother knew how he was feeling it would only make her even sadder.

"I think I will. I think the last time I had French toast was summer time." Sylvie drifted off as she remembered. "That seems such a long time ago. I just love summer." She walked over to the window and looked at the wind blowing the leaves around the garden. "I always seem to be waiting for summer." She seemed to be speaking to herself.

Alex, Markus and Marcy looked at each other a little puzzled.

"What do you mean Mum?" Alex was up by her side. He ran his hands through his hair as he spoke.

"It's just the best time of year. When you were young we used to spend every day at the beach. As you got older and you went to school, we all couldn't wait for the summer holidays to start. Because they were so long and it meant late nights and lazy days. It was the only time Dad and I could really relax. All construction stops in August, so we could be together, reconnect as a family. It's just the best time for me. We recharged our batteries and I always felt so... alive."

She went and sat at the table next to Markus. She helped herself to a slice of toast and poured maple syrup over it.

"I don't know about next summer though." She paused and looked at her plate as she tried to cut her toast. "We've got to get through winter and spring yet." She sighed. Markus was rubbing her back and Alex was staring into his coffee. "We'll manage though eh? Dad wouldn't want it any other way."

As she spoke the tears welled up and spilled over, however hard she tried to hold them back. The four of them sat there in silence, all deep in their own thoughts. Sylvie didn't want the boys to see her like this. It was making it harder for them. She knew they would feel guilty leaving her behind. But they had to and she had to get on with her life too.

"Zach called." Alex broke the silence. "About ten minutes before you came down. He said he was coming round."

"He must be exhausted. He hasn't stopped." Marcy chipped in. She had discreetly wiped her eyes but her eyelashes glistened with the residue of tears.

"I know, but he's insisting to do everything. I really don't know how we'd have managed without him. I hope he'll take a few days for himself before the company opens again." Sylvie was pushing away her half-finished plate.

"I think that's his way of coping with it all." Markus replied, "I actually think that's probably the best way. Keeping busy."

"You're right. We can't sit around all day moping. We should be doing things. I really think we need to keep an eye on Thea Miria. She was very bad yesterday."

"I've never seen her like that. She always so feisty. We should go round today and see her." Alex sipped his coffee and Markus nodded in agreement. "You're sure you're okay here on your own Mum?" Alex asked for the umpteenth . He wasn't comfortable leaving her alone.

"I'm not alone; Marcy's here and Zach will be over in a bit. You go and see her, I'm fine really. She'll need the company." Her tone was a lot chirpier. She forced a smile and kissed them goodbye.

Once they'd left Sylvie let her smile drop.

"Finish your toast. You've eaten nothing in three days." Marcy looked at Sylvie. She had always looked out for her. Mothered her even. They were roughly the same age, but Marcy took on the role as if she were a lot older. She pushed the plate back in front of her. "Don't make me feed you!" she scolded.

"I'm worried about them. They're trying so hard not to show how sad they are. I know it's because they don't want me to get upset. I wish they'd just tell me how they're feeling."

"Give them time, it hasn't sunk in yet. But they do need to be busy."

The door buzzed and Marcy went to let Zach in. He seemed to have aged over the last five days and his eyes were permanently bloodshot.

"Hello there, how are you?" The question was redundant and said more out of habit, he strained a smile as he spoke. It was strange seeing him in casuals. He was always in a suit or a shirt and trousers. Today he was in a black T-shirt and dark jeans and he hadn't shaved. It made him look older.

"A bit better today." Sylvie lied. "You didn't need to come over so early. You must need a break. I've got my boys. You don't need to babysit me."

"Where are they? I was hoping to see them too."

"I sent them to Thea Miria. I'm worried about her. It'll do her good to see them on her own." Zach looked a little edgy. "Do you want some breakfast? Coffee?"

"No um, I need to talk to you about something." He was fiddling with a fork as he spoke.

"Okay, do you want to go into the office?" Sylvie got up and Zach followed her but not before glancing at Marcy and straining a smile.

They settled on the settee.

"What is it, Zach?" Sylvie couldn't face another revelation.

"Well, it's just that the lawyers got in touch with me and as Chris's will states that you inherit everything; we need to draw up the correct papers to transfer everything to you."

Sylvie looked at Zach trying to work out what he'd said.

"He left the business to me?" she was a little stunned.

"I thought you knew that's what he'd wanted."

"To be honest I hadn't really thought about it. I just presumed he'd give it to… well, you, or at least some more shares in it. Sorry, is that a little insensitive? Did you expect something too?" She realised she wasn't really thinking before she spoke.

"Chris and I had discussed this many times or should I say argued. When we split the shares originally he gave me twenty five per cent, you had twenty four and he had the remaining fifty one. I didn't deserve the twenty five, he just gave them to me. That was Chris. I insisted though that he should make his will at the same time. I told him that in the event of his death all his shares should automatically go to you. He felt that I should get some too."

"Well yes, that's what I thought. You've been with the company from its start, Zach. It's only right." Sylvie was still in shock.

"That may be true, but it was Chris who started it with you. You two are 'Sapphire Developers' and on top of that you have two boys who are going to carry it on. I was just lucky to have been involved. I am lucky that I'm still part of it, but it's Alex and Markus's birth right. Their father built it. He was the one, without him and you by his side it wouldn't exist. Let's face it; I'd still be working with my father. So I told him I didn't want any more shares. The seventy five per cent you will have now can be split between the boys. Whenever that will be."

Sylvie was overcome. She knew Zach was and always had been one of their closest friends, but today he had shown to her that he was a lot more to her. She put her arms around him softly.

"Chris knew exactly what he was doing asking you to join the company. He knew you had his back and now you have mine. I still think that you should have been given some, it doesn't seem right." Zach pulled her gently back and looked at her.

"I had one hundred percent of nothing, and now I have twenty five percent of something. Something that's still growing. I'm very lucky. Now, I don't want to discuss it any more. Why I came was not to go over the will; I came to see when we can get everything signed over legally. Our lawyers want to do it as soon as possible. I just need you to tell me when you're up for it."

"We open a week on Monday, right?" Zach nodded, unsure where this was going.

"Then get them to have it all ready by then. Is that okay? Not too soon?" after all she didn't know how much work needed to be done.

"No that's fine. I'll get them to come here and it'll take about an hour, two tops."

"No, not at the house. At the office." Zach had a very bad feeling.

"Sylvie, is that such a good idea? It's going to be tough going into the office without this added pressure." Zach didn't want Sylvie to be faced with Dina as well as Chris's office. He was trying to avoid them seeing each other. He didn't know how long he'd be able to keep them apart.

"I think the staff need to see me. If I don't go in it'll make it even more awkward when they do see me." Sylvie knew why Zach was stressing. There was no way Dina was going to make her feel uncomfortable in her own company!

"Whatever you want. You may change your mind, let's decide nearer the time." Zach didn't want to push it.

"That's enough business for now. How are you? I mean I know this has been hard for you. Everyone's focusing on me and the boys, but you lost your best friend."

Zach sat for a while, not being able to say what he wanted. He wanted to be strong for everyone but Sylvie was the only one he could talk to. Not because Lilianna wouldn't understand, but because she didn't know the truth. He focused on his hands trying to summon up what was and had been going repeatedly through his mind over the last few days.

"I feel….I feel many things. Like you angry, disappointed. I also feel very alone. Chris and I didn't only work together we did pretty much everything together. From having morning coffee to watching football. But what I feel more than anything is guilt." He turned to her. She looked at him puzzled. Then with a sudden movement he was standing.

"I let you down. I let the boys down. I was with him every day. How did I not see it? How the hell was I so blind? I keep trying to remember situations. Anything at all that would have given me some inkling as to what he was up to. I keep going over things in my head. Over and over trying to find any clues I missed. If I'd just realised, I would have stopped him. He wouldn't have gone to Athens. He wouldn't have had an argument that caused him the heart attack." Sylvie flinched at his straight talking.

"I would have helped him sort it out, like the last time. And he'd be here. We wouldn't be talking about wills and shares and all this." He was almost shouting as he threw his hands in the air as he paced the room. "He left me too. Yes he left me to sort out all this mess. But I blame myself. In hindsight now it was obvious. She was always around. Not in your face but in the background, and she was familiar. You know what I mean… Oh shit, this is really insensitive of me. I'm so sorry, Sylvie, I just wasn't thinking." He'd turned to see her in the middle of his venting and saw her distraught expression.

"No, no carry on. I need to hear it and you need to get it off your chest." It was true. They had no one else to talk to. They really needed to get all their questions and their feelings out, how else would they be able to move forward?

"Familiar? What do you mean?"

"Well, they had stopped saying 'please' and 'thank you' to each other. I know it sounds strange, but Irene, whom we've all known for years, still says it to me and I to her. There's a respectful distance between us. I don't know; maybe I'm just trying to find something that's not there." He sat back down again and sighed.

"You shouldn't feel guilty. If anyone should it should be me." Sylvie rested her head back on the settee. "I confronted him and gave him an ultimatum. I put the pressure on him, knowing he'd be backed into a corner. Hell, I even enjoyed it. If I knew that he'd... Well, I would have buried my head in the sand and pretended I didn't know. The last words I spoke to him were so hard and angry. I told him I was done. We were over. He pleaded with me to forgive him. He told me that he loved me and that I was everything to him." She rubbed her face with her hands and sat up straight. "So if anyone should feel guilty it's me." She patted Zach's leg and he shook his head.

"I need a drink, is it too early?"

"Who cares, I'll go and get us one." Sylvie got up and headed for the door. "I'm glad you told me everything, Zach. It's made it easier. But don't beat yourself up about it. He knew what he was doing. Everyone has a choice to make and he made his. Unfortunately we're living with the consequences. You're a good man, Zach, with a very big heart. Don't carry his mistakes on your shoulders."

CHAPTER 7

JULIAN TO THE RESCUE

Sylvie had dragged herself into the office every day after the transfer. Originally, she was just going to keep a low profile until she felt she could face normality. But she watched her boys and knew that if she stayed at home they would also not find the courage to get back to their lives. She mainly sat in Chris's office and pretended to look at the paperwork. She spent a great many hours looking out of the window. Her favourite view, of the sea with the boats and yachts bobbing up and down. After the fourth day, Zach started getting a little concerned.

"She just comes in and sifts through the mail and paperwork. Drinks tea and stares out of the window. I don't know what to do." He was talking to Lilianna on the phone. He was hoping she might come up with something.

"She hasn't anything to do. Chris made that company a well-oiled machine. Everyone's getting on with what needs to be done. You have to give her something to do. Something she feels is hers. Right now, it's Chris's company. What about the club, what's happening there?"

"Well Stathis put it on hold. He didn't feel right pressuring us into getting it started. And to be honest I think he's still in shock too." It was true Stathis was finding it hard. Over twenty years Chris had been a close friend of his and where business was concerned they were always interconnected.

"Call him, Zach. If you tell him Sylvie's lost and needs something to get her going again, he'll help. Get Julian in too. You told me he offered to help. This is the only thing that'll do it, Zach. She needs to feel that she's needed. She's only coming in there so the boys think she's coping. She's just going through the motions and that's not good."

Zach knew she was right. He needed to make her feel as if she was part of the company and that her input was necessary.

"You're right, Lily. I'll get them both to subtly put a bit of pressure on her. Let's hope it jump-starts her. She seems to be in a daze most of the time." With that he put down the phone and immediately rang Julian. It took Julian ten minutes to drop what he was doing and get round to Sapphire Developers.

The intercom buzzed and brought Sylvie out of her daze.

"Yes Maria?"

"Julian's here to see you. Shall I send him in?" Maria tentatively asked.

"Err, yes. Thank you."

Maria looked up at Julian and smiled. He looked his usual smart, impeccable self in his dark blue shirt and dark suit. Maria really liked him; he was always so charming.

"You can go through."

"How's she been?" he asked her. She shrugged.

"Honestly? A little preoccupied and very quiet. Really quiet, actually. Understandable though, given the circumstances."

"Yes. Well let's see if we can do anything to change that, shall we? Thanks Maria."

Julian opened the office door and walked through. He tried not to show how shocked he was to see what seemed to be a shadow of her former self. Sylvie was wearing a black woollen V-necked dress which made her look gaunt and drawn. Her hair tied back in a ponytail, emphasizing her cheek bones and large brown eyes. She looked tired and her eyes had lost their sparkle. Something Julian wasn't used to.

"Hello Julian, it was nice of you to pop by." She stood up to greet him and he could see that she had lost weight. He couldn't believe that in the space of ten days she had deteriorated to such an extent. His heart broke as he hugged her feeling her rib cage through her dress.

"I should have come sooner. How have you been?"

"It's been hard but I really have to be strong. I need my boys to get on with their lives and they won't if they think I'm not. How are you? Family okay? How's the wedding preparations going?"

"Oh, I leave that to Maggie. She's enjoying every second!" Sylvie tried to smile but for some reason she couldn't get her lips to curl. Julian found himself staring at her as they stood in silence. He was trying hard not to succumb to his natural instinct to pull her into his arms, to comfort her.

"The reason why I dropped by, apart from wanting to see you, is that I got the visuals together for Stathis's club. I wanted to set up a meeting so we could show them to him." He knew he was throwing a lot at her but he felt that this was the only way. Zach said she was in a bad way, but nothing could have prepared him for this.

"Oh, didn't you talk to Zach about it. I'm not really sure… Should I say, I don't know how it was left." Sylvie had almost forgotten about the club.

"Yes I did. He said you were the one to talk to especially as you had the ideas for the interior. Do you want me to show you what I came up with? I have it in the car."

Sylvie had no idea what to say. She really couldn't face this right now, but she knew he'd come over especially to discuss it. "Alright, sure," she answered tentatively, good manners taking over.

Julian left in a flash to get his laptop while Sylvie tried to get hold of Zach.

"I can't find him Sylvie, he must have gone out," answered Irene, his assistant. Where the hell was he? She really wasn't up for this. Sylvie paced up and down until Julian returned. He was back within five minutes. They sat on the settees as Julian set up his Mac. He slipped off his jacket.

"Zach gave me all the ideas you discussed with Stathis and I've tried to incorporate them as best I could. But to be honest I really needed you to explain your ideas. Zach's not that, shall we say… eloquent when it comes to design." He chuckled. "I put in an entrance, like a tunnel and then here, look can you see how I incorporated the levels? Is that what you had in mind?"

He began guiding Sylvie through his virtual plan based on the information he was given. At first Sylvie gazed at the screen, not taking much in, but gradually Julian started to ask opinions which forced Sylvie take notice.

"The bars on the ground level. Zach said you wanted two, I wasn't sure where you wanted them so I put them down each wall." Sylvie moved forward and leaned closer to see.

"I'm not sure…" She looked at the plan. "Not sure about that, it looks a little sparse. It needs to be a feature. What about in the centre?" Julian leaned in and furrowed his brow.

"It will mean that the staff and supplies will have to walk through the club to get to it."

"Hmm… Doesn't it have a basement?"

"Yes." Julian looked at her, not sure where she was going with this. She raised her eyebrows at him as though she was willing him to guess. "Oh! I get it. Open it up so the staff enter from the basement up, supplies too. Genius!"

He beamed at her, and suddenly he saw her face slightly light up. It was working! He was getting her thinking again. He looked at her beautiful brown eyes that had once sparkled and felt his heart crack. He couldn't see her so broken, so empty and sad. He sat back and swallowed, trying to keep up the momentum.

"We're in two minds about the roof. What's your take on it?"

"I liked the idea of a glass roof so that you can see the sky. But what I really think is that, if we could make it a retractable roof, it would be ideal for the summer months. Make it open air. You'd have the best of both worlds then."

"Wow! I think that's a brilliant idea, Sylvie. In the summer everyone goes to the open air clubs and in the winter, they head for the indoor ones. Stathis would be the only club that works all year."

"It'll be pricey though, won't it?"

"Probably, but it'd be worth it. It'll be unique. That's Zach's department. He'll put all the costs together." Julian watched Sylvie start looking over the rest of his visuals and started to see a glimmer of the Sylvie he knew. Zach was right, she needed a project to kick start her. He studied her as he leaned backwards, giving her room. She really was quite beautiful, even in this state she was breathtaking. Julian shook his head bringing him back to the subject in hand.

"Let me call Stathis and arrange a meeting for tomorrow. If we get cracking we might get this club open by the end of April. Is that okay with you?" He'd purposely backed her into a corner, so that she'd have to say yes.

"If that suits you, sure. Tell him to come here around ten?"

He nodded his approval. "I'll make the changes and have them ready for tomorrow." He leaned back further and stretched.

"Great. I hope he likes it." Sylvie nervously looked back at Julian.

"He'll love it, Sylvie." He reached over to her and gently rubbed her back. Then, worried she might change her mind, he got up quickly and collected his things and made a quick exit. As soon as he was in his car he called Zach.

"Hi Julian. How did it go? How was she?" Zach sounded apprehensive.

"You were right. She really is in bad way. But I got her interested in the club again. And I've told her we need to meet Stathis tomorrow. I know its short notice, but if we leave it longer she'll cancel it."

"No, you did the right thing leave Stathis to me. I'll get him there. She tried to call me when you went to your car. But I avoided her call. If I'd have been there she would have backed off. She's too embarrassed to blow you off. You did really good Julian, thanks a lot." Zach was truly relieved.

"I told you, Zach; anytime you need help I'm here for you. For both of you. I really can't see her this way; whatever it takes we need to get her back to her own self again."

Zach put down the phone and dialled Stathis. It was nice to hear his voice. He'd avoided contacting him because he couldn't go over the past two weeks events again. But now he had another reason. After their initial pleasantries, Zach broached the subject.

"Stathis, I need a favour."

"Sure, whatever."

"We need to get the club going, and I need you to ask Sylvie to get involved."

"Oh. I thought it might be too soon. And what do you mean, get Sylvie involved? I thought she'd always been involved." Stathis was a little confused.

"Yes she is, but that's not what I mean. Chris and I were going to ask you if you'd let Sylvie do the interior design this time. She was really looking forward to it, then with everything that's happened. Well, she's not good, Stathis, really not good."

"Well it's understandable, Zach. We're all finding it hard." His voice was tight as he spoke.

"I know, I know. But she needs something to keep her mind off everything. Her boys are going and she'll just deteriorate. I know her. She needs something to get her going again. Stathis, she needs this."

"Of course Zach, it's always her ideas anyway that we use. She's really talented and apart from that... she's, well, you know." Stathis paused, feeling that maybe he'd said too much. Zach smiled; he knew how Stathis felt for Sylvie. "If you really think she's up for it, I wouldn't like anything more. I've already delayed the opening to the end of April. What do you need me to do?"

"We're going to have a meeting tomorrow. Julian, Sylvie, me and now you. We have to put her under a bit of pressure. Julian started the ball rolling today. So with any luck she'll start feeling a little more necessary."

"I'll be there. And thanks, Zach."

"Don't mention it."

Zach started feeling a little more optimistic. If all went to plan Sylvie would start coming round. His next problem was that air mattress Alex had told Lilianna about in her room!

CHAPTER 8

HOME ALONE

Over the next few weeks, Sylvie had been thrown in at the deep end. She had been figuratively bullied into overseeing the clubs reconstruction and redecoration. Stathis had simply pleaded with her to take it on as he trusted no-one else except Zach and her. Zach explained it was far too much for him to take on alone, so she relented, insisting that she get as much leeway as she could and that Julian took a more active role. Zach could not have orchestrated it any better.

Both Alex and Markus were thankful to see their mother start to come around. It was true, she was immersing herself into her work, but they were happy that she could be distracted by something. She was using the club as her crutch to keep her mind occupied and it seemed to be working. She stayed as long as she could at the office, anything to avoid the inevitable, coming back to their home.

Sylvie managed to convince Alex to resume his studies after the new year. He would need a lot of catching up, but she knew he could manage. Markus also decided that he should finish his military service, even though his commanding officer was happy for him to be excused from his remaining six months. She knew it was better for them to carry on as normal as soon as possible. So, once the terrible ordeal of Christmas and New Year without Chris had passed, she insisted that they stop worrying about her and start back into their own lives.

ON JANUARY SECOND, MARKUS resumed rank at the military base and Alex flew back to England. Sylvie drove home from the airport with tears rolling down her cheeks. She pulled into the garage and parked up her car next to the ever-stationary Mercedes. It was four o'clock and thankfully Marcy had left. She didn't want her clucking round her again. Sylvie got out of her car and walked into the kitchen. The house was silent.

Over the past two months, the house had never been quiet. From the day Chris had died there had been someone constantly there. Sylvie walked into the lounge and started to flick on lights. It would be getting dark soon. She walked back to the kitchen and saw some dinner Marcy had thoughtfully prepared.

The thought of sitting alone and eating filled her with dread. She'd promised herself that she would have to make small adjustments every day. But she really couldn't sit here for the next six hours. The easiest option was to ring Lilianna. She'd tell her to go over. But Sylvie had leaned on her and Zach enough these past two months. It was time for her to get used to being alone. She picked up her bag and headed back to her car. She'd go to the marina, look at the boats and have a coffee at Stathis's place, and maybe eat there. At least there would be noise and not this deathly silence.

It took her fifteen minutes to get there. She strolled down to the marina and looked at all the yachts and speedboats. They looked so beautiful bobbing in the calm sea. The whole area was buzzing. Many people were still on holiday and the weather had been unusually warm over the Christmas period. The sun was setting which sent a warm glow across the whole area. Eventually Sylvie walked into Stathis's place and ordered a drink. She sat in a booth. It didn't take long for the staff to call Stathis and before long he had joined her.

"What a lovely surprise Sylvie. You just missed Olga. She was here with the kids."

"That's a pity. I haven't seen her in ages. I thought I'd come and have a look at the boats."

She was glad she'd missed Olga. She really couldn't stomach watching happy couples together. It made her sadder than ever. And the truth be told she had very little in common with Olga. She was sweet and kind but there was very little they could talk about. Stathis, on the other hand, she could talk to for hours.

"I was about to have my late lunch, or should I say early dinner, will you join me?"

He'd sat down next to Sylvie and called one of his waiters over. He didn't even wait for an answer. "Dino, bring us some of that sea bream and a bottle of Chablis." Then he turned to Sylvie. "That's your favourite, isn't it?" He had an incredible memory for what his customers liked. Sylvie nodded, thankful she'd had the courage to come down.

NICK WALKED DOWN FROM his shop towards quay eight where his yacht was. He'd arranged to meet some of his friends for something to eat. He jumped into the shower and then quickly threw on his jeans and a shirt. He headed back to where all the cafés and restaurants were.

As he reached the café they were supposed to meet at his eye caught sight of a woman sat in a booth. He looked more closely and saw that it was Sylvie, the woman from his father's office. His friends were already sat outside, so he couldn't carry on staring. He joined them, but positioned himself so that he could see into the restaurant she was in.

He noticed that she was with a man, her husband he presumed. He had his back to the window so he couldn't see his face. Sylvie seemed to be a little preoccupied – or was it sad – and her face was pale. The man kept getting up and leaving her and on returning, her smile seemed forced. Nick couldn't quite work out was going on. What he didn't count on was how glad he was to see her again. The town was small and the chances of you falling on someone were pretty high, so it was strange that he hadn't seen her since that day at his father's office.

His friends continued talking and laughing around him, thankfully oblivious. Then he saw her get up to leave, she kissed the man goodbye and walked towards the door. He realised as the man turned that it was Stathis, a friend of his father's. Then he remembered something his father had told him about his new club. He'd have to check up on that.

He watched her leave the restaurant and cross over the road to his side. He almost held his breath as she passed by his table and walked off down the street to where her car was parked. She looked deep in thought, and her face looked tired and he noticed that she hadn't smiled, not once, but she still looked stunning.

"Are you alright, Nick? You looked miles away!" one of his friends asked.

"Yes er… I just saw someone I haven't seen in ages, that's all."

Sylvie got into her car and drove off. It was seven o' clock. At least she'd managed to occupy a couple of hours. Stathis had been good company, even if all they talked about was work. He probably didn't want to broach any other subject and kept it safe. Sylvie pulled into the garage and looked at the Mercedes. She was going to have to do something about that. If the boys were willing, she'd sell it. No one wanted to drive it. Petros just kept turning over the engine, to keep the battery working.

The phone was ringing as Sylvie entered the house.

"Hello?"

"Sylvie? Have you just got in?" It was Lilianna doing her evening check up call.

"Yes, just now."

"I rang earlier. What have you been up to?" She was trying to suss out her mood without being obvious.

"I went down to Stathis place. Had some dinner and sat and chatted about the club."

"I was worried you might feel crappy now that the boys have gone and Marcy told me that you asked her to leave as normal."

"I didn't want her fussing round me when I got back. I've got to get used to being here alone, however hard it is. I told you that after the new year I was determined to change something, however hard and however difficult." She sat down on the settee and kicked off her boots.

"What you got planned for tomorrow?"

"I'll pop into work for a bit. I know were closed but I left some samples in there that I need to take them back and then I'm not really sure." She was really going to find it hard to fill her days with the boys gone.

"Do you fancy going shopping with me? I need to find some new bedding for Electra's room and with sales started, I thought we'd be able to find some good bargains." Sylvie had a weird feeling about this. "You might find some bits you need, too." Sylvie realised where this was going. Lilianna had obviously been talking to Marcy.

"You're about as subtle as a sledgehammer. I know what you're trying to do."

"Crap, I was really trying to be delicate. You can't sleep on that airbed forever. You're going to have to eventually sleep on your bed. I know it's really hard sweetie, but it's been over two months. At least if you change the bedding it'll be different." Sylvie went quiet.

"Sylvie? Don't be cross. I just think you've suffered enough. New year, new beginning?"

"I know. It's just a lot harder than I thought it would be. The longer I leave it the harder it is. You're right though. At least if I buy some new bedding it's a step in the right direction."

"Baby steps sweetie." Lilianna was relieved. She really thought Sylvie might have reacted badly to her interfering. They arranged to meet the following morning.

Sylvie put the phone down and looked around. Every single part of the house screamed Chris to her. She poured herself a whisky and switched off the lights. She picked up a stack of magazines that she'd never even looked at and made her way to her bedroom with full intention of reading them. She opened the door to her room and switched on the lights. She glanced at the bed then went to run a bath. She loved having a bath at the end of the day. Especially in the winter and especially when she felt stressed or tired. She let the tub fill as she poured in her bath oil in and set the magazines close to the tub. She took a big gulp of her drink and set it down by the tub then returned to the bedroom.

Part Two – Winter

Sylvie walked over to what used to be Chris's side and pulled back the quilt, revealing the pillows. She picked one up and held it up to her face then buried her nose into it and took a deep breath. She sat down on the bed and wept into the pillow.

She couldn't smell him anymore. She reached for the second pillow and repeatedly took deep breaths in between her sobs to find any hint of his scent, but it was all in vain. Over the two months it had gone, disappeared, and she felt so hollow inside. She walked over to the bathroom again and turned off the water as she carried on heaving shallow sobs. She undressed and slipped into the bath, allowing the warm water to cover her shaking body. As the time passed her sobs subsided and she washed the tears from her face.

Before Sylvie padded back to the bedroom she dabbed some tissue with Chris's aftershave and took it to the air mattress. She slipped into the sheets and left the tissue on the bedside table. Within a few minutes the room smelt faintly of the scent evaporating from the tissue. Sylvie turned out the lights and cried herself to sleep again.

CHAPTER 9

A NEW FRIEND

S ylvie woke up to the sound of rain lightly pattering against the window. Her head felt heavy and her eyes tight. Her room was a mess. She couldn't believe she'd let it get to this state. She swiftly got out of bed and stripped the sheets off of the airbed. She moved over to the bed, took a deep breath as she stroked the pillows, before she stripped the sheets off that too.

Marcy was busying herself in the kitchen as she entered it. The radio was on and Sylvie scowled slightly. She reached over and turned it off. Since Chris had died she'd stopped listening to music. Every song seemed to mean something. Marcy had respected her wishes, but today she felt she might try again and had put it on.

"Morning Marcy."

"Morning." She was desperate to ask how her evening had gone, but she didn't. She had hardly slept, worrying about Sylvie. And at one point she'd nearly called her, but Petros had stopped her.

"If she needs you she'll call. She's got to get used to rattling around that house alone."

"Marcy, I put my bedding in the laundry. Could you ask Petros to take down the air bed, I won't be needing it anymore."

"Err, yes of course." Marcy found it very hard not to show how totally relieved she was.

"Don't remake the bed though. I'm off to buy new bedding today. I hope I can get it washed and dry by tonight. With this rain I think I may be pushing my luck." She took a sip of her tea, enjoying Marcy's loss for words. "It's okay Marcy just spit it out, I won't snap!" she smiled.

"Oh thank the Lord! That's the best news I've had all year." She moved over, hugging her. "Don't you worry about your new sheets, I'll stay until they're washed and dried."

"It's only the third of January Marcy. Don't you think you're setting the bar a little low?" she laughed. "Don't start pressuring me though. I said I'd try and do something small every day. So don't push me." Her eyes flitted over to the radio. "Like I said, when I'm ready. Today's a big step for me."

"I know, Mam. But it's a step in the right direction."

Lilianna was waiting for Sylvie in their usual coffee shop. After their customary kisses Lilianna broached the subject.

"Are we still going shopping?" she cocked her head to the side.

"Yes we are. You'll be pleased to know the airbed's gone. So let's go, I've got to get them washed, dried and ironed before tonight! I hate to think what else you've been plotting with Marcy!"

THEY MANAGED TO FIND two sets of bedding, which pleased Marcy no end. She got busy getting them ready. It was lunchtime and Sylvie started to feel a little redundant. Normally she'd either be cooking or working at the office. But their offices were closed until the seventh and there was no one to cook for. What was she going to do for the next three days? She'd spent all morning shopping now she didn't know what to do with herself. She decided to call Julian.

"Hello Sylvie, how are you? This is a nice surprise!" He'd stopped disguising his delight when she called.

"Not bad. You know; same shit, different day. Sorry to bother you. I know your offices are closed but I really wanted to look at the roof design for the club. I'm at a bit of a loose end, and…" She started to feel foolish. The man probably had plans. It was the holidays, he had family and she was harassing him.

"Sylvie, you never bother me. Meet me at my office. I'll be there in thirty minutes."

Smiling to herself, Sylvie reached for her bag and keys.

"He's a very good man," commented Marcy. Sylvie turned to look at her as she reached the door.

"Yes he is. He's been a good friend to me."

"I think he's hoping for something a little more" replied Marcy, with a knowing look.

"He's just a friend Marcy, don't you start as well!"

"Maybe for you, but I know very few men that would drop everything when they're supposed to be on holiday when a woman calls, just because he's a friend."

Sylvie knew she was right, but she really didn't want to think about it. She liked Julian, but her feelings were only Platonic. He was a perfect gentleman to her and she kept him at a respectful distance. "I'm just saying." Marcy raised her eyebrows and pursed her lips together. "Your bed will be done by the time you're back." And with that she scuttled off.

Julian jumped out of bed and jumped into the shower. Quickly he dried himself and threw his clothes on. Ellie looked up at him in surprise.

"Where you going? I thought we'd be spending all day in bed." She pouted.

"Sorry, it's work. Very urgent. I need to get to the office. But it's was nice… seeing you again. Let yourself out. I'll call." He felt bad running out on her like that, but she knew he was using her for sex, and so was she. That was their understanding. After all, he hadn't expected to hear from anyone today, especially Sylvie.

"Was that Sylvie?" she asked brightly as she stretched. Julian scowled.

"Err…yes. How do you know her?" He was sure he'd never mentioned her to Ellie.

"You mumbled her name in your sleep."

His face dropped. "I work with her, that's all." He muttered embarrassed.

"Cool. Call me when you're… Well, if you need anything." She blew him a kiss and he scuttled out of the bedroom, leaving her lying naked on his bed.

There was no one at his office apart from Julian. He was waiting for her in the car park.

"Is this really okay?" asked Sylvie.

"Of course, I told you. It's great to see you. Here, let me take your case." He kissed her on the cheek and took her laptop case.

They made their way up to his office. Julian turned on all the lights as it was overcast still. Sylvie started to feel a little unsettled. Whether it was what Marcy said or whether she could feel some sort of tension, she really couldn't work it out. She started to fidget and then she started twisting her rings as she always did when she felt nervous. Julian was hooking up his computer. He kept glancing over at her as she looked down at her rings. He couldn't believe how pleased he was to see her.

"Your hair's wet?"

"Yes, I was at the… gym when you called," he lied. He fiddled with the blinds so as not to look at her. "So, have the boys gone back?"

Sylvie looked up. "Yes, I'm sad to say. I got used to them being here. The house feels… Well, you know. It's not easy. How was your Christmas?" She really didn't want to answer too many questions about herself. She'd come here trying to get away from them.

"It wasn't bad. Quiet. I spent it with my ex, Maggie and our kids."

"That's nice. You get on with her then? You've got three children haven't you?" She tried to remember, she was sure he'd told her that.

"Yes Elenora is the one that's getting married in April. She's a teacher of art. She very like her mother. Vicki's the studious one. She's a lawyer, very ambitious."

"Like her father?" added Sylvie.

"I suppose so. And then there's Nick, he's the adventurer and entrepreneur. He has his own business in the marina and he lives most of the time on his yacht."

"How fascinating. They are all so individual. You must be very proud of them. And your ex-wife, Maggie, does she work?" After knowing Julian for all this time they'd never really spoken about his family. They touched on it from time to time, but Sylvie realised this was the first time he'd really spoken about them.

"She was always a mother first. But she studied textile design at university. She never used it because we got married and the kids came very quickly. Now she has her small business making her own pottery. She's very good. She's a free spirit and the kindest person I know. We always spent the holidays together as a family."

"You're very lucky Julian, there are not many divorced couples who can stand to be in the same room as each other, let alone spend Christmas together!" She felt the mood lighten and she gradually began to relax. Julian started to set up the program.

"It'll be ready in a minute. It takes a while to upload." He came and sat by her. "Sylvie, do you remember a few months back, I'm not sure if you do, what with everything and... Well... Anyway. I told you about Maggie needed some help with her bedroom and Elenora's room. Redesigning in preparation for the wedding? I suggested you could do it."

"Yes I remember. I just presumed, what with, well me not being altogether myself, that you'd found someone else."

"Not at all. It's just that, you've done amazingly well to get the club on schedule, and it's moving on really quickly. I was wondering if you had time now and could maybe start on that." He hoped he wasn't pressuring her. But he really wanted her to work on Maggie's house.

"Are you sure that Maggie would want me to do it? She doesn't know me. Maybe I should meet her first. You know you need to at least like your designer before you get them to work on your house," Sylvie joked.

"She'll love you, I know she will. But you're right, you should meet up first. Let me call her."

He reached for his phone.

"What, now?" Sylvie was taken aback at his impulsiveness. "I'm sure she's busy and it's such short notice." It was too late; he was already dialling.

"Hello Mags. Are you busy?"

To Sylvie's surprise Julian managed to persuade her to drop off her car back at her house and then drive up to Maggie's within twenty minutes. They pulled up outside the house which was set back from the main road. From the outside it looked understated but once inside, it was a very large home on many levels. It was a little bohemian for Sylvie's taste but it was definitely Maggie's style. Julian had designed the house twenty five years ago and when they had divorced he had been happy for her to keep it.

The house had a large garden with a heated swimming pool, which Maggie and the children used all year round. It had been designed with their three children in mind. They all loved the water except Julian, he much preferred the mountains so this had been his compromise. A house in the countryside with a huge pool.

The rain had thankfully stopped as they approached the front door and Sylvie could see Julian was a little anxious. It was very important to him that they got along. Sylvie was becoming more and more important to him. If things went the way he was hoping they would, Sylvie would be in Maggie's life too.

Maggie opened the door before they even knocked.

"Hello, you must be Sylvie. I've heard so much about you, come in, come in."

"I'm so pleased we've finally met. You have a beautiful home." Sylvie said as she walked through into the sitting room.

"It's always a mess. Forgive my state, I was working in the back." She showed them her hands which had paint on them. "I'll just wash up. Take her through to kitchen, Julian."

Maggie wasn't at all what she expected. She was tall, taller than her, and slim. She had fair skin and long, blonde wavy hair. Sylvie knew she was the same age as Julian but she looked in her early forties. She had a sense of calm around her and she seemed to float rather than walk. Sylvie noticed she was barefoot even though it was chilly and she was wearing ripped jeans and a floaty blouse. She could now understand how their relationship worked. Julian was the anxious, on the go, ambitious one and she was his opposite. The perfect yin and yang.

"I take it you designed this house." Sylvie was looking out to the pool. "It's really something."

"Well, I was designing for my family. It had to be perfect for them." He smiled. "Do you want something to drink? I'll put on the kettle."

He didn't even wait for an answer. He opened the cupboards, took out cups, and then went to the fridge. Sylvie watched him. This was still his home, she thought. He moved around the kitchen like it was still his. Even though she was happy to see him this way, she felt uneasy. What exactly was the relationship between Maggie and him?

"Great, you've started tea, or would you prefer something else? I only really drink tea, but Julian prefers coffee." Maggie had come back through.

"Tea's perfect."

Before long the two of them were chatting about what Maggie wanted in her room first. Elenora's would be done after the wedding. She wanted to update it as that was where the videoing would take place as Elenora would be getting ready.

"It hasn't changed in twenty-five years, so it's very eighties. Peach and cream with swags and tails. We can go up in a bit."

Julian sat back and observed. He watched as the two women switched from subject to subject. They moved to the wedding preparations and the problems they were having with where to have the pre-wedding dinner. Then they got on the subject of flowers and what would be the best combination. Maggie asked Sylvie about her boys and what they were doing. How was she coping now they were away? There were endless questions and they flitted from each subject with ease.

Then Sylvie asked about her work, so Maggie took her through to the studio at the back. Sylvie loved looking at all her designs. There were so many themes. Floral, abstract, plain, fruits and stripped.

"These are really beautiful Maggie. Julian said you were good." Sylvie was genuinely impressed.

"Thank you. Well, it started out as a hobby. When the kids were young I used to make cups and plates for them. I kept them all. I also have their hand and footprints on plates. Then a few friends asked me to do their kids some and it just went from there really. And now it's grown into this." She waved her arm around in the air.

"Are you going to do something to commemorate Elenora's wedding?"

"I never thought of that. But what a brilliant idea. Something with their initials on may be?"

They carried on discussing her work as Maggie took her on a full tour of the house. The girls lived permanently at the house, so their rooms were more lived in. Nick's room was immaculate. He only sometimes stayed over, but it was kept for him and obviously lovingly so by Maggie. They ended up in her bedroom which was all that she'd promised, a real flashback to the eighties!

It was only when they eventually came downstairs that they realised Julian had been left alone and it was dark outside.

"What time is it?" Sylvie looked at her watch. It was five o'clock. They'd been there nearly four hours and she hadn't even realised.

"It's five." Julian was laughing. "You two haven't stopped talking."

"Were you totally bored?" Sylvie started to feel bad for him. They had pretty much ignored him.

"I was fine. I watched some TV and caught up on my emails. Nick called and he'll be back by the sixth." Julian turned to Sylvie. "He left last night on a buying trip." He explained, then turned to Maggie. "He said the sale has gone through, he's just waiting for the transfer."

"That's brilliant news!" Maggie beamed.

"I take it then that you'd like to do this job then?" he was still laughing. "I knew you two would get on, but I wasn't expecting how much. My God, you two can talk!"

"Ignore him Sylvie, I do. So when will you have something to show me?"

"I'll need a couple of weeks. I'll be fitting it in around the club. Is that alright? I'll get you to come down to my office. I have some work that I've done before to show you, for ideas. Just to get me on the right track. I may be designing it but it needs to be your style, what you like."

"Sounds great and I'll bring the girls down. We'll do lunch or something."

"Maybe we should go then. Sorry we took so long." Sylvie said sheepishly to Julian.

"I'll forgive you this time!" He chuckled. They said their goodbyes and Julian and Sylvie headed back down to town.

"She's lovely, Julian. I'm so pleased I met her."

"Me too. It means a lot to me that you two got on so well." Sylvie somehow felt that she had been through some sort of test. She thought back to what both Marcy and Lilianna had said about Julian. She hoped that they might be over exaggerating, but she knew in the pit of her stomach that they were probably right. "Are you hungry? Shall we get some dinner?"

"Actually, Julian, I'm pretty shattered. I'd just like to go home. Is that okay?"

"No problem. All that talking, eh?" Julian was thankful it was dark. He didn't want Sylvie to see how disappointed he was.

He pulled into Sylvie's driveway and she tapped in the security code for the gate to open. The car stopped outside the door and Julian was out in a flash to open her door.

"Thanks for today. It was really good to get out of town." She walked up the steps to the door and opened it up. Julian walked with her.

"Goodnight then." He leant in and kissed her on the cheek but lingered a fraction.

"Goodnight, and thanks again." She walked into the hallway and waved him off as he drove away.

As Julian pulled off down the hill that had lead up to Sylvie's house, he dialled Maggie's number.

"Hello Julian," she answered.

"Well what did you think of her?" He sounded almost impatient.

"She's lovely Julian. I'm so pleased I met her." He laughed to himself. Uncanny, he thought. Her comment mirrored Sylvie's.

"I know, but she's had a rough time of it. She's pulling through though."

"You've been a good friend to her. Well good night and we'll speak tomorrow."

Maggie put down the phone and stood looking at it. After twenty years of having her ex -husband all to herself, she realised that she was in real danger of losing him. And losing him to such a worthy adversary.

Sylvie walked into the kitchen and poured herself a drink. She splashed a couple of ice cubes into the glass and opened the fridge to grab a plate with some chicken on. She just realised how hungry she was. She got down a jar of pickled gherkins and ate them from the jar. Before she could sit down her phone rang. It was Zach. Every night either Zach or Lilianna would call to check up on her.

"Hi Zach, you okay?"

"I'm fine, darling. I heard you went shopping today." His voice was a mixture of relief and mild sarcasm. "I'm glad to hear it. If you hadn't got rid of that airbed, I was going to come round and puncture it!"

"Oh shut up, Zach!" Sylvie laughed. He'd become like a big brother to her over the last few months.

"What's next on your list? Or is it going to be a surprise?" He carried on teasing.

"Zach I swear I'll ban Lilianna from telling you anything!"

"Okay, okay I'll back off, joking aside though, I'm glad for you. You really are trying. Can I make a suggestion though? No pressure?" His voice softened.

"Sure Zach, go ahead."

"I think it's time to ditch the black. I really can't see you in it anymore. I'm not used to it." He was worried he might have pushed his luck. There was silence on the other end of the phone.

"Sylvie?"

"Yes Zach, I'm still here. Give me until February and I promise I'll stop. Is that a good enough compromise?" It would be three months by then. She hoped she could keep her promise.

"Sure darling," he sighed.

Once she'd finished on the phone she walked upstairs to her bedroom and hesitantly opened the door. Marcy had made up the bed in her new lemon-coloured bedding. It was Sylvie's favourite of the two.

CHAPTER 10

WHEN SYLVIE MET NICK

The sun was beating down and reflecting off of the unusually calm sea. It was unseasonably warm for the middle of February. Sylvie was looking out of her office window. Every day she thanked her lucky stars she had this view to look at. The sun's reflection danced on the ripples of the sea. It was mesmerizing. She could literally watch them for hours.

She snapped herself out of her trance and started to collect her swatches and samples. It had been just over three months since Chris had died and Sylvie had kept her promise to Zach. She had put her mourning clothes away. It had been hard to reconcile but it upset Alex and Markus to see her in black. It had rained and been miserable all week, but this morning the sun broke through almost forcing Sylvie to make this difficult change. When she walked downstairs in one of her favourite dresses Marcy almost gasped.

"It's good to see you in that yellow dress again Mam. Alex and Markus will be so pleased."

Sylvie's spirit began to lift. "Thanks Marcy." She gently touched her arm as a form of acknowledgment.

She'd arranged to go up to Maggie's house at eleven o'clock to go over the refurbishment of her bedroom. It had been a month since Julian had introduced her to Maggie, and consequently Sylvie had become friends with his ex. They had spent the best part of that month trailing round furniture shops around town and basically getting to know one another. Sylvie also introduced Maggie to Lilianna and the three of them had become close.

It had been good for Sylvie especially as Maggie had never known Chris and she didn't associate her with him. It made it easier. There were never moments when Maggie might say, 'Do you remember when Chris...?' as Zach, Lilianna or Stathis would say.

Because of this new friendship, Julian was not only seeing Sylvie on work related subjects but also outside of work. He was interested in what she was putting together for Maggie. How much of that was real interest and how much of it was his way of getting closer to Sylvie was hard to tell.

Celle was on schedule, partly due to the fact that Sylvie was almost working round the clock. She was still avoiding being at home. Only on Sundays when Markus came out did she stay there. Then she would laze around watch films and cook for him. They both found it hard to eat out without Alex, so each weekend they'd try a new recipe and veg out all day.

She left her office and closed the door. The plaque read 'Managing Director, Chris Sapphiris'. She'd have to change that, but there never seemed to be the right time to do it.

"Bye Maria, have a good weekend. I won't be back today. I have my meeting with Maggie. If Zach needs me he can call me."

"Ok Sylvie, you too."

JULIAN WAS AT HIS office working on an office block he'd been asked to design. He looked at the time. He knew Sylvie was going up to Maggie's today with all the final plans and he'd really wanted to be there. But he'd fallen behind on some deadlines because he was spending so much time with her and he really couldn't spend the time away from the office. Well not today, anyway. He decided to call her instead. He made sure he saw her every day. But on days like today where he couldn't he'd call her. The weekends were the worst for him. Sylvie never left the house on Sunday because Markus was out and she spent it with him. He could never get anyone to work on Saturdays so that there would be no work related excuse to see her. At least when she was up at Maggie's he could pass by with any excuse. Three days without seeing her was going to be tough.

"Hello Julian, how are you today?" Sylvie had started to sound a lot like her old self again.

"Much better now I've heard your voice. You sound chirpy." This was their usual banter. Julian trying to push the boundaries of their relationship a little more every time.

"Yes, I am. The weather's changed at long last. I always feel better when the sun is out. I'm also pretty pleased with my design for Maggie. I'm just setting off to go there."

"Well let's hope she likes it, you need to get cracking. I was going to pop up too. But I'm really swamped. I'll call you later to see how it went. Have a good meeting." He put down the phone. He rubbed his eyes and looked back at his computer. How the hell was he going to concentrate now? All he could think about was that he'd have to wait three days to see her again and there was no denying that that made him feel wretched.

SYLVIE DROVE THE TWENTY minute journey to Maggie's house. The road was windy and lined with cypress trees which momentarily shaded the road from the brilliant sunlight. It was days like this she thought about buying a convertible car. She loved her BMW 4x4 but a convertible would be much more fun. Maybe… maybe not, Sylvie thought to herself. The air seemed so clean up here. She could understand why Maggie loved it, but Sylvie still preferred to be by the sea.

Sylvie had met both Elenora and Vicki while she had been discussing the redecoration of Maggie's bedroom. Even though Maggie's daughters were twins they were very different. Elenora was very feminine and gentle. She was always smiling and had a calmness about her. She was very much like Maggie.

Vicki was a lot more of a straight-shooter and reserved, but once you knew her she never stopped talking. People often mistook her for being shy, but that wasn't the case; she just was very selective. Sylvie liked them both straight away. It was a very different dynamic living in a predominately female environment, something Sylvie wasn't used to at all. She had three older brothers and then two sons.

There was great attention to detail in everything the twins said or did. If Sylvie asked her boys what they thought of something she'd cooked she'd get at best, 'Great Mum, thanks'. In complete contrast when Maggie asked her two girls they would start with, 'Mum this is so tasty, the tomatoes are so sweet and compliment the cheese, really well. You know what would work? Red peppers and caramelised onions....' And so it would go on.

Not that she'd change her sons for anything. She just hoped she'd get good daughter-in-laws.

The only member of the family Sylvie hadn't met was Nick. He lived mainly on his yacht in the marina. He was sometimes away on buying trips for clients. He had his own business, a shop which stocked all things from life jackets to jet skis to arranging the purchasing of speed boats and yachts. From what Sylvie understood he was doing very well.

Sylvie pulled up outside and parked next to a rather masculine, pristine-looking silver Jeep with a bumper sticker on the rear that said, "I like to do it at sea!" on it with a cartoon version of Poseidon winking and hold his trident. She laughed out loud as she read it then gathered all her samples heading for the front door. Before she managed to get all of them, Maggie was already outside.

"Morning! Let me give you a hand. Oh Sylvie, you look gorgeous in that dress. It's nice to see you in colour." Maggie was barefoot again, and she wore her ripped jeans and another one of her floaty tops. Her hair was the most beautiful shade of gold which was highlighted blonde. Her hands were stained with paint, as always.

"Thanks, I love yellow. It always makes me feel happy. I brought as many samples as I could lay my hands on." They walked into the open hallway and headed straight for the kitchen so that they could unload all the sample books.

"I'll put the kettle on. Tea or coffee?"

"Tea please. I'll open them up so you can see the different patterns, and I'll plug in my laptop so you can see the virtual image of your room."

Part Two – Winter

Sylvie looked round for a power point when something caught her eye, or rather, someone. A young man was pulling himself out of the pool. As he walked over to the chairs he towel-dried his hair. He was tall and tanned and his athletic body was toned. He had the bluest eyes and his hair was light brown, though she couldn't be sure as it was wet. He was stunning. Sylvie couldn't stop staring. Thankfully the window was tinted so she could not be seen.

"You'll meet Nick today. He came up to see us this morning. You haven't met him, have you?" Maggie was too busy fixing the tea to notice Sylvie staring.

"No, no, is that who's outside by the pool?" Sylvie tried to sound casual. Thankfully Maggie was rummaging in a cupboard for the cups to even notice that Sylvie was still looking at him.

"Yes, he came up at around nine this morning. Go out and introduce yourself, he knows all about you. I told him you were coming." She'd managed to get the cups out but couldn't find the biscuits.

"Maggie, what *are* you doing? All I want is tea, stop going to all that bother!"

"You go out and I'll be over in a sec." She waved her outside and went into the pantry to retrieve whatever she was fussing about.

Sylvie plugged in her laptop then pulled herself together, adjusting her wide belt slightly before she walked through the patio doors onto the terrace where Nick was now sat smoking.

"Hello." He had his back to her and her voice must have interrupted a deep thought, as he spun round, a little taken aback. "I'm sorry I didn't mean to startle you, I'm Sylvie, your Mum's friend."

Nick was instantly on his feet in one fluid movement, and he put down his cigarette and shook her hand. "That's okay, I was miles away. I'm Nick, very pleased to meet you Sylvie. Please, sit down." He waited until she sat down before he retook his seat. He suddenly felt very aware that he was only wearing trunks. "Excuse me; I should really put something on. I'll be back in a minute."

And with that he ran back into the house. He returned in what seemed like seconds rather than minutes wearing a white V-necked T-shirt and a pair of blue shorts. If Sylvie wasn't mistaken, he also looked like he'd tidied up his unruly hair and she could swear she could smell aftershave.

"Sorry about that." He had not dried himself properly and his T-shirt clung to his chest, outlining every muscle. "I didn't realise you were coming so early."

He looked up at her, and his amazing cobalt eyes locked on hers, and her heart lurched. *Oh Lord she was in trouble!*

"Really, you shouldn't have bothered." She actually meant it, she would rather he'd have stayed just in his trunks! It seemed a real shame to cover up such an incredible body.

He reached over to his cigarette, which had burned down to the filter, and stubbed it out. Then he picked up his packet of Dunhills and offered one to Sylvie. She was actually tempted to take one, anything to steady her nerves.

"Thanks, but I don't smoke."

"Good for you, it's a terrible vice." And with that he lit up another and dragged deep on it his eyes fixed on hers. *How sexy was that!*

"I can think of worse," said Sylvie with a slight smile. My God, what was she doing? She was flirting with Maggie's son. She really needed help! Nick gazed at her, his eyes seemed to sparkle mischievously and he arched his brow.

"So, have you introduced yourselves?" Maggie was coming out with a tray. She placed it on the table. "Move those horrible things, Nick." She pushed away the cigarettes. "I wish you'd quit."

"Sylvie just said she thought there were worse vices." He glanced over to her as he dragged on his cigarette again and held her gaze. For a split second she was totally blown away by how intensely he stared. She slowly looked away and smiled. Was he flirting with her? Surely not!

"Of course she'll say that; she's very polite. Just milk, right?" Maggie poured the tea. Just as she put down the pot, her phone rang. "That'll be Elenora, won't be a mo."

"Are you having tea?" Sylvie asked, not daring to look up at him. Her whole body was buzzing.

"Sure, thanks."

Sylvie tried to keep her hands steady as she poured the tea and handed it to him.

"So you're redecorating Mum's room? I hope you bring it into the twenty-first century, she's such a hippy." He picked up the cup without using the handle and took a gulp, before placing it back down.

"Maggie does have her own style, but I am hoping to make her room, shall we say, more contemporary." Nick laughed loudly. *Wow!* His whole face lit up. Holy shit, he was so good looking. She licked her lips nervously dragging her gaze away.

"Good luck with that!" He knew that would be quite an achievement.

"So what are you two laughing about, eh?" Maggie had a couple of samples in her hands.

"Sylvie was telling me how you've decided to go ultra-modern, very minimalistic; I totally approve." He was smiling as he took another drag from his cigarette and leaned back on his chair, flexing his legs.

Sylvie found it hard to pull her eyes off his taught thighs. *Stop it, stop it, stop it!* She repeated to herself.

"He's winding you up Maggie," Sylvie murmured. She couldn't bear to see her new friend stress as she turned slightly paler at the thought.

"That's my Nick for you; always messing with me. I was just looking at these floral designs, they look lovely…."

"Let me show you the design on my computer before you get too carried away, Maggie." Sylvie reluctantly got up to go back to the kitchen where her laptop was set up. She was ashamed to say she'd have much rather sat and ogled at Nick. As she walked back to the house with Maggie she glanced back to look at him, what she didn't expect was to see him staring straight back at her. She turned away, embarrassed. *Oh, hell. Busted!*

The two of them sat rehashing Sylvie's original design for the next hour while Nick sat out by the pool reading what seemed to be some report. He kept looking over to his mother and Sylvie as they carried on tweaking the design. He couldn't believe that the woman he had seen in his father's office a few months ago and again at the marina was actually a friend of his mother's too. He continued to stare at her until Maggie interrupted his thoughts.

"Nick, come and have a look at the design, tell us what you think." Maggie was ecstatic. "It's so beautiful, really Sylvie I would never have thought those elements would work so well together."

Nick came over and stood directly behind Sylvie, he leaned over her shoulder to look at the screen more closely, and his face was inches away from hers. He was so close she could smell him. God. he smelled good. She could feel the heat radiating off his body. Sylvie fixed her eyes on the screen so as not to turn and give herself away.

"So your evil plan worked. then." He was almost whispering. Sylvie was totally confused, what was he talking about? She really wished he'd move away she could feel herself sweating.

"I'm sorry. I'm not sure what you mean."

He turned and looked at her with his incredible blue eyes as she turned slightly to meet his gaze. "You pulled my Mum out of the eighties!" he held her gaze for a second then winked. He straightened himself and turned to his mother. "It looks great Mum. She's a genius."

With that he strolled back outside but not before turning back to look over his shoulder as Sylvie gaped after him. *Shit!* How embarrassing! She flushed, mortified that she'd been caught out again. *Get a freaking grip, girl!*

"Sylvie, how soon can we get started? I really want it done ASAP!"

Sylvie's hands were sweating and she was burning up. What the hell was going on? She really needed to cool down. She got up from the table. "I've got the workmen booked in next week. It'll be done in a week."

"Where are you going? You're not leaving... I've made lunch... You must stay. Nick, tell her she has to stay. Elenora and Vicki are on their way home."

"Oh no, I couldn't intrude... Really thanks, I should really be off." Sylvie's feeble attempt to leave was futile.

Nick had strolled back and was standing in the doorway, leaning against the frame.

"Don't bother arguing with her, she'll never let you go." He sauntered over to the fridge and opened it.

"Is it too early to open some wine?" asked Maggie. Nick reached into the fridge and pulled out a bottle.

"Who cares?" he said raising his eyebrow, his eyes fleetingly resting on Sylvie before he turned away as he searched for an opener.

So it was settled, Sylvie stayed and helped out with lunch. Once Elenora and Vicki arrived they all sat down to talk about their week. What they were up to, how the wedding preparations were going. Time passed and before Sylvie knew it she had started to relax. It probably had a lot to do with the wine. Out of sheer nervousness she had knocked back a couple of glasses before they had sat down to eat.

During the lunch Sylvie found out that Nick had been away consulting on a yacht refurbishment and closed a big sale. He had a very close relationship with all his family, but he was definitely closest to Maggie. She'd found it hard not to keep staring at him and on a few occasions he had caught her out again. He'd placed himself opposite her and it had made it doubly hard not to keep looking at him. She decided that maybe she should leave as she was sure she was making a fool out of herself and fuelled with a few glasses of wine she really wasn't sure if she could control herself.

"I really need to go. It was a lovely afternoon Maggie but it's already past four. I'm sure you've all got plans; I'll just call Petros to come and pick me up. I really shouldn't drive after all that wine." Sylvie got up from the sofa to find her phone.

"No way Sylvie, Nick will take you home. He's going down to the marina. He can drop you off on the way and tomorrow we'll arrange for you to pick up your car. That's okay isn't it Nick?"

Both Sylvie and Maggie turned to look at Nick who was stretched out on the sofa. His arms were behind his head, causing his T-shirt to rise up, revealing a section of his taut, tanned abdomen, mellow and sexy. His eyes seemed to widen and Sylvie tried her damnedest not to focus on the slight sprinkling of hair peeping over the waistband of his shorts.

"Of course it is." Before Sylvie could object Nick was up, gathering his keys and cigarettes. Maggie, Elenora and Vicki kissed them both goodbye and waved them off at the door. Nick opened the passenger door to his Jeep and Sylvie slipped into the seat. *Holy fucking crap!*

CHAPTER 11

AFTER THE LUNCH

A s Sylvie buckled her belt, she was ferociously listing topics to talk about on the ride home. She was feeling very uncomfortable being alone with him, and at such close proximity, too. He made her feel nervous. It wasn't how he behaved; it was more that she felt unbelievably attracted to him. Really attracted to him! She hadn't felt like that in a very long time and it was altogether alien to her. She knew it was completely inappropriate and that was why it made her so uneasy. It was just wrong.

"So, you live on a yacht at the marina? That's very unusual. It must be great to have that freedom though. I suppose if you get bored of the view you can change it. How long have you had it?" She hoped this would allow him to talk freely and avoid having to make any more small talk.

"Just a few months." *So much for that!*

"I love boats; in fact I have a boating licence. I got it over twenty years ago. Not that I ever used it. An old…friend gave me free lessons one summer in Corfu. It's only a speed boat license though, I'm sure it's probably obsolete now."

She babbled away, talking about anything so that there wouldn't be an awkward silence. She kept checking the clock, another ten minutes at least before they'd be at her house. He wasn't making it any easier either, with his short replies. He'd shifted in his seat a couple of times and Sylvie was glad he'd put the radio on so that it filled the gaps in their stilted conversation.

It was nice to hear music again; some love ballad that Sylvie vaguely recognised. She listened to the woman sing about being a little drunk and needing someone right now and she swallowed hard, thinking it was a little too close to home.

Trying desperately to avoid listening to the lyrics, Sylvie tried another tactic.

"So, Elenora seems very organised for her wedding. It's after Easter, isn't it?" she gazed out of the window as they drove downwards through the same villages and windy road. She was playing with her wedding and engagement ring, twisting it round as she did. *I really need to take these off*, she thought to herself. *Baby steps,* she reminded herself.

"Yes, the second Saturday after Easter."

Silence again. *Crap, how much longer?* Maybe she should just give up. He seemed to be preoccupied.

"I'm not exactly sure where you live. I know it's not far from the highway."

"Take the next exit and follow the road for a mile or so, it's that house on the hill." Thank God, they were close. Marcy and Petros would have left by now.

Nick pulled in through the open gates and stopped outside the front door. He turned to her and the atmosphere changed from polite and awkward to something intense as his eyes fixed on hers. Within a split second, he was out like a flash to open the door for her. The gesture caught her off guard.

"Thank you so much for the lift down. I'm sorry I took you out of your way. Won't you come in?" She offered purely out of politeness. She really wouldn't be able to handle any more time alone with him. He really did unnerve her.

"It was really my pleasure." He was smiling, "I'm afraid I can't, I need to get off. But maybe some other time." He looked at his watch. He obviously had a pressing prior engagement and she'd messed it up. For sure a hot date with some twenty year old. He was probably more like his father in that department.

"Sure, anytime." She hoped that she sounded casual as she set off to the door. She turned around to see him off and to her surprise he was still in front of her having followed her up the steps. His expression was a little odd, as though he was waiting, or hesitating. He put out his hand to shake Sylvie's, Sylvie moved forward, making his hand overshoot and catch her waist, and instinctively Sylvie leaned over and kissed him on the cheek, as she had done a hundred times to hundreds of people. The whole interaction only took a few seconds but it had felt as though time stood still. His cheek gently pressed against hers, leaving the smell of his cologne behind. His hand slipped further round her waist, and her hand softly ran down from his shoulder to his elbow. Sylvie took a deep breath and stepped back, trying to hold her balance. *Holy shit!*

"Drive carefully." she said softly. He seemed to want to say something, but then he turned to his car and got into the driver's seat.

"Bye," he said and drove off. Sylvie stayed on the driveway until he was out of sight. She stood there trying to understand what had just happened. Did she imagine it? She knew she was totally bowled over by him. Surely he wasn't interested in her, it was absurd. He was just being polite. It was customary to give a peck on the cheek when saying bye. That was it, obviously too much wine. She'd read far too much into it.

But she couldn't get that brief exchange out of her head. Had it been anyone else it would have felt awkward and embarrassing. This had felt very smooth and deliberate. Better she forget the whole thing, but the butterflies in her stomach jumped around and seemed to have other plans! She really needed to get her head together. She felt like a teenager, all breathy and jittery.

NICK'S HANDS GRIPPED THE steering wheel as he powered home to his boat in the marina. He couldn't get the image of Sylvie out of his head. He played their last five minutes back in his mind. Had he imagined it? Was he just being ridiculous? He could smell her still. The image of her playful smile and her chocolate eyes were imprinted in his mind. She couldn't be interested in him. He was sure she was married. He'd seen her playing with her rings. He really needed to find out more about her. He'd behaved like an idiot.

He'd hardly spoken to her on the journey down. The truth was he'd been knocked off balance, being with her at such close proximity he'd not been able to trust himself. He knew she was close to his father and didn't want to embarrass himself. He pulled into the parking area and got out of his car. He looked down at his watch; four forty five, he wasn't late.

He strolled over to his yacht and jumped onto the deck. The sun was starting to set. He stood there and took in the view. He loved this time of day twilight. The sun blazed orange leaving fiery stains across the sea. What was it that Sylvie said? 'Bored of the view'. No danger of that happening.

"Hello, anybody home?" He was always on time and always laden with bags.

"Hi Dad." He went over to help him up on deck and relieve him of his baggage. Every couple of weeks they would get together and catch up. They changed the venue, they usually went to a bar or restaurant, but today they arranged to meet on Nick's boat. Julian wasn't a big fan of the sea, he got nauseous just thinking about it, but he was totally in awe of his son's skill and talent where the sea was concerned. Nick had always been interested in boats he had loved them from very young and both Maggie and Julian encouraged him. They enrolled him in sailing clubs and as he got older he got his own boating license. He worked in the summer months as a water sports instructor and lifeguard. While most seventeen year olds were desperate to get their own car, Nick wanted his own boat. By the time he finished high school he had bought his first speedboat.

Over the next few years, he worked sourcing yachts and motor boats for clients, who had no time or the knowledge to do so for themselves. He had set up an office in a water sports outlet run by an ageing fisherman. Nick had eventually bought the shop and revamped it into very successful boating suppliers. He'd employed an old school friend of his to manage it. This left him free to travel around and build up his client base for his agency. It meant he could check out any yachts first hand and be able to advise his clients accordingly. He earned his commission from the seller, and the buyer would most certainly pay a finder's fee. Most of his clients were millionaires with more money than time, so they were more than willing to pay for his expertise.

Julian had wanted Nick to follow him in his business, but he had realized that he wasn't cut out for anything on land. So instead he had introduced all his wealthy clients to Nick and so helped him increase his local client base. Though their interests were very different they were both equally ambitious, both were very driven and enjoyed being in control.

"Do you need your seasick pills?" Nick joked. Julian was already looking green.

"Stop teasing your old man and open us up some beers. The only way I'll stay steady is if I'm half cut!" He threw his arms around his son and kissed him. They were roughly the same height but what was different about them was their physique. Nick was obviously well toned and had the body of a man who did physical work. He was also always tanned. Julian, in contrast, was paler and carried a little more weight.

He was also fit but it was obvious that he worked out in the gym rather than it being his lifestyle. The one thing that they had in common was their eyes, piercing blue.

Nick took the bags of food Julian had brought down to the galley and retrieved a couple of beers from the fridge. Julian was settled on the deck with his feet up on the table.

"So what you been up to? How was your trip?" Julian loved to hear what deals his son was putting together. It was an area he knew nothing about, but he was genuinely interested in his son's business.

They sat and chatted for a couple of hours. Nick told him that all had gone to plan and the Russian client had bought the yacht. It got dark and so they decided to move inside as it started to get chilly. They opened up the food Julian had got from his favourite sushi restaurant.

"So what's new with you Dad? Any new twenty-something in your life at the moment, or have you grown out of your twenty years of midlife crisis?" Nick and his sisters were forever teasing their father over his girlfriend choices. He never dated anyone over thirty. He really wasn't into commitment. So he was happy to have meaningless relationships with young women who enjoyed the fact he could spend enormous amounts of money on them.

"Nice to know I still amuse you, Nick!" Julian loved his children above everything and their approval was very important to him. He knew he must embarrass them on a regular basis but he did try to minimise their discomfort. He rarely introduced his 'girlfriends' to his children, but they were aware of his lifestyle. Nick was a little more accepting of his Dad's short comings than his sisters.

Nick picked up his cigarettes and walked onto the deck.

"I wish you'd fucking pack that in, Nick." It was the only thing Julian didn't approve of.

"I'll make you a deal Dad, I'll pack it in if you stop fucking twenty-two year-olds," laughed Nick. They both knew that neither one of them had a valid reason to quit their favourite vices. They were both neither willing nor able.

"Elenora's wedding seems to be on track. I was up at Mum's today and it was like they were on speed."

"I know that's all they talk about. Just another two months and it'll all be over." He shook his head smiling.

"I met that Sylvie, she was up there too. She's redecorating for Mum," he wondered if he knew much more about her. Maybe he could shed some light on what her story was.

"Yes she is. I introduced them not so long ago. I've known her a while. I do work for her husband's developing company. She's very good, she did my office too. I'm sure you've met her. You were there when she brought my painting."

"Oh yes. I didn't meet her though. Her husband's a developer?" He played along a bit; he remembered she was married to some developer that his father was friends with.

"Actually her late husband, he died last November. A week or so after that time actually. She's running his business along with his partner now. She's really something, isn't she? I've been working with her pretty closely over the past couple of months. She's had a lot to deal with. We've been out on business lunches and dinners, but it's always been work-related. I did invite her to the wedding though."

Nick turned to look at his father. As soon as he saw his face he realised that his father was obviously in love with Sylvie. What Nick didn't expect was the utter feeling of devastation that swept over him. He wanted to find out more. He'd have to ask, he had to know. He tried hard not to sound like he was interrogating.

"So you're seeing her then?"

"No I wouldn't say that, like I said just work stuff, but I'd really like to. It's a bit difficult, I knew Chris, her husband. We hung out together a lot. So I don't think she sees me as anything other than 'a friend of Chris's'. It was a pretty horrible thing for her to deal with too. I'm sure it'll take her a lot longer to get over his death." He paused and then said: "I can't compete with a dead man, can I?"

"No, I suppose you can't." So there it was. His father was in love with Sylvie, and he, in turn, was absolutely mad for her too. She, on the other hand, was still mourning her husband. Nick looked at his father. He was staring at the reflection of the moon on the sea.

"You like this Sylvie, then?" he gripped his beer, anticipating the response.

"You've met her, what's not to like. She's attractive, intelligent. She's very talented. Has a great sense of humour. She's nearly forty-four you know, but she looks ten years younger."

"So you haven't told her that you're interested then?"

"I just think it's too soon. To be honest I don't think she's ready and I'm not afraid to admit that I don't think I could face the rejection."

Nick slumped down in his chair and lit another cigarette. He dragged deeply on it and tried to absorb all the information he had gleaned.

"How about you? Any girlfriend?"

"No, no one at the moment Dad, I'm a bit fussier than you," joked Nick. He really needed to get off the subject. "Don't worry Dad there won't be another wedding for a while."

"Well I'd better be off, it's getting late, I enjoyed tonight. Next time somewhere on *terra ferma* though." He hugged and kissed Nick and made his way back to his car.

Nick sat in the dark, trying to make sense of what he was feeling. The problem was not so much that his father was obviously in love with Sylvie, but that once he had been aware of that, he realised how strongly he also felt about her. That was unsettling.

CHAPTER 12

STORMY WEATHER

Sylvie was going to arrange with Petros to take her up to the Maggie's to collect her car. However, Julian had somehow found out that she had needed a lift and rung her early and insisted that he would take her. She'd noticed over the last couple of weeks or so that he had done everything possible to spend as much time with her as he could without it really being totally necessary. She hoped he hadn't got the wrong idea. Or she hoped she hadn't given off the wrong vibe. She enjoyed his company, he was very charming and easy to talk to but she really felt nothing more than just friendship for him.

She heard his car roar up outside exactly on time. He climbed out to greet her as she closed the door behind her.

"Morning. You really didn't need to take me. Petros would have." She kissed him on the cheek and got into his car as he held the door open for her.

"It's really no bother. You look lovely. It's nice to see you in lighter colours again." He was just glad to see her even if it was just to taxi her. Sylvie scrunched up her nose at the compliment. Her hair was loose and she had put on her jeans and a cream, sleeveless sweater.

"Thanks."

The journey was only fifteen minutes, but they managed to talk about a huge amount of topics, mainly related to Stathis's club. He seemed nervous. As if he had something else to say, but instead he kept changing the subject. Sylvie rubbed her finger in the spot where her wedding and engagement ring had been. Sylvie had taken off her sapphire and diamond engagement ring along with her gold wedding band last night before she had her bath and decided to put them away.

Chris had purposely chosen a sapphire engagement ring. "A sapphire for the future Mrs Sapphiris." Sylvie remembered how his dark eyes had twinkled as she placed them back in their box. She loved blue, she thought wistfully.

It was again a very hard decision but she was determined to make the changes. If she held on to everything it would make it a hundred times harder later. She still felt the need to twist them around, as she always had. Force of habit.

They pulled up outside Maggie's house as clouds were gathering. Maggie was at the door.

"Morning. It looks like it's going to rain. Good job you came early. They're predicting a thunderstorm."

They went through to the kitchen and sitting room and Sylvie started to pack up her laptop.

"I won't be long I just need to put some pots into the kiln. Make yourselves at home, it'll only take five minutes." And with that, Maggie left Sylvie and Julian.

"Sylvie?" Julian looked over to where she was collecting her swatches.

"Yes Julian," she was preoccupied and didn't notice he had moved right by her side. She turned around and his closeness caught her off guard.

"Sorry, I didn't mean to startle you." His tone was very soft and he gently reached for her arm. "I need to talk to you about something, if that's okay. To be honest I've been putting it off for a while as I never seem to find the right time." He seemed a little tense as his eyes kept flitting around rather than settling on her face. Sylvie started to become concerned, she'd never seen him like this.

"Julian, is everything alright?" He took her hand and looked at her straight in the face.

"The truth is, Sylvie, I have had feelings for you for some time. If I'm to be perfectly honest I liked you a bit too much when Chris introduced us all that time ago. You were married then, and to a good friend of mine. So I put my feelings on the back burner, regardless of how hard that became as I got to know you more and more." He gently led her to the sofa where they both sat down. Sylvie was taken aback, but if she was honest with herself, she had known that Julian had a soft spot for her. Her conversation with Lilianna forced itself into her head.

"When Chris died, I watched you crumble and slowly build yourself up again. All the while I wanted to be closer to you. What I mean is that I wanted to be able to protect you and be someone you could rely on. But I realised if I pushed you, it would firstly be inappropriate and secondly, I needed to see that you might be ready, or at least more receptive should I make my feelings clear.

"Over the last month or so I have seen that you have come out of the other side. Not that you're over Chris, but that you've accepted that he has gone. I felt that I needed you to know how much I admire you in so many ways and that as I have got to know you even more, I realise that I am deeply in love with you. I know you see me as a friend and that's understandable, but I want you to understand that my feelings are true. I don't want you to feel like you need to respond to what I've said. What's important is that you know."

He stared at her with those blue eyes. His face showed signs of strain, but she could see he was being totally honest. Sylvie realised that it had taken a lot for him to admit this to her. After all, they would be working together and seeing each other a lot now.

"Julian... I really don't know what to say." She was being honest and he knew she had not been expecting this.

"You don't need to say anything. I just wanted you to know so that, maybe in the future, you might look at me in a different way other than friend and colleague. Sorry if I came on too strong, I didn't want to make you uncomfortable and I hope this won't change how we are. Actually I do, if you know what I mean." He cracked a smile at his own joke, which in turn made Sylvie laugh.

"Of course not, you are very important to me." She leant over to him and hugged him. He held on to her hoping he had done the right thing. She pulled away and he reluctantly let her go. Sylvie got up from the sofa then turned to Julian.

"I really am glad you told me Julian, I can't really say how I feel about it. Perhaps flattered. It won't change how we are," she reassured him as she repeated his words. "You'll always be a good friend to me. I don't think I could have gone through the past few months without your support. But right now that's all I can offer. I don't think I'm ready for anything, let's say, more complicated."

She hoped she'd let him down gently. It was true, she had relied on him a lot for her business. But she hadn't leant on him more than she had on Zach, Lilianna and recently Maggie. He was a good man, and they had so much in common, and had circumstances been different Sylvie was pretty sure that they could have been more than just friends.

He sat on the sofa looking at his hands. Maggie was still thankfully in her workshop, oblivious to their exchange. Sylvie wondered whether she knew how he felt. That might make things a little awkward, however friendly their relationship was.

Julian got up from the sofa and walked over to the table where Sylvie's swatches were and started to collect them for her. They could hear Maggie coming back through.

"Sorry I took so long. But I really needed to finish off the last of that order. The kiln took a while to get up to temperature. Shall I put the kettle on?"

"That's okay Maggie. I really should get off. I've disrupted yours and Julian's morning enough. I'll get my stuff into the car and set off home." Sylvie felt the sudden need to be as far away from them as possible. Firstly the strange exchange she'd had with Nick yesterday and now Julian's confession. It was all becoming a bit too much for her.

"Aw, I wanted to chat a bit more about my bedroom." She looked over at Julian. "Are you rushing off too?"

"Yes I've got to go, but maybe we'll catch up this week. Go and open your car I'll bring the rest."

Maggie came out with Sylvie to the car, as Julian collected the last swatches and followed them.

"I'll see you on Monday at my office. We've got a couple of things to look at. Zach needs to modify some plans." She said as he put everything in the boot.

Julian turned to Maggie and kissed her goodbye and then to Sylvie.

"Bye then. See you on Monday." He reluctantly kissed her goodbye and drove off. At least he'd got to see her today and given her something to think about. He wasn't sure why he'd decided to tell her how he felt. Maybe because he'd spoken to Nick last night and actually got it out in the open. Whatever had prompted him, he did feel better. At least she knew.

"Come in for a quick tea, the girls are out so we can chat about something other than the wedding!" Maggie laughed.

"Okay, I haven't anything to rush back for." So Sylvie followed Maggie back indoors.

They settled into the settee with their tea. Sylvie realised that they were in very similar circumstances. Their children were grown and they both didn't have a man in their life.

"Don't you get lonely up here on your own?" Sylvie had always enjoyed city life. The country didn't appeal to her at all.

"Sometimes I do. I've got used to my own company. While the kids were small I loved the tranquillity, especially at night. But now the house is pretty quiet all the time. The girls are at work and Nick's living mostly on his boat. My work keeps me busy though. Not that that can substitute some company. I have a few friends that pop in, but it's true a do feel that I need someone in my life. Elenora is leaving now and before long Vicki. I'll be totally alone." She looked over to Sylvie with sad eyes.

"What about Nick? Isn't he ready to settle down, or is more like his father?"

"Now that's altogether a different story. He's quite the opposite of Julian," replied Maggie.

"What do you mean?"

"Nick is a lot like me, when he falls in love he falls deep. He's only ever had two relationships that I know of; the first was a teenage, two-year love affair with a local girl from school. She broke it off with him because her father wanted her to only be with someone of her own background. He took it very badly and threw himself into his business. After a couple of years he fell in love with a Dutch woman. She was divorced with two younger children. They met when he sold her ex-husband's yacht. She was also twelve years older than him."

Maggie raised her eyebrows as she spoke. "Julian and I were not altogether supportive of the relationship. We didn't really like her. She was... how can I put it... very self-involved." Sylvie felt Maggie was hiding something as she spoke. But from her tone it was obvious she didn't like her.

"He was twenty-four and she was thirty-six. They were together for a year or so, and I know he really loved her, but I just didn't think it was right. He was prepared to take on the full responsibility of her kids and everything. It was Julian and I that really made it hard for him. She realised, and broke it off. She actually moved away, back to Amsterdam. He was absolutely devastated. He pulled away from us for a while. I was worried that we might lose him. It was the girls that brought him back round."

"Oh... So no one since her, then?" Sylvie couldn't help herself.

"Well if he has, we've never met her. Julian and I made a pact that we wouldn't interfere in our children's love lives again. Well we aren't exactly experts ourselves, looking at our track record! I think he keeps that part of his life very private. Do you blame him? He left the country for a couple of months after she left. We were distraught. He's forgiven us, but I think he's reluctant to let us be involved again so much."

"I suppose you do what you think's best for your children. When you're on the outside you can see things that they can't or won't. But yet again they need to live their own life, make mistakes and live with the consequences. Well at least Elenora's found a great guy."

"Yes he's such a sweetheart and they adore each other." Maggie lit back up again.

"What about you?"

"Me! Well that's even more complicated. My setup isn't exactly conventional," laughed Maggie.

'What do you mean?" Sylvie was puzzled. She thought that Maggie's relationship with Julian was one of the best she'd ever witnessed.

"As you know Julian was my college sweetheart, we got married pretty quickly then had the children even faster. I was totally in love with him and I had everything I ever wanted. It all proved too much for Julian, so we decided to separate for a while so he could get himself together. I realised that if I wanted him in my life I would have to let him go without a fight. He felt incredibly guilty, I know he did. But I think that's why he tried so hard to keep as close to a family as he could. He had the choice to spend time with us or not, and most of the time he chose to be around us. Of course there are very few men who could tolerate that kind of a relationship. So it made hard for me to find anyone else. I have had a couple of relationships. But like I said it's a very hard situation to come into." She looked into her cup and sighed.

"Do you think you'd ever get back with Julian?"

Maggie pressed her lips together as she tried to find the right response. "I honestly can't answer that. There are times that I can't think of anything else. Then there are times I think it would probably be the worst decision we could make. It works how we are at the moment. It might not if we were in a more conventional arrangement."

"You still love him though?"

"Well of course I do!"

"No, I mean you're still in love with him." Sylvie looked at her and really didn't need to hear the answer. Of course she was. Why would she put up with this situation if she wasn't? Sylvie put her arm around her and gave her squeeze. "He's crazy to have let you go. You can't choose who you fall in love with, it chooses you." They sat for a while in silence. If there was ever a reason she would never see Julian as anything more than just a friend it was this. She could never hurt Maggie.

The rain was starting to come down and the room had grown dark. They could hear the thunder in the distance. The smell of wet earth wafted in through the window. The drops came down gently at first, but there was the promise of heavier rainfall as the wind began to pick up and the thunder became louder. The raindrops started to sound like bullets ricocheting off every surface.

"Oh my, it's going to be a big one. Help me close the windows. We'll be drenched in no time." They both got up quickly and started closing up. With all the noise they hadn't heard the door open.

"I just made it!" It was Nick standing on the hallway mat, dripping.

"Goodness, you gave me a start, Nick! I didn't hear you come in," Maggie cried. "You're soaked, go and change. No wait. Take off those wet things here so you don't drip water everywhere and I'll go get you a towel. Don't move!" He stripped down to his boxers and she took his shirt and jeans and went to find him a towel for his hair.

Sylvie had gone to the living room and workshop to close the windows. When she came back through to the hallway she was confronted with the vision of Nick stood in his underwear, hair dripping down his back and chest. Sylvie let out a gasp.

"Sorry… I just came in and…"

Nick stood still in shock. He hadn't known Sylvie was there.

Maggie reappeared with a towel.

"Here you are darling, dry off and go get some dry clothes on. I put the wet ones in the laundry."

Sylvie stood there, paralysed. What the hell was going on? Every time she met Nick, he was half naked and wet! For the love of God! Was this some sick joke, playing with her emotions? She wasn't complaining, but it was very disarming. She could barely contain herself. She just hoped neither of them picked up on it.

Nick bolted up the stairs two at a time. He probably felt uncomfortable at the way she was gawking at him, *again*. How totally embarrassing! She really needed to get a grip.

"Poor thing got soaked. At least we got all the windows shut. Well it looks like you'll have to stay until it passes. You can't drive down in this!"

Great, now she'd have to make small talk with Nick. She'd already made an utter fool of herself and there was no quick get-away. Especially after yesterday's strange interaction, she hoped Maggie would be prattling away so as to take the pressure off.

Sylvie went through to the sitting room and collected their tea cups.

"Shall we have another? Or would you prefer a coffee?"

"Tea, I think. I get the shakes with too much coffee." *That and a hefty dose of half-naked, dripping wet Nick!*

Nick came into the kitchen dressed in a light blue shirt and a pair of jeans. The blue of his shirt made his eyes pop and his cheeks had a glow. He looked absolutely delicious. A perfect combination of his mother and father. Sylvie pried her gaze away from him. She felt herself getting hot. The rain was hammering down outside and the lightning and thunder was getting closer.

"Wow, it's crazy out there." Maggie was looking out of the window. "I wasn't expecting you today darling. Nice surprise though." Maggie turned to Nick.

"I was up this way and thought I'd pop in. Just made before it really started teaming down! They said it's going to last a couple of hours." He was sitting on a stool leaning his chin on his hands. He turned to Sylvie, "Sorry about earlier, you must think I always walk around half naked!" He joked.

"I was beginning to wonder," she replied, relieved that he was joking about it.

"You came to get your car then?"

"Yes, but I think I'm stuck here for a little while longer."

"You'll stay as long as you like, you said you had nothing pressing. I'll put us together some lunch. I just need to take my pots out of the kiln. Nick, make Sylvie some tea, I'll be five minutes." She left, leaving the two of them behind.

Nick got up from the stool and put the kettle on.

"Just milk, isn't it?" he asked.

Sylvie was looking out of the window at the pool so that she didn't have to look at him. "Err, yes. Thanks." He remembered, Sylvie thought. For some reason that mattered to her. She watched the raindrops splash into the pool, like mini bombs. The water was overflowing and running like a river down the pathway. She felt him come up beside her. He handed her the cup. "Thank you." She tried hard to keep her hand steady as she took it from him avoiding his eyes.

They stood in silence just looking at the rain. Sylvie was beginning to feel more and more uncomfortable. He was the first to break.

"So, when are you starting on the decorating?" He turned to her as he spoke.

"We hope on Thursday. The workmen will come up on Tuesday, to check what they need. Then they'll need a day before they start."

"How long will it take?"

"It shouldn't take more than a week. There's no structural work."

"Isn't Mum doing out the en suite too?"

"She never mentioned that. Just her room for now."

"She should do that too. In for a penny, in for a pound. The place will be upside down anyway. Will you be here to over-look the work? Or do they just get on with it?"

"The men I use are very good and normally I wouldn't need to be around as much once their brief has been given. But this case is a little different. Maggie's a friend so I'll probably be here quite a bit."

Why did she feel like she was being interrogated? He seemed to have questions lined up. He took a sip from his tea again ignoring the handle and holding from the rim again.

"How long have you been doing this business?" *Again with questions!*

"About twenty years."

"Oh, I thought you'd only recently started. Weren't my father's offices done by you?" *He was very well informed.*

"I've only recently started getting paid for it. I've always been designing and redecorating. Your father's offices were one of my first paid jobs. I mostly do out shops, boutiques and houses. I'm branching out a bit now though."

"How so?"

"I've been asked to decorate a nightclub." Sylvie took a sip of tea. Maybe he might ease up on her.

"That must be quite a challenge and a lot of work." He looked genuinely impressed.

"It is. But your Dad's been very helpful."

"He's been involved too then?" Was he fishing now, she wasn't sure.

"Yes, he did all the plans for the remodel and we worked together so that I could get the right effect the club owner and I wanted." Sylvie moved over to the kitchen and put down her cup. Her hands were ice cold and sweating and she was worried that the cup might slip. He'd hardly spoken yesterday and today he was firing questions at her almost like a lawyer's cross-examination.

"So you work closely with my Dad?"

"Yes, that's why he recommended me to Maggie." Sylvie couldn't work out if it bothered him that she worked with his father as he seemed to scowl slightly.

Suddenly there was an almighty crash of thunder. It shook the whole house. Sylvie jumped out of her skin.

"Jesus, that was loud," Nick murmured.

Maggie came running through.

"The electricity just went out. Luckily my pots got fired before it stopped. Looks like it's a cold lunch then. What have you two been talking about?"

"The redecoration. Why aren't you doing your bathroom too Mum?"

"I hadn't really thought about it. But now that you mention it, I suppose I should. Can you do that too Sylvie?"

"Err. Yes, if you want to."

"Well, yes I think it'll look shabby once my room's done. Do you want to go and look at it now? I'll put us together lunch while you come up with what you think will work."

"Ok, I'll go up." Sylvie headed for the stairs which lead to Maggie's room. She was glad to get out of the interrogation.

Nick watched her leave and sat back down on the stool. He really needed a cigarette. He couldn't smoke in the house Maggie hated it and it was still pouring down outside.

"She works closely with Dad." It was a statement rather than a question.

"Yes, especially over the last couple of months."

"I thought she was a friend of yours. But Dad introduced you?" He wanted to know if his mother had realised that his Dad was in love with her.

"That's right. But I feel like I've known her for ages. I like her, don't you?" She'd got out some cheeses and salad and was cutting up a baguette.

"Yes, she's very nice." That wasn't the right word at all but he felt it was the best word he could use.

"Take up that pencil and pad for her, she may want to jot something down. All her stuff's in her car." She handed him them and he went through to the hallway and ran up the stairs taking them two by two. As he got to the doorway of the bedroom he could hear Sylvie mumbling to herself. He couldn't make out what she was saying. He walked through to the doorway of the en suite and found her counting her strides. She hadn't heard him as he was barefoot and she jumped when she saw him.

"Sorry, I startled you again. Mum said you might need these to jot something down." He handed her the pad and pencil.

"Actually yes, I do. I was trying to see if we could fit a tub and a walk-in shower. I don't have my tape measure so it's an estimate." She carried on averting her eyes as he watched.

"Does she need a tub? Who takes baths these days?" He walked into the bathroom and perched himself on the edge of the bath.

"I love to have a bath. I have one all the time, it relaxes me. Especially on a day like today." She looked over to him briefly, glad the lighting was dim, then she wrote down some measurements. He looked straight at her. He was having a hard time getting the image of her laid naked in a bubble bath out of his head.

"Really?" his eyes narrowed as he spoke.

"Yes, a glass of wine, candles, bubbles and oil. I suppose it's a woman thing," Sylvie knelt onto the floor so that she could rest the paper on the toilet seat. "I take it you don't, then?"

He shook his head slowly. The room was badly lit due to the lack of light and the dark rain clouds stopping any natural light. Sylvie tried to concentrate on what she was doing, but it was hard. She could feel his presence. She felt him edge a little closer and he leant over to see what she was sketching.

"That looks completely different," he leaned in closer. Thank goodness the light was bad and he couldn't see how flushed she was. His hand came over to point at something on the paper which threw Sylvie off balance and she fell back onto her heels. He steadied her by gently placing his hand on the small of her back. Her pulse started speeding up as though an electric current had passed through her entire body.

"Sorry, about that. I was just going to ask you what that was." He turned to look at her. His face was six inches away from hers. She looked at him sideways, trying not to fully turn and face him.

"It's a heated towel rail. They come in different shapes and sizes now." She started to get up and he took her arm to help her. "Thanks, I should go down and see if your mother approves."

They both started to leave for downstairs. As they left the bedroom and headed for the top of the stairs Nick said something which Sylvie didn't expect.

"I can understand why Dad wants you."

Sylvie quickly turned to look at him. Had she heard him right? Had he actually said that, she could see he had a hard expression on his face and she could see he was almost gritting his teeth. Had his father told him how he felt about her?

"You're very good." His face softened. He'd got the reaction he wanted. She was shocked and had picked up on the double meaning. "At your job. He knew what he was doing recommending you to Mum."

Once Sylvie realised what he was actually saying, she replied. "Julian's just helping me out. Trying to keep me busy." She tried to make light of it. "He's a good friend."

"Oh, I think it may be more than that." Sylvie wasn't quite sure what he meant by that but there was no way she was going to ask for an explanation.

CHAPTER 13

SILVER LINING

***

S ylvie stepped out of the elevator and into the reception area of Sapphire Developers. She was usually the first one in. Today was her forty fourth birthday day and she brought in some small cakes she'd made for all the staff. She loved to bake but she didn't have anyone to do that for now so it was a great excuse. She took them through to the kitchen area and flicked on the kettle and coffee machine.

She enjoyed being there without any interruptions. She walked up to her office and looked up at the plaque. 'Chris Sapphiris. Managing Director.' She promised herself a small change every day. So today she would need to change that. A birthday present to herself, she mused, not that she felt like celebrating much. Both her boys were away, but at least she'd be having lunch with Lilianna. She put her bags down and opened the blinds to reveal her favourite part of this office, the view. The sun was sending its rays onto the water's surface making it glisten, it was mesmerizing.

Dragging herself away from the window, Sylvie turned back to her desk. She had a lot to organise today. She had her meeting with Julian and Zach about the plans for Celle and she also needed to get everything prepared for the en suite at Maggie's. She spent all day yesterday modifying the rough sketch she had put together. She had also spent all day yesterday re-enacting her exchange with Nick.

She really couldn't work it out. He was always very polite and courteous to her. Asking the right questions and behaving like a gentleman. Then he would say something that was unexpected, something that revealed a part of him or what he was feeling. He made her feel uncomfortable, not because he was behaving badly, but because of how she felt about him. He kept his distance, even ignoring her. Then suddenly he would be awkwardly near to her in a familiar way that you could only be with someone you were very close to. Sylvie felt that maybe a lot of this was her overactive imagination. She probably read too much into every gesture. But the fact was, Nick's presence affected her, affected her in a way that she felt was inappropriate.

Saturday had been strange, being with him at Maggie's. After their awkward moment at the top of the stairs Nick had almost backed off. He sat in the sitting room while Sylvie showed Maggie her rough sketch. Then once they'd had lunch and the electricity had come back on he'd sat in the sitting room and watched some match on the TV, occasionally looking over to where Maggie and Sylvie were talking.

Once the rain had died down Sylvie made her excuses and got up to leave. She would have much preferred to stay but Nick's presence was making her nervous. He had gone out on the terrace for a cigarette and Sylvie knew she'd have to go out and say bye.

Maggie had rushed into her workshop leaving her alone. She stood and watched him for a moment taking in his profile as he dragged on his cigarette. He really was unbelievably handsome. He looked deep in thought then something made him turn to where she was standing, making her fluster. *Caught out again!* He furrowed his brow then smiled.

"I just came to say bye."

"You're leaving?" Sylvie nodded as he stubbed out his cigarette.

"Well it was great seeing you again." He gracefully moved towards her and Sylvie felt her whole body start to heat up. He held out his hand for her to shake and she tentatively took it. He hesitated for a second then leaned down and kissed her cheek. Holy hell, her heart bashed against her chest as she inhaled deeply taking in that heady scent of cigarette smoke and aftershave. "Hope to see you soon." He stared at her in that way he did so intensely she had to turn away.

"Bye then." And with that she quickly hugged and kissed Maggie and drove away, his eyes still burning in the very front of her mind.

Sylvie tried hard to stop her mind wandering and set to work on Maggie's en suite. Before long Sylvie had created a virtual image of the bathroom and put together a sample board to show Maggie later on today. Zach had arrived and walked into her office.

"Happy birthday darling!" He came in and kissed her.

"Thanks Zach." She screwed up her nose.

"What?"

"I just don't feel like celebrating."

"I know darling. Doesn't help the boys being away either." Sylvie shook her head. "You've been busy. What are you working on?" He looked at her desk and picked up some samples. He had the most relaxed air about him. Nothing seemed to faze him.

"Maggie's doing her en suite too, so I've put some ideas together for her. What time's Julian coming?"

"He's on his way. We need to see if we can put that electric ceiling in. After you mentioned it to Stathis he's determined to have it. I just need to see about the cost."

"Zach, can you do something for me? I don't want to dump things on you but I'd feel better if you did it for me." She was worried that Zach might get upset at the plaque change.

"Name it." He'd sat down and was swinging on the chair.

"Would you arrange for the plaque on my door to get changed?" She watched him uncomfortably shift in his chair. "I promised myself that I needed to start moving forward. If it's awkward for you I can ask..."

"No, no! It's not awkward. I'm just surprised. That's good. You're feeling more at home here. To be honest I wanted to suggest it a while back. I'll do it for you, consider it done." He leaned forward and smiled. "You've got a little bit of your sparkle back today. What did you get up to this weekend?"

"I was up at Maggie's Friday and Saturday. Sorting out her room. It was really nice being up there. They're good people, the kids, well you know." She was shuffling papers nervously.

"And then Markus was out yesterday and we had a lovely day." Why was she feeling so embarrassed? It was Zach for goodness sake.

"Hmm, I think it's something more than that." He was grinning.

"Whatever do you mean?" *Crap how could he know about Nick.* He didn't even know him. Good God she was being paranoid!

"Never mind, let's get to work. I'm waiting for our quantity surveyor's estimate. The engineers feel they can pull it off in time too. So if the cost is okayed by Stathis, it's a go. Julian's also bringing the revised entrance. I think the glass tunnel works better, like you suggested, so that's another cost we need to revise. Stathis is going to freak."

There was a knock at the door and Julian popped his head round.

"Am I too early? No one's out here yet." His face lit up when he saw Sylvie.

"Come in, we were just talking about the entrance changes."

"Happy birthday!" He walked in with an enormous bouquet of pink flowers. He headed straight to Sylvie and kissed her on both cheeks. Sylvie flushed.

"Thank you, Julian. They're beautiful." Zach raised his eyebrows so only Sylvie could see and she glared at him.

"Beautiful flowers for a beautiful lady." Sylvie flushed and Zach stifled a snort.

Before long the three of them had finalised all the plans and costs. All that was needed was to pass them by Stathis so that the final stages of the club's remodel could get underway and be ready for the middle of May.

"I'll take them to him at lunchtime. I'm supposed to be meeting Lilianna there, so I can go through them with him." With all her work these past couple of days she'd hardly seen her. "I better get going it's nearly one, I don't want her waiting for me." She said her goodbyes and left.

Once Julian knew she was out of earshot, he turned to Zach.

"Did she say anything?" He was hoping that Zach may have got an idea of how Sylvie was feeling about his confession on Saturday. After Julian had told Sylvie how he felt about her he had called Zach. He was worried that firstly it was inappropriate, and as he was the closest person to her, he wanted to know if he'd overstepped his position. Secondly he wanted to know if he thought there was any chance she may see him differently. He hadn't wanted to spring it on her. But after he'd spoken openly to Nick about her he felt compelled to. He just hoped he hadn't blown his chances.

"She didn't, no. But she's in a lot better mood. She asked me to change the plaque on the door today, and didn't you notice? No wedding ring." Zach raised his eyebrows and wiggled his wedding ring finger. "That's got to be a good sign. But I'd suggest not pushing her anymore. She knows how you feel. When and if she's ready, I'm sure she'll give you the sign."

Julian sighed with relief. So there was some hope. Zach was right though, she might pull back if he pushed.

"Thanks for that Zach. I'm not so good with this kind of stuff. Well not with some as important as Sylvie anyway. And this isn't your usual case scenario. She's worth the stress though."

"I've always thought so. And don't beat yourself up. None of us are good at this stuff. Believe me. At least you've got an inside man. Most of us had to find out the hard way. If anyone will know anything Lilianna will."

SYLVIE PULLED UP INTO the marina car park, picked up her briefcase, actually Chris's briefcase, and walked over to Stathis's restaurant where Lilianna was sitting at a table on the outside terrace.

"Hi there sweetie, happy birthday! I've missed you." She hugged and kissed her friend then handed her a beautifully wrapped box with 'Chanel' written on the top. "Just something small, I know you don't want a fuss today." Sylvie opened up the ribbon and lifted off the box lid. Inside was a small red handbag with a long chain handle. Sylvie's eye widened.

"Lily it's… oh, it's too much. Thank you!" She hugged her tightly.

"I remember you always liked it and well…now you're wearing colours again I thought why not go for the brightest. Zach said you'd ditched the black. Well done, you look great, nearly back to normal. She couldn't help but notice her rings were off. She picked up her hand. "Well there's a surprise, I thought they might never come off. That must have been hard."

"It was. But I figure that the longer I hold on to stuff, the harder it'll be to let go. The rings aren't Chris, nor are the black clothes. I won't remember him because of them. He's never out of my thoughts, ever. Whatever I wear or do, he's there."

"I know, sweetie. It's so easy for everyone to make a judgement or have expectations. You do what you feel. If you feel it; and if you feel it strongly, then to hell with everyone."

Lilianna always hit the nail on the head. She was the only one who really spoke to her straight when it came to Chris. Everyone else was careful not to hurt her feelings. Sylvie snorted.

"I don't think I'll ever wear a wedding ring again." She muttered.

"Sylvie! Don't say that. Your only forty-four, not a hundred and four." Lilianna chastised.

"I feel it sometimes. No, I just don't think I ever want to get married again. I've done that. Maybe I should just be on my own. Not have to answer to anyone. Be selfish. I'm too set in my ways to compromise anymore." Lilianna raised her eyebrows in shock.

"Jesus Sylvie. Since when did you become such a cynic? You've always been such a romantic. You're the only woman I know who loves tradition, having a man take care of you." Sylvie snorted again.

"Maybe it's an age thing or circumstances. Or maybe I just woke up and smelled the coffee." Sylvie rubbed her finger searching for her rings. *Or maybe it's since my husband cheated on me.* God she felt old, old and washed up.

They caught up on their children and what they'd been up to. Sylvie told her about Maggie's redecoration and that she was doing her bathroom too. She avoided mentioning Nick as she was afraid she might pick up on something. What, she wasn't actually sure, but she thought it was for the best.

"I have got something to tell you, but I'm not sure I can be bothered with your relentless teasing."

"Ooh now you've got me excited, come on spill it. You know I've got to get off and *now* you mention you've something to tell me!" Lilianna pulled her seat closer to her, "Come on then, what is it?"

"It's about Julian." She was immediately interrupted.

"He didn't make a move did he?" Lilianna's eyes were as wide as saucers.

"Can I tell you please and calm down! No he didn't, but he did confess that he had feelings for me." It was no use; Sylvie knew she wouldn't be able to shut her up.

"I told you. I said it way back when. I'm never wrong. I've never seen such a love struck puppy. I swear. You remember the barbecue? He was building you up to Chris. He wanted you to do Celle, he suggested it, remember? And then he wanted you to do Maggie's. He hasn't been away from you for the last couple of months. He rings you all the time. When anyone who was just a friend would have given you space, not him he's been there, helping you, guiding you. Oh my God, what are you going to do?"

Sylvie was shaking her head. "Did you even take a breath? How long have you been keeping that inside you?" She had her hand over her mouth as she continued to shake her head. "I'm not going to do anything. I don't see him that way. He was Chris's friend, he's a colleague and yes he's become a friend. But you know what? I can't really go there right now. I just thought you should know. Please don't say anything, especially to Zach. I don't want an atmosphere. Things are starting to get a little more normal. I'm settling in. I don't want to set the cat amongst the pigeons!"

''Don't rule him out sweetie. You're still not ready. You know he's pretty much perfect for you don't you? You've so much in common, he's very good looking, a gentleman. And if all those young girls are anything to go by…"

Sylvie squirmed at Lilianna's frankness. "Lily! Stop it!'

ONCE THEY'D FINISHED LUNCH and Lilianna had calmed down she left to go pick up the girls, which left Sylvie to go over all the final plans with Stathis.

She got out all the final costs and sat down with him.

"So, what do you think? Is it within your budget? I know it's over what we originally discussed. I'll leave them with you to think it through in your own time."

He was quietly reading everything thoroughly. Sylvie didn't want him to be over stretched. She really believed it would look amazing but she also knew it was a good twenty per cent over the original budget. He put the papers down.

"You know, every project I have ever done I've always gone over budget. With this place it went fifteen percent and the bar, eighteen. I know the amounts are a lot greater, but it's still twenty per cent. I love it Sylvie, and the buzz it's already creating is phenomenal. Tell Zach to get cracking, just go ahead. It's going to be sensational! You and Julian make a great team." Sylvie beamed. She really was excited about Celle. It was a huge project for her. She'd really put her heart and soul into it. She left the restaurant and wandered to the marina. She dialled the office and got through to Zach.

"He wants to go ahead, Zach. He loves it and he's okay about the cost. So that's it then full steam ahead!" She squealed. She couldn't hide her excitement. Maybe it wasn't such a bad birthday after all.

She put her phone away and sat down on a bench just to take it all in. She must have been sitting there for ten minutes before she felt someone behind her.

"Sylvie?" she felt herself get hot within a millisecond. His voice was unmistakable. She turned around to see him standing there in all his glory. All dazzling smiles and casually dressed in a white T-shirt and faded jeans.

"Nick, what a surprise." She tried to keep her voice steady and was thankful that she was seated and that she had her sunglasses on. He walked round and sat next to her.

"What are you doing round here?" He actually seemed pleased to see her. *Surely not!*

"I was going over some figures with a customer of mine and decided to take in the view. What are you doing down here?" She felt her hands start to sweat and she searched again for her non-existent rings.

"I live down here. Just over there, quay eight. That's my yacht, the one with the jet-ski tied at the back." He was pointing to what seemed to be an enormous white yacht.

"That's yours?" She couldn't hide how impressed she was. "It's amazing." It truly was. It was pristine white with sleek tinted windows and big, really big.

"Thank you." Nick looked over to the woman who he hadn't stopped thinking about and blurted out. "Do you want to come and have a look?"

Without even thinking, Sylvie replied. "I'd love to." She was up on her feet within an instant. He quickly got up and led her to his home.

They reached where it was moored and Sylvie stopped to take a good look at it.

"What a very poignant name for a yacht, *Silver Lining*. Did you choose it?"

"No, but I thought the same thing. I think that's what made me buy her."

He'd jumped onto the deck and turned to help Sylvie onto the gangplank. She held out her hand and he took it. Ever so gently he helped her up as she struggled restricted by her blue pinstriped pencil skirt and stilettos. She lost her balance and he grabbed her with both his hands.

"I'm not wearing appropriate shoes or clothes for this." She slipped off her stilettos and left them on the deck. "That's better."

Nick was still holding her. Once he realised, he let her go and straightened himself up. His eye caught the bag she was holding with her present from Lilianna.

"It's a birthday present," she explained.

"It's your birthday today?" Nick's eyes glittered as he spoke and Sylvie couldn't drag her gaze from them. She nodded feebly.

"Well happy birthday." He hesitated for a split second then leaned over and kissed her cheek. Sylvie felt herself involuntarily lean into him and she took a deep breath; savouring their far-too brief contact, drinking in that unmistakable scent of cigarettes and his aftershave.

"Thanks," she breathed softly. As Nick pulled back his smile looked strained then he seemed to compose himself.

"Do you want the grand tour?" he said in an overly posh accent. He was trying to diffuse the tension with humour.

"Of course." Sylvie over exaggerated her reply to continue the joke. Her heart was pounding and she worried that her knees would buckle. How was he having such a profound effect on her? It was ludicrous and a little humiliating. Thank goodness no-one was witnessing her ridiculous behaviour!

He guided her down the narrow wooden stairs to what was the sitting area. It was surprisingly roomy and beautifully equipped. It was predominately wooden, light oak and had everything you could ever need. A plasma screen, leather cream sofas, a stereo system, DVD player and a coffee table, further in was a breakfast bar, a dining area which led to a fully fitted kitchen. It even had a wine fridge! Though it had more beers in than wine. Nick showed her the bathroom which was a beautifully decorated wet room.

"What, no tub?" Sylvie joked.

"Hey if I want to relax I just jump in the sea!" Sylvie nodded and smirked at him.

To the right was one bedroom with two beds and fully fitted wardrobes. The second bedroom which also had two beds in it, but Nick was using it as an office come work area.

Nick then took her through to the master bedroom. It was larger than she expected with a king sized bed and fully fitted cupboards along with a flat screen and windows. It also had its own wet room.

"Nick, it's absolutely magnificent. It's stunning, really." She gushed.

"Well, thank you very much, that really means a lot to me." Sylvie looked at him, wondering why on earth her opinion should matter so much. "I refurbished the interior myself, so that's a great compliment coming from a professional."

Sylvie smiled, realizing her overactive imagination was going into overdrive.

"You have very good taste and an exceptional eye, Nick." Sylvie chose her words carefully.

"Thank you." Nick couldn't quite read what was going on but he knew he was in real danger of making a fool out of himself if he wasn't careful. He suddenly felt very conscious that they were in his bedroom. "Shall we go back up on deck?" He motioned to the doorway.

They walked back through the sitting area and went back up to where Sylvie had left her shoes.

"That was really kind of you to show me round, but I think I should be going. I've a lot to prepare for your Mum." She headed towards where she'd got on.

"Maybe next time I could take you out. When you're not so busy?"

"I'd love to." Her reply was a little too enthusiastic and she quickly turned to go. She could feel her ears buzzing and her whole body was on fire, she had to get out of there.

"Don't forget your shoes!" he picked them up and handed them back to her. He expertly jumped on to the quay and held out his hand to her. She took a deep breath and placed her hand in his. He leant over and grabbed her waist with his free hand and lifted her on to the quay.

Once she was on the quay he hurriedly jumped back on his yacht.

"Thanks again for the tour, bye." She smiled at him as she slipped on her shoes.

"Anytime." Nick tried to sound blasé as he waved his goodbye and watched her walk away, wiggling quickly in that pencil skirt outlining every curve and back to where her car was parked. He shook his head, trying hard to clear his thoughts. But there was no doubt in his mind that he was utterly and totally captivated by her.

Sylvie all but ran to her car and quickly got in. She felt giddy and she couldn't wipe the huge grin off her face. Her heart was racing and she had an overwhelming urge to scream from excitement. Maybe it wasn't such a bad birthday after all.

PART THREE

SPRING

Earth, teach me to forget myself as melted snow forgets its life. Earth, teach me resignation as the leaves which die in the fall. Earth, teach me courage as the tree which stands all alone. Earth teach, me regeneration as the seed which rises in the spring.

William Alexander

CHAPTER 1

TIMES ARE CHANGING

S ylvie stretched as she turned to look at the clock by her bedside. Seven o'clock.

She smiled to herself. It was the last Sunday in March and Sylvie had thankfully remembered to put all the clocks forward before she came to bed the night before. Markus would be home soon and she'd have both her boys together. Alex had come over for a short visit, which meant they would spend the day out. Sylvie had also arranged for Thea Miria to come out with them.

The sun was peeping through the curtains, sending shards of hazy light onto her bed. She sat and thought back to the morning she had put the clocks back. A simple action had started off a series of events that snowballed into the unthinkable. She still couldn't process the last five months. It was easier to immerse herself in her work; if she thought about it too much she would start to feel the guilt, the anger and the utter devastation. Shaking her head, trying to erase her thoughts, she got herself out of bed.

Things had become progressively easier as the time had passed, but then something would appear out of nowhere and almost knock her back to five months ago. She was thankful of the people she had around her. They were always on hand to pick her up when she was brought down to her knees.

Today would be hard because Sylvie had decided it was time to sort out some of Chris's belongings. But before she went ahead she wanted to know Alex and Markus were ready. She knew she wasn't, but that was not the issue. Things had to move forward, so she would, however hard it was, need to instigate it. She was also hoping Thea Miria would be a positive influence on them. Chris's death had affected her very deeply, but she was an objective woman. A woman of reason and she knew she would feel it was also the right thing to do.

Alex had gone to pick up Thea Miria and arranged to meet Sylvie and Markus at Stathis's restaurant. It was a beautiful spring day and the marina was alive with tourists and locals. Yachts were spreading out to sea, scattering their sails out as far as the eye could see. They seated themselves outside on the terrace and waited for their drinks to arrive.

"It's so lovely here Sylvie, it's like a whole other world." Thea Miria was looking around in wonder. "I don't get to come here that often. I remember it in the old days. It wasn't much then, but now it's like being on the French Riviera."

"Mum's favourite place. I think if she could live down here she would." remarked Alex.

"Dad hated the sea. Don't you remember that holiday in Santorini where we went on a small boat trip to that secluded bay? Dad threw up so many times on the way and slept on the return. It was a nightmare!" Markus was laughing and shaking his head. "He really wasn't good near the sea."

They all sat there, obviously remembering personal things about Chris. It was times like this that the boys missed him the most. Their times together were on days like today. Whatever Sylvie tried to do, there was always a huge gaping hole where he should have been.

"I need to ask you both something, and to be honest I'm not sure how you'll take it." Sylvie broke their train of thoughts. She reached and took a gulp of wine.

"What is it, Mum? Just tell us." Alex was the first to respond.

"It's about Dad's things. I think maybe, if you're ready, it's time to sort them out." She really didn't want to upset them today but she needed to get things in some sort of order. She was faced with them every day and it wasn't helping her at all.

"You mean Dad's clothes and stuff?" Markus asked in a soft voice.

"Well yes, and a few other things."

"What do you want to do with them?" It was Markus again, Alex sat in silence, his eyes fixed on his beer bottle.

"I'm not sure. I was hoping you may have some idea or suggestions."

Again silence.

"I know it's hard. It's a huge step for us all, but, if I'm honest. It's hard for me to look at them every day." The waiter arrived with their food, which luckily drew their attention away but once he was gone it was Thea Miria who spoke.

"Your mother's right. His things need to be sorted. No one wants to do it, but it has to done and it's better you do it together, you all need some sort of closure."

As she spoke Sylvie could see Alex's muscle pulse in his cheek and he stared out to sea. He was finding it harder than Markus. He had been strong for everyone when Chris had died and put his own feelings on hold. But now, as Markus was beginning to accept Chris's death, Alex was not. It also didn't help him being away and then coming back into. It was almost as if he kept reliving it.

"Your Dad isn't his things. He's your memories and what you feel inside," Thea Miria added softly.

As she spoke, her eyes started to well up. Sylvie took hold of her hand and squeezed it. Both Alex and Markus had tears in their eyes. Markus was the first to speak.

"Can we keep some of his things?" he croaked.

"Whatever you want; that's why I wanted us to do it together. I don't know what you'd like to have."

"I think you might be right Thea, we should do it together. Mum's had to do most of this alone." Markus turned to Sylvie and smiled.

"Alex, we don't have to do it if you're not ready." Sylvie reached and took his hand. He turned to her and tried to smile.

"I just feel that I missed out. Being at Uni, you know. You two have started to get used to him not being here. But I still expect him to be home when I'm back."

"I know, darling." Sylvie was still holding his hand.

"But, maybe if we do it, it'll make me get used to it, if that's ever possible."

"I'd like to help too, if that's okay." Thea Miria wiped her eyes and took a gulp of her wine.

"Of course you can." Sylvie squeezed Alex's shoulders. "Now come on, let's eat. This is supposed to be a nice day out." She smiled at them all.

It didn't take long before their mood started to lighten up as they started to eat and talk about a number of random topics. When Thea Miria was there she always seemed to open up conversations which led to big discussions. Today she wanted to understand the whole social networking phenomenon. Alex tried to convince her to get her own Facebook account, so that she could stay in contact with all her former students. Sylvie watched him as he reached over to her plate and forked a prawn and ate it. Then Markus picked up a mussel she'd purposely set aside for him. She sighed inwardly; they were finally relaxing.

It was getting late, so Sylvie paid the bill and they set off towards their cars. Sylvie walked slowly with Thea Miria while the boys were just a little ahead.

"Thanks for supporting me today. It was a hard subject to broach, but it needed to be sorted." Sylvie had her arms linked with her as they walked.

"You're going to have to move on sometime, they need to know that. You're still young. You've plenty of time in front of you. And don't think I don't know that life with Chris wasn't all a bed of roses. It's easy for people to look back and see only the good. He was a handful, always was." She patted Sylvie's arm.

Alex and Markus were by their cars and as they approached Sylvie was stunned to see Nick's Jeep parking up next to them. Her heart started to race as he got out and waved at her. He was wearing sunglasses which unfortunately shaded those magnificent eyes.

"Hi there! What a surprise, I keep bumping into you down here." Sylvie couldn't hide her delight.

"This is my neighbourhood, you know," he replied, with a mega-watt smile.

"Let me introduce you, Alex, Markus Thea this is Nick, Julian's son. These are my boys and my aunt." They all shook hands. "He lives on a yacht in the marina." Alex raised his eyebrows, suitably impressed.

Nick almost seemed embarrassed. Thea Miria left Sylvie, realising that they wanted to talk.

"It was nice to meet you Nick, give my regards to Julian. He's a good man your father, he's been a good friend to Sylvie." She lowered herself into Alex's car as Nick walked up closer to Sylvie.

"We'll meet you back home, Mum. Bye Nick, nice to meet you," called out Alex as he got into his car then, Markus and Thea Miria drove off leaving Sylvie behind.

"I'm going up to your Mum's tomorrow. She wants to look at some ideas for Elenora's room." She wasn't exactly sure why she felt the need to tell him what her plans were, but she couldn't stop herself.

"Have you spoken to her today?" he removed his sunglasses and looked straight at her, making her catch her breath.

"Err... no." She felt the temperature rising. He was doing that thing that he did, getting uncomfortably close to her.

"Oh... so you haven't heard the latest." Sylvie looked puzzled at him. "The restaurant we booked the pre-wedding dinner for has been burned down, some electrical fault. So you can imagine what Mum and Elenora are like!"

"That's terrible, have they found somewhere else?" Sylvie could only imagine what state Maggie would be in. She'd need to call her as soon as she got home.

"No, it's short notice. And they'll be over sixty people." Nick leant back against her car.

"Why don't they do it at the house? The garden's big enough. They could get someone to cater. It'd be really lovely." Sylvie started looking for her rings again. Why did she always feel so uneasy when they were alone?

"That's actually a really good idea. You should call and tell Mum. Not sure we've got much of a choice; it's in less than three weeks." He straightened up and came towards her. "I better let you get back home." He put his hand on her arm and leant in to kiss her cheek.

Sylvie took a deep breath, capturing every molecule of his scent as he pulled away. "Bye then. See you soon hopefully." His hand gently caressed her arm as it drew away. Sylvie's felt her whole body heat up and her stomach go into free fall.

"Yes, bye bye," she answered weakly. He turned and walked towards quay eight. Sylvie got into her car and drove home in a daze. He'd done it again. He'd behaved like they had some close relationship. He'd behaved like there were no boundaries. She really couldn't fathom out what was going on, the only thing she knew was she liked it, she liked it *a lot*.

She pulled into the garage next to Chris's Mercedes. She got out and stood by the front wing and ran her hand over it. It was a lovely car. But no-one wanted to drive it. What was the point in keeping it? She walked back to the house where she found all of them in the kitchen.

"So, shall we get to work?" Her question was mainly directed to Alex. He was the one who needed to be comfortable with it.

"Yes let's go, before I change my mind." He smiled, Thea Miria winked at Sylvie. She had a strong feeling that she had had a lot to do with his sudden acceptance.

AT FIRST IT WAS hard sifting through Chris's clothes. Each one of them could remember him wearing certain items. But they all shared different memories and it started to get a little easier. Alex took a couple of suits which said he liked. He thought he might wear them at his graduation. Markus also picked a sweatshirt he loved and a suit. Sylvie put Chris's watches, cufflinks, wedding ring and crucifix away. She thought that she would like to give them to the boys at a later stage. Thea Miria picked up one of his scarves and rubbed it on her hands.

"If it's alright, I'd like to take this."

They packed the clothes that were to be given away in boxes and the few items that they wanted to hang on to were moved to the spare room. Alex and Markus took their items to their rooms. As Sylvie tided up the wardrobe Thea Miria straightened up the bed.

"Julian's son is a handsome man." The comment caught Sylvie off guard and she stopped dead in her tracks.

"Yes, he is." She decided not to turn round and continued to unnecessarily keep rearranging the shelves and hangers.

"Is he married?"

"No."

"Seeing anyone?"

"Not that I'm aware of."

"He must be very successful." Thea Miria wasn't going to give up.

"Yes, I suppose he must be." She tried to sound indifferent, but she knew she was fooling no one.

"You've spent a lot of time with Julian and his family these past few months. It's done you a lot of good. You've got that twinkle in your eye again." Thea Miria was trying another tactic.

"Well I work with Julian and I redecorated his ex-wife's house, so they've been quite present in my life."

"That's good. Julian and his ex are friendly then? That's quite unusual. She must be a tolerant woman. Does his ex-wife know he's in love with you?" *Bang there it was*. She'd seen Julian only a handful of times, but she'd seen enough to realise what his intentions were.

"Thea!"

"Come on, it's as plain as the nose on your face. He's helped you so much over the last few months. He's introduced you to his children. You know everything about his life, he's brought you in. Even his own son has a close relationship with you! I may wear glasses but I'm not blind." She'd almost hit the nail on the head. What she'd mistaken for Sylvie's interest in Nick, was not because he was Julian's son though, it was purely because she was interested in him. Thankfully she hadn't worked that part out, yet.

"Julian is a friend and a colleague. I don't see him as anything more. If he has feelings for me, as you seem to think, it is not because I've encouraged it. I've only recently started to feel myself again!" She hoped that would be the end of the conversation.

"Maybe it's because of Julian that you are feeling like yourself again."

Sylvie was shaking her head and rubbing forehead. She really wanted to change the subject.

"Thea, please don't. I really don't want to get into this. I'm sorry I know you mean well, but it's not going to happen. I just don't see him that way."

"You know he's perfect for you? He's the right age. He's not interested in having a family. He's very well established, charming and very easy on the eye! But, I'll say no more." She sighed and straightened her blouse. After a moment she looked at Sylvie and smiled resigned to the fact that this conversation was finished for now. "Now then, are you going to tell them about the car now?"

"How did you know I was going to ask them that?" Sylvie looked at her in total shock.

"Strike now while the iron's hot. That's really the only thing left to sort out. Come on, stop putting it off. It's just a hunk of metal!"

Sylvie looked at Thea Miria and chuckled. Thank goodness she had her to kick her into action.

CHAPTER 2

THE CAR

***

P etros was packing the boxes into the back of his truck as Sylvie came down to the kitchen. Markus had left early in the morning and Alex was showering.

"Morning Petros. Thank you so much for doing this." She'd arranged to take them herself but Marcy insisted Petros take them. She felt that maybe they may regret what they'd done and leave them in the spare room.

"It's really no problem. I know a few poor families who could really do with these."

He carried on putting the boxes in his work truck as Marcy hurried him along.

After they had sorted the clothes last night Sylvie had spoken to Alex and Markus about the car. There initial reaction was not to get rid of it.

"Mum, it's a great car." Markus cried. "Can't we just keep it?'

"If you want to, but we need to drive it. It can't just sit there."

"I've got my pickup truck, I couldn't drive it. It wouldn't feel right." Markus replied feeling decidedly uncomfortable.

"Alex, what about you then?' Sylvie turned to look at him.

"I've got my car too. And to be honest I really don't want to drive it either." He was shifting in his seat.

"That's why I said we should sell it. I could buy something else. I have my car that I need for work, but I thought I could trade it in for another car. Like a spare. One we could all drive, or at least feel comfortable driving. What do you say?" She hoped they'd come round. It really was a waste for the car just to sit there. She'd asked Zach if he wanted it. But she'd had pretty much the same response as she'd had from the boys.

Part Three – Spring

"I suppose it makes sense," Alex reluctantly answered. "It's worth quite a bit, Dad really looked after it. None of us feel comfortable driving it. Maybe you're right Mum."

"We can take it together, before you go back to Uni." She came and sat by him and put her arms around him. "It's really shitty I know, but we need to be practical. The car's going to deteriorate if it doesn't get used." She kissed his head. Markus came over and sat with them. Sylvie put her arm around his shoulders.

"You've really had a lot to deal with these past few months but I know one thing for sure. Your Dad would have been very proud of you. You've both been so incredibly strong. I don't think I could have done half the things I've had to do if it wasn't for you two."

The three of them sat there in the quiet. Even though the day had been filled with sadness, the day had also been filled with memories. Good memories. They had all been able to share them without the uncontrollable emotions that they had felt in the first couple of months after Chris had died. There was calm and peace, something they hadn't felt for what seemed a very long time.

SYLVIE DECIDED TO TAKE Chris's car early, before Alex was down. Initially she thought they could go together, but in hindsight she thought it would only make it harder to part with it. She didn't feel it was necessary for him to see her drive the car away either. So she retrieved the keys from the drawer and made her way to the garage. Her heart was thumping and she wasn't sure why. It was true she wasn't comfortable with the idea of driving the car, but it was more than that. It hadn't been moved since he'd died. Only Petros had turned over the engine. She opened the door and slipped into the driver seat. She was instantly overcome with the smell of Chris's aftershave. She swallowed hard and tried not to allow the tears that pricked her eyes spill over. She turned the key and the engine roared its familiar roar. Her hands were trembling as she put it into gear. She gripped the steering wheel to steady them. She slowly reversed out of the garage and gently drove down the driveway and onto the road.

Her heart was still thumping and the engine's familiar roar was almost deafening to her. She turned on the radio and cranked up the volume in an attempt to drown out the engine. As she drove she heard a low beeping sound coming through the speakers. Sylvie slowed down to pull over to see if she could discover what the sound was. It sounded like a message coming through on her phone. She checked it, but there was nothing. Then something caught her eye on the dashboard. It was the car phone.

Once she'd turned on the radio, the phone had automatically turned on. The message was flashing on the dashboard control panel. She closed her eyes, knowing full well who the message was from. The tears were now uncontrollably streaming down her face. As she tried to wipe them, the smell of Chris's aftershave became stronger. It was on her hands. The aftershave must have been on the steering wheel. She began to sob with total abandon. All she could remember was the messages and that now, five months on, there was another.

She didn't know if she had the courage to read it. When could it have been sent? Why? Sylvie pulled over to the curb then opened up the compartment that housed the phone and selected the inbox. There was that familiar number. Her finger hovered over the 'open' button as she squeezed her eyes shut, as if it might make it disappear. Her finger depressed the button and the message shone back at her.

'Can't wait to see you. These past 48hrs have been hell. All I want is to have you in my arms again. To be with you for 2 whole days. Love you. See you at the airport xxxxx'

Dina must have sent it to Chris after they'd had the confrontation and he'd never read it. She scrolled back to see if he'd sent a message to her first. Sylvie pressed the 'Sent' box. There it was, as she knew deep down it would be. After all she had known first-hand Chris's ways. How he made a woman feel. How he made you truly believe you were the only one for him.

> 'Counting down the minutes until I see you and then it'll be just you and me. x'

She dropped the phone and shook violently. Her stomach cramped and she just managed to open the car door as she began to heave. She allowed herself to cry, her tears constantly streamed down her face as she unsuccessfully kept wiping them away. She felt many things, anger, grief, humiliation and sorrow. But what she felt most of all was the unbelievable and excruciating pain in her heart. Chris had managed, even after his death, to break her heart once again. This morning she had felt that she was finally moving forward, making steps in the right direction to get on with her life. Now it was as though she was back to five months ago. She buried her face in her hands and let her pain wash out of her. She was just thankful Alex had not come with her.

ZACH AND JULIAN WERE sat in Julian's office going over a new project they were working on when Zach received a call on his mobile. He looked at the number and his face turned white.

'Chris' said his phone. What was going on, how could that be? Julian looked at him worried as to why his friend looked like he'd seen a ghost. Zach turned the phone for him to see. He looked bemused at Zach.

"Answer it." Julian held his breath as he waited.

"Hello?"

"Zach I'm so sorry to call you so early but I'm…" Sylvie was still heaving for her sobs as she spoke.

"My God Sylvie, where are you, what is it?" Zach looked relieved and concerned with in a split second of each other. Julian began to breathe again. He hadn't realised he'd been holding his breath.

"I'm down by the Mercedes garage. I brought Chris's car to part exchange it. But it's just a little too much for me and I could do with…"

"I'm on my way. Don't move!" Zach put down his phone and looked at Julian.

"Christ, I thought it was some sick joke. It's Sylvie. She was on Chris's car phone, she's hysterical. I'm off to go calm her down." Zach explained and within a split second Julian was up.

"I'll come too."

They found Sylvie parked outside trying hard to compose herself. Zach was there first. He turned to Julian and asked him to give him a moment with her alone. He had a bad feeling about what he might find as he slipped into the passenger's seat. Julian nodded and waited by his car. Sylvie had somewhat pulled herself together but her eyes were swollen from crying and her face had lost its colour.

"Come here darling." He put his arms around her as she relaxed into him. "Want to tell me what's going on?"

Sylvie picked up the car phone and opened the messages for him to read. He stiffened and shook his head in disbelief.

"How many more slaps in the face am I going to get, Zach? I thought I was coming through. I was making progress. And today I was ready to take the car, the final really hard decision, and then this." She pointed to the phone. "I really feel like I've jumped back ten steps." She was playing with the tissue in her hand.

"I don't know what to say to you, really I don't. I thought that there were no more surprises. That we'd eliminated all of them. But it would seem……Oh Sylvie, darling. This is so cruel."

They sat for a moment. Zach trying to digest what he had just seen, Sylvie in a daze trying hard not to break down again.

"What do you want to do? Shall I go and talk to the garage. Andreas will give you a good price. He knows the car." Sylvie shrugged her shoulders. "Julian's here too; I'll get him to go in, and you can get in my car. You don't need to talk or see anyone. What do you say?" She nodded weakly her acceptance. Zach got out of the car and made the necessary arrangements. Sylvie picked up the car phone and dropped it into her bag.

Within five minutes Zach was ushering her into his car while Julian spoke to the dealer. Sylvie pulled down the windshield and looked at herself in the mirror. Her eyes were still puffy but at least her nose had lost its redness. She reached into her bag and applied some cover up to disguise as much of the black circles as possible and dabbed some rouge on her cheeks. She turned to Zach as he watched.

"That's better." He rubbed her hand as he spoke. "Are you ready to face Julian at least? I think he's arranged to leave the car here until you've decided what to do." Sylvie took a deep breath and closed her eyes. She had to hold it together.

"I think I should make a decision on what to exchange it for now. If I leave, I'll never do it. And at least you're here now." She opened the car door and stepped out into the sunlight. She quickly put on her sunglasses and waited for Zach to show her where to go.

Julian was already looking at a number of saloons on the forecourt as they approached he turned and smiled at Sylvie. He tried hard not to show how shocked he was at her sombre appearance. It was like he was back to five months ago. His heart broke to see her like this again.

"There you are!" he tried his best to seem as normal as he could. He leant over and kissed her on the cheek. "Andreas has given us a brilliant deal, so you can pretty much choose whatever." He put a guiding arm around her and led her round the lot.

Sylvie walked around in a state of semi awareness. She really had no interest in any of them. They'd walked round for a second time when Sylvie's eyes focused on a silver car parked behind the sales annex.

"Is that car for sale?" she inquired to the assistant.

"I suppose so. It's being sent to the Jaguar dealer. Customers that come here only want Mercedes so we trade off with them when we part exchange another make of car."

Sylvie walked over to it and ran her fingers over the bonnet. It was a beautiful Jaguar XR convertible. Sylvie opened up the driver's side and lowered herself into the cream leather seat. Her hands slowly caressed the steering wheel. The sales assistant came over to her.

"Start it up if you like, and I'll show you how the top goes down."

Sylvie took the card key from him and started up the engine. It purred. He leant in and pressed a button near the gear box and the top slowly began to fold itself away. Sylvie felt the sun on her face and a light breeze blew through her hair and she knew that this was the car she wanted.

Zach and Julian watched on, all the while keeping a distance. They looked at each other with relief in their eyes. Julian went straight inside to talk to the owner. Within five minutes he'd thrashed out a deal and arranged the car to be ready to be picked up in a couple of days. Zach went over to Sylvie as she opened up the glove compartment. It was immaculate.

"One lady owner. Some diplomat's wife. Only had it for a year and then she traded it in for a new Mercedes. It suits you. If you're sure it'll be ready on Wednesday. Julian's sorting it out."

"I'm sure." She nodded with a slight smile. Zach took a deep breath filled with relief. Thank goodness he thought. This had gone better than he'd hoped. He turned to Julian and winked a nod at him, who turned to Andreas and nodded his approval.

CHAPTER 3

A NEW PROJECT

By the time they'd finished up at the garage it was eleven o'clock. Sylvie felt exhausted and totally drained. She really couldn't face the office. She sat in Zach's car looking for her rings again.

"Let me take you home. You don't need to go in today. Spend time with Alex." Zach opened the door to his car.

"Alex has gone to see some friends this morning. But it's true, I can't face the office." Her face had lost some of its puffiness but the dark circles were still evident. Julian came over to tell them what the final arrangements were.

"Thanks again Julian." Sylvie spoke softly as she closed the door.

"Maggie just called. She said you suggested that we should have the pre-wedding dinner up at the house. She seems awfully excited. I think it's a marvellous idea." He wanted to change the subject. It had worked in the past with her. He hoped that he could manage it again.

Sylvie remembered she'd called her late last night and promised she'd be up there in the afternoon to go over it with her. With everything that had happened she had totally forgotten. Julian knelt down to her level and looked at her through the open window. He could see that she was agonising over what to do. Determined not to let her regress backwards he made the decision to put a bit of pressure on. He knew once she was arranging something else, something totally detached from what she was now going through, she would start to come round.

"She was in such a state about it until you called her yesterday. You really saved the day. Of course, there's loads to organise. Catering, decorations and the invites will need to be sent out again." He watched her nod her agreement. "Let's hope we can pull it off."

"Maybe I should go up there this afternoon as arranged. I wouldn't want to let her down." Sylvie thought that under the circumstances, and after everything he'd done today, it was the least she could do.

"Only if you're up to it. I know it's been a rough morning." He started to feel a little guilty for pressuring her.

"No, it's okay. It'd probably do me some good. Change of environment."

Zach said his goodbyes and got into the car. They drove home without talking. Zach felt that whatever he said would probably be redundant. They'd both said all they wanted to and there was no point upsetting her anymore.

They got to the house and Sylvie saw Alex's Mini was still home. Sylvie panicked. She'd thought he would have already left. She turned to Zach.

"Do I look like I've been crying? I don't want him to see me like this. He's had a lot to deal with."

"You look fine. Just tired. I'll come in with you and I'll distract him if you want to get yourself together." Sylvie nodded and went directly upstairs avoiding the living room where Alex was sitting. She heard Zach go in and start talking to him. She went to her bathroom and washed her hands and face. Then she reapplied her make up. Even with concealer and blusher she still looked haggard, but at least her eyes weren't red anymore. She then changed into a pair of cropped trousers and T-shirt, discarding her business clothes on the bed. She pinched her cheeks, encouraging them to blush some more.

They were talking about Celle when she eventually came downstairs to join them. Alex was totally engrossed in what Zach was telling him. He'd explained how the club had been redone and that it would be ready in five weeks, which was right on schedule. Zach offered to take him down to see it before he left and they began to arrange a suitable time. Sylvie started to relax. It was twelve thirty by the time Zach left.

"Thanks for this morning Zach, and for now." Sylvie was seeing him to the door.

"I told him that we took the car so there won't be any awkward questions. He was remarkably accepting, so don't worry. He actually was impressed that you'd chosen the car already. I'll call you later. Now, get up to Maggie's and sort out that dinner. It'll take your mind off everything." He hugged and kissed her, then drove off waving out of the window.

As she walked back into the house Alex came out.

"Zach told me about the car." He came over to her, giving her a hug. "You did the right thing." He pulled back from her so he could look at her. "He also told me about Celle. Now that really sounds unbelievable, can't wait to see it."

"It's been hard work, but it's coming together." She shrugged.

"I've got to get off now Mum. I'm meeting up with some friends and I'm already late."

She smiled. "You get off and have a good time. We'll speak later." She kissed him goodbye and then headed to the garage.

Sylvie opened the door and looked at the empty space next to her car. Her stomach tightened. That was going to take a lot of getting used to. She took a deep breath and set off up to Maggie's. At least there she could lose her thoughts in whatever state of panic Maggie was in.

NICK WAS SITTING IN his shop going over some paper work while Christian, his shop manager, was telling him about his weekend. He'd been jabbering on for what seemed like the best part of an hour. Nick wasn't really listening but he nodded and laughed in the right places, giving the illusion that he was. He kept looking at the clock; it was one o'clock. They should be closing for lunch.

Normally he'd grab a sandwich and stay in the shop, especially when he had all this paperwork to sort out. It was coming to the end of the business year and he needed to get everything off to the accountant. The problem was, all he wanted to do was go up to his Mum's house. Sylvie had said that she'd be there this afternoon. He really wanted to see her again. All the time she'd been redecorating and remodelling Maggie's bedroom and bathroom, he'd made unnecessary visits to his mother's house. Any excuse just to be near her. With all the upheaval and the constant talk of the wedding no one notice that he was spending an unusual amount of time there.

He would go under the pretence that he wanted to use the pool. He tried to go around lunchtime, knowing that Sylvie turned up around two. He knew she was working on the club, so she used to organise anything that needed to be done in the morning, leaving the afternoons free for Maggie's. The whole refurbishment had taken two and a half weeks and he had got used to seeing her practically every day. Now that it had been finished the chances of bumping into her were less likely.

He really couldn't concentrate. *Fuck it!* He thought and with that he collected his papers and put them in the desk drawer.

"I'm out for lunch, not sure what time I'll be back so lock up tonight for me." He ran back to his yacht to change his clothes and then set off up to Maggie's.

SYLVIE PULLED UP OUTSIDE Maggie's house after the fifteen minute drive through the winding roads that had become so familiar to her. She started to feel better just with the thought of being in her house. It was so alive and full of happiness. It really was the best place for her today after the harrowing morning she'd had. After she had finished Maggie's redecoration she had really missed coming up there. They spoke on the phone every day, but Sylvie hadn't had a reason to come up for a visit. She'd also been busy with Celle so it was hard to get away. Of course the other reason why she loved being there was that there was always the chance she'd see Nick.

While she'd been working on Maggie's house she had been lucky enough to see him. She didn't realise he spent so much time up there. Not that she was complaining! Most of the time he was in the pool, swimming lengths. Then he'd come and sit with them after the workmen had left. There were days he was ready to talk about anything and then there were days he'd just say hello and get on with something else away from her. She still couldn't work him out. Even Maggie commented on his hot and cold temperament.

"He's very sensitive at the moment. I don't know, lately he's sociable and happy one day and then the next you can hardly get him to talk. I'm afraid it might be down to a woman!"

That came as quite a bombshell to Sylvie. She was astounded as to how bad that statement made her feel. She didn't have any right to feel that way. He was just her friend's son. But deep down she knew that the thought of Nick with another woman made her feel sick. She hadn't seen him for over two weeks and then yesterday they had that chance meeting at the marina. That was why she'd told him she'd be here today, in the hope that he might come up. She felt embarrassed just thinking about how silly she was behaving. She got out of her car and walked up to the front door.

Maggie was over the moon when she saw her.

"I've not been able to stop thinking of what we should do. Thank goodness you came up with the idea to do it here. Elenora was absolutely devastated when we heard about the fire. Admittedly she's a little sceptical of whether it will work here. But after the magic you pulled off in my bedroom, I have no doubt it will be perfect."

Instantly Sylvie started to feel better. Maggie didn't even mention that Julian had explained what sort of a morning she'd had. Or that the puffiness of her eyes gave away the fact that she'd been crying. Maggie took her out to the garden and went to make tea. She left her there with a pad and pencil to get her ideas down. She was just about to get the tray when she heard the familiar sound of Nick's Jeep pull up.

Thank goodness, she thought. He'd be able to talk to her while she prepared lunch. He always seemed to lift her spirits. They always seemed to find a multitude of subjects to talk about. It would be just what she needed.

"Hello darling, this is a nice surprise. You haven't been up in ages, what's the occasion?" She hugged and kissed him.

"Well err…" he hadn't thought of a feasible excuse and her comment caught him off guard. Before he could answer Maggie, hugged and kissed him.

"Like I care! Just happy to see you. Sylvie's here. She's out on the patio. We're going to see what we can do in the garden for the dinner. Go and take this out for me so I can get lunch on, you're staying aren't you?"

"Yes, sure." He took the tray, glad not to have to make up a reason for his visit.

"And Nick, be really nice to her, she's had a very rough morning." Maggie added, Nick tilted his head looking for a reason.

"Your Dad called. Said he had to help her this morning. She was in state because she was selling her husband's car."

"Oh. Okay." Nick nodded and headed for the patio with mixed emotions. He was thrilled that he'd get to be with Sylvie, but at the same time he felt a pang of envy that his father had been there and helped her out today. It was something he was finding difficult to accept. His father was obviously very present in her life. Though he knew they were just friends, he knew his father's feelings were more. He was ashamed to say that this bothered him. It bothered him far too much. Well, he had her here now he'd better make the most of it.

"Did someone order tea?" His comment made her jump. She'd been scribbling on a pad, engrossed in whatever she was doing. "Sorry. I didn't mean to startle you. I seem to do that a lot." His whole face beamed at her as he put the tray down then leant over her shoulder to see what she was doing. The oh-so familiar smell of his aftershave hit her and she breathed it in slightly, closing her eyes.

"Hi. I was miles away." He was doing that thing again, invading her space, and she absolutely *loved* it. She couldn't believe how much her mood changed when he was so near to her. He looked delicious in a light blue polo shirt and faded jeans.

"That looks like a completely different garden. Do you think we'll be able to do it, I mean, at such short notice? I'm not disputing your capability!" he laughed. His eyes were so vibrant, they lit up his whole face as he laughed, and Sylvie could do nothing else but gaze at him. She dragged herself out of her trance.

"I was going to be very offended if you were doubting my ability." Sylvie replied in mock horror. "The biggest problem is the catering. Luckily I've someone that can do it for us, especially because it's a Friday. The flowers need to be ordered pretty fast, but I'm leaning towards flowers that are in season and can be found locally. The band will stay the same, thankfully." Nick turned the sketch towards him, so as to see it better.

"Are these lanterns?" he pointed to the pad. Sylvie had to move closer to see what he was pointing at. Their shoulders were almost touching and she could feel the heat radiating off his skin through his shirt. Sylvie picked up the pencil and pointed to them.

"That's right. I've put them round what would be the dance floor, see here and by the bar. And up here I thought we could use fairy lights rather than strong lighting. It'll be more romantic."

She looked at him sideways as he looked at her. She really could get used to this, she thought.

"It looks…" He was trying to find the right words.

"Oh, Sylvie… that looks amazing." They hadn't even heard Maggie come out. They instantly pulled back from one another.

"Yes it looks amazing," repeated Nick.

"I just hope Elenora will like it," mumbled Sylvie.

"She'll love it. You didn't pour the tea. Too engrossed, I suppose." She sat down and poured everyone a cup. "You'll both be staying for lunch I hope; I just made some spaghetti carbonara." She sat back looking at Sylvie. Her face had lost that sallowness and her eyes were perking up again. She just needed to keep busy and have people around her and she'd come back round again, she thought.

CHAPTER 4

HERE COMES THE SUN

Easter had passed, and Alex had gone back to university. The house was empty again. The quiet was deafening, and Sylvie still found it difficult to handle. She'd taken to putting on the radio back on again. Another change that had been difficult.

Listening to music was hard for her. Most songs held some memory that pulled at her heart but she couldn't stand the silence any more so she put it on very low so that there was background noise. Easter had been tough on all of them. Normally everyone would come to their house for a huge barbeque. Zach, Lilianna and their girls would come round early and they'd all finish late, usually rounding up the day by playing cards.

This year Sylvie hadn't wanted to go anywhere, but Zach insisted they get together at his house. Both he and Lilianna tried their best to make it as easy as possible and Sylvie had been glad they pressed her and the boys to go. For a split-second she kept expecting Chris to walk in. Then she'd turn and expect him to be sitting next to her. Every occasion was a milestone for her to get over. The only good thing that Sylvie was pleased about was that Alex and Markus seemed more relaxed, more like themselves again.

Sylvie was sitting at her desk, going through some invoices that she needed to pass. She had a busy three weeks ahead of her and she needed to get all her paperwork organised. Elenora's wedding was at the end of the week and she would need to be up there practically every afternoon making sure everything was going to plan. Maggie was already busy with the actual wedding so Sylvie had taken control of the Friday pre-wedding dinner. Celle was opening two weeks after the wedding, meaning that she, along with Zach and Julian, were also back and forth from the site. Sylvie was putting in a twelve hour day, which suited her fine. It meant less time at her empty home.

She couldn't wait for summer to be here. Alex would be back and Markus would have finished his national service. She'd have them for three whole months. That thought allowed a smile to creep across her face. She quickly gulped down her tea and headed out of her office.

Sylvie closed her door behind her and looked up at the plaque. Sylvie Sapphiris. M.D. That was still hard to get used to. She still felt the title was wasted on her. Yes, it was her company, but it was difficult being put in the spotlight. Over the last five months all of the company's customers, associates and suppliers had started to make the transition from only dealing with Zach to including her in any business matters. It had been daunting for her. She didn't want to make a fool out of herself and she didn't want to let anyone down. But over the last couple of months she'd become more confident. Celle had been the catalyst which had propelled her into this new field and, consequently, a new chapter in her life.

"Maria, I left all the invoices on my desk if you need them. I'm off to Celle, then to Maggie's. If you need anything call me." Sylvie called over to her as she passed her newly-created office. Thank goodness for Maria. She had been a Godsend to Sylvie. She had taken on the position of assistant like a duck to water. Actually more like a serene swan, calm and graceful on the surface but powering away underneath. Nothing was too hard or too much trouble for her. She thrived in her new role.

Sylvie thought it was only right she had her own office rather than just a desk in the reception area. So Zach arranged for a part of the open reception area to be closed off creating a small office for Maria.

"Okay, good luck. I'm sure it'll be fabulous!" Maria called back.

Sylvie walked out into the sunshine and admired her newly acquired car. She'd had it a couple of weeks now. It was perfect for days like today. She jumped into the driver's seat, put down the top and, full of excitement, headed off to Celle.

Most of the construction was finished. Today the roof was being tested and Sylvie was excited to see it finally working. It had been a technical nightmare to get the glass roof to retract so as to expose the sky, but between Zach, Julian and their engineers, they had eventually ironed out any foreseeable problems. The building itself was slightly set back from the road, allowing a driveway to be created allowing cars to pull up right outside the entrance for guests to be dropped off. The entrance was a glass walkway leading into the club. This was so that if it was raining, the guest would be protected. Once inside the entrance, reception area was open yet warm and luxurious. There was a cloakroom and reception area where the hosts and hostesses would be waiting to take the guests to their reserved tables. The door leading into the club was tinted glass, allowing you to see into the club, but once inside the light was obstructed so that you could not see out into the entrance area.

There were steps down to the main dance floor. The bar, which was situated in the centre, was in the shape of a circle. The only way to get into it was underground. Sylvie had suggested that the basement could house the kitchen and storage areas. All the staff could come in and out of the bar via the underground corridors and the internal stairs. This also meant that the staff didn't need to trail supplies and rubbish through the club. They could disappear down the stairs to the stores and kitchen and then out to the trade entrance.

The second level ran the whole length and width of the club and was for the private tables. It provided a bird's eye view of the club. This area had once been the offices and the holding cells. The bars had all gone, to Stathis's relief! Sylvie did, however, create cages raised up off the floor for dancers to use and these *did* look like elevated holding cells!

There was also a third floor, which was sectioned off with glass for private parties. On the opposite side was a 'chill out' area for exclusive guests to enjoy.

Today Sylvie would see the glass roof retract, which would be perfect in the summer time. She pulled up outside the entrance and started to feel excited. She felt like a child going to a funfair for the first time. It really had felt like a rollercoaster ride these past few months. Sylvie walked inside where Stathis, Zach, Julian and the engineers were waiting.

"Morning!" she called. "So, does it work?" she couldn't conceal her apprehension.

"Morning, Sylvie. We waited for you before we tried it out." Stathis came over to her, giving her a kiss. "I couldn't sleep last night," he added.

"Tell me about it," whispered Sylvie. She hooked her arm around him and squeezed his waist.

"Come on you guys, have a little faith. We've got the best team here," chuckled Zach, in his ever-relaxed manner. Sylvie envied his calmness. He never seemed to get stressed.

"So, Stathis, are you ready to see it in action?" Julian was revelling in his anxiety.

"Just do it already!" Stathis snapped, looking nervous.

Zach called to the engineer to set it in motion and everyone's eyes in the club looked upwards to the tinted glass ceiling. The roof slowly glided open, allowing the glorious sunshine to come through. It moved gradually and smoothly into the remaining roof and became totally concealed.

"Wow, that's incredible." Stathis was punching the air with his fist. He squeezed Sylvie and lifted her off the air. "You're a genius!"

"I didn't construct it," she giggled, totally swept away by his reaction and that it worked so well. "You have to thank Zach and his team for that.'

"Our team," Zach corrected her. "I told you it was going to be fine." Stathis crossed over to him, hugging his shoulders, his relief obvious. A total contrast to the calm Zach.

"The best part of it though is that as you open and close it, the glass is automatically cleaned," Julian added. "So that's another headache solved too. Close it now!" he shouted. "Or did you forget that we also need to see it close?" He turned to Stathis with raised eyebrows.

"Oh God, I forgot about that." Everyone looked skyward again, this time shielding their eyes from the sun. The glass slowly began to reappear and smoothly closed the hole, creating a semi-light hue like an eclipse. Stathis beamed. "Fantastic job guys, really."

The rest of the morning was taken up with checking that the floor was being laid before the furnishings were put in at the end of the week. There were only twenty days until the opening and Stathis wanted it all finished so that his staff could be trained up before the official opening.

"I've brought your official invitations for the opening." He reached into his jacket pocket and handed them each an envelope. "If you need more, let me know." He watched Sylvie as she turned the envelope in her hands. He went up close to her and in a low voice said, "I know this will be your first opening since... well, you know. But I really want you to be there. You've been to every one of my openings. You're like my good luck charm."

Sylvie took a deep breath.

"I don't know, Stathis. It'll be... well, hard. You know under normal circumstances, of course I'd love to be there. I can't promise."

Both Zach and Julian were listening as Sylvie mumbled her response. Julian looked over at Zach with raised eyebrows. Zach looked back, shaking his head and struggling to think of what to say.

"It's a couple of weeks yet, don't decide just yet." He left her still staring at the envelope.

When he was sure she was out of earshot he went and quietly spoke to Zach. "What do you think? Is she up to it?"

"I'm really not sure, Stathis. She's up and down. But I was thinking that maybe we could get a group from work to go with her. Like a thank you for all their work. I think she'd like that. She's become quite close to a few girls at the office, and it would be something different from the usual openings for her. You know that I don't usually come to these events, they're not my kind of thing. It was always Chris and Sylvie that did the P.R., so she'll feel that she should show her face, even if it's just for a bit."

"Yes, that might make her feel like it's more work related rather than a personal invite," agreed Stathis.

"Besides, I think the staff would love to come. Definitely more their scene than mine!" he chuckled.

Julian slipped his invite into his pocket and walked over to where Sylvie was. She'd been talking to the floor fitter trying to get a time of completion so she could get the upholsterer booked in. He'd initially wanted to ask Sylvie to the opening. In fact he'd planned to try and broach the subject over the wedding, where he hoped she might be more open to his advances. But after hearing the conversation Stathis and Zach had just had, he really wasn't so sure. He had no intention of going with anyone else. He'd had no liaison with any other woman in the last few months, except for the odd 'booty call' from Ellie, and he really didn't want to go with anyone other than Sylvie. If she was going to make it a work night out, he didn't want to encroach on that either. He'd just rather not go at all.

"I'm off back to my office. I've a lot to finish before this weekend. Are you off to Maggie's later?"

"Yes, I'll be heading up as soon as I've finished here. I'm so pleased about the roof. It's really magnificent."

Julian nodded his agreement. "Yes, the place is really coming together. You've done an amazing job, Sylvie."

"*We've* done," she corrected him.

Julian said his goodbyes and left. He made up his mind to wait and see what she decided to do before he spoke to her. It would be a difficult decision for her to make and he didn't want to make it worse. He hoped that she might feel a little less intimidated and more excited as the opening drew closer.

CHAPTER 5

JUST DESSERTS

Sylvie drove up the winding roads up to Maggie's for what seemed like the hundredth time this past week. It was the day before the pre-wedding dinner and Sylvie had dedicated the next forty-eight hours to Maggie and Elenora. The tables, bar, dance floor and lighting were being put in today, leaving the flowers and table settings for the day of the dinner.

The house was a hive of activity, but luckily everything was being set up with minimum fuss. Sylvie walked into the house, as the door was wide open, and found Maggie in the kitchen. She'd decided to make the dessert herself, to make it feel like a big family dinner. She had her glasses on and was leafing through a cookbook. Sylvie looked over to the lounge and saw hundreds of ivory, satin-covered boxes.

"Hello! What are you doing?" Maggie looked up and beamed at Sylvie.

"I was just checking out a recipe. I hope you came to help out. Elenora is useless and Vicki's working. Nick is the only one that's any good in the kitchen and I've no idea where he is. So I've been left to make them on my own. I've been given my list of all the desserts Elenora wants. Thankfully Pavlos's mum is making a couple too."

"Sure I'll help, what's on your list?" Sylvie hardly ever made desserts now that Alex was away and Markus only came out for a day so it wasn't worth it.

"Chocolate Mousse, crème caramel, strawberry trifle and tiramisu. Rita's making some Greek desserts." Maggie raised her eyebrows and grinned. "Simple girl, my Elenora!" she added sarcastically. "Well better start cracking on."

Sylvie laughed as she put her bag down.

"Are those the finished product?" Sylvie motioned to the boxes.

"Yes! They arrived late last night. Let me show you!" Maggie couldn't hide her pure excitement.

Maggie had designed a favour to commemorate Elenora and Pavlos' wedding. Each family would receive a set of six cream and gold Greek coffee cups and saucers, which were presented in a satin box with the traditional sugared almonds. She reached for a box and untied the ribbon. She opened the box to reveal her handcrafted work. The cup had their initials tastefully inscribed on it and on the base of the cup was the date of the wedding. They were exquisite.

"Oh, Maggie, they are stunning. What a fabulous job, really, they really are special." Maggie beamed and nodded, totally overcome.

"Thanks," she choked, and wiped a tear with the back of her hand.

"Let me just check on everything outside and I'll expect you to give me my orders when I come back." Sylvie hugged her before she left.

She went through the French doors outside to where the dance floor was being finished off and the lights were being wired. She spoke to the workmen who seemed to be getting on a lot faster than she'd hoped. The bar had already been erected and the lanterns were being secured. She heard a vehicle pull up.

That must be all the tables and chairs, she thought. They were supposed to be coming any minute and so she went around to see. To her surprise she fell on Nick jumping out of his Jeep. She had to catch her breath as he fixed her with his eyes. Why oh why couldn't she get used to seeing him? She really hoped this crush would have subsided by now, as it was it seemed to be getting worse. Seeing him every day didn't help either.

"Oh! Hello, I thought you'd be keeping well away from here and all the commotion!" She couldn't believe how pleased she was to see him. He looked mouth-watering in a white T-shirt and camel slacks. His hair was dishevelled and the blonde streaks from the sun were more prominent. He stared at her with his amazing eyes and smiled a crooked smile.

"No chance of that, I got a call last night from Elenora saying she wanted me here to make sure Mum was getting everything done and to plan. She knows that Mum can be a little laid back. How's it going?" Sylvie searched for her non-existent rings again and tried desperately to ease her pounding heart.

"Everything's right on schedule. I just checked the back garden. I'm going to go and help your Mum with the desserts Elenora wanted. There's an awful lot to make."

"I hope there crème caramel on that list. That's my favourite," he joked and his whole face lit up as he spoke to her.

"Well if you want it so badly, you should help."

They both went into the house and found Maggie whipping up butter and sugar for the sponge.

"I've brought another helper." Sylvie nodded towards Nick. "I thought we might need him."

"The more the merrier," Maggie beamed, and with that they started to crack on with the list.

Sylvie loved to cook. She didn't have reason to these days, so to create desserts was the perfect way to spend an afternoon, and of course the company made it even more perfect. The three of them worked away without a break.

Sylvie kept checking up on the garden periodically. As she walked back into the kitchen Maggie put down a mixing bowl and went over to turn on the oven.

"Taste the tiramisu Sylvie, is there enough Masala in it?" Sylvie unconsciously walked over to the bowl deep in thought and trailed her middle finger around the top edge of the mixing bowl, gathering the creamy mixture and then popped it into her mouth. Nick stared on, mesmerized.

"Mmm, that's delicious." Sylvie momentarily closed her eyes. Nick held on to the sink and turned away, trying desperately not to look again. He left the kitchen and went to have a cigarette.

Maggie scowled as he left and Sylvie glanced over to him. *Strange*, thought Maggie; he looked strained again. For the past couple of hours he'd been laughing and his mood had been almost playful, now his eyes were tight and he was ferociously dragging deeply on his cigarette. She turned to Sylvie.

"Good. Well let me assemble it and then it can chill with the mousse. Just got to pop in the crème caramel and we're done."

Once the mousse and tiramisu were chilling and the crème caramels were baking, Maggie started to assemble the trifle. She expertly poured the custard over the fruit and then covered it with cellophane wrap and placed it in the fridge.

"I need to sit down!" she moaned. "Let's have a cup of tea and put our feet up, it's nearly six. The girls should be back any minute."

Nick sauntered back in from the terrace, his face had softened again. "I'll do it Mum. Sit down." He put his arm around her and hugged her. "Go on," he guided her to the settee.

"You're such a good boy." She flopped onto the settee and put her feet up on the coffee table. Sylvie sat down beside her.

"Well I think we did those pretty fast, another ten minutes and the crème caramels will be done too. That was fun. I haven't done so much cooking in ages." Sylvie looked out to the garden and saw all the tables and chairs set out as per her instructions. The garden was slowly being transformed into the romantic setting she'd envisaged. As she watched the lights were put on and the whole garden looked beautiful. She stood up to get a better look. "Look at that, Maggie. Isn't it lovely, and the flowers aren't here yet and the tables aren't set. I hope Elenora likes it."

"Oh Sylvie, it doesn't even look like the same garden." Suddenly there was a shriek from outside.

"Mum, Mum… *Mum*! Have you seen the garden?" It was Elenora, back from town with Vicki. They ran into the kitchen like a couple of overexcited teenagers. "Have you seen it? It looks so romantic. Sylvie it's amazing!" She ran over to Sylvie and hugged her so hard. "Thank you, thank you so much. I didn't think it would look this good. Come on Mum, let's go and have a better look." She pulled her off the settee and dragged her outside, followed by Vicki.

"Well I *think* she's happy." Nick laughed with a hint of sarcasm. "I thought she was going to explode!" He brought over her tea and placed it on the coffee table. "When it's all over I really don't know what they're going to do. I'm sure Mum will go into a depression. She's been, eating, drinking and breathing this wedding for nearly a year now. It'll hit her hard when it's over."

"She'll need to find a new project to occupy her." Sylvie gazed up at him, relishing every minute that Nick spoke to her. His presence today was less intimidating and she could see his softer side; a side he didn't often share with her. He seemed more relaxed today, and definitely less intense. The past couple of hours had been really fun, joking and working together. She almost started to feel comfortable around him. Well, maybe comfortable was too strong a word. He seemed happy to be near her. Sometimes he behaved like he couldn't be anywhere near her. Not today though. Today he definitely seemed happy, and that thought made her heart soar.

"You should get her to start on Elenora's room. That'll keep her busy," he mused. That would be exactly what his Mum would need, and of course he'd be able to see more of Sylvie. His thoughts were interrupted by the oven timer as it buzzed. "Better get them out of the oven." He shot up and went over to the kitchen to retrieve the crème caramels. As he slowly pulled them out when one of the dishes collided with the other, causing the boiling water from the bain-marie to splash onto his forearm.

"Ouch, shit!" he cried as he carefully put them down. Without thinking, Sylvie was over in seconds to examine the burn. She pulled him over to the sink and opened up the cold tap, thrusting his arm under it.

"Keep it there while I get some ice." She opened up the freezer and quickly threw a couple of ice cubes onto some kitchen paper and wrapped them up. Then she opened up a couple of drawers in search of burn cream which she found. Nick, all the while, was spellbound by her as he watched.

"It's not so bad, really."

She took his arm gently and placed the ice on it. He winced. "You need to keep it cool. I hope it doesn't blister." She was still holding his arm. When she realised she let go as if it had scorched her. She couldn't look up at him embarrassed at her reaction, when she did catch sight of his face his eyes were boring into her and his cheek muscle was twitching. She stepped back, feeling how close she was to him. Everything had happened so fast; her instinct to protect him was so strong she couldn't explain it.

In a feeble attempt to rectify her hasty retreat she lifted off the ice to examine the wound. "I think the ice will have helped a lot. Does it still sting?" Her heart was thumping so hard she thought it would burst out of her chest.

"It's calming down now." He was almost whispering. She fumbled with the cream cap and unscrewed it. She squeezed some cream onto her finger and started to dab it ever so gently on the burn. Nick involuntarily clenched his fist.

"Sorry, does it hurt?" She'd mistaken his reaction as pain from the burn. She continued to softly rub in the cream and as she did she leant closer to gently blow on it in an attempt to soothe it. He shook his head, still clenching his teeth.

"No, no it's really nothing," he made an attempt to pull back from her, but then stopped, allowing her to carry on blowing on to his arm he closed his eyes and exhaled almost in surrender. Sylvie released his arm and he opened his eyes.

"How's it feel?" she asked as she stepped backwards and then awkwardly turned away to put the cap back onto the tube so that she wouldn't need to look at his face.

"A lot better, thanks." His tone was strained as if he really didn't want to answer, as if it pained him to speak.

Maggie and the girls were approaching the kitchen and their voices made Sylvie jump. She'd totally forgotten about them. She'd been so wrapped up in Nick that she'd forgotten they were even there.

"Sylvie, what a fantastic job, really." Vicki was the first in.

"I forgot the crème caramels. Did you get them out?" Maggie directed the question to Sylvie.

"Err… Actually Nick got them out and, umm…"

"Oh my God, what happened, Nick?" Maggie took one look at his arm and the ice and was over to him to inspect it.

"It's nothing Mum, just a bit of hot water splashed on my arm as I got them out." Maggie turned to Sylvie for more information.

"I put it under cold water and then some ice. I think it should be okay. I found the burn cream too." Satisfied, Maggie turned back to Nick, still holding his arm.

"Mum, it's nothing. Stop fussing." He was almost agitated or embarrassed and his eyes momentarily met with Sylvie's.

"Okay, okay." She backed off.

"Well, I'd better be off. I've a lot to get through tomorrow." Sylvie went over to where her bag was and picked it up. "I'm so glad you liked everything Elenora. It'll be even better when everything's in place." She started to head for the door.

"Oh don't leave now, stay for dinner at least." Maggie pleaded.

"No really I can't. I'll be up early tomorrow though to make sure everything's done right." She allowed her eyes to flit over to Nick's direction. He still had his jaw clenched and his eyes were blazing at her. She couldn't get out fast enough. She wasn't exactly sure what had happened. He'd been so talkative and fun all afternoon then suddenly he turned into the monosyllabic, intense Nick again. Had she offended him by tending to his burn? Whatever she'd done, he seemed extremely irritated.

Sylvie said her goodbyes and Maggie accompanied her to the door.

"Thank you so much for today; you were so much help. I don't think I would have managed on my own." They hugged and kissed and Maggie waved her off as she drove away back home.

Part Three – Spring

NICK WENT OUTSIDE AND sat on the terrace. He took a drag on his cigarette as he tried to calm his nerves. He felt such an idiot. He'd managed to spend an amazing afternoon with Sylvie. He was beginning to feel less awkward around her, relaxed even. He enjoyed her company so much he didn't know how he was going to cope once all the wedding drama was over. He knew that was why he suggested she press his mother to start on Elenora's room.

And then when she had tended his burn, her touch and close proximity, her incredible tenderness and concern had made him want to pull her close to him. How he hadn't grasped at her... He shook his head, marvelling at his self-control.

He looked down at his arm and could almost feel her gentle fingertips on his arm and her cooling breath on his wound as he closed his eyes. What was he going to do? He couldn't avoid her anymore, and that didn't seem to work anyway. All he did was think about her. If he spent time with her it exposed him to situations like today that he found unbearable to keep himself in control. What a mess! Another couple of days and she really wouldn't be around as much. His heart ached as that thought passed through his mind.

All the drive down back to her home, Sylvie played the final scene in her head. She couldn't figure out what was going on. He was running hot and cold with her and she didn't understand why. All she knew for sure was that she loved being around him and a lot of her drive to be around Maggie was because of that. She parked her car and stepped into her beautiful, but quiet home again. Sylvie poured herself a stiff drink and went straight upstairs to her room. She kicked off her shoes and went into her bathroom. She turned on the bath taps and allowed the water to flow into the tub. After Saturdays wedding though, she'd have less reason to go up to visit Maggie, she'd be busy with Celle. The chances of her bumping into Nick would be very slim and that thought made her heart ache.

Chapter 6

PRE-WEDDING DINNER

After all the chaos over the last week, the pre-wedding dinner had finally arrived. Sylvie had left Maggie's at around three o'clock giving her enough time to relax and get ready at a leisurely pace so that she could be back up there for six. It had been a stressful week, what with the wedding arrangements and Celle in its final stages. Sylvie had been totally occupied by her work.

Sylvie had managed to transform her back garden into the right kind of setting for the dinner. She was only too happy to help out. In fact, she thrived on the pressure. The whole experience of being involved in the organisation had brought Sylvie back to her normal self. Plus, the fact Nick had been around her constantly probably also had a lot to do with her elated mood. He hadn't been around that morning though and Sylvie felt sure that he was avoiding her on purpose after yesterday's strange episode. Well, he'd have to face her tonight however much she'd upset him.

Sylvie had supervised the whole morning ensuring that the tables and chairs around the garden were perfectly set and the thousands of fairy lights adorning all the trees were correctly positioned. There were huge lanterns lighting the dance floor where a small band would be playing. The whole garden smelled of orange blossoms and jasmine and each table had gardenias and candles floating in glass bowls. Sylvie had placed floating candles in the pool along with magnolia flowers. The food was catered for by her good friend Stathis.

There were approximately sixty guests in total and all but a handful were from the two families. Sylvie was one of the honoured special friends that had been invited. Tomorrow at the wedding there would be over three hundred guests, so tonight really was a special, intimate evening.

The guests arrived early at around six. It was still light, which meant that pictures could be taken in natural light. Elenora looked radiant. She had chosen a long floaty chiffon dress in blue which made her eyes sparkle. She had her father's colouring, pale skin and light brown hair. Pavlos looked so proud of her standing next to her smartly dressed in a casual suit and open necked cream shirt. In her heels they were the same height. They really made a beautiful couple.

Vicki, who normally wore business suits all day, had pulled out all the stops. She had a figure hugging, off-the–shoulder, black, knee-length dress. Her blonde hair was swept up in a soft pleat with wisps falling around her pretty face. Maggie had decided to break away from her usual floaty bohemian style and had opted for a maxi slim fitting, dark blue dress which showed off her slender figure perfectly.

Julian looked handsome as always in a dark grey suit and a sky blue shirt. His eyes shone as he greeted the guests with Maggie. They both looked unbelievably happy. Everyone who came gushed at how wonderful it was to be there.

Vicki was propping up the bar with Nick. He, of course, looked breathtaking. He was wearing a pale blue, open-necked shirt that matched his eyes and a pair of dark blue slacks that clung to his toned thighs. He was holding his customary beer in one hand and his cigarette in the other. He'd ditched his designer stubble and was clean shaven, emphasising his strong, chiselled jaw line. He was in a deep conversation with his sister when Sylvie walked into the garden. He stopped dead when he saw her.

Sylvie looked stunning in a long, backless, Grecian-style, honey coloured dress that draped around her body. Her hair was put up softly, revealing her bare back. She went straight over to Maggie and kissed her.

"You look gorgeous Maggie, is this a new look for you?" she teased her.

"So do you, and no, I'm just being a little more conventional." She was beaming.

"Hello Julian, you must feel so proud today. They look great, don't they?" He held her close as she kissed him too.

"They do. You look stunning." He pulled back to appraise her, making Sylvie flush.

Over by the bar, Nick was watching. He tensed up when he saw the exchange between his father and Sylvie. Vicki was talking away about some cock up at work that she'd had to stay and fix, totally oblivious to her brother's distraction. Some other family member came over and started talking to the both of them.

Nick's eyes kept checking back to Sylvie. She was talking to Elenora and Pavlos now. She had her back to him so he could stare in her direction without her realising. As she turned around to speak to Pavlos' mother Rita, she caught him staring at her. He didn't look away. He just smiled and nodded his hello. All of a sudden she felt very hot. His look always seemed to do that to her. She had spent a tremendous amount of time with him these past few days, and his manner had been friendly, making it easier to be around him. But then, like now, he would look at her in a certain way and she would feel unbearably awkward. So much so that she had to ask Pavlos' mother to repeat what she had just said. She carried on talking to her when she felt someone close behind her.

"Thought you might need a drink." He was holding out a glass of champagne for her. He looked straight at her.

"Oh, he's such a gentleman. How come you haven't got married yet, Nick?" Rita nudged him with a twinkle in her eye.

"Thank you; I haven't met the right girl yet. All the good ones are taken." He was smiling to himself and then he looked at Sylvie. "Can I get you something too, Rita?"

"No, I'm fine your father's already given me two and that's nearly my limit, in fact I'm going to have to sit down."

As Rita moved away to sit in a chair Sylvie turned to Nick. Her heart skipped a beat as she looked at him.

"Thanks for the drink." She took a sip, even though she really wanted to knock it back in one gulp.

"The place looks amazing, you did a fabulous job. Elenora was a bit worried it would be too casual at home, but it's just right. Where are you sitting?"

"I haven't a clue." This was true; she hadn't even thought about it.

"Come sit with me and Vicki, we're on the table near the bar." He put his arm very gently around her and guided her to his table. She could feel the heat of his hand through her dress. A centimetre higher and he would be touching her bare back. She could feel herself beginning to flush. So much for him being angry with her, what was he playing at now?

Nick pulled out her chair so that she could sit down. Before she did she gave Vicki a hug and a kiss.

"You look stunning Vicki. I've never seen you look so radiant!"

Vicki coiled back in embarrassment and went red. "Thanks a lot Sylvie. So do you. I love your dress, doesn't she look lovely Nick? You always look lovely." Vicki looked at her brother as he admired Sylvie.

"Yes she really does." He pushed in her chair and his hand lingered on the back as he sat next to her.

"The garden has been totally transformed. We should keep it like this, it's so romantic. God I'm starving! Do you think everyone's here?"

"I think so, once everyone sits down, Dad's going to give a small speech and then you can eat, Vicki." Nick passed her some bread that was on the table. "Here; nibble on that, otherwise the champagne will go to your head." Sylvie witnessed a different side to Nick. He was very much their older brother. He had taken that role very seriously. He always seemed to be checking up on his sisters and looking out for them.

"How's your arm?" Sylvie asked tentatively. Nick's eyes looked at her through his lashes, but she kept his gaze and waited for a response.

"It's fine, thanks." He smiled slightly and lifted his shirt sleeve so that she could see.

"I'm glad." There was a slight red blotch, but it hadn't blistered and she was tempted to stroke it but restrained herself. He reluctantly turned his attention back to Vicki as she babbled away.

Sylvie turned to Vicki as she munched on her bread and carried on talking, all the while Nick sat and observed. Sylvie could feel him watching her even though she was slightly turned away from him. A few cousins of theirs came and joined their table and, before long, everyone was seated.

Julian and Maggie were seated at the top table alongside Pavlos' parents. Pavlos' brother also sat with them as he was his best man and there was an empty seat left.

"Vicki?" Sylvie interrupted her conversation.

"Yes, Sylvie." Vicki turned to Sylvie.

"That empty chair up there, isn't that your place? You *are* the maid of honour, aren't you?" The look of shock on Vicki's face was priceless.

"Shit, I forgot!" And with that she hurriedly got up and ran to her seat. Nick was rolling his eyes. Sylvie was laughing under her breath.

Nick leaned in to say something to Sylvie. His nose brushed up against her ear and Sylvie felt his hot breath sending shivers down her spine. "I hope she remembers everything tomorrow. Mum and Elenora will kill her if she doesn't."

Sylvie felt herself start heating up. This was really getting ridiculous. She couldn't even look at him without blushing or sweating. Thankfully Julian got up and made his speech which meant Sylvie didn't need to talk or look at him for a while.

Julian's speech was short, but full of emotion. He was obviously moved and both Maggie and Elenora had tears in their eyes as he spoke of how proud he was of Elenora. He credited Maggie for being an unbelievable parent and for organising the wedding. He also expressed his family's happiness in Pavlos and his family. He then went on to thank Sylvie for creating a beautiful setting for the dinner and wished everyone a pleasant evening.

Part Three – Spring

The band started playing and the food started to be served. Nick played the perfect host, talking to everyone at the table and introducing Sylvie as a friend of the family. She spent most of the dinner talking to a cousin of Nick's who had recently set up an estate agency.

"So you're Sylvie Sapphiris? Sapphiris Developers?" Nick's cousin asked. Sylvie nodded as Nick turned his head slightly towards them listening. "A girl I worked with went to work for you a few years back, Dina, Dina Psaras. Do you know her?"

Sylvie froze for a split second and felt the colour drain from her face. Reaching over to her glass she took a gulp of wine. Then placing her glass back down she smiled tightly as she answered.

"Yes, she used to work for us but left in November." Nick watched as Sylvie fumbled with her fingers nervously, rubbing her ring finger, her expression unreadable but her eyes seemed to be welling with tears as she spoke and she looked down at her plate. Nick's attention was momentarily distracted by one of the guests on their table as Sylvie carried on speaking to his cousin. He turned back to them only to find that Sylvie had vacated her seat. Looking around for her he asked his cousin where she had gone and he shrugged saying she excused herself. Then he spotted her talking to the caterer.

Sylvie stood by the buffet table talking banalities with the one of Stathis's staff, anything to calm her racing heart. Dina hadn't come into her life for six months, and Nick's cousin's comment had thrown her. It just went to show how small this city was and that her past was ever present in her life. Sylvie glanced over to her table and caught Nick watching her and he motioned to her asking if she was alright. He looked concerned and she smiled weakly at him. His gesture instantly made her feel better as his eyes searched her face for some explanation, and coming up blank.

After that incident, the evening progressed and Sylvie hardly spoke to Nick even though she was sitting next to him. He was being constantly bombarded with questions from the guests at their table. Did he have a girlfriend? How was his business? Most of them hadn't seen him in a while so were very interested in what he was up to. A few people had got up to dance, including some people from their table. Once everyone had had dessert Maggie came over to Sylvie.

"Everything turned out wonderful Sylvie, I'm so pleased. Are you having a good time? I know you don't know many people here but at least Nick's been with you. I hope he's been looking after you."

"Don't worry about me I'm fine, honestly. You should be looking after your guests. Nick's been the perfect host, really."

"Actually I came over to get him to dance, he'll kill me I know but I don't often get a chance to dance with him." She looked over at him. "Come on Nick, come and dance with your old Mum!" She was getting up and coaxing him with her hand. "I won't embarrass you much, promise."

Nick pretended it was such a chore to get up.

"Oh, okay Mum, if I really have to." He turned round to the table and winked, making the table laugh at his exaggerated gesture. He put his arms around his Mum and led her to the dance floor.

It was already filling up with couples swaying to the soft music. Sylvie turned to her dessert plate and began to fiddle with her fork. She didn't want to be caught staring after them. It was times like this she realised she missed having someone. Everyone here was either in a couple or they were young. She didn't fit into either category.

It wasn't the fact that she was alone. It was just that she felt like she was the odd one out. That she didn't belong. Just then her thoughts were interrupted.

"How are you enjoying your evening?" Julian was standing by her. He slipped into Nick's chair.

"It really has been a lovely evening, your speech was perfect." He really was a good man, she thought.

"I thought I'd come over and ask you to dance; you looked a little lonely."

"Not at all. I've got to know all your relatives, they've been very sweet."

"I can imagine!" He laughed. "Come, let's dance." He stood up and took her hand. The last thing Sylvie wanted to do was dance, but his expression was very insistent. He guided her to the dance floor where he took her by the waist and moved her expertly round the dance floor. They passed Maggie and Nick, who had swapped partners with Elenora and Pavlos.

"You look incredible, Sylvie," Julian whispered in a low, loaded voice. Sylvie realised that if she behaved in any way receptive, Julian would see that as a green light for him to further his advances. Her reaction would have to make him understand that they were only ever going to be friends.

"Thank you, that's very kind of you. I think everything went well tonight. It'll be a fabulous wedding tomorrow. Maggie and Elenora seem to have everything under control." She was trying to be polite and hoping to steer the conversation in another direction.

"Yes… Um… Sylvie, I was wondering whether..."Sylvie knew where this was going and really didn't want to let him down when he was obviously in a good mood. She'd have to think of something before he asked her anything. Elenora and Nick were just passing when Elenora thankfully interrupted.

"Will you dance with me, Dad? Nick's nowhere near as good as you. I swear he stepped on me a hundred times!"

Nick shook his head in despair.

"Of course sweetheart, I'll just take Sylvie back to her seat."

"She can dance with Nick, Dad. Watch your toes Sylvie!" Elenora teased. Julian reluctantly let Sylvie go, passing her over to a nervous looking Nick and took his daughter in his arms.

Nick looked at Sylvie and clenched a smile, then raised his eyebrows.

"Are you wearing steel toe caps?" He was trying to diffuse what was an awkward moment with humour. Sylvie lifted her dress slightly to reveal her gold peep toe shoes and shrugged.

"No, but I'll take my chances." She also felt that humour was the only way to handle it. He slipped his hand around her waist and took her hand gently in the other, flinching a little.

"Sorry my hands are always cold, bad circulation," she added as way of explanation.

"Warm heart then? That's how the saying goes, isn't it?" He cocked his head to one side, his gaze intense and Sylvie felt herself heat up. Her heart pumped. *Was he flirting? No! Surely not! Overactive imagination.....again!*

They moved slowly around the dance floor, as the band played 'Sway'. Luckily it had become quite crowded so there was no need to move around so much. "Well I really don't know what Elenora was talking about. You dance just fine." Sylvie looked at Nick and his face was set hard, his oh-so blue eyes blazing.

"Mmm... But not as good as my Dad, though." He stared deep into her eyes, and Sylvie realised he meant something entirely different. She could feel her heart racing again as they slowly moved in time to the music. He kept readjusting his hold at the base of her back sending shivers up Sylvie's spine.

The distance between them becoming smaller, and Sylvie was torn between wishing the song would finish quickly and wishing it would never end. She could smell the heady combination of his cologne and cigarettes and she found it almost impossible to stop herself from stroking his shoulder, feeling his flexed muscles under his shirt. His proximity was intoxicating as he breathed deeply, close to her ear. *Get a grip girl!*

The song finished, and Sylvie really felt like she needed to get out of there. She reluctantly released herself and they walked back to the table.

"It's getting late, I think I should go." She turned to Nick, and he was looking at her in that way that made her feel uneasy. He was clenching his teeth and almost looked angry. "I'll go and say bye to your Mum and Dad, thanks for looking after me tonight."

His face softened and as she was about to turn away he said, "I'll see you tomorrow then." His blue eyes boring into her, making her blood pulse faster. She smiled weakly and nodded.

Sylvie walked off to find Maggie. She was talking to Pavlos' dad, Harry.

"Maggie sweetie, it was lovely, but I need to get home. I've an early meeting in the morning and then I need to get ready for the main event tomorrow." She said her byes and headed off to her car. As she got in, Julian caught up with her. He knelt down so he was on the same level.

"I couldn't find you to say bye," she apologised.

"You're leaving so soon? I didn't have a chance to spend time with you." He looked disappointed. He'd really wanted to talk to her about the opening tonight, to try and at least make a date.

"I'm just tired. I have a meeting at Celle early in the morning and want to be alright for the big day, so it's better that I head off." He picked up her hand and kissed it.

"I'll see you tomorrow then." His blue eyes stared at her.

Whoa! It felt like déjà vu. With that she closed her door and drove off.

CHAPTER 7

THE WEDDING

After tireless preparation and months of hard work, Elenora's wedding day had finally arrived. The whole family had all slept over at Maggie's house, including Julian and Nick.

They had all wanted to experience the whole day together. It was a testament to how well Maggie and Julian had raised their children and how they themselves had set the example. Even after their divorce twenty years ago they were very close friends. The fact that Maggie had never remarried, had made things easier and it was obvious she was more than content with that choice. Maggie and Julian truly loved each other but she realised that they were not the same people they had been when they first met at university. They had married young and jumped into parenthood immediately. Maggie was more than happy to do so, but Julian had felt very restricted. They parted ways as best they could and since grown closer because of it. Maggie couldn't imagine her life without Julian he was the most important man in her life.

As always, the sun was shining but, thankfully, the temperature was going to stay in the mid-twenties. The only sign that there had been a party the evening before were the glorious flowers that had been moved into the house for today, and the carefully stacked tables and chairs that had been left in the driveway to be collected this morning.

Nick was up first. He'd stayed in his own bedroom, not that he'd slept much. He had watched his father as he had kept checking up on Sylvie and then he'd seen him dancing with her. It was obvious that his father was still deeply in love with her, and that they did seem to have a special relationship. How far that had gone or how much it had been reciprocated he wasn't sure. Never the less, it had bothered him to see them together. He'd rarely seen them together so it had really grated on him last night. He slipped downstairs and put the kettle and coffee machine on. While he waited for them to heat up he sat at the kitchen table and held his head in his hands. He'd hoped that either his feelings would have changed or his father's. But after last night it had been perfectly clear that neither had. Nick put together three cups of tea for Elenora, Maggie and himself and two cups of coffee for Vicki and Julian on a tray.

It was eight o'clock already, and in approximately eight hours they would need to be at the church. He gently woke up Maggie and left her tea for her. He then walked over to Vicki's room where Julian had spent the night and left his coffee after waking him. Finally he walked into Elenora's room where both his sisters had slept.

"Morning, sleepy heads." He kissed them both as they lay there.

"Aren't you *finally* getting married today?" he joked, emphasising the 'finally'. They both raised themselves onto their pillows and stretched. He passed them their drinks and sat on the bed with them.

"What time is it, Nick? I slept like a log." Vicki was still trying to come round.

"After eight. Thought we could have our last few minutes together. Calm before the storm. You know it's going to be mad around here in the next hour. Isn't everyone arriving around nine-thirty?"

"So you *have* been listening to our arrangements then." Elenora was beaming, "I can't believe it's finally here, I'm actually getting married!" With that, she and Vicki squealed.

"Oh my God! Too much oestrogen for this time in the morning!"

He was laughing at them, revelling in their obvious delight. They sat there for a while chatting about last night and the last-minute instructions for today. Before long, Maggie was in the room too. She had left her children a little time alone. After all, after today all their lives would change. She was just so thankful that Pavlos was such a worthy partner for Elenora and that both her children cared for him as much as she did. Things would be changing for all of them but in the best possible way. It was a new chapter for her family.

As the morning progressed, people arrived with more flowers. Hairdressers, photographers and video men arrived. The house became a hub of activity. Luckily everyone was truly enjoying the day. There was a constant supply of drinks and food laid out for anyone who got hungry. It was going to be a long day and the dinner wasn't until seven.

Maggie was on hand making sure everyone was looked after and, more importantly, that Elenora was enjoying every moment. Julian was predominately looking after the travel arrangements to the church, and then on to the hotel. Elenora and Pavlos had chosen a small church on a hill which overlooked the whole of the town covering a twelve kilometre coastline; the view was breath taking. Even though Elenora wasn't of Greek Cypriot origin, she had decided to adopt Pavlos' religion. After all, she had lived here all her life and had grown up knowing all about their traditions and it was important to him and his family.

Nick was coordinating the photographer and video man, while Vicki helped Elenora. Before they knew it was three thirty and time to set off to church. Julian accompanied Elenora to the church in a white Mercedes, while the rest left in a second car with Nick driving.

Everyone was waiting outside the church for the bride to arrive. Nick arrived first with Maggie and Vicki. He looked immaculate in his black, slim-fitting suit with a white shirt, sky blue waistcoat, and matching tie. Maggie was in a light blue, knee-length dress with a matching jacket that showed off her shapely legs, and Vicki was wearing an ivory chiffon floor-length dress with a light blue sash at the waist She carried a small bouquet of stephanotis, jasmine and gardenias.

They all moved to the door of the church to where Pavlos and his brother Aris, who were dressed the same as Nick, were waiting with the rest of his family. They all hugged and kissed each other, all of them immensely happy that this day had finally come.

The bridal car pulled up outside the church to cheers. Julian turned to Elenora, his eyes full of emotion.

"Well sweetheart, this is it. Are you ready?" He smiled at her as he squeezed her hand.

"I'm ready, Dad." With that, she gave him a kiss and the driver opened the door. As Julian stepped out and turned to help his daughter out a hundred clicks of cameras went off. They were totally overwhelmed.

"Oh Dad, I feel like a movie star!" She was genuinely overcome. Elenora had chosen a simple ivory gown which had capped sleeves and a sweetheart neckline. It was fitted at the waist and then slightly opened out, skimming her body. It opened at the back to form a small train. Her veil was also ivory. It was fitted at the back of her head and floated down the whole length of her dress.

"I see what you mean."

The cameras kept clicking as they walked up to the church door where Pavlos was waiting with her bouquet, a larger version of Vicki's. He kissed her and, as he handed her the flowers, he said, "You look so beautiful, darling." He was clearly overwhelmed and Elenora blushed shyly.

The guests were taking their seats as the couple prepared to walk down the aisle. The church was a sea of people, all anticipating the ceremony. As the couple walked in everyone turned to watch. Nick was already in his seat. He scanned the church to see if he could see Sylvie, but there were so many people he couldn't see her anywhere.

Then he spotted her, right at the back in a royal blue dress which had cut-away sleeves, showing off her smooth, toned shoulders. His eyes fixed on her as she chatted to the couple next to her. He'd seen them before but couldn't remember where. The ceremony began to commence and everyone in the church stood up.

SYLVIE LOVED WEDDINGS. She loved the whole experience of them. She had always been an incurable romantic. What she loved most was how all the families rallied round to make the day special. After last night she was feeling a little less awkward. Zach and Lilianna had also been invited to the wedding, so she wasn't as lost today. Zach was fidgeting in the church and Lilianna kept nudging him to stop.

"He's worse than a child, he hates being confined," Lilianna giggled.

Luckily for Zach the ceremony didn't take too long, and before they knew it they were in the car driving down to the hotel where the reception was to be held. It was already six o'clock and the sun was going down. The guests were served champagne and canapés while the photos were taken, then they were lead to where the dinner was to be held. Each and every guest passed by the newly married couple and their parents to congratulate them.

Eventually everyone was seated and dinner was served. Lilianna and Sylvie chatted constantly about how lovely everything had turned out and Sylvie explained to her who everyone was.

"Elenora is so elegant. She looked lovely, and her sister... Vicki, isn't it?" Lilanna was trying to remember. "But Nick is something else, he's stunning. He *does* get his looks from his father." Sylvie just nodded, trying not to give too much away. Lilianna was her oldest friend and no fool. She only needed to say one word, or comment on Nick and she'd pick up on it like a bloodhound.

The couple cut the cake and had their first dance. Dessert was served and everyone was able to relax and enjoy the evening. Maggie and Julian were doing the rounds talking to everyone. Eventually Maggie came over and sat with Sylvie.

"Well, I can't believe today has actually come." Maggie was beaming.

"Everything was perfect, really fabulous. Your hard work paid off, now sit with us and have a drink." Sylvie reached over to get her a glass and pour her some wine. "Cheers, sweetie."

Within a few minutes Julian was over. "Is everyone having a good time? I don't see any of you lot dancing." He pulled up a chair and sat next to Zach.

"We're waiting for you to show us how it's done!" Zach replied, and the two of them started their usual banter, ribbing each other. It was good to see how close Julian had become with Zach over the last few months. Julian had, in some way, filled the huge void that Chris had left in Zach's life. Their relationship had become closer and Sylvie was happy to see her dearest friend joking again like he used to.

The night wore on and slowly people began to head off home. It was already past midnight. Zach and Lilianna had already left and Sylvie was getting ready to bid goodnight to everyone.

"Don't leave yet, let's have a last drink. I've only just managed to sit with you." Maggie pleaded. "Come on Sylvie, just one drink."

"Okay, okay."

Maggie was very persuasive. They sat down and poured a couple of glasses of wine. "I have had far too much wine tonight." She sipped her wine. "I suppose it won't be long before Vicki finds someone, and Nick, and then I really will be alone. Where are those two? They're probably by the bar."

She looked over to see if she was right. Vicki was dancing with some of her friends but Nick wasn't anywhere around. "I wonder where he's got to." she turned again and then she caught sight of him. He was coming back from the hotel foyer. She called over to him.

"Nick come and join us, Sylvie was about to leave and I convinced her to stay for another drink." He looked a little irritated, but he came anyway. He'd avoided Sylvie all night and was anxious not to have to spend too much time near her after yesterday. He sat down next to Maggie. "I was looking for you. Where were you?"

"I went to get some cigarettes from the foyer." He was opening the packet as he spoke. "Everything went well, didn't it?" The question was directed at Maggie, but somehow his eyes focused on Sylvie, making her feel uncomfortable. He lit up his cigarette and poured himself some wine.

"Nick, I wish you'd pack it in. It's such a nasty habit, isn't it, Sylvie?"

He carried on looking at her as he took a deep drag.

Sylvie flushed as his eyes blazed at her. She smiled stiffly and then, summoning her alcohol induced courage, she answered.

"I actually think it's one of those really bad habits that's quite sexy. You know the way people drag on the cigarette and when slowly exhale a stream of smoke." She paused for a moment. Nick was totally transfixed on what she was saying. "I never smoked myself. But it never bothered me that others did though."

She was looking at Maggie the whole time. "I can understand its appeal though. It must give you quite a rush," she turned to look at Nick, "Having said all that, you really should quit. You're too young and far too handsome to ruin your health and good looks. Start it up again when you're sixty, then it won't matter so much."

She smiled at him and steadied her gaze on him. Nick took another deep drag and exhaled a steady stream of smoke, meeting her gaze. He licked his lips thoughtfully. *Fuck he was so hot!* Sylvie felt herself heat up instantly.

Maggie was trying to work out what exactly Sylvie was saying through her fuzzy head from too much wine, when suddenly Nick leant forward and deliberately stubbed out his half-smoked cigarette.

"Since you put it like that, I'll stop, then." He fixed her again with his gaze. He seized up his new packet and broke it two, disintegrating it into small pieces and then sprinkling them into the ashtray. His action seemed like a challenge. As if he felt he'd been goaded into stopping. Sylvie dragged her eyes away from his and fumbled with her glass. *Holy hell, how sexy was that!*

Maggie turned to Sylvie, totally in shock. "I don't believe it. For ten years we've been nagging him to stop, and one word from you and he quits!"

Sylvie started to feel a little awkward. She didn't really understand what was going on. She knew she'd flirted with him. *That would be the alcohol, no doubt.* But now she almost regretted it. *Time for a quick getaway!*

"Well, I need to get off. It was a lovely wedding, Maggie." She got up to leave. Julian was on his way over to the table as she hugged Maggie goodbye.

"You're leaving so soon, I hardly saw you." He couldn't hide his disappointment.

"'Fraid so. I'm really tired, but everything was really lovely. I just need to organise a cab." She leaned over to kiss him on the cheek. As she pulled back from him, his hand stayed around her waist a while before he let her go.

"Goodnight then." Sylvie turned to where Nick was now standing. His face was set hard except for his flinching jaw. He nodded stiffly. She walked away trying hard not to give away how quickly she needed to get out of there. She really didn't understand what was going on. Yesterday Nick had been the perfect host, talking to her and being very attentive. Today he had hardly said two words to her and looked as though he really didn't want to be around her.

Then there was that whole 'stopping smoking' incident. *What was that all about?* She really had no idea what was going on. He was obviously being polite to her because of his parents, and everything else that had gone on was probably her vivid imagination and the drink. She got into the cab and put her head back; well, she probably wouldn't see him as often now seeing as the redecoration was done and the wedding was over. She'd only have to deal with her other problem, Julian. She'd have to make it clear to him that they could only ever be friends.

Maggie sat looking at the remains of the crushed packet of cigarettes on the table. She couldn't understand what had made Nick so adamantly decide to stop smoking. She was over the moon, but she still wondered.

"Nick?" He was staring into his glass, he seemed miles away. He looked up at her, "Nick, are you serious about quitting smoking?"

"I said I would, didn't I?" he almost snapped as her question disrupted him. His eyes looked thoughtful.

"I know you did, I just can't believe that with one word from Sylvie, after all our nagging, you decided so easily." She smiled at him gently.

"She gave a very interesting and convincing point of view, that's all." He got up to leave. "I'm bushed. I think I'll head off home Mum. Everything was perfect." He bent down and kissed her, then headed off to say bye to the rest of his family.

Maggie sat there, staring after him as he walked off.

And then to her horror, it began to dawn on her. She looked down at the cigarettes, then up to where he was heading. *Her son was in love with Sylvie.* She watched him go to say bye to Julian. As they hugged goodbye, Maggie began to realise the severity of that. She'd known for a while of Julian's feelings for Sylvie. Though he'd never openly admitted it to her she knew him well enough to see how besotted he was with her. It hurt, a lot. But what could she do? But now Nick, too – that really complicated things. She put her hand to her mouth and took a deep breath.

CHAPTER 8

THE INVITATIONS

The days had flown by after the wedding, and everyone at Sapphire Developers were excited about the impending opening of Celle. It was the talk of the city and there was a real buzz surrounding the club. Stathis was in full panic mode trying to get his staff trained up, whilst Sylvie was tweaking all her finishing touches.

Sylvie walked into Zach's office as he was checking over some invoices for a new build that their company was involved with in Athens. The same build that Chris had gone to consult on on his fated last trip. Zach shuffled the papers to the side when he saw Sylvie so that she couldn't see them.

"Hi there. What you up to?" She'd seen him quickly hide the papers.

"Just some invoices for the Glifada project." He wasn't going to lie. She knew they were still working on it.

"How's it going? It should be nearly finished." She tried her hardest not to show any emotion, but Zach was no fool. She sat opposite him and started to rub fingers again, where her absent wedding ring should have been.

"Yes, first week in June we hand over the keys. I'll have to go over for that. Just to sign it over to the owners. Procedure, that's all. What are you up to? I thought you'd be with Stathis."

"I was, but it's pretty much under control. He's flapping around there getting the staff all trained up, so I left him to it. I've started to put plans together for Maggie's other room, but to be honest, I want to wait until after the opening."

"Have you decided to go?" Zach had been pressuring her all week to make up her mind. He'd tried a number of tactics, from emotional blackmail to plain bullying.

"Just go, for the love of God. Take Maria and the other office staff, they're desperate to go. It's the hottest ticket in Limassol. Don't stay long; just show your face, have a couple of drinks and go. If only Alex and Markus were here, you could have taken them. You know Lilianna and I hate these things, you're so much better at the P.R. stuff than we are. Unless you want to go with Julian?"

Sylvie eyes shot up to Zach's face; he was smirking. "Very funny Zach!" Not him as well. It was almost a conspiracy. First Lilianna, then Marcy, then Thea Miria, and now Zach!

"What? He's been a part of it too. Maybe it'd do you good." He carried on teasing her. But now he'd planted the thought, Sylvie started to worry. How would she get out of that one?

"No, no you're right. I should take the staff and, like you said, I can leave early." She got up to go and thought she'd better get it all arranged as fast as possible. She really couldn't face having to let down Julian again. Zach smiled.

"That's great. I'll let Stathis know how many people as soon as you get the number." Sylvie nodded. She set off back to her office. She knew he'd tried to back her into a corner but after all, she owed her staff this much. They had been incredibly supportive and understanding over the last six months. It was the least she could do. She'd go with them and then leave early.

"Maria, can you come in please?" She called through to her.

"Yes, Sylvie?"

"I was wondering if you and a few of the office staff would like to go to Celle's opening with me tomorrow? I know its short notice but I thought it'd be a nice way for me to say thank you to all of you. You've all been so good to me and I thought it would be a good way to celebrate the end of my first big job here."

Maria's faced lit up instantly. "Oh Sylvie, I'd love to! We'd all love to. That's all everyone's talking about, really. How many of us do you think? It's going to be hard to decide who can come." She couldn't hide her excitement.

"Well, I think we should restrict it to staff only... So no partners, I'm afraid. After all, it is a work thing. There are roughly ten of you, aren't there? So ask them all. You're all the ones that worked on getting it done. Stathis is absolutely ecstatic with how quickly and well it turned out. So you all deserve it. Can I leave it with you to get the numbers together?"

"Of course, you'll know by the morning. Everyone's going to be so surprised Sylvie. Thanks, really, thanks a lot." And with that Maria sped out to her office to start organising everything.

Sylvie turned to look at her favourite view. There were yachts bobbing in the sea and she allowed her mind to wander again to Nick. It had become a regular pastime for her. She'd daydream and remember the way he laughed. How he half smiled at her and the way he smelled whenever he invaded her space of second hand smoke and his cologne. If she closed her eyes she could even see his sun kissed cheeks below those unbelievable eyes.

She hadn't seen him since the wedding almost two weeks ago and she couldn't believe how much she missed him and how it was upsetting her. She'd been very busy with the club but she'd thought about him constantly. Many times she had contemplated going down to the marina in the hope of bumping into him. But she realised she was being foolish. It was borderline stalking! But she was finding it hard.

It didn't help that Maggie had called her everyday pushing her to get Elenora's room done. Sylvie had asked to wait until Celle was finished and then she'd give it her full attention. The truth was she couldn't trust herself going up to Maggie's. She was trying to get some distance. She was hoping that if she didn't see him, her girlish crush would subside and she'd probably get some perspective. It didn't seem to be working much. Her thoughts were rudely interrupted by her intercom. It was Maria. Surely she hadn't got the numbers already!

"Yes Maria?"

"Julian's on the phone, shall I put him through?"

"Yes, sure. Thanks." She smiled to herself. If only she could feel that way about Julian. He was perfect for her on paper. Even if she did feel that way for him she could never do that to Maggie.

"Hi there Julian, how are you?"

"Fine, and you?" His voice was so smooth and gentle. He had the kindest manner; no wonder he had women fawning for his attention.

"Not bad, just trying to finish up a few things before Friday's big night."

"The reason I'm calling, well, actually, it's a couple of things. I'm going through all the invoices that I have to pay for the wedding and Maggie put in a note to remind me to ask you for your invoice."

"My invoice? Whatever for?" Sylvie was puzzled. He'd already paid her for Maggie's redecoration, which she felt awkward about and she hadn't started Elenora's room yet.

"Well, for the pre-wedding dinner. You organised everything. I've got all the other invoices for the flowers, catering, band and tables hire, plus the other bits and pieces, but your fee isn't in here."

"I didn't do it as a job Julian. I did it because you're my friends. I wasn't going to charge you for my services. It was my pleasure. I just wanted to help you out, what with the restaurant being burnt down and everything. I can't believe you thought it was a job. Really Julian!" Sylvie scolded. "I'm just glad Elenora was happy with it."

"But you spent so much time on it. I feel like we took advantage of you. I really don't feel right about it. I know you're a good friend but business is business." He really was uncomfortable with the idea that Sylvie didn't want to be paid.

"Julian, it's bad enough you paid me for the redecoration. I felt a little uneasy about that as it was. But this, this was part of my wedding present to Elenora. I won't hear another word about it. Unless you want us to fall out?" Sylvie joked.

"No, no, not at all okay. I'll say no more about it except thank you so very much. You really did a wonderful job. I don't think I could ever thank you enough for getting us out of a jam like that." He was leaning back in his chair as he spoke to her.

"Like I said, it really was my pleasure. It was great fun for me too, you know?"

"The other thing I needed to ask you was about the opening night." He hoped his voice was still steady, he couldn't believe how nervous he was. It was tomorrow and he knew he'd have to bite the bullet and ask her to go with him today, he'd left it as late as possible.

"Oh, not you as well. Don't worry I've decided to go. I've organised with the guys from work to get a party together and take them. They've had to put up with a lot these past six months, so I thought this would be a kind of thank you."

She'd obviously misunderstood why he was asking, and her reply had thrown him. She'd thought he was also badgering her to go, when he was actually hoping they would go together. He needed to make sure she didn't realise that was what he was asking.

"Oh, that's great. Good idea, I'm sure you'll have a fabulous time. Stathis is a great host." His voice had lost its smoothness and he was talking a lot faster.

"Will you be coming too?"

"Err, no. Not really my kind of thing. Well, I'll let you get back to whatever you were doing and no doubt we'll speak later." He wanted to get off the phone. He didn't want her to hear the disappointment in his voice. He was only happy he hadn't spoken to her in person for her to see the mortification in his face.

Nick watched as his father put down the receiver. He watched as his father unsuccessfully tried not to show how he was really feeling. Julian was playing with the invitation in is his hands, deep in thought. He just couldn't catch a break with her. It took him a minute before he realised that Nick was watching him.

"Oh well. Looks like I won't be needing these invitations after all." Julian was trying to sound blasé. Nick was desperate to find out what Sylvie had said to upset his father. He swallowed hard.

"So you're not going?" Nick asked.

"No. I was going to ask Sylvie, you know, to go together. But she's already arranged to go with some friends." He was slumped back in his chair, and Nick could see how disappointed he was. Their relationship had obviously stayed at friendship. "Shame for them to go to waste. Would you like them? There are four of them so you could go with your friends. Should be a good night."

Nick shrugged and took them hesitantly from his father.

"Thanks. Everyone's talking about it. I'll take some friends out for my birthday!"

Julian nodded but it was obvious his mind was elsewhere. "Oh yes it's your birthday tomorrow. Twenty eight."

Nick nodded. "So, I brought you that invoice from the photographer." Nick handed his father the envelope, he'd almost forgotten why he'd come. Julian opened it then put it on the rest of the pile almost in a daze.

"That's a hell of a pile Dad, are they all for the wedding?" Julian had his elbows on his desk and had rested his chin on them. "Dad?"

"Sorry Nick, what was that?" He seemed to come out of his daydream.

"The pile, they're all for the wedding?" Nick motioned to the pile on the desk.

"Yes. Well, it was quite a do. Worth every penny just to see how happy Elenora was, though," he said thoughtfully. "You know Sylvie didn't charge me for the organising of the dinner? She wouldn't have it. She said it was part of her wedding present to Elenora." He shook his head as if he still couldn't believe it. "Bloody generous wedding gift! I should know, I advised her on what to charge her other clients!" He chuckled.

"Very generous," agreed Nick, as he watched his father fiddle with the letter opener, trying to judge what he was thinking.

"I should send her something to say thank you. It's only right." He sat up and started looking through the invoices.

"Where is it?" He pulled out every invoice one by one. "Ah, there we are." He put on his glasses and pick up the phone to dial. "Hello, this is Julian Steed... Yes, thank you, I received your invoice. I'll be sending the cheque out tonight. I was wondering whether you knew what Sylvie Sapphiris's favourite flowers were, seeing as she deals with you... Oh yes, white stargazer lilies and yellow roses. Could you send her two dozen of each to her home? Do you have her address? I'll put the cost on to the cheque I'm sending you."

He jotted down the additional figure. "The card? Err... Yes, just write: 'Thank you for making my daughter's day so special. I will always be indebted to you. Yours, as always, Julian.' And she'll get them tomorrow? Perfect, thank you very much."

He put the phone down with a huge smile on his face. The muscle in Nick's cheek was flexing and he rummaged around for some chewing gum. He shoved two pieces in his mouth and chewed hard. He needed to change the subject.

"I spoke to Pavlos and Elenora this morning. They're having a great time. They were off to Versailles today. I think Pavlos is putting on a brave face actually. She's dragging him to the Louvre and all these historical sites. He's probably really bored." Nick smirked.

"I can imagine, poor man. You put up with a lot when you're in love though, Nick. Believe me." He spoke as if he'd experienced it.

"Apparently," Nick answered, as though he also understood what that was like. "Well, I better get off. I can pick up the photos and video next Wednesday, the photographer told me. They're in the last stages of editing. So we'll have them for when they get back from Paris." Nick got up to leave.

"How's the not smoking going?" Julian raised his eyebrows as he looked at Nick.

"I need to buy shares in the chewing gum business to cover my chewing gum addiction! That's all I can say."

"Never mind, it'll get better. It's only been a couple of weeks."

NICK GOT INTO HIS Jeep and headed off to his shop. He parked up and sat for a moment as he pulled out and looked at the invitations Julian had given him.

He hadn't seen Sylvie for nearly two weeks and the thought that she would be at Celle tomorrow night made his heart start to race. He'd called by his mothers on the off-chance that she'd be there periodically after the wedding, but he'd been bitterly disappointed every time. He'd hoped she'd started work up there again, but Maggie told him she was going to start after the opening. Now he knew there was a guaranteed chance that he would see her again.

He knew he would be going; that had never been an option. His problem was that he knew it was pointless. After seeing his father's reaction today he realised that it was probably only a matter of time before he tried to further his relationship with Sylvie. That aside, he didn't have the strength to stop himself going tomorrow, regardless of how difficult it would be. All he knew was that he was in love with her, and the thought of not being able to see her caused him incredible pain. He just needed to see her again. The urge was beyond his control.

His father had been right; you put up with a lot when you're in love.

CHAPTER 9

OPENING NIGHT

Sylvie's work load had started to take over her life. It was really the only way that she could shut out her true feelings. Over the last six months she had a lot to reconcile; the betrayal of her husband, then his consequent death. Then she had to portray, for the sake of her sons and the rest of the family, that their marriage was idyllic. She had been the grieving widow, though the tears were of anger and true heartbreak. She had held the family together and encouraged Alex and Markus to continue with their lives in spite of all that had happened.

With the constant help of Lilianna, Zach and Julian, Sylvie had managed to find her way within Chris's company and as a result her own business had flourished. Luckily the developments that Chris had started were well on track. He had managed to employ and delegate project managers for overseas and the local market was pretty well covered with Zach and a couple trusted employees. Zach and Julian had also been key to introducing Sylvie to a number of clients that needed interior design services, from prestigious offices to luxury houses.

Stathis's new nightclub, Celle, was, however, Sylvie's labour of love. Though this had been instigated by Julian and Zach, Stathis himself had wanted Sylvie on board. He wanted to be close to Sylvie after Chris's death. Her opinion was very important to him, she had always been around along with Chris on all his ventures and he missed him badly. The club had been scheduled to finish in March, but because of Chris's death, Stathis waited until Zach and Sylvie were able to get back to work. Stathis had insisted that Sylvie attend the opening, as she had always done with Chris.

Tonight was the opening, and under normal circumstances Sylvie would have been looking forward to such an event. When Chris had been alive they attended every opening of Stathis's businesses. In fact, they attended all the opening ceremonies of every building Chris had been responsible for. This alone was going to prove difficult.

But that was not the only reason Sylvie felt in trepidation. The last place she had seen Chris had been at the derelict site before his fated trip to Athens. Every time she had gone there over the last six months, the image of him in her rear view mirror came flooding back.

After the constant bullying from Zach, Sylvie had decided to go. Maria had arranged for the ten staff who had been involved in Celle's reconstruction to come out to the opening. They were all extremely excited. It was a perfect opportunity to invite all the young staff who had been incredibly supportive over the past six months, helping her settle into Chris's position. They were at different stages in their life to her and on occasions like this, even though Sylvie had enjoyed going out to bars and clubs, she felt that maybe her time had passed. They were all in their late twenties and early thirties and Sylvie felt incredibly old next to them. Zach and Lilianna offered to come too, more out of politeness, but Sylvie felt that maybe it was time she went out alone without her loyal babysitters.

Having said that, Stathis had made a huge fuss and insisted that she attend. So Sylvie had decided the most pain-free way to get through this evening, would be to have a large, familiar crowd around her; after all, this would be the first time she would be seen in public after Chris's death.

In true style Stathis had arranged a Limo for Sylvie and her party, so it meant that they would all arrive together.

"Sylvie, I'm so happy you made it, you look amazing… Welcome, we've put you in our V.I.P section. Everyone's so impressed with the look of the club, you did an unbelievable job!" Stathis was looking as handsome as ever. He was always charming, sociable but above all he had a real flair. Anyone who went to his establishments felt they were the most important customer. Sylvie admired him for being able to juggle an antisocial career and yet have a happy home life.

"It's packed out Stathis, that's brilliant; and you have all the press here too!"

"You know how it is; the more pictures get out there, the more people want to see for themselves! It takes me back to when I opened 101. Do you remember?" He smiled, squeezing her.

Sylvie nodded and half smiled at him as her thoughts were catapulted back in time to the opening of his first club over ten years ago. "Chris drank so much that night. He never got off the dance floor." It was true. Chris had known how to have a good time. He loved being out and he had always been the centre of attention. People were always drawn to him and he had revelled in it. "That club was an instant hit. Just like this one will be. Thanks to you, Sylvie." He squeezed her again and Sylvie could see his genuine emotion.

"That's over ten years ago now. Olga was eight months pregnant, how she didn't give birth that night I'll never know!" Sylvie remembered. "A lot's happened since then," she mused

"Time flies, eh?" He put his arm around her waist. "She'll be down later. She's so pleased you're here. We both are." As they headed towards the door the photographer stopped them to take their photo. The photographer clicked two or three times. "Sylvie Sapphiris, the interior designer." He called to the photographer's assistant as he jotted down her name. Sylvie flushed. "Get used to it, Sylvie after this everyone will want you." He squeezed her as they entered the club.

Stathis took all of them into the club and across to their table, where champagne was already chilling.

"Laurent Perrier Rose… that's right, isn't it? And of course your Chivas will be on the way. What else would you like?" Sylvie reeled at his incredible ability to remember everyone's favourite drink.

"That's okay Stathis, we'll be fine for now, we'll order from the waiter. You go to your guests and stop wasting your time on us." And with a kiss on the cheek he left Sylvie.

ACROSS FROM THEIR TABLE, at the other side of club sat Nick with a couple of his friends at the bar. They were absolutely blown away that he'd managed to get invites to tonight and were busy taking in the club and scanning the club for talent!

It was very crowded and he could not be clearly seen, but he had a clear view of Sylvie's table. She looked amazing in a slinky red dress. His feelings towards her were becoming increasingly undeniable but he'd hoped that she was unaware. He'd tried his utmost to be extremely careful. There had been the odd moment when he'd found it difficult, especially while she had been at his mother's. What was more important, he hoped his father hadn't noticed, after all *she'd* only known him weeks, and not his entire life!

He sat staring at her every move. She must have been older than the women she was with, not that you could tell; it was more her composure rather than her look. She was confident and secure. He'd never observed her without her knowing. He'd never seen her in her own environment. Maybe he would see a side to her that he didn't like. Perhaps she'd behave differently. Perhaps she wasn't who she seemed. Nick clutched his drink, perhaps that's what he hoped to see so that he could stop feeling what he was feeling.

How had this happened? He still couldn't understand how he'd allowed it to happen. He felt like some teenager having a crush on a school teacher; for Christ's sake, she was nearly old enough to be his mother! But that wasn't the worst of it. His father was also in love with her...

It was unbearable to think of. His father had had many girlfriends over the years, all ridiculously younger than him; more suited to his age, in fact, than his father's. The irony! And now when his father had finally met someone 'age appropriate', *he'd* fallen in love with *her*. His father was obviously serious about her; he'd introduced her to his mother. As if almost seeking her approval. Now here he was in a nightclub, watching Sylvie drinking champagne and dancing with her friends.

Part Three – Spring

As he watched on he noticed that Sylvie had seemed a little tense at the beginning, but as the evening wore on he saw her begin to relax. She seemed comfortable with her group and they all equally seemed to enjoy her company. Her staff joked freely with her and it was a joy to watch her laughing; he'd never really seen her laugh before.

He watched as Stathis came over and introduced her to an endless array of people. Some seemed to know her, some did not. The photographer came over and took various pictures of her with each and every one that came. Then finally Stathis brought over a young pretty woman. Sylvie hugged her warmly and she seemed genuinely pleased to see her. Then Stathis motioned something to the D.J. and a moment later he saw Sylvie react to a song that obviously seemed to mean something to all three of them. The young woman squealed as she clapped her hands and dragged Sylvie to the dance area and Stathis beamed across at them as they started to dance to Usher's 'Yeah'.

Sylvie started off tentatively at first, then, as the song continued, he watched in awe as she allowed herself to be swept away, closing her eyes and dancing in perfect time with the rhythm, as if she was dancing alone, oblivious to her surroundings.

Nick was totally mesmerised. He watched, unable to take his eyes off her. Once the music changed Sylvie seemed to transport herself back to the present and she turned to the young girl and motioned that she wanted to return to her party. She took a drink of her champagne, then poured herself a whisky and sat down as the young woman left with Stathis.

As she stared into her glass, he watched a tall slim woman with dark hair walk over to Sylvie's table. She seemed to know everyone there and they all seemed pleased to see her, except Sylvie. No one at the party noticed, but Sylvie stiffened as the woman approached. Nick watched her as she politely shook hands with the woman and then hastily sat back down. The woman only stayed for a few minutes, then, saying her goodbyes, she left.

Nick watched on and he saw Sylvie sink into the couch. She looked around nervously. She was laughing with her friends and duly dancing when a song came on they liked, but she looked like she wasn't altogether there. She looked like she was faking it, not like before.

Something had changed. At one point Nick could swear he saw her brush a tear from her face. It was almost one o'clock and Nick had realised he'd been watching her for over an hour. Stathis, the owner, kept checking on them, and Nick had noticed a few men eyeing up the party. He was ashamed to admit to himself how jealous and protective that made him feel. His friends hadn't particularly noticed that his attention was distracted, until one of them commented on how Sylvie was probably the best looking woman in the club.

"Isn't that your Dad's girlfriend?" said his manager Christian, who was clearly in shock. "Jesus man, she's…"

"Yes, she's just a friend of his. They work together." he corrected him stiffly. "She did the interior design for the club… I should really go and say hi, it'd be rude not to." Nick was glad it was dark in the club and the light hid his strained expression. He was looking for any excuse to go to talk to her; thankfully, Christian had provided it.

He put down his beer and started off towards Sylvie's table. Once he was sure he was out of earshot one of his friends turned to Christian

"Fuck me, talk about a MILF!"

"Watch it! If Nick hears you say that he'll break your neck…he's very touchy about his father's… friends."

Sylvie was about to pour herself another scotch when Nick gently picked up the bottle.

"Here, let me do that for you."

"Nick! What a surprise, I didn't know you were coming tonight." And with that she jumped up from her seat, put her arms around him and kissed him on the cheek. Nick was totally caught off guard. He was, thankfully, holding the bottle of whisky in his hand, so he was unable to fully put his arms around Sylvie the way he would have liked to, but he awkwardly held her for a split second too long, taking a deep breath and taking in her scent.

Maybe only he noticed, because Sylvie most certainly didn't show it.

"I can't believe you're here… Hey, everybody, let me introduce you to Nick, he's Julian's son."

Nick dutifully shook hands with all of them. Maria and the rest of the girls gawked at him, forgetting themselves. He looked stunning in a blue shirt, dark jeans and his designer stubble. He turned away from them and sat next to Sylvie.

"What are you drinking?" Sylvie grabbed a clean glass and put ice in it; he noticed her hands were shaking.

"No don't bother Sylvie, I had a beer and I shouldn't have another. I'm driving, so I'll just have some of that soda." He helped himself and took the glass from her hands. "Let me pour yours, though." He slowly poured her drink and passed it to her. "Cheers to a job well done; it's really something else."

"Thanks Nick, that's really sweet of you."

Sylvie's friends reluctantly carried on with their conversations, trying hard not to make it obvious that they were straining to hear their conversation. They hadn't noticed that Sylvie was obviously not herself. As she took a sip of her drink, Nick saw again that her hands were shaking.

"Are you alright?" He'd had to lean in very close to talk into her ear and all he could smell was her distinct perfume. She smiled stiffly and nodded; scared her voice would give her away. "Do you need some air…shall I take you outside?"

Tears started welling in her eyes; she quickly wiped them away and nodded. He handed her a napkin, she discreetly dabbed her eyes and then turned to her party and made an excuse that she had a headache and that Nick would take her home. Before they could ask too many questions Nick moved Sylvie out of the firing line and said goodnight to them all.

He gently put his arm around her to protect her through the crowds until they got to the side fire exit which brought them out on a side street where Nick had parked his Jeep. He opened the passenger door for her and ensured she was safely inside. Once he was in and started the car, Sylvie started quietly crying, trying hard to stifle it. Nick drove as quickly and smoothly out of the town until he reached a quiet place to stop. At this point he pulled out some tissues that he'd left in his car and passed them to Sylvie.

"I'm so sorry." Sylvie eventually caught her breath and the tightness in her throat had subsided.

"You don't need to apologise, I'm glad I was there to get you out. Did someone upset you?" He wanted to put his arms around her so badly, but he didn't think he'd be able to let her go. He couldn't understand what was going through her mind, she wasn't giving anything away and he didn't want to push her.

"No. No, it's not that… Well, yes they have, but… Oh, it's very complicated. I really shouldn't have come out tonight. I'm just being morbid, do you mind taking me home?"

What on earth was she doing? How could she begin to explain what was going on in her head? All these secrets and all those horrible memories came flooding back. And then, as if that wasn't enough, Dina turning up at the club was like rubbing salt into an open wound. She hadn't seen her since her last day at the office, and to see her tonight, of all nights. At least she'd looked a little nervous. Probably worried that Sylvie might snub her or even make a scene. She wouldn't have given her the satisfaction.

Was this feeling of utter despair and total humiliation ever going to go away? Seeing her made her feel like nothing. It brought back the pain of betrayal and she felt worthless again.

Then out of the blue, Nick had magically appeared just at the right time to get her out of a place that held so much heartache. Where she had argued over the texts she'd seen. And where she had confronted Chris before he'd set off to go Athens. Where she had told him that his things would be packed by the time he'd reach his destination and where, finally, she'd found the strength to tell him that they were through, that she wouldn't forgive him, not this time.

"Of course I will." And with that Nick drove off towards her home.

CHAPTER 10

THE DRIVE HOME

The journey home was a ten minute drive and both Nick and Sylvie were silent. Nick had thankfully put the radio on and had tuned it to a local, easy listening channel. Sylvie noted that he didn't listen to the English radio from the bases, which surprised her, since most ex pats did. Nat King Cole was singing 'When I fall in love', which put less pressure on her to speak. She looked out of the window and tried to control her cramps.

Nick had so many questions he wanted answered. He was unable to work out what was upsetting her so much; no one at the club had bothered her, he'd been watching from the minute she'd walked in. All her friends had behaved impeccably and Stathis had spent what seemed to be an extraordinary amount of time making sure she was well looked after. They arrived at her home. The electric gates needed a pass code.

"It's 0109," whispered Sylvie. She'd pulled herself together by now.

She really needed to change that code. It was the date of her wedding anniversary. Chris was still everywhere in her life and she really needed to start pushing him out. It had been six months now. She was still very angry at him, but tonight had been the last straw. He'd hurt her so immeasurably, even now beyond the grave, but she needed to let it go. Everywhere she went there was a constant reminder of him; their home, his office, and again, tonight at Celle.

Of course a lot of it was the fact she couldn't talk about it to anyone. Only Zach knew all the truth, and of course Dina. But she had said everything she could to Zach; he had been with her practically all the time, letting her vent her anger. But he had also lost his best friend too, and however understanding he was, it was hard for him to hear Sylvie's anger. Sylvie couldn't expect him to feel or comprehend the extent of her feelings.

Nick had stopped the car and sat waiting for her.

"Sorry, Nick, for dragging you out here." She was fumbling in her bag for her keys.

"Let me take you in, make sure you're okay." He took the keys from her and jumped out of the car, walking around and opening the car door. The gesture took her by surprise.

"I'm fine, really. A little embarrassed, maybe, but fine."

He had a gentle smile on his face, or maybe it was relief that she genuinely looked better. He fixed her with his steely blue eyes still luminous even in the dark then smiled softly at her.

"Humour me." And with that he led her up to the doorway. He pulled out the keys. Sylvie went to show him which key it was, and when their hands touched, his were burning hot compared to her cold hands. He jumped as if she'd passed a current through him.

"Sorry my hands are freezing, they always are." It wasn't their temperature that had made him jump, rather her proximity. He really was feeling very vulnerable around her.

They walked through the hallway and into the kitchen as Sylvie flicked on the lights. Sylvie dropped her bag on the counter next to one of the vases housing Julian's glorious flowers. The smell filled the whole house. Nick eyed them as she walked behind the kitchen counter.

"I'd offer you a drink, but you're driving. What about a coffee? Or tea maybe?" She turned to look at him. His eyes were scanning the room, flitting from each vase of flowers to the next.

"Water will be fine. Thanks. Your home is really lovely." Nick stood ill at ease by the settee as Sylvie nervously opened the fridge, retrieving a bottle of water.

"Thanks. It's a work in progress." She shrugged.

"How are you feeling?" he asked tentatively hoping if he asked she might tell him something, anything that would reveal what was really upsetting her. She gathered up a couple of glasses and the bottle of water and scrunched up her nose, indicating that she wasn't so good, then shook her head slightly. She walked over and sat down on the settee, placing the glasses and bottle on the coffee table amongst the magazines and a large bowl filled with chocolates. He looked awkwardly down at the space next to her then edged over and joined her. Nick reached over and picked up the bottle and started pouring the water. The room was silent, but it was Sylvie who spoke first.

"Have you ever had something that you couldn't tell anyone? Something that if the people you really loved knew about, they would be devastated?" Her voice was barely audible. It was almost rhetorical, but Nick felt he needed to answer.

"Is that why you were upset tonight, you're keeping a secret?" Desperate to understand her, he watched her as she scanned the room. There were pictures of her sons scattered around the room at various ages, and on the mantelpiece there was also a picture of Sylvie and Chris, he presumed, in each other's arms at the beach. Her eyes had rested on the picture and he gazed at it also.

"That's Chris and me this summer just passed. The kids complained that we never had pictures together as I always take them, so Alex took this one of us. They insisted we put it up."

She paused, then drank some water. "He died last October, of a heart attack. He was away on… business. Stress, they say caused it. Too much pressure." She almost smiled as she said it, but then thought better of it.

"I'm really sorry. It must be very hard for you. He was young. I suppose nights like tonight can get to you." Nick looked over at the smiling picture. "You both look very happy."

"It looks that way, doesn't it?" Nick looked confused. *What an odd response!* He thought.

Sylvie looked into her glass. She felt like she needed to give Nick some explanation. She looked up at him and he was looking straight at her with those stunning eyes and his excruciatingly handsome, young face.

Jesus, what was she doing? He was in his twenties; she really was making a fool out of herself. The poor man was being kind, helping out his parent's friend, and she was behaving like a love-struck teenager. She found it hard not to focus on his mouth as he kept licking his lips. *Get a grip girl!*

"Sylvie, what did you mean earlier?" He shuffled closer to her but she didn't seem to mind.

"Oh don't mind me, I'm just tired." She leant her head back on the sofa and closed her eyes. He wanted so badly to tell her that he knew exactly how it felt to harbour a secret that could potentially hurt everyone he loved. He looked at her profile. She looked so relaxed and so calm. She looked breathtakingly beautiful.

"I'd better go, it's really late." If he stayed any longer while she seemed so vulnerable he really wouldn't be able to trust himself. She opened her eyes and put her hand on his arm, he froze.

"Don't go," she whispered. "Stay a little longer."

Swallowing hard, he sat back into the settee and Sylvie put her head on his shoulder. She was exhausted. A combination of the stress of tonight, the drink and the crying had made her suddenly very tired. Mmm, she had drunk an awful lot tonight. Was that why she was being unguarded?

She sighed as she allowed herself to relax against his firm shoulder. He smelled delicious, and his breathing was very heavy. It was so soothing, he made her feel safe. He'd slipped his arm around her shoulders and she pulled herself in closer. She could hear his heart beating quickly and she suddenly realised that his hand was ever so gently stroking her arm. Her heart was doing somersaults into her throat and she really didn't want him to leave.

They must have been sitting there for a few minutes when her phone began to ring, breaking through the silence. Sylvie's eyes flew open, and she shot up suddenly. *Talk about wakeup call!*

Nick moved his arm off her as she hurriedly rose, then stumbled to the table to retrieve her phone from her bag. Nick clenched his jaw and, with great effort, calmed himself; taking deep breaths as he closely watched her.

"Hello? Yes Stathis, no, no, I'm fine thanks … Yes, Nick drove me home… Julian's son… Yes, he was there too… Just a headache, getting too old for that shit I think… Yeah… No I'm fine, really. In fact I feel bad. Poor guy got roped into taking home his parent's friend. I probably ruined his evening… Okay, I'll call you… Goodnight, sweetie. Thanks for calling, enjoy the rest of the night, bye."

Sylvie put down the phone and turned around to find Nick six inches from her. His eyes were the most intense she'd ever seen them and his brow was deeply furrowed.

"Is that what you think? That I brought you home because you're friends with my parents." Sylvie stared wide eyed at him, totally confused. He looked so angry.

"Well, yes. I didn't mean to upset you, but I'm sure you have better things to do than taxi service me around. I…"

He seemed genuinely hurt and Sylvie was completely baffled. Nick leaned in closer and gently took hold of Sylvie's shoulders with both his hands.

"Sylvie, have you no idea how I feel about you?" His eyes were boring into her, his voice quiet and cautious. "Jesus, I can't stop thinking about you. From the first time I saw you at my father's office; I have done everything possible to keep away from you."

Whoa! Where did that come from? Sylvie blinked rapidly, trying to focus through the alcohol-induced fuzziness. This wasn't her imagination – no, no, he was actually saying this.

"I've tried to avoid being alone with you, when all I wanted was the complete opposite. But it's been impossible. You were at my Mum's house *all* the time. Even at the marina, where I thought I'd never see you, I bumped into you. Then with all the wedding and the arrangements, the redecoration, I just never caught a break. You were *everywhere*. It was… It was torture!" He swallowed hard and caught his breath.

Holy fucking… Her heart was banging against her ribs.

"I didn't want to give anything away. I obviously succeeded. I wasn't even going to come tonight. But then my Dad gave me his invites. I kept trying to find an excuse not to, but in the end I just had to see you again." Nick closed his eyes and took a deep breath in an attempt to compose himself.

"In answer to your previous question, yes; I do know something that would hurt everyone I love if they knew. The fact that I want to be with you, that I have these incredibly strong feelings for you, that I want to…!" He felt a weight lift off him as he spoke the words he'd so often wanted to say to her.

He stopped himself, dropped his hands from her, and stepped back. He turned and ran his fingers through his hair. His back was facing Sylvie. He seemed to be trying to gather his composure. Then he leaned onto the table with both hands and dropped his head, taking deep breaths. Maybe he should have just kept quiet, he realised that now he'd said what he felt, their relationship would change. The question was, which way would it go?

"Nick? I don't know what to say. I had no idea. I thought you were being aloof. You always kept your distance. Other times you were so charming, talking to me and joking; then you'd turn back to being distant and indifferent. Tonight, I thought you were just being polite again. Nick?"

Her heart was racing. It seemed ludicrous that he had feelings for her too. She knew how she felt, ridiculous as it was, but this was insane. He was so young, and she… Well, she wasn't. There was Julian to consider, and Maggie. Oh my God, Maggie! This was far too complicated.

"Nick, I…" She edged closer to him, wanting to touch him. "I really don't know how this happened. I…"

Nick turned around and looked at her, his eyes never wavering from hers. Sylvie stared at his beautiful face agonising over the right words to say. She knew what she wanted to say, but never in a million years did she believe a time would come that she'd be able to. Now, being propelled into that exact situation, she had to make a choice. Either to tell him she felt the same way, or to not.

Part Three – Spring

That from the second she'd laid eyes on him hauling himself out of Maggie's pool, she'd thought about nothing else. Should she take the high road and let him down gently, safe in the knowledge that she would be doing the right thing by all? She'd be making the moral choice. She shut her eyes, and in a rare selfish moment, Sylvie knew what her Hobson's choice was.

Nick watched intently as Sylvie's eyes opened again, gazing softly at him. She wasn't angry, or upset; in fact, her eyes stared back at him gently. With one swift movement he was inches from her again. This time, his hands took her face and after a slight pause he pressed his lips against hers.

Sylvie had no choice but to surrender as she melted into him. Her arms and hands reached up and clung to his neck, her whole body pressed against him. Nick's hands ran down the length of her now-trembling body stopping at her waist as he lifted her onto the table, never losing their contact. He kissed and caressed her neck, allowing Sylvie to gasp for air; all the while she was kissing his head, his cheek then back to his lips as he moaned. He tasted delicious and their mouths locked together again and Nick deepened the kiss with renewed urgency. He held her so closely she thought she might suffocate. All the pent-up desire, the wanting, the unspoken emotions were all concentrated in this first kiss.

Nick reluctantly pulled back and looked at her, his face pained. He kept gritting his teeth and the muscle tensed at his jaw line, as if he was still unsure. His eyes dropped to his hands. Sylvie took them both and gently kissed them and he met her gaze again.

"Oh Nick, you realise that this is… wrong, madness, insane?" she breathed, as she looked into his blazing eyes.

"What do you mean?" he looked hurt as he spoke, it was almost a whisper.

"Nick, I'm forty-four for the love of God! I'm seventeen years older than you. How can you honestly say that that isn't an issue? What kind of future is there? That's even before we start on your father and mother!"

Reality hit her like a wrecking ball; what was he thinking? Trying to be reasonable, she realised that he probably had a crush, and it really couldn't be more than that. Her heart was thumping away, she realised that this was the only way. Her initial selfish, self-centred reaction was probably the alcohol clouding her judgement. Self-preservation. If she let him in he would eventually hurt her, or equally, she could hurt him. However much she felt for him she didn't want to do that, and she couldn't have her heart broken again.

"What are you saying? I..." He was trying desperately to understand what she was thinking. All he knew was that for the last four months, this had been what he'd wanted. He wanted to hold her, kiss her. He looked deep into her worried eyes.

"Does it bother you, the age difference?" He pulled up her face by the chin and desperately searched it for answers. "Sylvie, I don't give a shit what age you are. All I know is that I have never felt this way about anyone. I saw you talking to so many different men tonight... I really didn't like it. Stathis was practically with you every moment he could. It drove me insane. Tonight when I saw you so upset all I wanted to do was take you in my arms.

"I cannot begin to tell you how difficult it has been these last few weeks to see you, yet not be with you. I couldn't keep away any more. The only thing that really matters is..." He took a pause before he finished his sentence. "Do you feel the same way?"

He held her gaze, and Sylvie could see that he needed to hear the truth. She stared at this incredible man who had opened up to her, being totally honest; it was disarming. It was something she'd never encountered before. Rather than say it out loud, she showed him. She put her hand onto his cheek then gently pulled him to her. This time it was Nick gasping for breath. The only thing Sylvie could think of was how this young man had made her feel alive again. That she wanted only to be with him, and by some miracle he felt the same way. It was probably the stupidest thing she had ever done but it felt unbelievably right. Nick took her down from the table and looked deep into her eyes.

"Sylvie, this is real for me; I don't mess around."

"Do I look like someone who does? I have far more to lose than you do."

"You know what? At this moment I don't care about anything or anyone, just you." And with that he took her hand. "You'll need to lead the way. I don't know where the bedroom is."

"Sod the bedroom!" To Nick's surprise, Sylvie reached up and started to unbutton his shirt. It was almost as if the walk upstairs may have made her stop and rethink. She wasn't risking it. She had never wanted a man so much, and her urgency only made Nick sure that they had only avoided the inevitable.

Sylvie pulled off his shirt, exposing his tanned, toned chest. She caressed it softly and kissed him. Nick moaned, then moved her to the sofa. Sylvie kicked off her heels while Nick removed his shoes and socks. He then unbuttoned his trousers, dropping them and then stepping out of them.

Their eyes locked on each other, desire burning white-hot between them. He reached up to her face and pulled her close, then kissed her neck, and then down to her throat whilst unzipping her dress slowly and smoothly. He gently pulled down the straps and then let it drop to the floor. Sylvie was standing in her red silk bra and panties, totally overcome. She held on to him so tight, scared that he might change his mind. Lifting her gently, he placed her slowly onto the settee.

"Oh Sylvie, you smell like heaven." He nuzzled her ear. Nick never expected, never hoped that she would feel this way, this intense desire that was equally matched to his.

He couldn't get enough of her dark, honey skin, so smooth, and her sweet smell. Both of them were breathing deep and urgently. He slowly unhooked her bra and gently eased it off her shoulders. Her back arched up to meet him as he stroked and kissed the length of her body, trailing his tongue downwards, over her breasts. Her hands holding on to his hair, he pulled her up slightly so that he could slide off her panties.

Sylvie groaned and he covered her in kisses as he worked up her stomach and back to her mouth.

Nick expertly slipped off his boxers, allowing them to drop on the floor. Sylvie pulled him back to her and kissed him deeply, his hands cupping her face. He slightly moved back from her and looked deep into her eyes, as if asking her permission. He wanted to be sure. She closed her eyes, marvelling at the fact that this incredible man wanted her and she arched into him as he became totally overwhelmed. Nick moaned as their bodies fused, proving there was never any doubt about her feelings or his. He sunk deep into her and Sylvie groaned, grasping on to his taut back as he moved slowly at first. Sylvie wrapped her legs around him and he began to quicken the pace, all the while kissing her mouth, her neck, along her shoulder then back to her mouth.

"Ah!" Sylvie gasped as she ran her hands down to the small of his back. He was perfect.

Nick rose slightly so he could see her, his eyes bore into hers. His gaze was almost triumphant as he revelled in her. Sylvie's hands moved up to his face as he continued to move deeper, her body bowing in perfect unison to his as she felt herself climbing. Nick momentarily closed his eyes in an attempt to control himself. The sight of him was enough to tilt Sylvie over the edge and as she gripped onto his back surrendering to her sweet release. Nick almost instantly let himself go, crying out her name and collapsing against her breathing hard and fast.

"Oh Sylvie!"

As their breathing slowed Nick reluctantly pulled himself a fraction up, just to allow Sylvie to catch her breath.

"No, don't move, stay exactly where you are." She whispered. He leant onto his elbow so that he could see every feature on her glowing face. He stroked back her hair off her face where his sweat had set it there, then kissed her.

"I don't want to crush you," he answered tenderly.

"Oh I think that ship has sailed." Sylvie's face cracked into a huge smile as she laughed.

Part Three – Spring

Nick wrapped his arms around her and squeezed her. "You are my heaven." He nuzzled her neck and planted kisses from her temple down her cheek to her lips. "You're incredible Sylvie; how the hell am I going to ever leave from here?" His face beamed at her, his expression was almost euphoric.

"Well you don't need to leave yet..." she said mockingly. "No one gets in 'til seven thirty; that gives us at least another four and a half hours!"

"And then I need to slip off like a thief in the night?" He kissed her lips softly. "You know, there's actually only a sixteen years difference between us. It's my birthday today." He was stroking her cheek as he spoke.

She took his face in her hands and pulled him to her lips. *Wow, he was here in her arms, naked!* "Well, happy birthday." She looked into his eyes, and he smirked.

"Best birthday present I've ever had."

Sylvie giggled, somehow she thought that maybe it was the other way round. "Really? You know what?" Sylvie turned and wriggled under him. "I'm too old for this... I've got a huge bed upstairs which would be a hell of a lot more comfortable. That's if you want more birthday present?"

"Didn't I say that about half an hour ago?"

Before he could finish, Sylvie pulled herself up and strolled towards the stairs. Nick sat up and admired her as she walked naked towards the hallway.

"I'll show you the way," she purred coyly over her shoulder as he quickly got up and ran up behind her, chasing her up the stairs.

CHAPTER 11

THE MORNING AFTER

The light from the gap in the curtains fell across Sylvie's face as she started to wake up. She took a few seconds to come round. She looked at the clock on her bedside table, eight twenty five! Shit, she had never slept past six before. She looked around her room and to the empty side of the bed. There on the pillow was a note.

Leaving you this morning was the
hardest thing I've ever done. Call me
Nick x

She rolled over to his side and buried her head in the pillow. The smell of his skin lingered on the pillow and Sylvie couldn't get enough of it as she took deep breaths.

Shit, she had it bad. As she played over what happened last night she remembered that they had started downstairs. That meant her clothes would still be strewn over the living room! Marcy would have seen them. Shit! What must she think?

Sylvie sat up and looked around her room. There on the chaise were all her clothes and her shoes carefully placed underneath. Nick must have brought them up before he left. She threw herself back on the bed and hugged his pillow.

What was she thinking, really? She reread the note. He'd put his number at the bottom thankfully, because she had no way of finding it. She couldn't very well call Maggie or Julian. *Oh God, Maggie and Julian; what would they make of it? What would anyone make of it!*

Sylvie padded over to the bathroom and washed her face. She looked at herself in the mirror. If Nick had hung around until morning, he may not have felt the same way about her after seeing her now. She looked tired, with black circles under her eyes. Granted, she had only had three hours sleep. But there was a time that she could have not slept at all and still looked great. Sylvie splashed more cold water on her face and brushed her teeth.

She kept replaying last night in her head. Sylvie had led Nick up to her bedroom where they had spent the remainder of the night making love. It hadn't been as urgent as the first time in the living room, but it was just as intense. Nick couldn't seem to get enough of her. He'd caressed her body softly and deliberately, savouring every moment. He'd kissed her with such passion that Sylvie had to pull away just so she could breath. He had held her with great tenderness and looked deep into her eyes, all the while saying her name. Eventually, they had both fallen asleep wrapped in each other's arms. Nick must have left before Marcy arrived at seven thirty. That would have been extremely awkward.

Sylvie reluctantly turned on the shower. She didn't want to wash off his smell. The thought of him made her whole body glow.

Once she was dressed she decided to go downstairs. Was it too early to call him? What if he was sleeping? Oh, she really was far too old for games. She wanted to talk to him so badly. She wanted to make sure she wasn't making a fool out of herself.

Marcy had made tea and left it in the pot. Sylvie poured herself a cup and walked over to the sofa. Sylvie smiled to herself as she nestled into where they had only a few hours previously been entwined. She picked up her phone. It had six missed calls and three messages. The calls were from her friends checking in on her this morning. They knew she was an early riser. Two of the messages were from Lilianna arranging lunch for Sunday and one was from Julian. He wanted to meet for dinner tonight.

Sylvie sat on the couch and gazed at the phone. She realised that Julian wanted more than just friendship from her and she had made it clear that she really wasn't ready for anything other than what they already had. In fact, she *was* ready. It would seem, though, just not with him.

There was no putting it off; she would need to call him and make some excuse as to why she couldn't make it tonight. She firstly called her friends from last night, otherwise they wouldn't leave her alone. They were all duly concerned about her, but she assured them she was fine. She then returned Lilianna's message saying she was on for lunch. She actually thought that she might be able to confide in her.

She dialled Julian's number and waited for him to answer.

"Hello there, how are you?" Julian answered.

"Oh I'm fine, just a little tired, you?"

"A lot better for hearing your voice. How was your opening last night?" Should she tell him that she saw Nick? Plenty of people saw them there. She really wasn't any good at this.

"It was really good, loads of people. But I think I'm a little old for that kind of thing. Stathis was in his element."

"I bet he was. Did you see Nick? I gave him my invites. He told me he was going."

"Yes I did, he was with some of his friends."

"He doesn't normally go to those kinds of things, but his friends like to. So, about tonight; do you fancy going to that Japanese restaurant on the beach?"

"To be honest Julian, I really don't feel like going anywhere tonight. Last night took it out of me, and I have a lunch tomorrow with Lilianna. So I'd rather just stay in, thanks though." Sylvie felt horrible. How did people do this? She hated having to blow him off. She hated herself more because of the reason why.

"That's okay, some other time then." She could hear his disappointment in his voice.

"Ok Julian, speak soon, bye." She put down the phone and cringed.

Julian was actually perfect for her. He was the right age, for a start. They worked in similar fields. He was a very attractive man who looked after himself and had no baggage. He had a wicked sense of humour and didn't take himself so seriously. The problem was that she saw him as Chris's friend, and that element freaked her out. They used to hang out together. It made Sylvie unable to see him any other way. There was also the added complication that she was totally, and indisputably, madly in love with his son.

Sylvie sat on the couch looking at her phone when Marcy walked in.

"Morning Mam! How are you this morning?" Since Chris had died she'd very much taken on a motherly role. She made sure everything was as it should be and tried to anticipate any forthcoming problems. She had helped her immensely throughout the weeks that followed his death. She helped pack his things and helped with the children. Even though they were young men now, she mothered them like they were her own and they treated her very much like an aunty rather than their housekeeper.

"Oh, I'm okay Marcy, you?"

"Same as usual; I cut some fruit salad for you and put it in the fridge. How was the opening?" She knew all Sylvie's engagements as she wrote them all down on a calendar.

"It was really good, but I had a really late night. I feel a little tired."

"Well it's about time you went out a bit. All you do is work and sit at home. It's not right. You need to enjoy yourself too you know. The boys are away and you have time to do your own thing now. Thank God you have Lilianna and Maggie."

It was true; had it not been for them she wouldn't even leave the house. She had a few other friends too, like the ones she was out with last night, but they were more work related.

"Did Mr Julian come too?" Sylvie knew where she was going with the leading question.

"No Marcy, he didn't. He doesn't go to that kind of thing." She gave her a knowing smile. Marcy liked Julian, and she made it perfectly obvious that she thought Sylvie should like him too.

"Oh that's a shame." She smiled cheekily back.

"Marcy, I'm not interested in him! He's just a friend, really." It didn't matter how many times she explained to

Marcy about Julian, she still held on to hope that Sylvie might change her mind.

"You know he likes you Mam, he's such a gentleman."

"Marcy!" Sylvie mockingly chastised her.

"Okay, okay I won't say anymore, I'm just saying what I see." And with that she walked off into the laundry room.

It was eleven o'clock and Sylvie wondered if it was too early to call Nick. After all, he'd hardly slept too. She didn't want to wake him. She didn't want to seem eager... Oh crap, she really wasn't cut out for this. The butterflies in her stomach were doing aerobics!

She ran upstairs to her room and closed the door. She picked up the note and looked at it again. What the hell, she was already in deeper than she ever expected, what was the worst he could say? It was a mistake? We shouldn't see each other? Not knowing was a hundred times worse. She picked up her phone and dialled the number. It rang only once.

"Hello?"

Her heart jumped as she heard his voice. "Hi, it's me."

"Jesus, I thought you'd never call!" He couldn't hide the relief in his voice. That was all Sylvie needed to hear.

"I didn't want to wake you," she apologised.

"Are you under the impression I slept? I just couldn't. I meant what I wrote. I really didn't want to leave you. I just thought it would be better, less awkward. I know you have people in and out of your house."

"That was incredibly thoughtful. Yes, it would have been hard to explain."

"I really need to see you. We need to talk. Come over."

"Now?" she hoped that was what he meant.

"Yes, now... I would have preferred four hours ago, but I'll settle for now." He was joking with her to ease the tension. "Do you remember where my boat is?"

"Yes, quay eight." How could she forget?

"Ok, I'll be waiting; and Sylvie?"

"Yes, Nick?"

'Hurry!'

Part Three – Spring

WOW! She put down her phone and flung herself on her bed shrieking with joy into the covers, like a teenager.

CHAPTER 12

TOGETHER

Nick had spent the best part of the morning pacing up and down, waiting for his phone to ring. He'd left Sylvie sleeping at around six thirty, but not before he'd tidied up down stairs. He knew she wouldn't want to give any explanations.

He'd come back to the *Silver Lining* and started to tidy that as well, purely out of nervousness. He scrubbed down the deck, all the while checking his phone. He made himself some tea and jumped into the shower. After he'd dried himself and quickly dressed he sat on the deck staring at his phone.

He was desperate for a cigarette. It had been three weeks since he'd quit. He rummaged around for some chewing gum and stuffed it into his mouth; not much of a substitute, but he'd have to live with it. What if she didn't call, what if she thought it was all a big mistake? He was going out of his mind.

He looked at the time. Ten thirty. Why hadn't she called? She woke early, he knew she did. He couldn't call her, he didn't have her number. He picked up the phone for the hundredth time to check it. He chewed harder on his gum. Maybe he should ring his Mum and ask for her number, but she'd ask him why. He'd have to sit it out. He threw his gum into the bin and shoved a new piece in his mouth. Christ, he needed a cigarette!

He stood up and started to pace again. He was about to pick up his phone when an unknown number came through; he didn't let it ring more than once.

"Hello?"

Nick raced round the yacht, making sure everything was perfect. He ran to the bathroom and checked himself over. Why, oh why was he so nervous? He went up on deck and started up the engine. He decided that he'd take Sylvie out, so that they'd be guaranteed privacy and that she wouldn't get away! Maybe he'd better ask her first; she might think he was kidnapping her. He shoved more gum in his mouth and scanned the marina for the umpteenth time.

Then, as he looked over to where the restaurants were, he saw a silver convertible turn into the parking area. His heart pounded in his chest. He tried to compose himself as he watched her put the top up of her car and then, after a moment, she opened her car door. She smoothed down her jeans and then headed towards quay eight. Her hair flowed behind her as the breeze gently blew and from where Nick was watching she looked like a young woman. She had a skip in her step and the sweetest smile, as though she was the only one who knew a wonderful secret. She looked over to where Nick was now standing and her smile grew.

She waved and quickened her step. Nick got down from the yacht and walked quickly to meet her. Within seconds he was up to her and his arms were holding her as she kissed him tenderly.

"I thought you'd never get here. Come on." He put his arm around her and led her to his yacht. "Fancy a little boat trip?" He lifted her onto the deck and then he untied the ropes.

"That sounds perfect," she replied, hardly able to contain herself.

It wasn't long before Nick had taken them out and was heading towards a secluded bay he knew. Sylvie sat on his knee as he steered the boat. She had her arms draped around his neck and her head rested on his shoulder. He smelt divine.

"Can you see that small cove?" Nick pointed to what looked like a sandy beach enclosed by sheer rocks all around. Sylvie nodded as she shielded her eyes and looked to where he was pointing. "Five more minutes and we'll be there."

He turned to look at her. "Do you want something to drink?"

"Sure, shall I get you something?"

"Just mineral water. I'm driving, remember!"

Sylvie reluctantly uncoiled herself from him and went below deck and into the galley. She was amazed at how well equipped it was, and surprisingly spacious. Opening Nick's fridge was a revelation. She'd expected it to be stocked with beer and nothing else, but to her surprise it had everything, from fresh fruit and vegetables to yogurts, cheeses and hams. Sylvie grabbed a mineral water for Nick and poured herself a glass of wine.

"I see you're very domesticated." She handed him his drink as she settled back on his lap.

"Surprised?"

"Well… Yes, to be honest. I thought you bachelors lived off of take out and beer." She gulped her wine. She felt like a teenager on a first date, which was ridiculous in the light of what had happened last night.

"I'm not your average bachelor." He grinned as he cut the engine and pressed a button to drop the anchor.

That he most certainly was not! thought Sylvie.

"Well, here we are." Sylvie looked out and saw that they were at least one hundred metres from the cove.

"How are we going to get to the cove?" She looked down at the sea, which was crystal clear and looked extremely deep. She was a good swimmer, but it was an altogether different thing swimming in the sea, and so far out, too.

"Jet-ski. It's tied up at the stern."

Sylvie suddenly felt very old. "I can't go on that, I'm scared to death!"

Nick looked at her, amused by her obvious fear. "I'll be driving it. I won't go fast. Would you rather we swam?"

"Oh God, I really didn't think this through. I haven't my swimming costume, I'm really not prepared." She was starting to panic a bit.

Nick was revelling in her obvious discomfort. He came over to her and took her in his arms. He kissed her gently, then rubbed his nose down hers. "We don't need swimming costumes." He arched his eyebrows. He watched the dread creep across Sylvie's face as she realised what he was saying. He burst out laughing. "Too soon?"

"Are you trying to make me feel even more uncomfortable?" She playfully pushed him away, but his grip was too strong and he squeezed her tighter.

"After last night I didn't think you were going to be so shy," he teased.

"It was alcohol-induced," she teased back. "You took advantage of me."

"Really? That's not how I remember it." He kissed her again and she let herself be totally swept away.

"Let me show you *my* bedroom today," he whispered in her ear, and with that he took her hand and led her below deck.

Sylvie followed in a love–struck, daze still unable to comprehend how this sexy, young, handsome man was still interested in her.

NICK PROPPED HIMSELF UP, resting his head on his hands as he looked deep into Sylvie's eyes. She couldn't believe that this man was actually lying next to her. She turned so that she could fully appreciate him.

What was going to come of this? She really didn't want to think about it, but unfortunately it was there, always in the back of her mind. He did a brilliant job of distracting her, but afterwards her mind only had thoughts of how this was ever going to work.

"What are you thinking?" He was running his finger slowly down her body, making every nerve in her burst into flames as she trembled under his touch. A smile crept over his face. He bent down to kiss her shoulder and across her collarbone.

Sylvie exhaled and closed her eyes. Would she ever tire of his touch? She couldn't think that that was possible. She wanted his hands on her every waking moment.

He lowered himself gently on top of her and brushed back her hair from her face, then kissed her forehead. He raised his eyebrows to indicate that he was waiting for an answer.

"I don't want to spoil the mood," she answered, placing her arms around his neck.

He took a deep breath and smiled slightly. "Listen, I'll make a deal with you. We can talk about whatever you want.

Get it all out there in the open. But once we've said everything, we get back to this." He kissed her lips again softly, then more urgently, until Sylvie had to gasp for air.

"Deal," she whispered.

"So, where do you want to start?"

Sylvie slightly shrugged her shoulders.

"Age difference?" Nick asked.

"Well, it is an issue."

"Not for me it isn't. I don't see you as an age, Sylvie; I see you as you. It's you I want."

"Yes but for you, what kind of future would you have with me? I'm forty four; in ten years I'll be fifty four and you'll only be thirty eight. Don't you want to be with someone who will be able to give you a family, children? I know now it's seems a long way off and right now this might not be your priority, but it will one day.

"And, from a selfish point of view, if you're only in this for the short term, to be honest I can't deal with that. That's not who I am. I'd rather know now than envisage a life with you forever, then have that all shattered five years down the line."

Crap, was that too much? She'd have to learn to be less candid.

"Sylvie, I can't tell you what I'll be like when I'm forty. What I can tell you is that I can't imagine my life without you in it. I didn't see you for two weeks and I thought I was dying! As for children, that's something we'd need to discuss. Would you want any more?"

Sylvie shot up and stared at him. "What are you saying? That you'd want me to have your..." She couldn't even say it. They'd been together not even twenty four hours and he was talking babies! Maybe she'd misunderstood. Surely not!

"Well, if you wanted to," he said tentatively.

Sylvie flopped back on the bed and covered her face with her arm. *Well, fuck a duck!* She'd never expected that.

"You've actually thought about it?" she asked in disbelief.

"Yes, is that weird?" He was so calm, so serene, and she was totally freaking out.

"To be honest, yes! We haven't spent a whole day together and you're talking children!" She turned to look at him. "You're not screwing with me, are you?"

"No I'm not. But please don't use that word when you're inches from me stark naked; it's very distracting, and I thought we had a few more topics to cover!"

He reached over and pulled her close to him. "So, next. What about my parents? That is the next issue, right?"

So that was that, then? Age no problem and now children?

"How can you be so calm?" She couldn't believe how matter of fact he was.

"Look, I don't know if you know, but both my parents have interfered in my private life in the past. It happened a few years back, but nevertheless it was very hard for me. They are well aware that if they do it again I will not forgive them. So they are going to have to accept whatever decision I make in my private life. It's my life, Sylvie, and to be honest they really are no experts on relationships.

"My Mum will be shocked but she'll get used to it. She loves you already. As for my Dad, that's a lot trickier. I know he has feelings for you, but I also know you've made it clear that you're not interested, because if you were you wouldn't be here, with me."

He pulled her even closer, and kissed her temple and ran his nose down her cheek. "He'll take it badly and it'll be awkward, especially because you work together, but he'll have to accept it."

"Nick, I don't want to be the one that comes between you and your family. I know what it's like to be hurt in a way that can never be cured or mended. And this *will* be like that, Nick." Sylvie rubbed her face, trying to fathom out what was the best solution; if there actually was one.

"Listen Sylvie, like you said, we've not even been together a day and we're trying to work out problems that at the moment we can't really solve, or even evaluate. Can't we just enjoy the fact that we've actually managed to be together?" He pulled her hand away from her face and turned it to face him.

"Sylvie?" His beautiful eyes were pleading with her and she was done for again.

"We're going to have to keep this quiet Nick, just for a while." It was the only way. Maybe in time, things might be easier.

"This is only so we can see how best to handle it, right? Not because you think we'll fizzle out and then it won't matter?" She could see he was genuinely hurt. "Because it won't, Sylvie. Not on my part, anyway." He was doubting her, his beautiful eyes searching hers.

"Nick, oh Nick; are you kidding me? In my adult life I have been with three men. A water ski instructor that I met while working in Corfu on my gap year when I was eighteen. I left him because I went to study and was heartbroken as a result; my late husband Chris, who I met while studying when I was twenty, and you. I hardly think I qualify as the 'love 'em and leave 'em' type!"

Relief washed over his face as she spoke the words he had desperately wanted to hear. "I see," He whispered softly, fixing her with his eyes.

"This is all very new to me. I'm reeling from so many emotions, and…"

Before she could finish, he crushed her lips with his as he held on to her. "Enough talking, please. Can we just enjoy the day? It's going to be torture not being able to be with you. I'm not sure I'll be able to cope. God, I need a cigarette!" He shook his head trying to rid himself of the thought.

"So you've really quit?"

"Yes, funny really, I started smoking because my girlfriend dumped me when I was eighteen and now I've quit because my girlfriend told me I should."

"Girlfriend? That sounds bizarre!" Sylvie laughed; she hadn't laughed for what seemed like ages. And the term 'girlfriend' in reference to her tickled her. She laughed so hard that tears ran down her face.

Nick shook his head and laughed as he watched her squirm under him. "Come on, let's go to the cove. It's so peaceful, you'll love it."

"How can I? I can't go like this." She motioned to her naked body. "And I can't go in those." She pointed to her jeans and her silky, aqua, halter-necked top.

"Let me see what I've got." Nick got up and went over to his wardrobe. He stood in front of his open wardrobe naked as Sylvie sat back on the bed and marvelled at him. God, he was in good shape. She pulled the sheet around her, suddenly feeling inadequate.

"I'm not wearing some ex-girlfriends teeny weeny thong she left behind!" Sylvie warned.

"Don't be silly, I got rid of all of those!" he teased, looking at her over his shoulder. She picked up a pillow and threw it at him. He ducked so that she missed.

"Here, wear that and your t-shirt." He passed her some black stretch cotton boxer shorts. Sylvie reluctantly put them on. "There, you look fabulous." He'd slipped on a pair of light blue board shorts.

"Don't push your luck!" She followed him up on deck and to where the jet-ski was tied.

Sylvie looked down at it and started to feel very uneasy. She wasn't a huge fan of anything that went fast and that wasn't covered. Nick expertly got down and reached out his hand to help her. He could see she was hesitant.

"Come on baby, give me your hand." She looked at his handsome face as he smiled at her reassuringly. He was calling her *baby*, Nick was calling *her* baby! She smiled at the irony.

"Don't you trust me?"

She reached out to grab his hand and realised that she'd probably swim in shark infested waters if he asked her. She felt her heart fall into his hands as she got on and sat behind him, clinging for dear life onto his waist. "I'll go slowly, I promise."

And true to his word, he started up the jet-ski and gently drove it to the shore.

CHAPTER 13

THE COVE

Nick helped Sylvie down from the jet-ski and on to the secluded beach. He pulled out a couple of towels and put them down.

"It's beautiful here, really. And you can't get to it any other way?" Sylvie looked up and around as she shielded her eyes.

"No, just from the sea. It's absolutely private." He came up behind her and put his arms around her; his hands slowly moved up under her top. She giggled as he kissed her neck. "Perfect for us. Let's go for a swim," he whispered in her ear. He took her hand and guided her to the water's edge.

Sylvie began to feel a little daunted at the prospect of removing her clothes in the blazing glare of the midday sun. What did he have to worry about? He was perfect. Every part of him was toned, tanned, tight and taut! All she could think of was that once she was in the water her makeup would be washed away, revealing her dark circles and wrinkles. Her body looked fine in clothes. After all, they held you in and smoothed out all the bumps, lumps and wobbly bits. And laying down, things always looked svelte. But to be stood up, naked; just the thought made her sweat. Everything dropping, without the correct scaffolding to keep it held up and perky! She really didn't think she could do it.

Nick looked at her trying to read her thoughts. "What's wrong?"

"Honestly?"

He nodded, a puzzled look on his face.

"The last man who saw me naked in daylight was Chris. He'd seen me age slowly and steady over twenty years. I don't feel particularly thrilled revealing myself to a twenty eight year old with the body of a Greek god. You don't make it any easier looking like you do!"

Nick shook his head and rubbed his eyes, took a deep breath and turned to her. "Sylvie, listen to me. I don't want to sound like some kind of stud or a player even, but I have had many opportunities to be with younger women. They have never interested me, because they have nothing to offer me. They don't challenge me.

"You, on the other hand are everything I want and desire in a woman. You're sure of who you are, you don't play games. You're honest and extremely loving. You don't take yourself seriously, you're intelligent and your heart is huge. You're the sexiest woman I've ever come across, and as for seeing you in daylight, I already have. This very morning I looked over every inch of you while you slept!"

Sylvie cringed as he said the last words. Nick lifted up her face to look at him. "You had better get used to showing me your beautiful body in the sunshine right through to the moonlight, because I'm going to want to see that as often as possible!" He wrapped his arms around her and kissed her head. "Come on, let's go in."

He took her hand as they stepped into the clear water. Sylvie instantly felt better as the cool water refreshed her warm skin. The water was so still it hardly lapped the shore.

"It's really beautiful and peaceful here. Like a completely different part of the world." Sylvie put her head back into the water to cool it down. The temperature was in the high twenties now.

Nick came up close to her. He pulled her towards him and she wrapped her legs around his waist. He caressed her back and kissed her neck as she held on to him and allowed the sea to support her.

"Hmm," he moaned, as his hands moved up through her top, and Sylvie surrendered to him. As he peeled it off her she floated back. Then he expertly slid off her shorts. Sylvie was thankful she was mostly underwater.

She swam a little away from him, playfully insinuating she was trying to escape. But he was fast, of course he was; she knew there was no contest. Nick grabbed her ankle and pulled her to him. He'd managed to already remove his trunks with ease and had thrown their clothes to shore.

"You can't escape," he teased and again she tried to wriggle away. He let her just a little and then he ran after her through the water, then he plunged himself underwater and skilfully swam to where she was. He resurfaced and wrapped himself around her. Sylvie squealed and turned to face him. He loosened his hold on her only to hold her face as he kissed her with such overpowering passion she almost forgot where she was. Nick looked deep into her eyes as he pulled away slightly.

"You're killing me!" His face was so full of agony, so intense. It was as if he couldn't bear to let her go.

Sylvie leaned into him and kissed him so ardently there was no question of how she felt. Nick lifted her onto him and Sylvie moaned as he made love to her with formidable intensity. All the while, his eyes were staring directly into hers.

Sylvie had never experienced anything so sensual, so spiritual. She felt like they were on a different plane. He held her close and, as they moved in the weightless sea, Nick held her face and rested his head on her forehead as he tried to control himself. The sight of his pent up passion was her undoing and she gasped out, knowing no one could hear and almost instantly Nick found his release too.

Nick held her close as they waded towards the shore, leaving her momentarily to bring a towel to wrap her in. Her legs felt like they would buckle if he didn't support her. He slipped the towel around his waist and collected their belongings.

"Are you okay?" He looked at her with a worried expression.

Sylvie smiled slightly and nodded. "I'm fine." The truth was, she was *more* than fine. This man had somehow made her feel so vibrant and so full of incredible joy, it worried her beyond belief. She had let him in with complete abandon and let down all her barriers. It scared her. She felt so exposed.

Part Three – Spring

It was four o'clock by the time they got back onto the *Silver Lining*. Nick ran the shower for Sylvie while he put together some sandwiches for them to eat.

Sylvie washed the salt water out of her hair and reluctantly washed the smell of Nick from her body. She combed back her hair and borrowed some moisturizing lotion she found in the bathroom cabinet to try and plump up her face. She reached into her bag and applied a little cover up stick onto her dark circles. She emerged from the bathroom still in a towel. Her top was wet and the rest of her clothes were in the bedroom.

"Is that better?" Nick called from the galley. "What do you want to drink?"

"Water's fine. I might need to borrow a shirt. Mine's still wet."

Nick came through to where she was. "Open my wardrobe and take whatever you need." He tenderly touched her shoulders. "You've caught the sun. Let me get you some after sun to cool it down."

Sylvie padded through to the bedroom and opened up Nick's wardrobe. There were hundreds of t-shirts and shorts and above them hung a few of his suits and shirts. She recognised the suit we'd worn to the wedding as she ran her fingers over it, and the blue shirt he'd worn to the dinner. She pulled it from the hanger and slipped it on. Sylvie rolled back the sleeves and let the shirt drop, covering her bottom and coming down to just above her knees. She could hear Nick in the shower as she slipped on her panties and she walked through towards the galley. Her stomach was rumbling. She'd eaten nothing since last night.

As she passed the bathroom, she saw that Nick had left the door wide open. She stood there for a while, admiring him as he allowed the water to rinse away the soap suds from his impeccable body. He rubbed the shampoo vigorously out of his hair then turned off the water. As he reached for his towel he saw Sylvie, who at this point had forgotten how hungry she was. Her stomach was reacting in a totally different way.

"That shirt looks good on you, except I'd have preferred it unbuttoned," he mused, with a cheeky grin.

Sylvie shook her head in disbelief. "You're really terrible."

She went to the lounge area and flopped down on the sofa. She thought he might want some privacy. Within what seemed like seconds, he was next to her in a pair of shorts. He looked unbelievable with his hair still damp and his toned chest still glistening from the water that hadn't quite been towelled off. He smelled delicious. He was carrying a bottle of after sun.

"Hungry?"

"I'm starving. Let me give you a hand. I'm a little out of sorts. I'm not used to being looked after."

"Stay where you are; It's all ready. I just need to bring the plates." He'd managed to prepare a selection of sandwiches and some salad. He placed them on the table and brought over their mineral waters. It didn't take long before they'd polished off everything.

"That was wonderful; just what I needed." Sylvie stretched her arms and winced a little; her shoulders felt tight. She got up to clear the things.

"Leave those. How are your shoulders?" Nick lightly pulled back his shirt off her to see.

"A bit tender."

"Come on, let me put some after sun on."

He led her through to the bedroom and she let the shirt slip down off her shoulders. "Lay down, baby." Sylvie unbuttoned the shirt and he slipped it off as she lay down. Nick gently rubbed the cooling lotion onto her shoulders as she lay face-down on the bed. It felt glorious. She really needed to get more prepared if they were going to be enjoying a lot more outdoor activities! She made a mental note to always have sun lotion, a swimming costume and at least a spare t-shirt always in her bag.

Nick carried on smoothing more lotion on and blowing on her shoulders to cool down the sunburn. It was so relaxing that before she knew it she had drifted off to sleep. A combination of a very late night, inordinate amount of sex and sun had finally worn her out. Nick carefully covered her with a sheet and went to clear up the plates.

Part Three – Spring

NICK STILL COULDN'T BELIEVE she was here. That she had felt the same way as him, and that she was prepared to overcome the obvious hurdles that they were guaranteed to face. He didn't want to think about it. Today had been the most perfect day, and the only thing that was worrying him was that she was going to have to leave and he wouldn't be able to see her again until she thought it was safe. How was he going to survive the next twenty four hours, or forty eight, until he could see her again? When would he be able to touch her, feel her, hold her?

He slumped down on the sofa and held his face in his hands. They'd not even been together for a day, yet he felt like he'd been with her his whole life. He instinctively knew that there would never be anyone in his life that he'd ever want to be with other than Sylvie.

Nick looked at the clock. It was almost six. He knew he'd have to start heading back. He didn't want to. He was happy to stay here, away from the real world. Here was all that mattered to him, all he ever wanted and everything he'd ever needed. He crept back to his bedroom and gazed at her for the second time today as she slept peacefully. He quietly and tentatively lay down beside her. She stirred momentarily as she rolled over to him and snuggled into the crook of his arm. He pulled her closer and kissed the top of her head. How was he ever going to let her go?

Sylvie opened her eyes and took a couple of seconds to register where she was. Once the realisation began to sink in, a content smile crept onto her face.

"How long did I sleep?" she croaked.

"About an hour and a half." Nick wrapped himself around her.

"That was a little rude of me," she replied. "I haven't slept in the afternoon since I was a child. Too much sun, not enough sleep and a lot of exercise," she chuckled.

"I suppose you need to get back." His voice was tight as he spoke the words. Sylvie nodded but avoided speaking. She didn't trust herself. Nick peeled himself away from her, and

Sylvie sat up. "I'll go and start up the engine. It'll take us about three quarters of an hour to get back."

His face had disappointment written all over it. As he walked out of the room, Sylvie's heart lurched. This was going to be a lot harder than she'd ever imagined. The secrecy was going to get to them, and every time they had to part, it would become more difficult.

She quickly got dressed and went up on deck to at least spend their last minutes together. Nick was steering with one hand and he was vigorously chewing gum. He gave her a weary smile and she clambered onto his knee, draping her arms around his neck again. Resting her head on his bare shoulder, she said, "Markus leaves around seven tomorrow night. Do you think you'd be able to come? That is, if you want to." She didn't want to sound presumptuous, but her heart was beating so hard hoping he'd say yes.

Nick squeezed her. "There's nowhere else I'd rather be."

He kissed her tenderly on her lips and her heart went into turbo boost. God, she wanted him again! How was it possible? How would she be able to wait until tomorrow? She squeezed him tighter.

"Do you want to steer? Just put your hands on this, like that, and hold them steady." He got up so that she could sit properly. She pulled a face, as though she was upset that he'd moved away from her. He smiled at her and positioned her hands on the wheel and stood back. "There you are; not bad for an amateur. Give me a minute. I need to get a t-shirt on, it's getting chilly!"

Sylvie looked horrified. "Don't leave me, what if something happens?" It was too late – he'd already sped down the stairs. In the distance she was sure she could hear a phone ringing.

"Nick! Nick! Is that my phone?" He ran back up wearing his t-shirt and carrying her bag. "Pull it out for me," she called.

He put down the bag and rummaged in it. The phone had stopped ringing by then. Sylvie watched him as he pulled out her phone in one hand and another in his other hand. He showed them to her and shrugged his shoulders.

"I don't know which one it was. How come you've got two?" Sylvie's face dropped slightly as she remembered that she'd put Chris's car phone in her bag the day she took his car to the garage. He walked over to her with them and handed them over. Sylvie slipped out of the driving seat to allow Nick to sit back down.

She checked her phone and saw that it was Zach doing his regular evening check in call. Sylvie put her phone back into her bag; she'd call him later when she was on her way home. She then looked down at Chris's. She went to the edge of the deck and took a deep breath, then threw it as hard as she could into the sea. Nick looked at her, even more puzzled than before.

"It was an old phone I had. It broke, beyond repair. So it needed to be gotten rid of."

Sylvie went over and took back her position on Nick's knee. "I don't need to get home just yet. That sleep has given me a second wind."

She started kissing his neck, and moved up to his ear. Nick started shifting in his seat. She smiled, knowing that he was finding it hard to keep himself composed. She stood up and unbuttoned her shirt, allowing him to see her breasts. He moaned and cupped them in his hands as she straddled him, and he cut the engine. He kissed her exposed breasts and she arched her back, bringing them closer to him.

'Oh, fuck! Let me drop the anchor,' he whispered.

Sylvie giggled. "Is that some sort of innuendo?" She got up from him as he laughed at her comment.

As she walked towards the stairs that led down to the bedroom, she left a trail of clothes. Nick speedily flicked the switch to drop the anchor and hastily followed the trail.

CHAPTER 14

MR X

Sylvie finished her twenty lengths and pulled herself out of the pool. Thank goodness it was warming up again, and she could enjoy her morning swim without the shivering she'd had to endure over the cooler months. Having said that, she had only recently had the energy to start up her swimming again; she'd pretty much avoided it over this winter. She towelled herself dry and strolled back into the house. Markus was standing in front of a wide open fridge.

"Morning sweetheart, I didn't hear you come in." She went over to him, kissing him on the cheek, and avoiding getting him wet.

"Morning Mum. I just got in. I'm starving. I thought I'd make us some pancakes." He ate like a horse. He'd always had an unbelievable appetite. Good job she'd taught him how to cook.

"Good idea."

Markus turned and looked at Sylvie and cocked his head to one side. "You're looking good, Mum. You've caught the sun, have you been sunbathing?"

Sylvie almost felt embarrassed. "I was out in it yesterday. I should have put lotion on. I'll go and get showered; I'll be down in a bit." Sylvie ran up to her room. Why on earth did she feel so guilty? She looked at her phone. There were three messages. She opened them up and saw they were all from Nick.

'Hope you slept well x'
'What am I going to do with myself until 7 ☹ x'

Part Three – Spring

'If u don't answer me soon, I'll light up a cig!'

Sylvie giggled to herself. Just the thought of him made her glow. God, she had it bad. She pressed 'call' and waited for it to connect.

"Just in time; I'd just lit a match."

Sylvie hadn't even heard it ring. "Well you'd better blow it out then, hadn't you? Is that what you're going to be doing from now on, blackmail me?"

He could hear the smile in her voice. "Whatever it takes. I really have no shame. I thought you'd have worked that out by now."

"I see, so you have no scruples when it comes to grabbing my attention?"

"Well I pretty much kidnapped you yesterday. Or maybe you hadn't realised."

Wow, his voice made her giddy. She could picture him lying on his bed with his arm behind his head. She was finding it hard not to blow off lunch and go over. "Now that you mention it, I hadn't thought about it. I'll need to be a lot more careful next time."

"Next time? So when exactly will that be?"

"That all depends."

"Depends on what?"

"On how well you behave tonight." She was loving it, teasing him. He made her feel playful and flirty again. She flopped back onto her bed.

"I swear I'll be over in a flash if you carry on. Family or no family! What the hell am I going to do for ten hours? God, I want you!"

"Chew your gum!" she giggled, rolling around on the bed.

"I can think of nicer things to chew."

Sylvie closed her eyes and took a deep breath. "Nick, you really shouldn't say things like that. It's very unfair."

"Well, today when you're having lunch I want you to think about that. All the places I could be chewing!" His voice was intense and oh-so disarming.

"Nick stop, please," she whispered. Ten hours seemed like an age away.

"I want you so much."

"Me too. This is hell. Shit, I need to go. I'll call you as soon as you can come." Sylvie sighed. Two days and she was in deep.

"Bye baby."

Nick hung up and reached for his gum. He'd have to do something until tonight, otherwise he'd go mad. He shoved the gum in his mouth and chewed. Maybe he should go and see his Mum. Vicki would be there, and hopefully they'd both keep his mind occupied until seven o clock. He rubbed his jaw. It ached from his perpetual chewing.

ZACH AND LILIANNA WERE waiting at Stathis's restaurant as Marcus and Sylvie pulled up into the marina. She was glad that they were all meeting up. It would hopefully help pass the time until she could be with Nick again. Sylvie felt guilty for almost wishing her time away with her son and her dearest friends. She hoped she wouldn't pay for it later. Why did she always feel so guilty?

"Sylvie, you look lovely. You've caught the sun and you look so... Well, like old Sylvie again!" Lilianna was genuinely happy to see her best friend back to her old self. Sylvie wrinkled her nose, feeling embarrassed. She wasn't good at taking compliments.

"Thanks. I have to say, I do feel a lot like my old self."

They sat down and enjoyed their time talking about their week and plans they were making for the summer. Zach touched on their work schedule and mentioned that he'd need to go off to Athens, though he really couldn't afford the time off what with all the extra workload he'd taken on.

"Why don't you send Sylvie?" Sylvie spun her head round to Lilianna in surprise. "You said it was just a formality. Someone from the company just needs to sign over the deeds. She *is* the M.D. It'd do her good; it'll be a change of scenery, and they'd get to know her too."

"It would help me out. I just thought that maybe it would be... well... a little upsetting. You know." Zach watched Sylvie as he saw her process the idea.

"That's all it is, signing the documentation?" she asked.

"Pretty much. It's a week tomorrow, so you could fly out Sunday and be back Tuesday."

Sylvie mulled the idea in her head. It would be weird going over; she'd only ever been with Chris before. But the idea of a fancy hotel room and time away from familiar surroundings sounded very appealing, especially as she might be able to persuade a certain someone to join her.

"I think I'd like that, Zach. I might even make it a long weekend. Markus won't be out next Sunday as he's switched days off with a friend. I could leave Friday afternoon and be back on Tuesday."

Four whole nights with Nick. How glorious!

"Good for you. You could have your spa treatments and take in the museum. I know you love the old part of town, and the shops. It'll be wonderful. Shame I can't join you."

Sylvie's heart stopped. Normally she would have loved Lilianna to come with her, but she was ashamed to say she really was glad she couldn't.

"Electra's got exams and I really need to be around to help her and Melita's got her prize giving ceremony, so I can't abandon them." Lilianna added sadly.

"Oh, I'm sure we'll be able to do it again. Once I get the hang of everything." Sylvie was glad that Stathis decided to come to their table in that moment. She didn't want to give away too much. Lilianna knew her very well, and it wouldn't take long before she would put two and two together.

Stathis sat with them for a while and began to talk with Zach and Markus. He'd got the proof shots of the opening night and was showing them off proudly.

"So, who is it then?" Lilianna whispered over to Sylvie.

Sylvie's face froze.

"Oh, come on, Sylvie. It's obvious. You've got that sparkle in your eye. You've got that goofy grin. You're walking with a spring in your step."

Sylvie's eyes widened and she motioned to the men talking.

"Let's go for a little walk, then." Lilianna grabbed her hand and pulled her in the direction of the shops.

"Jeez Lilianna, you really need to learn discretion!"

"So it is a man, then? Someone I know, someone who…"

Sylvie put up her hand to make her stop. She knew where this was going. "It's not what you think."

"So you haven't had sex yet!" Sylvie shook her head in disbelief. She wanted to die from embarrassment. "What? You're both consenting adults, he's been hot for you for… how long, and finally you've let him in. There's nothing wrong with that at all. You'd have to be mad not to. He's sexy, handsome, rich, *and* has a great sense of humour."

"Will you please be quiet for a second? For the love of all that is holy, Lily! It's not who you think." Lilianna stepped back in shock. "No, it's not Julian!"

"It's not Julian, well who the fuck is it?"

Sylvie swallowed hard. She wasn't ready to confess all yet. She wanted to see how they were going to handle everything before she spilled the beans. "You don't know him. It's early stages and I'm not entirely sure where it's going. I'm trying to be careful."

"Well knock me down with a feather! Well, whoever he is he's doing wonders. I've never seen you look so good."

Sylvie blushed a little.

"Oh my God!" Lilianna said. "This is more, this is way more. You've fallen for him. I've only ever seen that face on you when you were doe-eyed over Chris. When did this happen?"

"A few months ago."

"You've been with him for a few months?!" cried Lilianna, reeling at the news. Her sweet, innocent, faithful friend had been carrying on, and she'd been oblivious.

"No! No! I've known him a few months; we've only, well, you know. Well, it's just at the beginning."

"You little minx, you've slept with him. Well I never. Good for you. I can't believe it. Are we going to meet him?"

"Look Lily, I'm just getting used to the idea myself. No one knows, and I want to keep it that way. Don't tell Zach, he'll worry. And I have to think of the kids too. It's a lot more complicated. So please just keep it to yourself."

"Sure, sweetie. Whatever you say. But I know you. You're an all or nothing person. He must be really important to you for you to take the plunge."

"He is, and that's what's scary. I don't want to get hurt. And more importantly I don't want to hurt anyone else."

Lilianna looked at her, puzzled. "What do you mean, 'anyone else'?"

"Like I said, it's a lot more complicated. Let's just leave it at that."

"Well, at least tell me his name."

Sylvie shook her head.

"Okay, we'll need to give a code name." She laughed.. "I'll call him Mr X until you tell me. Well, I can't refer to him as 'your lover'!" She emphasized the last two words all breathy.

Sylvie giggled and put her hands to her face.

"Listen Sylvie, I know this is all a bit new and it obviously agrees with you, but remember; don't over-think things. You've had a shitty six months. You need this. Let yourself go a bit. Have fun."

Lilianna reached over and squeezed her best friend. "You deserve this, Sylvie, so don't do the guilt thing."

"Thanks Lily. I'll try."

"Let's get back to the table."

Stathis was still there when they got back, though he was about to leave.

"Sylvie, were you down here yesterday? I could have sworn I saw you leaving around eight o clock last night."

Sylvie struggled to keep the surprise out of her face. She didn't want to lie. "Yes, I popped down and had a walk around the yachts." She kept her face as steady as she could.

Lilianna looked across at Sylvie with a smirk on her face and mouthed 'Mr X?'

Sylvie turned to Stathis and smiled. "I find it very relaxing down here."

Lilianna stifled a cough and Sylvie threw her a murderous stare.

IT WAS SIX THIRTY, and Markus was packing up the last of his things. He'd be out again on Thursday this week as he'd traded days off with a fellow soldier whose sister was getting married on Sunday.

"See you Thursday, then. I think it's great you're going away, Mum. You really deserve it. And whatever you're doing to make you look so good, keep doing it. It obviously agrees with you." He flung his arms around her and headed back to camp.

Sylvie picked up her phone and scrolled to Nick's number. She hurriedly texted him.

> `'Coast is clear x'`

Within seconds her phone bleeped a reply.

> `'On my way! Full steam ahead x'`

She felt her whole body tingle at the thought of him. As she put her phone down she realised she hadn't saved his number to her memory. She picked it back up again and pressed the save button. Instantly the 'Name' option came up. She considered what she should save him as.

She smiled to herself and typed in 'Mr X'.

CHAPTER 15

CUSTOM-MADE

Nick was sitting on the terrace at Maggie's; he'd been there since eleven. He was thankful that Vicki was home too and they messed around in the pool and watched a couple of films she'd rented. Maggie was busy cooking and sorting out her garden. She looked over to Nick as he was checking his phone. Vicki was helping her plant some bedding plants.

"It must be a girl, Mum," Vicki whispered to Maggie. "He's never been so preoccupied with his phone before. He's been clock-watching, too."

"Oh, hell. I hope he doesn't get hurt again. He's been so up and down these past few months."

"He's been okay today, though."

"Yes, he has. In fact he's been great. Full of energy, and he seems happy. Really happy. And he's keeping off the cigarettes."

"Don't get all worried, Mum. He's a big boy now. You've got to let him get on with it."

Vicki put her arm around Maggie and squeezed. She knew only too well how her mother was feeling. She didn't want to live through Nick disappearing again.

It was twenty past six, and Nick had chewed his way through four packets of various flavoured gum. He felt like he would explode if Sylvie didn't call. He got up and went to get himself a mineral water. As he closed the fridge, his phone beeped. He turned and sped to the terrace table to pick up his phone. Maggie and Vicki watched his face light up as he read the message and type back his reply.

"Got to go." He kissed them both goodbye and ran to his Jeep.

"Definitely a girl!" Vicki laughed.

NICK PULLED UP OUTSIDE Sylvie's house and was about to get out of his car when he saw that the garage was open. Sylvie was inside, and she motioned him to park his car inside. His heart crashed into his chest as he saw her standing there wrapped in the yellow dress she had worn the first time he'd spoken to her at his Mum's.

"I thought it might be better." She almost felt foolish. After all, she could have anyone over, but it just made her feel better knowing his car was out of sight.

Nick got out of his Jeep and was next to her in seconds. He placed his hands on either side of her face and pulled her to his lips. Sylvie flung her arms around his neck and kissed him back. He pushed her up against her car and let herself slouch back against the bonnet.

"That has been the longest ten hours of my life," he breathed into her ear. Sylvie looked at him as he pulled back and she could see his eyes blaze.

"Heaven," he breathed, as he closed his eyes again. "Let's go to bed." It wasn't a request.

Nick released her and took her hand. They were in her room so fast that Sylvie was almost out of breath. He gently unzipped her dress as he kissed her shoulders. Sylvie moaned and rested her head back against him as her dress fell to the floor. She turned around to face him and reached down to the bottom of his t-shirt and lifted it over his head. He took a deep breath and closed his eyes. Sylvie lowered herself down so that she could unbutton his jeans, then slowly peeled them down his legs.

Nick kicked off his shoes and stepped out of them. Sylvie lowered herself onto the bed and propped herself on her elbows so that she could admire him as he slipped off his boxers. Mr X? More like Mr Sex! She smiled to herself. Nick raised his eyebrow as if wanting to know what the joke was. He positioned himself over her and pushed back her hair.

"I'm so glad I amuse you."

"That you do."

He kissed her as he reached behind her to unhook her bra.

"I saved your number in my phone today." Her words were soft and raspy. "I didn't want to use your name." He trailed his hands down her body to her panties, and ever-so gently slid them off. Sylvie gasped and Nick began to kiss his way up her from her hips. "So I saved you as Mr X."

A smile spread across his face. "Mr X, eh? That makes me sound very... mysterious." He lowered himself onto her naked, trembling body. "Is that why you were smiling?"

She could feel the full force of him against her body. "Yes, but I was thinking of a more appropriate title." Sylvie reached up and grabbed the back of his head and pulled him to her so that she could kiss him.

Nick was overwhelmed by the gesture. As she released him and he drew a deep breath, she held his gaze. "What would that be?" His eyes burned into her, full of passion.

"Mr Sex," she whispered into his ear.

He clenched his teeth as if he couldn't bear it any more. "Oh, Sylvie."

And he was lost, lost in her. She moaned as he savoured every cell of her, every fibre. His penetrating gaze made her whole body quiver as she arched up to meet him. She didn't want him to ever stop. He kept calling her name as he made love to her, as though he needed to be able to say it over and over. All the while his eyes held her gaze, looking deep into her. They both collapsed from the sheer intensity.

"You're going to wear me out," Nick gasped, as he pressed his forehead against hers. The sweat glistened on his chest and Sylvie could feel the heat radiating off him. It was delicious.

"Don't move," Sylvie pleaded. "I want to feel you on me."

He kissed her slowly and deliberately, tasting her sweet skin. She held on to him tighter. He gently brushed back her hair. "So, how was your day?" he asked, with a grin on his face.

"Oh, so now you remember the pleasantries!" Sylvie's eyes looked skywards.

"I'm sorry, but you seem to have this effect on me. How I ever held it together these last few weeks I'll never know." He slid himself off her and Sylvie pulled a face. "I must be crushing you. So, really how was lunch? And Markus, right?" He'd remembered, and he really *was* interested.

"It was lovely."

He could see that she was hesitant. She looked down at her hands and rubbed her finger. He took her hand and kissed it. There was a slight, lighter band round her finger where her rings had obviously been. He remembered that on the first time he'd met her and driven her home, she'd nervously fiddled with them then.

"What's wrong? Why are you so nervous? Did something happen?"

"I'm not nervous."

"You always fiddle with your finger when you're nervous." *How did he know that?*

"Lilianna guessed that I'm seeing someone."

Nick raised his eyebrows. "Did she know who?"

Sylvie shook her head.

"Did you tell her?"

She shook it again. "I thought I could, but then I decided to wait. I told her it was complicated. She seemed to be pacified, for now anyway. But I know her; she'll badger me until I crack."

"Does that make you feel sad?" Nick lifted her head up.

"Sad?"

"Well, you don't sound too happy about it."

"It just made me realise how complex this is. Normally I'd have rushed to tell her something like this and today, well, I couldn't. That did make me think."

He pulled her close and she laid her head on his chest. He stroked her head and kissed it. They lay there for a moment in the quiet; Sylvie could hear Nick's heartbeat rhythmically and the sound soothed her. Lilianna's words came to her mind. *Live a little. Don't overthink things. Have fun.* Sylvie swallowed hard. *Oh well, here goes!*

"Shall I introduce you to one of my favourite pastimes?"

Nick looked at her, puzzled. Sylvie got up and headed towards her bathroom. He sat up to get a better look. He could hear the taps being turned on. He stood up and entered the bathroom and leaned up against the door frame. He watched as Sylvie poured in bubble bath into a huge tub. "I seem to remember that you thought no one used these." She'd slipped on a thin bathrobe that clung to her.

"That's all I need – a hot bath! I'm already sweaty. It's really big!" His mouth curled up into a smile as he admired her.

"You'll love it, trust me. I had it custom made."

"Of course you did. I wouldn't have expected anything less!"

"What can I say; it's one of *my* guilty pleasures. Give me minute to go and get some drinks. Will you have a beer, or would you prefer something else; wine, maybe?'

"Whatever you're having will be fine."

Sylvie left the bath filling as she ran downstairs to collect a bottle of Sancerre, glasses and some water. By the time she was back the tub was filled, and Nick was closing off the taps. Sylvie handed him a glass then took a huge gulp of hers. Dutch courage! She slipped off her robe, and Nick took in a deep breath.

"Any pastime that lets me see you naked is fine by me." He had a wicked look in his eye.

She stepped into the bath and lowered herself in. Nick put down his glass and stepped in.

"Lay back on me." Sylvie opened her arms so that he could nestle against her and then she slowly opened her legs so that he'd be able to sit between them.

"Oh, fuck! I thought this was going to be relaxing! I'll never relax if I'm sitting in between your thighs. This is torture."

Sylvie giggled and beckoned to him to sit. "Just turn around and sit down."

He did as he was told, and as he rested back on her she rested her legs along his, and wrapped her arms under his. He let out a moan.

"How's that feel?" Her face was nestled against his hair.

"Honestly? It feels as sexy as hell."

"So, how was your day?"

"Oh, now *you're* doing the pleasantries. We're naked and you're rubbing up against me, and you're asking me about my day?"

She stroked his chest, and ran her fingers through the light covering of hair. "Just relax." She pulled him even closer as he closed his eyes, and she stroked his forehead. His breathing deepened.

"I went to my Mum's and passed my time there. Vicki was home, so we watched videos and chilled. I was going out of my mind until your text."

Sylvie squeezed him, and he took hold of her arms and wrapped them about him. Now she needed to see about the weekend. She reached over to her wine glass and drained the contents. She put down her glass and took a deep breath.

"Have you got plans for next weekend?" She was glad he couldn't see her face. She'd never asked a man out in her life, let alone to spend the weekend with her.

"Well, I was hoping to see you. Why?"

"Well, I need to go to Athens for work. It's only a day really, but I thought, if you..."

He turned around to look at her. The water sloshed as he lay on top of her, face to face.

"Are you asking me to come with you?" He couldn't hide the surprise in his voice.

"I was thinking we could leave on Friday afternoon and be back on Tuesday." She couldn't get used to being able to look at his face. She could feel herself warming up and she dropped her gaze. He looked incredible; the redness in his cheeks made his eyes pop. He slid up to her and lifted her face so that he could kiss her softly on her lips.

"Four days together? Just you and me? Wild horses couldn't drag me away." He knelt up in the bath and kissed her with more force. "How will I last 'til then?"

Sylvie put her arms around his neck and pulled him to her. "Is this why you had this specially made?" he muttered gently. He didn't need to hear an answer. Sylvie gently kissed his chest, moving from his neck down and then back up to his collarbone. He pulled her to him as he manoeuvred himself into a sitting position. Her legs wrapped around him. "Oh, baby, how am I going to ever leave?"

She cupped water in her hands, and slowly trickled it down his shoulders and down his chest. All the while, Nick's eyes were transfixed on her. It was so sensual, the act of being bathed and being entwined so intimately. He was totally mesmerized. "This is insanely sexy."

"So you like it?" She leant over, closer to him so that she could talk into his ear. Her breasts touched his chest and he gasped.

"I think you can feel how much I like it."

A wry smile crept over her face and he tried to cup her breasts, but she stopped him.

"I have to bathe you all over first, and then you can touch me."

His eyes widened. *Fuck me, she's teasing me!* Nick thought, and groaned as she slowly rubbed his arms and then his legs with a soft sponge; all the while sitting astride him. Nick was totally in awe of this woman. He could barely control himself as she started to rinse him.

All the while, her eyes kept flitting back to his. When she was finished, she leant back close to him, took his face in her hands and kissed him ever so gently, then whispered: "Now touch me."

CHAPTER 16

TRAVEL PLANS

S ylvie opened her eyes and immediately reached around her bed. Her heart sank, he'd left already. She checked the time. Five forty-five.

Propping herself up her elbows, she surveyed her room. Her clothes were neatly folded on the chaise and the towels were hanging. She got up to check the wreckage in the bathroom. The floor was a little damp, but apart from that, everything looked tidy. She shook her head. Had he really cleared everything away before he left? She really had no energy to swim this morning. After all, she'd exercised in the water enough last night! She jumped back on the bed and pushed her face onto the pillow where he'd lain and took a deep breath. It smelled wonderful.

Sylvie got herself showered and dressed and made her way to the office. She wanted to avoid Marcy this morning. She was worried she might realise that she'd had company last night, and Sylvie really didn't want to face that conversation. She was in such a good mood, she didn't want to start thinking about how this was all going to work out.

She checked her phone. There were two messages, both from Nick.

'Morning baby you look like an angel when u
sleep x'
'Call me when u r up x'

She plugged in her hands free and pressed the call button. Again, it only rang once.

"Hi," His voice was a little craggy.

"Were you sleeping? I'm sorry."

"I told you to call. I wanted to hear your voice."

"What time did you leave last night?"

"Around three thirty."

"Why did you tidy up? I would have done it."

"I didn't want you running around this morning trying to get everything back in order."

"We made quite a mess in there," Sylvie chuckled.

"It's fair to say that I'm a bathing convert! Not sure I could fit one in the *Silver Lining* though! God, I miss you."

"It's only been four hours!"

"Are you going to the office?"

"Yes, I'm driving there now. I'm going to book our flights and the hotel once I'm there. And then I've a couple of things to clear up; documentation mainly. What are you doing today?"

"I need to be down the shop today; summers coming and I need to make sure all my stock's in. When am I going to see you?"

"I've got a bit of planning to organise for your Mum's. I'm having meetings with the contractors. They start next week. I hope to be done by five, so if you've no other plans you could come over." She winced. hoping she didn't sound needy.

"Just so you know, I never have other plans when it comes to you. I don't play games. Sylvie. I want to be with you twenty four seven."

"Oh." His response took her by surprise; her heart leapt and her face beamed.

"What are you wearing?" His comment came out of the blue.

"I'm sorry?"

"What are you wearing? I want to picture you in my head."

"Oh, I see. A white, sleeveless blouse, a camel pencil skirt and a pair of camel stilettos." She felt awkward, but giddy at the same time.

"I bet you look stunning."

She blushed, even though no one could see her. "What are *you* wearing?" Well, if he was playing with her then so could she.

"A smile." Sylvie gasped, and she could hear Nick's laughter. "Think about that in your meetings this morning."

"You really are bad. That's so unfair." She'd started to sweat again, and he wasn't even there. "I'll call you when I get home. I've just pulled up outside the office."

"Another ten hours of hell, and then heaven." His voice was loaded as he spoke. "I better go buy some gum. Shit, I miss you. See you later baby."

Sylvie sat in her car, staring out into space. Wow, he really was turning her inside out. She looked at her clock. Eight o'clock. She turned to reach for her bag and was faced with Julian pulling up next to her.

Oh no, the guilt came flooding back. She felt herself start sweating even more. She hoped he was meeting Zach, she couldn't cope.

Julian beamed at her, and all she could see were Nick's eyes looking back at her. Those mesmerizing sapphire blue eyes. She'd never realised before but both their eyes seemed to change colour depending on what they were wearing. Today Julian was wearing a navy blue linen shirt which made his eyes darker.

"Morning! You look very cheery today." Julian had come over to her and opened the door for her. He leant and kissed her cheek. "I take it you had a good weekend."

Sylvie swallowed hard and smiled. Then she realised he meant the opening and lunch. Oh, the guilt!

"Yes, it went very well. And lunch was great."

"You've caught the sun. Been swimming?"

Her heart was bouncing off her rib cage. "I swam at home, so I must have caught it then. You're here early, are you meeting Zach?" She needed to change the subject; her palms were clamming up.

"Yes, we've got to go over some plans for the new offices. There's a lot to get through this week and I think he has to leave at some point for Athens; so we're trying to get things settled before he goes."

"Well actually, Zach suggested I go instead, so he'll be here."

"You're going?" He looked surprised.

"Yes; apparently it's just a formality, so I can do the signing. I'm going for a long weekend. Recharge my batteries. You know; spas, shopping and museums." She was prattling, but she could see the Julian was a little disappointed.

"For how long?" They stepped into the elevator.

"I leave Friday afternoon and I'll be back on Tuesday."

"You're going alone?" Sylvie couldn't even look at him.

"Yes," she lied.

"Oh. Well I'm sure you'll have a great time. You're familiar with the city?"

Sylvie nodded as the doors opened up onto the reception area. Maria was already in.

"Coffee? I'll get Maria to make you one. Zach will be in any minute." She escaped to the kitchen area, where Maria was starting up the coffee machine.

"Morning Maria, how was the rest of your weekend?"

"Morning. Great, Sylvie, and yours?"

"Pretty good, actually." Sylvie grinned. "Can you make Julian a coffee? He's meeting Zach this morning."

"Of course; and I'll bring your tea too."

Sylvie walked through to her office, and was surprised to see Julian waiting there.

"Zach just called. He's running late and he'll be here in fifteen minutes. So, I'll keep you company until he comes. Is that alright?" He was sitting on the couch, looking a little nervous. Sylvie had a bad feeling.

"Of course you can." Sylvie opened up her laptop and rearranged the papers on her desk. How was she going to book flights and hotels now? Maria walked in with their drinks and placed them where Julian was seated.

"Do you need anything else, Sylvie?"

"No that's fine. What time is Yiannis coming this morning?"

"Nine. I'll buzz you when he gets here." Maria, left closing the door behind her.

"Is that the contractor who's doing Maggie's house?"

Sylvie nodded. She could kill Zach for being late. She would have to make small talk now, and she really couldn't look at him.

"I was wondering," Julian shifted in his seat nervously, "whether you might be free on Wednesday night."

Oh crap, here it comes!

"We're going to have the wedding photos and video back. Elenora and Pavlos will be back too, so we thought we could watch them altogether. Pavlos' parents will be there, and, well; you were a very integral part of the arrangements. I thought you might like to be there."

"Oh, um, well I'm not sure. Don't you think that it's better you see it as a family? I wouldn't want to intrude."

"Don't be ridiculous. You're a very close friend of ours. They'd all be upset if you didn't come."

"That's very sweet of you. Wednesday? What time?" There was no avoiding it. She'd have to go. She knew Maggie would ring her and insist she be there anyway.

"Around seven. I'll pick up, so you'll be able to drink."

Oh no – how was she going to get out of that?

"That's alright, I'll be tee total. I don't want to bother you and make you go out of your way." He was really making this hard!

"I've told you a hundred times, Sylvie, you are never a bother to me. So it's settled. I was hoping we might get to go out sometime over the weekend. When you get back, maybe?"

Sylvie shuffled every paper she could lay her hands on. Sometimes she wished Maria wasn't so damn efficient!

"Yes. Next week, maybe?" Hell why couldn't she just be more non-committal!

Crap. Double crap!

"You're starting Maggie's next week, aren't you?"

"Hopefully. That's why I'm meeting Yiannis today. He's busy but he promised to help me out."

He took a sip of his coffee and carried on watching her as she started to look through her desk drawers.

"Are you alright? You seem a little… Well, flustered."

"Just got a lot on. I'm sorry, I'm being rude."

Guilt, guilt, guilt! He'd been so good to her. He really didn't deserve to be treated this way. She got up and went to sit by him where her tea was.

"What have you got on this week?" At least she could ask about his week, to take the focus off her.

"There's a lot in the pipeline. Celle was very good publicity." He put down his cup and leant forward and rested his arm on the couch back. "It was fun working together again. I'm going to miss that, a lot. We work well as a team. Well, I suppose now you're more involved in the developing part of the business we'll be working together more often."

"I'm not sure if I'm quite up to that yet. I'm still learning." The buzzer went on her desk. "Excuse me." She went over to her desk. "Yes Maria?"

"Zach's in his office if Julian wants to know." *Thank you God!* Sylvie was really starting to panic.

"Okay, I'd better leave you to get on. If I don't see you before, I'll see you Wednesday at six thirty." He came over to her and kissed her goodbye.

Sylvie sank in her chair and put her face in her hands. What a mess. She hoped Nick would be okay about it. Playing happy families and being escorted by Julian. What choice did he have? She felt like she was having an affair, for goodness sake! How did people do it? Keep up the lies and keep things secret? How had Chris managed it so well? She mused sadly. How indeed?

Sylvie quickly called the travel agent and booked her flight to Athens, business class. Then she asked them to arrange a suite in the usual hotel they used. Well, if she was going to have four days in Athens then she was most certainly going to do it in style.

Once they were booked she then purchased a second ticket for Nick online on the same flight using her personal credit card. That way, no one would realise from the company when the invoice came that she had gone with anyone. She was sure that was probably what Chris used to do when he was going with Dina. That thought made her heart sink. It really was incredibly easy to deceive people, after all. Especially if they trusted you, if they never suspected anything. If they loved you.

She shook her head, trying to rid herself of her errant thoughts.

Once all the bookings were confirmed she picked up her phone to text Nick.

'We're booked ☺x'

Within a couple of seconds he replied.

'Can't wait x'

AFTER A HECTIC DAY trying to negotiate all the contractors for Maggie and then arranging all the correct documentation for Athens, Sylvie was glad her day had come to an end. She'd asked Marcy to get in some supplies in for tonight. She was planning to cook for Nick. It felt wonderful to have someone to cook for again.

She got home as early as she could to prepare a crème caramel. She remembered it was his favourite. While it baked she put on some rice and prepared the prawns. It was already five o' clock, so she reached for her phone to text him.

'Hungry? x'

She pressed send. Instantly her phone beeped a reply.

'For you yes. On my way. Be there in 10'

The butterflies in her stomach went into overdrive as she rushed around the house trying to get everything in order. The table was set, the crème caramel was chilling and the prawns just needed to be finished off before they were served. She sprinted upstairs to check her makeup and squirted some more perfume.

The buzzer went and Sylvie ran to the hall to open up the gates.

"Park it in the garage again," she called through the intercom and then ran back downstairs again.

As she entered the kitchen, Nick walked through from the garage adjoining door. He strode over to her with such purpose and wanting in his eyes, Sylvie was taken aback by his sheer forcefulness. He took her face between his hands and kissed her tenderly at first, then more eagerly. As he let her go, Sylvie gasped.

"Hi." Nick's face broke into a smile.

"Hi." He took her hand and led her to the couch and she lowered herself onto it. "Are we going to do the pleasantries again?"

Sylvie smiled embarrassedly.

"So, how was your day?" She carried on their little game.

"God, you smell good." He nuzzled her ear as he leant over to her and kissed her neck. His hand caressed her. "My day was boring and tedious and all I could think about was you wiggling around in this pencil skirt." He ran his hand down her skirt, and then up under it. Sylvie moaned.

"I cooked," she breathed back into his ear, as she let her fingers run through his hair. He pushed up her skirt so he could feel her thighs and started undoing her blouse.

"Good. I'm starving." He pulled back slightly, only to remove his t-shirt. Sylvie kicked off her shoes and slipped out of her blouse. Nick stood up to remove his jeans and sneakers, then he helped Sylvie up and unzipped her skirt.

"I like a man with a healthy appetite," Sylvie whispered back.

Nick pulled her skirt down as he sat back on the couch, all the while looking deep into her eyes. Sylvie stepped out of it and then knelt onto the couch and pushed Nick back into it so that she was over him.

"I can wait," he moaned.

"Good."

THEY ENDED UP ON the floor amongst their discarded clothes. Nick rolled over onto his back and ran his hand over his face. He was breathing hard and his face glistened with sweat.

"I swear you're going to kill me." He had his eyes closed and Sylvie could see his perfect profile. He was far too handsome, it really wasn't fair. "God, I'm hot."

How very true!

"Go jump in the pool while I get dinner ready."

He turned to her and gave her one of his sensational smiles, stroking her hair off her face. "So, you cooked for me?" Sylvie nodded. "I love that you did that. I can cool off later. Let me help you." He kissed her head as he got up and threw on his boxers. Sylvie slipped on her panties and put on her blouse. Nick took her hand to help her up.

"So, what else is on the menu?" He raised his eyebrows at her.

"Open some wine and I'll bring it over. It just needs warming through."

He caught sight of the set table as he went to the fridge. He then watched Sylvie stirring cream into a pan that was wafting an incredible smell of prawns and wine.

This is what he wanted. He wanted to be with her and live moments like this. Sylvie tipped the prawns into a dish and then gathered up the rice. She placed them on the table and then mixed the salad. Nick pulled out a chair for her and then sat down.

As Nick poured the wine, Sylvie reached over to pick up a warm roll, splitting it in half. Then she slowly, but deliberately buttered it and placed it on Nick's side plate. Nick was totally hypnotized by the gesture. Sylvie picked up another roll and repeated the action, this time putting it on her own plate. Nick picked up her hand and kissed the inside of her wrist. Sylvie spooned the rice and creamy prawns onto his plate and then served herself.

"It smells wonderful. And you did this for me?" He picked up his fork and took a mouthful. "Wow, this is amazing."

"You sound surprised."

"Well to be honest, I didn't have you down as a domestic goddess."

"Oh really. Why's that?" Sylvie sat back, eyeing him and waiting for an explanation.

"Well I suppose because you have staff, and you work and you look like you do. Sorry, have I offended you? It's just been my experience that women like that tend to be less... How shall I put it? Capable."

"I'm not offended. I didn't always have 'staff'" Sylvie made air quotes. "I'm just lucky I do now. I've always loved cooking. It relaxes me. I love it more when I have someone to cook for. Recently that hasn't been the case. You really don't know that much about me. And what did you mean by 'the way I look'?"

"Well, you're sexy as hell and so un-housewife-like!" He picked up her hand kissed it. "I'm hoping to get to know you very well over this weekend." His piercing blue eyes looked deep into hers.

"So, we will be talking then? It won't just be about sex?" Sylvie gave a little laugh.

"Oh no, it'll be about the sex. But we can talk in between!" Sylvie shook her head as Nick carried on eating. "This is really good."

"There's dessert too, so don't fill up." Now he really was shocked.

Sylvie took a forkful and smirked. Once they'd eaten Sylvie cleared their plates and took them into the kitchen. She turned over the crème caramel and collected desert plates on her way back to the table.

Nick took one look at it and gasped. "You remembered? It's my favourite," he breathed, totally taken aback. Sylvie spooned it into the dishes. "I'm touched."

"It really was my pleasure. I told you, I love cooking."

He sat back in his chair and looked at her in wonder. He shifted round so that he could gently stroke her cheek. Sylvie stared at him, wondering what he was agonising over. His face looked tortured, as though he didn't know what to do or say.

"Hey, what's wrong?" She couldn't see him this way. "What is it, Nick?" She lifted her hand and ran her fingers into his soft hair, and he closed his eyes, relishing her touch. He opened his eyes and they blazed, white hot and raw.

"I love you, Sylvie." And he reached over to her and kissed her deeply and fully on her mouth.

Holy shit!

Before she could even think she replied.

"I love you too," she rasped, because it was true.

CHAPTER 17

MISUNDERSTOOD

S ylvie's hair flew around her as she headed up to Maggie's in her car, the top down, music blazing. Rihanna was singing something about feeling like the only girl in the world; that was how Nick made her feel when they were together, like she was the only girl again. She really couldn't believe that he wanted to be with her. He'd left late last night after she'd fallen asleep in his arms. This morning she had woken only to find a note on his pillow.

I'll call you.
You're beautiful when you sleep
Love you, Mr X! X

Summer was nearly here and she felt elated. As usual Maggie was in her ripped jeans, floaty top and barefoot.

"Sylvie, you look great. If I didn't know better, I'd think you were in love." The pang of guilt swept over her as she watched her friend assess her. "Come on I've just made tea."

They went straight to the kitchen and Sylvie walked over to the French doors and looked at the pool. She closed her eyes and summoned the scene of the first time she'd seen Nick hauling himself out of the pool. That seemed like an age ago.

"Yiannis will start next Wednesday. Is that okay? I'll be away until Tuesday so it works well for me."

"Where are you going?"

"Athens, for work. Signing over a building we've just completed. It's my first official duty as M.D."

"Sounds very official. Are you going alone?"

Sylvie kept her eyes on the pool.

"Yes. I thought it'd be good for me. Get away. See the sights and pamper myself. I've had quite a busy couple of months. I leave on Friday."

Her hands were fidgeting and clamming up. God, she hated lying. She wasn't good at it and that feeling of guilt has still pushing down on her shoulders.

"Good for you. Everyone seems to be either coming or going at the moment. Elenora and Pavlos are coming back tomorrow.

"You're going off on Friday. Nick's flying off at a moment's notice to the South of France. I can't keep up." Sylvie's heart stopped for a split second. *He was going to the South of France? Why hadn't he mentioned it? I thought he didn't play games. What about Athens?*

"It'll be great to have everyone back tomorrow night, all under one roof again. It's going to take a while for me to get used to not having Elenora around. Vicki's always working and Nick comes in fits and starts. I got used to him being here over the wedding and the redecoration. But I have a feeling I'll be seeing much less of him."

Sylvie turned round to try and work out what Maggie was saying. She couldn't stop herself. "Oh? Why's that?" She flushed as she spoke, but luckily Maggie was carrying the tray and her eyes were focused on it.

"Vicki and I reckon he has a girl." She placed the tray down onto the table and looked up at her with her eyebrows raised.

"Oh?"

"I thought he was acting weird. Hot and cold. His mood swings were getting hard to handle, I can tell you. I actually got very worried about him. I thought he had feelings for someone else actually... He looked tortured, or at least..."

She stopped herself and she looked up at Sylvie, thinking back to the wedding and seeing Nick's reaction to her, and the way that he'd stopped smoking just on her say so. She shook her head, as though she was trying to rid herself of her thoughts.

"Well, it doesn't matter now, because over the last few days he's been unbelievably happy. So he obviously got over that and has found someone."

Sylvie sat in silence. This was really getting to be too much for her.

"I hope she doesn't hurt him. I couldn't see him broken again."

Sylvie swallowed hard and reached over to her tea.

"He comes across confident, and he is" Maggie continued. "He's brilliant at his work. He can charm the socks off of anyone, but in his personal life he seems to get swept away. He really throws himself into a relationship. It's always been that way with him." She looked at Sylvie and smiled. "Sorry; you're supposed to be showing me the plans and I'm prattling on about my family. So, what did you decide on?"

Sylvie reached into her briefcase and opened up her laptop, thankful that Maggie had stopped talking. She showed her three different options, and as Maggie mulled over them Sylvie started to process what Maggie had said. She knew they'd only been together a few days, but he never mentioned he was going away. Oh, she really wasn't cut out for this. Her stomach was cramping again. Maggie was worried about him getting hurt! Three days in and she was already getting stomach cramps. Maggie's phone rang and she went to answer it.

"Hi, darling... Fine. And you? No, Sylvie's here. We're going through my plans... Yes, I will. Ok... Bye." She put down the phone. "That was Nick, checking that I'm ok. He says hi."

Sylvie felt herself flush. God, how was she going to cope tomorrow with everyone here? Why had she agreed to come? Sylvie quickly got her samples out and pressed Maggie for a decision. She needed to get out of there.

ONCE MAGGIE DECIDED ON the finished design, Sylvie packed up and set off down back into town. It was five o'clock and there was a little traffic.

She toyed with the idea of calling Nick. After his revelation yesterday she was beginning to feel a little more relaxed. Why hadn't he called, or texted? And why had he kept his trip from her? They hadn't made any plans to see each other and she was starting to feel that maybe she was running before she could walk. She picked up her phone while she was stationary in traffic. To her horror, she saw it was switched off! It must have been pressed up against something which had turned it off. She hurriedly turned it back on again. Within seconds, five messages beeped in.

'Another 10 hrs of hell til I c u x'
'Come to the SL after work x'
'R u ok?'
'Yr phones off. I'm worried'
'I just rang Mum and yr there call me when yr done x'

She put on her hands free and hit the call button and waited. It didn't even ring.

"Sylvie?"

Her pulse was beating double speed. "Hi. My phone got switched off, I only just realised."

"Jeez, I was going out of my mind. I was about to set off up there. That's why I called Mum, to see if you were still there. Are you okay?" He couldn't hide the concern in his voice.

"Yes I'm fine. I'm on my way down. Traffic's manic." Sylvie felt a-glow. He was really concerned for her.

"You're coming down to mine, aren't you?"

"If you'd like me to." Sylvie sounded cool.

"I'd love you to. Sylvie? What's wrong? Has anything happened? You sound funny."

"Nothing," she lied. Her voice was tight and Nick could hear it.

"Just get here. You can tell me then. God, I missed you today. I really need to touch you."

The butterflies in Sylvie's stomach starting dancing, pushing the cramps out of the way. "I'll be there in ten."

Sylvie pulled up into the parking area and headed to quay eight. Nick was sitting on deck, holding a beer and chewing frantically on his gum. As soon as he saw her he took out his gum and tossed into the bin where it landed on the heap of discarded chewing gum wrappers. He jumped on to the quay and grabbed her face in his hands, planting a hard kiss on her lips.

"I thought I would go mad if you didn't call. This is driving me crazy. I can't do this hiding. I just need to be with you, be able to talk to you and see you."

He kissed her again, softer this time. "Come on, let's go sailing." He lifted her on deck and untied the ropes. Sylvie beamed at him. God; he looked amazing in a white shirt and faded jeans. His golden, tanned face and those blonde streaks from the sun in his hair. It really wasn't fair; all that handsome poured into one person.

Nick expertly pulled out of the marina and headed out. The sun was low in the sky and its rays bounced off of the crests of the waves. Sylvie was sitting on his lap as he steered; it was fast becoming one of her favourite places.

"It's so bright." Sylvie shielded her eyes.

Nick kissed her head and wrapped himself closer to her. "Now, are you going to tell me what's wrong? Don't lie to me, I know something's up."

Sylvie squirmed on his lap. What the hell, she might as well just get it out. "You're going away. Your Mum told me today." God, she felt like a spoilt teenager. He probably had work.

"Yes I am. I told her yesterday." He looked puzzled.

"You never mentioned it to me, that's all." She tried hard to keep the crack in her voice together.

He pulled her round so that he could see her face. He had a confused look on his own face as reached over and slowed the yacht right down.

"I told her that I'm going to the South of France on a business trip this Friday and I'll be back on Wednesday, because I couldn't tell her I was going with you to Athens. Is this why you're so upset? Oh, baby. I had to lie to her because she'd be calling me all weekend."

He pulled her close to him, and then kissed her cheeks repeatedly and then back to her mouth.

Sylvie threw her arms around him and kissed him passionately back, the relief flowing over her. "I thought you were keeping it from me; I didn't even think about our weekend. God, I'm not good at this lying shit. I had your Mum telling me she thinks you have a girlfriend and that she's worried about you, and all the while I was wondering why you hadn't told me you were leaving. What a mess."

He put his arms inside her blouse and rubbed the bare skin on her back. Sylvie pulled herself closer to him.

"Sylvie, I don't play games. That's just not me. I do and say what I mean. Why don't you get that? God, Sylvie, I watched and waited for nearly four months. I play for keeps. Let me drop the anchor." He reached over and pressed the button, then cut the engine. Sylvie smiled and Nick arched his brow.

"Drop the anchor?" she remarked. "That sounds… interesting!"

"You're very naughty, Sylvie. I'll never be able to say that without thinking of what it means to you."

She laughed. He took her hand and pulled her up. He gently raised it to his lips and kissed it tenderly. His blazing eyes fixed on her as she stared at him wide eyed. "Bed," he whispered, and led her below deck.

NICK'S STOMACH RUMBLED AS he laid on the bed, his arm cradling Sylvie.

"I think someone's hungry," Sylvie giggled.

"I didn't eat a thing today. I was so wound up, I forgot. I'll take us closer to shore and get some kebabs. In fact, I'll teach you to steer."

"I do have a boating licence, you know." Sylvie faked being deeply offended.

"Hmm… and how long ago did you get that? And have you ever used it?" Nick teased.

"That better not be a dig at my age. Twenty-five years ago, if you must know. He was a very good teacher.'

"I bet he was!" laughed Nick. "But I'm talking about steering a yacht, not whatever else he was good at teaching you!" He raised his eyebrows in pretend disapproval. "I'm sure he taught you everything you needed to know..." he paused for effect, "for a speed boat. But I'm talking about a completely different kind of equipment! I have to say, I'm a little jealous that you're not a complete novice. I would have loved to have been the first to introduce you to the joys of... sailing."

Sylvie shifted onto her side and propped up her head looked at him. She was smiling at his obvious double entendre. "Oh, you know how it is, being young and in love!" She smirked back. "Have you taught all your girlfriends how to sail?"

"Brigitte, my last serious girlfriend, knew a bit about sailing because her ex-husband had yachts. She wasn't really that enthusiastic about it though. The others were impressed that I had my own boat, even though then it was a much smaller one than this. But to be honest I didn't really want to teach any of them, only Brigitte."

"Maggie said you were very serious about her."

"Yes, I was." He obviously didn't want to explain.

"Sorry, I didn't mean to pry." Sylvie lifted herself up and started to retrieve her discarded clothes. Nick lay on the bed and watched her intently.

"You're not prying. It's in the past. It wasn't a particularly happy time for me. In fact I'd have to say it was probably a time I'd rather wipe from my memory. Though I blame my parents for meddling, looking back she didn't really fight for me. When she saw their resistance she just broke it off and left."

His eyes looked sorrowful, and Sylvie could see that it was painful for him to talk about. She also realised that she was in a very similar position. There was no doubt that there would be resistance when Maggie and Julian found out about them. What worried her was that she knew she'd have to make the decision whether to stay or leave.

Nick kept his eyes on her, trying to read what she was thinking. "I wasn't very good at handling the fallout, so I disappeared for a while. I checked in with Elenora and Vicki; I didn't want them to worry. But it was hard for me to forgive my parents."

"Where did you go?"

"Nowhere in particular. I drifted. The yacht I had then wasn't like this; it was smaller, so I was limited. I stayed for a while in the south of France, built up some contacts there. After a couple of months I came back and told them that if they ever meddled again, they'd lose me."

He pulled himself off the bed and dressed. Then he came up close to where Sylvie was standing and gently brushed her cheek with the back of his hand. She leaned into it and put her arms around him, pulling him close to her. "Come on. Let me show you some of the controls." He lifted her chin up and kissed her. "And then we'll get kebabs." She nodded and smiled.

They got up on deck and Nick started to lift the anchor. "I hear you're coming tomorrow for the wedding video show!"

Crap! She'd forgotten to tell him.

"Yes. Your Dad insisted I be there. I'm not sure that's a good idea. I didn't know how to get out of it and, to be honest, your Mum would have insisted too."

"It'll be fine. They have no reason to suspect anything. Should be interesting." Nick smirked and held her gaze.

"Oh God, this really isn't such a good idea." Sylvie started to panic. "You know your father's bringing me, don't you?"

Nick arched his eyebrow. Obviously this was news to him. "Really?" he pursed his lips together and his eyes clouded over. "No, I didn't know that."

"He insisted he pick me up so that I could drink. Not that I'd touch a drop. I'm going to need my wits about me! What could I say?"

Nick took a deep breath and clenched his jaw. She could see he wasn't happy. He reached for his gum and started to chew. Oh, he was really not pleased.

"Well, I'll have to live with it." He ran his hands through his hair and braved a smile. "I don't think I'll be able to keep this up for long. You know he's going to try and make a move on you. He's been waiting for the right moment. And it'll only make it worse.'

"Let's see how things go this next week, and then we'll tell them. I need to talk to my boys first, and Alex gets back next week. So can we at least wait until then?" Sylvie had her arms draped around his shoulders as she'd repositioned herself on his lap.

"Okay, sure. But then we tell them." He kissed her forehead and squeezed her close.

CHAPTER 18

REVELATIONS

Lilianna was waiting in their usual coffee shop, talking on her phone as Sylvie sat down next to her. She quickly finished her call and turned her full attention to Sylvie.

"Oh my, oh my. Someone looks good."

"Whatever do you mean?" Sylvie flushed, knowing she was going to be bombarded and there was no escape.

"Sylvie, you look like the cat that got the cream. You've got it bad. Boy, have you got it bad. Mr X certainly agrees with you!"

"Will you stop it!" She started fiddling with her spoon. But, to be honest, she was pleased she could talk about it, even if she was emitting the most important detail.

"Come on, spill; you know I won't let up 'til you do. I take it you've seen him a lot, then?"

"Uhuh."

"Come on… and?"

"Well, it's been pretty intense. Something I didn't expect."

"Do you think it's going somewhere? Is there a future, I mean, or is it just… Well, sex, really?"

"Shit, Lilianna!" Sylvie flushed.

"You know I'm not going to pussyfoot around. Well?"

"I'd like it to be more than, well, you know. He says it is for him, but it's complicated. I need to be sure and I really need to talk to the boys too. This will affect them. You know me. I'm not into casual. I'm just not. I'm afraid to be honest, that I'll get hurt and I don't know if I'm up for the heartache. I can feel myself falling in deep and I just hope that what he says is true."

"You love him, don't you?" Lilianna's expression changed. It dawned on her that her dearest friend was not just having a fling, or getting hot and heavy to pass her time. She was serious about this man, whoever it was. Sylvie looked up at her through her lashes and nodded. "God, Sylvie, I thought you were just having a bit of fun at last. What's complicated? He's not married, is he?"

"No, nothing like that," she answered, shocked that Lilianna would even think that. "I really don't want to say right now. It's just that circumstances are not ideal and I'm trying, or should I say *we* are trying, to handle them as best we can."

"How does he feel?"

"He says he wants me. I mean, that he wants to be with me." Lilianna took a deep breath and sat back in her chair. "He said... he loves me." It was a whisper.

"You don't sound convinced."

"That's one of my worries. He says he does, but I don't see how he can."

Lilianna flew forward in her chair and stared directly at Sylvie. "Are you insane, why wouldn't he be in love with you? Why do you have such a low opinion of yourself? You're beautiful, kind, generous and talented. You're a fantastic mother and a loyal friend. Please will you get that? I really don't get why you doubt yourself so much."

Her tone was stern, but her words were sincere. "What happened to you to make you feel that way?" She shook her head and reached for Sylvie's hands.

Sylvie was trying hard not to cry. She wanted to tell her so badly why she felt this way. *Oh, by the way, my husband cheated on me* twice. *First with a young psycho, and then with his secretary! All younger than me! A lot younger than me!*

"Jeez, Sylvie just enjoy it; don't overthink things. If he says he wants to be with you... If I knew who it was, maybe I could help. But I get it. You need to talk to the boys first. They'll find it hard whoever it is, you know that."

Sylvie nodded, blinking back the tears.

"God, I hate seeing you like this." Lilianna squeezed her hands before releasing them.

"There's a lot of baggage Lily. That's all," Sylvie whispered, forcing the tears back.

"Everyone comes with baggage, sweetie. You just need to find someone who loves you enough to help you unpack it. You need and deserve that."

Sylvie looked up at her dearest friend. She always seemed to hit the nail on the head. "Listen, I'll tell you once the boys know. I really have to pass it by them first." Sylvie wiped her eyes as she spoke.

"If they're negative, will you break it off?"

Sylvie shrugged and shook her head, as though the thought was too painful.

"You can't, then. If the thought of it makes you feel like that, they'll have to lump it. They're old enough to be objective. They'll be getting on with their lives soon enough, and you'll be alone."

"I have to think of him, too. My boys might be accepting, but his family might not. They might make it hard for him too. Like I said, it's complicated."

Lilianna nodded, but Sylvie knew that her comment had made Lilianna think that her Mr X had children, rather than over protective parents!

NICK HAD PASSED BY the photographers and collected the proof albums and DVD for the evening's soiree.

He'd got up early to Maggie's, mainly because he wanted to be there when Sylvie turned up. He wasn't at all happy that she was being driven up by Julian. It was going to be hard not being natural around her as it was. But with the added pressure of his father being all doe eyed over her, it really was going to test him. His blood was beginning to boil at just the thought of it, so he decided to cool off in the pool.

He swam twenty lengths and hauled himself out and reached for his towel. Maggie had just finished putting together the nibbles and food for her guests and had decided to join him on the terrace. It was still very warm as the sun was receding. She had brought him out a beer and retrieved some more chewing gum. He seemed to be chewing his way through an extraordinary amount these days.

"Nick? I want to ask you something, but I don't want you to jump down my throat. It's just that you know I worry about you, and that's the only reason. I'm not trying to pry." Maggie kept her eyes on him as he continued to dry himself off. She could tell he was feeling uneasy.

"What is it, Mum?" Nick knew where this conversation was going, and he really didn't like it. He knew his Mum wasn't a fool, so he didn't want to lie, but he was most definitely not ready to tell her what she wanted to know. He'd have to tread carefully.

"I've noticed that over the last couple of days you've been a lot more… Um… I'm not sure, really… Happier. It's more than that, actually; you seem very happy. I'm not saying you were miserable before, it's just you seemed to have mood swings. Happy one minute, then you'd go into your quiet mode. Like something was getting to you. Anyway, you just seem… Well… It's really great seeing you like this. Back to your old self again."

She wasn't actually asking the question she wanted to. Maggie waited to see his response before she pressed him.

He sat down and reached for his chewing gum. He was getting his nicotine cravings again.

"Is that a bad thing?" He smiled slightly, trying to make a joke of it.

"Of course not, silly!" She placed herself opposite him and took his hand that was fidgeting with the wrapper. "I was wondering what had changed. For it to have such a significant effect on you."

He was looking down at their hands, and his cheek muscle started to twitch as he clenched and unclenched his jaw. He couldn't answer her. To be honest, he didn't know what to say; how could he? His situation was something he couldn't talk about, and especially to Maggie.

Maggie knew she'd have to just ask him straight out, however uncomfortable it made them both feel. She was worried about him and she didn't want him to get hurt, not again.

"I just thought that it might be because you'd found someone. A girl, I mean. Is that what it is?"

Nick pulled his hand away and rested both of them behind his head and took a deep breath. How was he going to answer this?

"Look Mum, I know you're worried. I know because of what's gone on in my past that you're a little wary of my personal life. But I can handle it fine without you or anyone else getting involved."

"I know darling, I'm not trying to be nosey. I just don't want you to get hurt again. I'm not trying to get involved; I promised myself that I'd never do that again. I'm really pleased you've found someone that makes you feel the way you so obviously feel."

He knew she meant it, but he wasn't sure she'd feel the same way if she knew who it was.

"Well if you really want to know, Mum, she's the best thing that's ever happened to me." He took another deep breath as he spoke the words. "It's not some fling, or something that happened overnight. I've known her a while. But it's only recently become more." He didn't trust himself to say any more than that, but he felt unbelievable relief being able to say even that much.

"Well, that's great. So you were friends first. That's really wonderful." Maggie was a little relieved. "It's important to have more than just attraction in a relationship."

She leaned back in her chair. Nick shifted uneasily. He loved his mother deeply and they had a very unique relationship, but he did feel awkward talking about his personal life with her sometimes. She was very much a 'sharer'; something he wasn't altogether comfortable with.

"Whoever she is, Nick, she definitely has a good effect on you. I'm sure she's wonderful; anyone who can make you shine like you have over the past couple of days is fine in my books!"

Nick leaned back forward and rested his arms on the table again. "I'm glad you feel that way, Mum, because I really think this is it for me. I can't imagine being with anyone else."

He paused to let his words sink in. "It's important to me that you remember this conversation, Mum. What I mean is that you can see how happy she makes me." He was trying to prepare her. Maggie cocked her to one side trying to assess what he was saying. "Like I said, it's not some whirlwind romance. She's been in my life a while, and I fell in love with her as I got to know her. She means everything to me."

Maggie looked at him, and softly smiled. She could see that he was being totally honest with her, which she knew was hard for her. After his past relationships, she knew he didn't want anyone interfering again. She made the decision that whoever this mystery girl was, she would accept her if only because she could see how totally in love her son was, and that she'd managed to bring back the happy man he had once been.

He got up and kissed her head. "I'd better get showered and changed. They'll all be here in half an hour." He picked up his beer and phone and headed up to his room.

JULIAN PARKED UP OUTSIDE Sapphire Developers and tried to gather his thoughts. He was nervous, which was very unlike him. He was ten minutes early but he really couldn't sit in the car park until six thirty. He decided to pop and see Zach. His car was still here.

Sylvie had asked him to pick her up from the office as she'd had a late meeting with the lawyers in preparation for her trip to Athens. Markus was out tomorrow so she wasn't going to be at work, and then she was leaving on Friday. She'd arranged for her car to be taken home so that she would have it in the morning. He got out of his car and headed for Zach's office.

Julian walked to the reception area and found Zach seeing off the lawyers.

"So once Sylvie has signed the papers, the final funds will be transferred to our account?"

He was confirming the last details with two young lawyers. They re-confirmed all the details as Zach's eye caught Julian. He smiled and motioned him to go to his office.

Julian sat himself down on the leather couch and started fidgeting with the coasters on the coffee table.

"Hello, there. I wasn't expecting you today. I didn't miss an appointment, did I? I'm afraid with everything going on I'm a little absent minded." He leaned over to shake Julian's hand.

"No, nothing like that. I'm picking up Sylvie and we're off up to Maggie's to see the wedding photos and DVD. I was a bit early so I thought I'd drop in and see you."

Zach eyed him up before he sat down next to him. "You look a little... well, nervous, to be honest. Are you alright?"

Julian exhaled and leaned forward as if he didn't want anyone to hear what he was about to say, even though they were alone. "Well, you see... Sylvie seems to be a lot better these past few days, and I thought that I might ask her out over the weekend. But with Markus out tomorrow and her leaving for four days, I haven't really found a window of opportunity. So I thought I'd... Oh shit, I feel like a teenager! I wanted to see if she wanted to take it further than just friends. At least let her think about it while she's away." He looked up at Zach nervously as he leaned back.

Zach had his eyebrows raised. "Oh, I see. Well she does seem a lot like her old self again. So you're going to spring this on her tonight?"

Julian nodded and looked for Zach's approval.

"Christ Julian, I don't know. I was never any good at this stuff. *Lilianna* asked *me* out, for fuck's sake! I'm sure I would have still been single if she hadn't." He laughed, thinking back. "I mean it. Thank God." He shook his head, smiling.

"Well I have to make my move. She knows how I feel so it won't be a shock. What's the worst she can say... no? I'll have to live with the rejection. Better than hanging around and waiting. It's been... Well it's been hell, actually. I'd rather know."

Part Three – Spring

Zach shrugged, as though he really was at a loss. "I don't know what to say. Good luck then?" Zach arched his eyebrows as he spoke.

"I'd better go and tell her I'm here." And with that he got up and headed for Sylvie's office, leaving Zach staring after him.

Thank God he had Lilianna! Poor bugger! he mused.

SYLVIE WAS PUTTING HER papers in her briefcase. Actually, it was Chris's briefcase; she'd never got round to getting her own. Yet another reminder of him. She really should get herself a new one. She ran her fingers over the monograms; C.S.

She logged off her computer and looked at the time. Six twenty five; Julian would be here any minute. She really wasn't looking forward to this evening. She'd tried to get out of it, but Nick insisted that she come. As she sat there, her phone beeped a message. She knew instantly who it was.

'Can't wait to c u x'

She smiled and felt those butterflies leaping about in her stomach again. How was it that just the slightest contact with him made her feel like this? Friday seemed an age away. She had tonight to get through, and then Thursday. At least Markus would keep her busy.

'R u there?'

She replied as a huge smile spread across her face. The reply was almost instant.

'Yes, ready and waiting… impatiently!'

She chuckled to herself and didn't hear Julian come through her open door.

"Hi, what's made you so happy?" Sylvie jumped out of her skin and then felt her whole body heat up. "Sorry, I startled you."

She nervously stood up, dropping her phone. "Yes, I was miles away and didn't hear you." He was walking over to her, and leaned in to kiss her cheek as he always did. His arm lingered around her waist. Sylvie stepped back to pick up her phone, but he managed to get there first.

She could feel herself start to panic as he slowly handed it back to her. His eyes were locked on hers as he gently placed the phone into her outstretched hand.

"You were lucky, no harm done," he smiled, as his eyes flitted momentarily over the phone. She quickly closed her fingers around the screen so that the message was hidden from sight.

"I'm so clumsy sometimes. I just need to reply and we can get off."

She knew that if she didn't Nick would text her again or, even worse, call. She felt so guilty, and they weren't even in the same vicinity! She took a deep breath, trying to calm her heart beat which was hammering against her chest.

`'Just setting off now x'`

"There, let's go." She forced a smile. As she picked up her bag and briefcase they headed towards the door; Julian took her briefcase and gently placed his hand against the small of her back, guiding her to the elevator.

Oh no – he was most definitely more touchy feely today!

THE DRIVE UP TO Maggie's was torture. Throughout the whole journey Sylvie babbled incessantly about anything she could think of so that Julian was unable to start up any kind of conversation. Thank goodness he was well-mannered and didn't interrupt her. She managed to cover a multitude of topics, from Maggie's redecoration, to the Athens trip, and she even touched on the weather!

They pulled up outside Maggie's and Sylvie sighed inwardly. Well, at least they had got there without Julian asking her any questions. He turned off the ignition and speedily turned to face Sylvie as she released her seat belt. He raised his hand and stroked her cheek. Sylvie felt like a rabbit caught in headlights. She tensed up involuntarily and stared into his amazing blue eyes.

"God, you're beautiful, Sylvie."

She swallowed hard and blinked repeatedly as though she was trying to make sure she was actually experiencing this unexpected outburst.

"I know you said that you weren't ready for anything more than just friendship. But I have to be honest, as everyday slips by I can think of nothing else but you. I'm crazy about you; you know that, don't you?"

Sylvie sat perfectly still, her brown eyes still fixed on his. She closed them and took a deep breath. *Crap!*

If she was honest with herself, she did have feelings for Julian. She had grown used to him being around her, looking out for her. She'd loved his company too and the fact that he was so refreshingly honest about himself. She didn't want to hurt him; that idea filled her with dread. He was perfect for her, she knew he was, but yet she couldn't get past the idea that he was Chris's friend, and that made it weird somehow.

She also knew that Maggie was still in love with him, and Sylvie believed that Julian probably still had strong feelings for her too. Apart from that, she could never hurt Maggie. She opened up her eyes and was met by his blazing gaze again. His face broke into a soft smile.

"Too much? Well, I had to give you something to think about over the next few days," he joked. "I'm not saying you're over Chris; it's just that I can see you're back to the Sylvie I first met. So that's why I felt I needed you to know that my feelings are still the same for you."

Sylvie placed her hand over his. "Julian, you know how really very special you are to me. And if I'm honest, my feelings for you have changed, but not in the way you want."

His eyes narrowed as he tried to comprehend what she was saying.

"We've grown so close over the last few months, and I feel that we have a… unique relationship. But I think what you have unfortunately not realised is that in getting to know you I have also got to know Maggie."

Julian leant back a fraction and tilted his head, as though he was trying to work out where this was going.

"She has become a dear and valued friend, to me and I would find it very difficult to have a more serious relationship with you because of her."

Julian reached for her hands and pulled her a little closer. "Why? She thinks you're wonderful; she loves you, Sylvie." Julian felt a glimmer of hope. If the only reason was Maggie that was holding her back, he knew it was a non-issue. She adored Sylvie.

"I know, and I her. Julian… For such an intelligent man, though, you really are stupid." Sylvie spoke gently as she looked deep into his piercing blue eyes. "She's still in love with you; she never stopped. How have you never realised?"

His eyes widened in disbelief and he shook his head.

"Yes, she does. No one would put up with your way of life and still have you so much a part of her life. You only put up with that if you really love someone."

Julian let go of her hands and ran his hands through his hair. *He really didn't know. Shit, had she done the right thing?.*

There was a tap at the window, and Sylvie shot round to see who it was. Vicki's face beamed at them. They hadn't realised she'd pulled up next to them. Sylvie opened her door.

"Hi there. Did you just get here too?"

"Yes, we were just going in." Sylvie stepped out of the car, relieved by the interruption. Julian gradually got out of the car, still with a puzzled look on his face.

"Hi Dad, are you okay? You look like you've seen a ghost!"

He managed a smile and recovered some of his usual composure. "Fine, darling. Just tired." He walked round to where she was and kissed her.

She quickly linked his arm and they set off to the door. Julian turned back to look at Sylvie. His face was still pained from the revelation, and he nodded his response to Sylvie as she mouthed 'Are you alright?'

They all got to the door, which was almost immediately opened by Nick.

"Hi Nick." Julian hugged his son tightly and passed through followed by Vicki. Sylvie saw him walk straight through to the lounge and say: "I need a drink."

Nick blocked the doorway and looked down at Sylvie. His eyes bore into her full of questions that he couldn't ask.

Sylvie leaned up to him, as she always did to kiss his cheek. "Hi."

He held her close, knowing that everyone was out of sight. They were just inside the doorway. "Hi. Is everything okay?" he whispered into her ear. "You were sitting out there for ages."

"Fine. We'll talk later." Sylvie gave him a reassuring smile.

He squeezed her tighter and allowed his hand to slip down to her bottom. "You smell amazing and feel incredible," he murmured into her ear.

"Behave!"

This was going to be a very difficult evening.

"What's it worth?" Nick pulled back and winked at her. His expression was a mixture of total yearning and mischief.

CHAPTER 19

PARIS IN THE SPRINGTIME

Maggie was sitting on the terrace drinking a glass of white wine. There was a slight breeze that rustled the fallen petals around the garden. Julian momentarily stopped to watch her. She looked serene and peaceful, as she always did.

Looking at her now, he realised that he depended on her totally, how had he never realised that their lives had never really ever separated? They had always been through everything together, hand in hand, in unison. He shook his head, trying to process Sylvie's recent revelations. He loved Maggie, deeply; they had shared so much throughout their lives, but the idea that Maggie was still in love with him had shaken him like a thunderbolt. He thought that that part of their lives was gone, finished with.

Knowing that Sylvie knew about Maggie's feelings towards him made things impossible. He knew that Sylvie was loyal and that she could never hurt Maggie. It was a lot to take in, even harder coming from Sylvie. His feelings for her he knew. He'd been keeping them in check for what seemed like an eternity. With this latest piece of information, though, he really didn't know how he felt.

Vicki's voice alerted Maggie's attention that her guests were arriving, and she turned to look over into the house. This prompted Julian to walk out to her. Her face instantly broke into her radiant smile.

"Hi Mags." He leant down and kissed her cheek.

"Hi, did you just come? I'm sure I heard Vicki's voice."

"Yes, we arrive the same time. I brought Sylvie; she's talking to Nick I think."

"Do you want a drink? Wine, beer? Elenora and Pavlos are on the way, they just called. They're picking up Rita and Harry."

"I'll get myself a whisky, you stay here, I'll get it."

She stared at him, trying to fathom out his mood. He seemed out of sorts. "Are you alright? You look a little stressed."

"Just been a bit of a rough day. A drink will help, and seeing Elenora, too."

Maggie grinned at him. "It's been very weird her not being around. I've missed her too."

Julian nodded in agreement. He walked back to the house. Sylvie was making her way to the terrace to see Maggie. She stopped at the threshold of the French windows that lead out to the terrace.

"Sorry, I thought you knew. I shouldn't have sprung it on you."

He shook his head as though he was trying to clear it, and forced a grin. He put his hand on her arm as a way of reassuring her that he was alright with her for telling him, and his eyes locked onto hers. He was very handsome, and he had a vulnerability about him that made it hard not to be drawn to him. But his eyes were saying so many things right now that she couldn't quite grasp which emotion he was feeling. Was it hurt, confusion? Maybe acceptance? She couldn't quite put her finger on it. Vicki and Nick were coming through from the kitchen, and Julian let go of Sylvie's arm.

"What would you like to drink? I'm just going to get myself a whisky," he asked her, so as not to alert anyone to their exchange.

"It's alright, Dad, I've got Sylvie one," Nick interrupted, before Sylvie could answer.

She slowly turned round to look at Nick and tried not to glare at him. He was holding a large whisky with ice and his face was hard set.

Oh crap, he wasn't going to make this easy.

"That looks perfect; I think I'll get one of those too."

Julian headed to the drinks cabinet as Vicki passed by her to meet her Mum out on the terrace. Nick walked up to Sylvie and handed her the drink. His eyes were blazing and Sylvie could feel her pulse start to race. His cheek muscle was moving as he clenched his teeth.

"Do you need some chewing gum?" Sylvie asked, overly sweetly. He took a deep breath and closed his eyes. When he opened his eyes, Sylvie could see he was searching for the answers. "Nick, please don't make this harder than it already is. Nothing's happened, really."

"I thought I'd be able to handle your being here, but it's fucking torture," he whispered as he touched her arm; sending electric sparks throughout her whole body. They could hear Elenora opening the front door letting herself, Pavlos and her parents-in-law in.

"Showtime!"

He dropped his hand and arched his eyebrows. Sylvie took a huge gulp of her drink.

Within seconds, the house was buzzing. Elenora looked radiant as she handed out small gifts for everyone. Pavlos was getting everyone a drink as he admired his new wife. They looked so much in love, it was a pleasure to watch. They were constantly touching each other, and it made Sylvie feel a pang of jealousy and made her even more uneasy.

Vicki and Maggie were getting out the nuts and olives as Nick set up the DVD and Julian was sat with Rita and Harry. Sylvie clutched her drink and watched the family move comfortably around one another.

She had that feeling again, the feeling that she didn't belong. Her heart lurched thinking, about how things would change if Nick and she were together. The whole family would be ripped apart. She really shouldn't be here. Why had she said that she would come? She should have feigned a headache and kept away.

The worst thing was that she couldn't leave as she'd come with Julian. Maggie spotted her looking into her drink, and she felt a huge sense of sorrow for her friend.

"Sylvie, do you mind coming and checking on the roast in the oven?" she asked. Her friend looked out of sorts, and she wanted her to get involved. Maggie realised that events like this were hard for her.

"Sure."

Nick allowed his eyes to follow her as she moved over to the kitchen. He could see she was feeling uncomfortable.

Sylvie went over to the oven and opened it. "It needs a bit longer."

Maggie nodded. Of course, she'd already known it did.

"Well in that case, we can start watching the DVD, then we can eat in about an hour. Here, take these bowls for me and I'll get the rest."

Nick was drawing the curtains so that the room became dark, and Julian had rearranged all the chairs for everyone to sit down. Pavlos was sat on the armchair with Elenora curled up on his lap. Harry and Rita were sitting on one sofa, and Vicki joined them. Sylvie chose one of the wing-backed chairs, which were positioned between the two sofas. Maggie sat on the adjacent sofa and Julian joined her so that he was between Sylvie and Maggie.

Nick adjusted the picture and turned to find a seat. His eyes flitted from Julian to Sylvie then he walked purposefully in the direction of the sofa on the other side of Sylvie. He perched himself on the armrest, allowing himself to be as close as he could to Sylvie without it being obvious. Vicki tried to make room for him but he told her he was fine. His leg was inches away from Sylvie's hand.

"Okay, ready?" Nick said, and he pointed the remote to TV and pressed it, starting the DVD.

Sylvie's pulse was racing again. If she moved her hand just a little, she'd be able to touch him. The urge was so strong that it frightened her. Nick shifted on the armrest, allowing his leg to rest up against the armchair. He was doing it on purpose. Everyone was so transfixed on the screen that his movements were totally undetected by anyone, apart from Sylvie.

Sylvie sat frozen, her drink in one hand and the other resting on the armrest. His taut, denim-clad thigh was only an inch away.

The DVD carried on playing, showing all of the activity from before the service. There was Pavlos' parents' house, where he was getting ready, and all their traditional preparations. Then it moved to Maggie's house, showing all the commotion of Elenora getting ready. Nick rested his hand on his leg, and ever-so slowly allowed his hand to graze Sylvie's hand. She gasped as the surge of electricity passed through her whole body. She saw Nick's slight smile from the corner of her eye.

He really wasn't playing fair!

The video shifted to outside the church and focused on the various guests. Nick's hand slid back down his leg again and this time he squeezed her hand. Sylvie took a deep breath and squeezed back then pulled her hand away. Within a second, Nick paused the video.

Oh crap, what was he going to do?

"Intermission! We should eat and watch the rest after." His voice was playful, even though his expression was strained. There was a collective moan, but they were all in agreement. Maggie got up to go check on dinner and Vicki pulled open the curtains.

"Let me help, Maggie. Shall I set the table?" Sylvie got out of her chair. She couldn't sit so close to Nick, she was on fire! She was sure she was flushed. The temperature in the room seemed to have risen.

"Oh, that would be great. Nick, can you get all the mats and stuff out?"

Oh no! She was trying to get distance from him, and now they'd be alone.

"Sure, Mum." He got up and headed to the dining-room, Sylvie reluctantly followed. Nick opened up the drawers of the sideboard and lifted out a tablecloth and mats. He turned around and handed them to Sylvie, ensuring that their hands touched and his eyes, his incredible eyes, bore into her.

"Stop it," Sylvie mouthed, her eyes widening.

He winked at her. She took them to the table and started to open up the tablecloth. Nick collected up the cutlery and they started to place everything around the table. Nick purposely brushed up against Sylvie at every opportunity, causing a chaotic surge of emotions every time.

"Nick, will you please behave," Sylvie pleaded.

"Oh I am. Believe me." His eyebrows arched again. "What were you talking about in the car?" He was very close to her as he placed the knives and forks at the place settings as Sylvie expertly folded the napkins. "Sylvie, I'm cracking up here. Did he try anything?"

Sylvie took a deep breath and looked at him. His face was ashen with worry, or was it panic? She knew she couldn't go into details now.

"Can we talk later? I can't tell you everything in a few seconds, please, Nick. It's fine really, but it isn't the time or the place." She tried to reassure him with a smile, and she reached over to squeeze his hand.

Nick clenched his jaw and ran his hand through his hair, but his face seemed to relax a little. He nodded and strained a smile. "Forty-eight hours of hell," he turned and stared at her, "then heaven?" he murmured. He looked so torn, it made Sylvie's heart ache. She was making him miserable, why had she come?

"I should have never come tonight."

"I'd rather see you under these circumstances, than not at all. Jesus, I've got to get through tonight and tomorrow yet. This is even harder than when we weren't together. I wish I could fast forward, like the video." He grinned.

"Or better still, pause and rewind to yesterday afternoon," Sylvie giggled. It took all her strength not to wrap her arms around him and kiss him. He really made her feel alive and being so close to him was intoxicating. When it was just them, everything seemed to pale into insignificance. It was as though they were in their own cocoon.

"I really want to kiss you. Shit, this is…" He looked at her as he leaned onto the table with both his hands, his eyes scorching. He let go of the table and stalked into the kitchen.

What was that all about?

Sylvie walked back to the lounge, keeping her distance from Nick. She found everyone apart from Maggie and Nick still sitting there, discussing the photos. There were around four albums of proofs, and everyone was poring over them.

Julian looked up as Sylvie came in. "Everything okay?"

"Yes, I think we should go sit down. I'll give Maggie a hand."

Rita got up and volunteered her help too. At least there would be someone else in the kitchen too!

Maggie was putting all the food on the serving platters. "Oh great, you can take these out. Nick, open up the wine and see what everyone wants to drink."

Nick was leaning broodily up against the kitchen counter, his eyes fixed on Sylvie. He looked stunning even when he was pissed off. He opened up the fridge to retrieve a bottle of wine and rummaged in the drawer for the opener, only allowing his eyes to move from Sylvie momentarily. Sylvie quickly picked up the platters and took them through to the dining room, closely followed by Rita.

"Everything smells and looks wonderful, Maggie," Rita gushed. "You really shouldn't have gone to so much trouble."

Before long, everyone was sitting down and passing around the food. Sylvie sat between Harry and Vicki, trying to put as much distance between her and Nick. He came and placed himself directly opposite her next to Maggie. She didn't know what was worse; that he was opposite her, or that Maggie would be able to see her squirm under his intense gaze.

"Tell us about Paris, Elenora. Did you bore Pavlos to death trailing round all the galleries and museums?" Julian joked.

"Dad! He loves going to them, don't you?" Elenora put her head lovingly on Pavlos shoulder.

"Of course I do, sweetheart." He winked at Julian, as though he was in on a private joke.

"See. It was beautiful. The trees were in blossom. It's true what they say; Paris is beautiful in the spring time."

"I love Paris in the springtime!" Maggie commented wistfully, and looked at Julian. He smiled back, as though remembering something.

"Dum di dum di dum da," Julian added, and Maggie started to laugh.

"Now I feel old!"

"What are you two talking about?" Elenora looked between her parents.

"It's from a song, darling. When Dad and I were at university we were huge fans of Genesis. One of their songs has that line in it, on the live album."

"The Wardrobe song!" Julian laughed, "We loved that song. Though I think Phil Collins stole the quote from someone else." He was shaking his head, Maggie beamed at him, obviously remembering a shared memory.

"Cole Porter," Sylvie murmured.

Julian spun round and looked at her. "Really, was it his quote?"

Maggie looked stunned at her, surprised that she would know.

"Yes, from Can Can the musical. But Frank Sinatra said it in the film." The whole table looked at Sylvie. Nick smiled and seemed to relish the idea that she was so knowledgeable. Sylvie chuckled. "Now I feel old! I loved that song. The Genesis one, I mean; well, both actually."

"Never heard of it." Vicki looked over to Sylvie.

"We went to see them... how many times?" asked Julian.

"Four," answered Maggie. "We went to loads of concerts when we were dating. The Rolling Stones, Elton John, even Bruce Springsteen."

"Oh my God, you really *are* old!" Vicki laughed, and Elenora joined in.

Sylvie smiled to herself. Well there it was, the age gap gaping like the Grand Canyon. Maggie and Julian were smirking at each other. Their connection was obvious to everyone, and Sylvie once again felt out of place. She couldn't bring herself to look up at Nick. She could feel his eyes on her.

She picked up her drink and drained it. So much for keeping a level head!

Sylvie kept her eyes on her plate as Julian and Maggie spoke of their honeymoon in Paris.

"We stayed in this cheap hotel not far from the Eiffel tower. I remember the sheets!" Maggie giggled.

"Oh my… I forgot about those. They were starched within in an inch of their lives. We both had burn marks from the friction!" Julian shook his head and laughed. "And you dragged me round all the art galleries. We went to the Louvre at least four times. We ate kilos of snails and oysters and chocolate mousse. Oh, and the Calvados!" He fiddled with his fork and looked wistful. "Seems like a lifetime ago."

His eyes rose up to meet Maggie's. They were met by hers, and their look spoke a thousand words.

Elenora, Vicki and Nick watched their parents reminisce, and then in unison they turned to each other, unspoken emotions passing from each of them.

"We only went twice to the Louvre, so I got off lightly then," joked Pavlos. Everyone laughed as Elenora playfully punched his arm.

"Let me give you a hand." Sylvie rose from her chair as Maggie began to collect the plates. Rita and the girls also stood, picking up platters and plates as they left the table.

"I'll bring the dessert into the lounge so we can watch the last part of the video," called Maggie.

Nick moved swiftly to the lounge and watched Sylvie as she helped load the dishwasher. Her face was set hard and he could tell she was tense. She went over to her bag and rummaged for something. He saw her pull out a small plastic bottle. Opening it, she then popped two large tablets into her mouth. She glanced over to Nick, feeling his stare and smiled weakly. Then she picked up her bag and headed for the bathroom.

Nick scanned the room quickly. Harry and Pavlos were poring over the photos. Julian was preparing coffee with Vicki and Elenora. Rita and Maggie were putting out the desserts. He decided, in that split second, to see where Sylvie was. He slipped through the dining room door to the hallway and headed to the downstairs bathroom. As he reached the door, Sylvie was just opening the door to come back out.

"Oh," she gasped.

"Are you alright? You were looking a little off in there. I was worried." He lifted his hand to her cheek and gently stroked it.

"I'm fine, just an upset stomach." She swallowed, trying to keep the burning sensation in check. She had the most sensitive stomach, and with any kind of upset or stress she'd automatically cramp or, at worst, vomit. She took a deep breath. "We'd better get back; they'll be looking for us."

"Let me take you home if you're not feeling well." His eyes searched hers for some inkling as to what was really troubling her.

"No, no. I'm fine; I don't want to spoil tonight for all of you. Really, come on; let's go back in."

He leant into her and gently kissed her soft lips. She closed her eyes and sighed as she allowed herself to fall back against the door. Nick held her face as his kiss became more urgent and Sylvie dropped her bag so that she could grab his hair. He pushed up against her, pinning her hard up against the door, and she could feel his built up tension being released. She craved his touch, his hands on her, and being so close to him and not being able to was torture. He pulled away, gasping, shaking his head and stepping back as though he needed distance.

"Fuck, I want you so bad. Let me take you home." He ran his hands through his hair and rested them on his head as he exhaled.

Sylvie shook her head and clenched her eyes shut. "Just go back in. Please, Nick."

He looked at her, his eyes burning with emotion. He took a moment to calm himself down then he stalked back to the lounge. He knew she was right, but he couldn't bear it. What was worse was that he knew his Dad was going to take her home.

Sylvie went back into the bathroom and splashed water on her face, then carefully patted it dry. The antacids had done nothing. Her stomach felt like there was someone having a sword fight in there! She picked up her bag and made her way back to the lounge. She was met by Julian, who had come to see if she was alright.

"There you are. We're about to start the second half. Are you alright? You look at little pale." His face was full of concern.

"Just an upset stomach. I'll be fine."

"Let me take you home. I can watch it another day." He put his arm around her, guiding her to where everyone else was.

"No, no, please don't fuss. Really, I'm fine." Sylvie's eye caught Nick staring at them as he chewed vigorously on his gum.

"If you're sure. I think there's only an hour left."

Sylvie nodded and smiled at him, hoping that would pacify him. She really didn't want to leave earlier. She knew Nick would be on tenterhooks. Sylvie sat herself down in the armchair and sat rigid as the video was restarted by a stony-faced Nick who was gripping a beer.

Sylvie placed her hands on her lap and searched for her rings.

CHAPTER 20

MIXED EMOTIONS

Julian pulled up outside of Sylvie's, and switched off the engine. They'd just exchanged small talk on the journey home, but Sylvie knew he was going to carry on the conversation that Vicki had interrupted a few hours earlier.

"Thank you for bringing me home. It was a lovely evening." Sylvie unbuckled her seat belt, and Julian grasped at her hand and held it tightly. Her eyes looked up at him, and in the pale moonlight she could see his pained expression.

"Sylvie, I meant what I said earlier." He took a deep breath. "My feelings for you are still the same. I'm in love with you, and even in the light of what you told me they won't change. Maggie and I are complicated. I love her, but to be honest, I'm not sure I can go back; especially because of my feelings for you.

"It's ironic, really. I wanted you both to become friends so that if you and I became more it wouldn't be awkward. I wanted her to like you for you, not as my... Well, it would seem like that's backfired on me." He let go of her hand and rubbed his face as he thought about how differently he'd envisaged this evening going.

"Julian, I'm sorry; truly, I am. If circumstances had been different... It's not only because of Maggie. I don't want you to resent her. I never told her about what you said to be me, about how you felt. It's true, I could never hurt her like that, but I only see you as a friend, a very dear friend. You're a good man, Julian. You mean a lot to me, and how you've been over the last six months has proven to me that I'm unbelievably lucky to have you in my life."

Julian gripped the steering wheel as she spoke.

"Julian?" Sylvie rested her hand on his tense arm and he turned back again to face her, his eyes full of sorrow. However, he managed a weak smile.

"I'm sorry," she murmured

He nodded and undid his belt, and climbed out of the car. He swiftly opened the door for her and stepped back for her to get out. Then within a split second he put his arm around her waist and she gasped. She gazed up at him, his expression determined. Then he reached up to her face and gently caressed her cheek.

Sylvie's heart pounded against her chest. *Oh no, what was he doing?*

Julian hesitated for a millisecond then leant down to her and kissed her on the lips; gently at first as if he was testing the water. Sylvie stilled for a second, but didn't resist, allowing Julian to hold her even closer. Feeling that this was a signal, that she was receptive, he took the kiss deeper.

Sylvie was dumbfounded, and it took her a few seconds to realise what was happening. She tightened her mouth and pulled back from him, and immediately he let her go and stepped back. His eyes were wary, and he waited for a backlash as he realised that he'd stepped over the line.

Sylvie stood with her eyes clenched shut as a multitude of emotions swept over her. She was shocked, then angry, but as the seconds slipped by she felt her stomach churn and the butterflies skipped softly around.

Oh, God, what the hell was going on?

"I'm sorry Sylvie, please forgive me. I've behaved… Well, actually, I haven't behaved. I just needed to see what it felt like, to kiss you. I'm so sorry, I couldn't help myself. I've behaved like an adolescent and stepped way over the line."

She could hear the panic in his voice. Sylvie opened up her eyes and carefully looked up at him. His eyes were scared, and tainted with a little shame. Sylvie really couldn't see him this way. He had never looked vulnerable to her, and his stance made her heart melt. She had caused him this pain. Julian had always been so confident and strong in her eyes. Someone she could depend on. And now she was witnessing him in a new light.

"Don't, Julian." She held up her hand, motioning him to stop his apology. "It's okay, really. It's been a long, difficult day. I think I had better go in now. I'll speak to you later."

She turned away from him and turned her key into the door. She turned round and strained a smile at him, and then quickly entered the threshold and closed the door behind her. She leant against the door and closed her eyes, waiting to hear his car pull away. Within what seemed an age she heard the roar of the engine as Julian's Maserati pulled out of the driveway and down the hill.

Sylvie let herself slide down the door and she collapsed in a heap at the bottom. What had happened? She felt giddy and confused. Was it from the shock? Or was it from... Oh, she didn't want to go there! Oh God, why was she feeling like this?

She sat up straight and shook her head. She felt ashamed to admit – it even to herself – that she, for a split second, had reciprocated the kiss. And, what was worse, she had felt something. How was that possible? She focused on Nick and summoned up how she felt for him. Her heart beat faster and her stomach lurched, making her whole body glow. So, no doubt there then. So what was that, then? What was the feeling she felt for Julian?

As if on cue her phone rang, and she knew instantly who it was.

"Hi."

"Hi. Are you okay?" Nick's voice was strained and cautious.

"I'm fine, just my stomach. It'll pass."

"Sylvie, are you going to tell me what the hell went down tonight? I'm dying here."

"We just talked, Nick. Cleared the air. That's all." She was thankful he couldn't see her as her face flushed, thinking back to only a few moments ago. The last thing she needed was Nick knowing about his father's declaration and her revelations, not to mention that kiss!

"I wanted to come over but I've had too much to drink and really shouldn't drive. I'm still up at my Mum's. I've been going out of my mind. I won't get to see you tomorrow either because you're tied up all day." He paused, and Sylvie could tell he was waiting for some sort of answer. "Sylvie please, talk to me. Tell me what happened. It can't be any worse than what I'm imagining!"

She knew she'd have to tell him something, even if she omitted some of the disturbing details. "Your Dad is a very good friend of mine, Nick. We work together closely and to be honest, he's been a huge help to me over the last six months. So I had to speak to him and make him realise that we were just that. Very good friends and I really hope that never changes, whatever happens. I don't want to hurt anyone, Nick, your father included. What we actually spoke about is really immaterial. Having said that, your Dad knows and understands that we can only ever be friends."

"Did he...?"

"Nick please don't ask for details. Julian and I have a history that's never going to change, so please don't make it harder than it already is. It's been a rough day and, to be perfectly truthful, I really can't deal with any more tonight."

"You're angry."

"No I'm not. It's just been stressful."

"I know what you're thinking about, please don't. Don't put a cloud over us. Tonight I saw how you looked, how you felt."

"Well it was hard to avoid, Nick. We're a generation apart. That was patently clear tonight, there's no point in hiding it. Half the things we talked about tonight happened before you were born!" Sylvie rested her head on her bent knees and sighed. "Everyone was happy and comfortable together, and all I could think about was how that would be shattered."

"Sylvie, my family are going to have to accept it. If they want to see me happy, they're going to have to live with it. I can't live my life for them, not anymore. And I've told you I don't care about the age. Why don't you get that?"

Sylvie fell silent as she sat in the darkness on the floor in her hallway. Her emotions were raw, and she was glad that Markus would be here tomorrow. He would distract her from all of this as only Markus could.

"I'm really tired, Nick. I need to get some sleep."

"Alright baby, you get to bed."

"Goodnight Nick," she sighed.

"Goodnight baby, sweet dreams."

Sylvie looked down at her phone and saw three missed calls from Julian. *Crap!* She couldn't deal with him now. She picked herself off the floor and went straight upstairs and crawled into bed. She rolled over to the side that Nick had slept on, and drank in his smell. Whatever had gone tonight with Julian didn't compare to the glorious mix of emotions she felt when she thought of Nick.

AFTER A RESTLESS NIGHT'S sleep, Sylvie dragged herself out of bed. It was five thirty. She checked herself in the mirror and shook her head. She looked tired.

After brushing her teeth, she slipped on her costume and padded downstairs. She needed to clear her head, and the only way she knew how was to swim. She opened up the French doors that lead out to the pool. The air was fresh and she took a deep breath. Her lungs filled up and she was already feeling better. She stood by the water's edge and dove into the clear, cool water. The water seemed to soothe her as she began to swim up and down the pool. After her twenty lengths she pulled herself out and sat on the edge, gently kicking the water.

She focused on what had happened last night. What exactly did she feel? She thought about Julian and how vulnerable he looked, and she felt a pang of guilt. She hoped she hadn't given him the wrong impression, led him on in any way. He was special to her, that was something she was sure of, but in the cold light of day she realised that her feelings for him paled in comparison to the intense feelings she had for Nick.

Pleased to have found her resolve, she made her way back to the house.

By seven thirty Markus was pulling up the driveway. He made his way into the kitchen and immediately opened the fridge.

"Morning Markus, can I get you anything?" Marcy was coming in from the garden with a handful of roses that she had cut.

"Hi Marcy. Um… I'm not sure, is Mum up yet?"

"Yes, she's just showering. She'll be down in a bit. Have you any clothes to be washed?"

"Yes, I put them in the laundry room. I'll wait for her, then, and we can have breakfast together."

Marcy smiled as she headed to the laundry room. She loved having him home. Markus slouched on the sofa and flicked on the TV.

"Markus. Is that you?" Sylvie was skipping down the stairs.

"In here, Mum."

Sylvie walked into the lounge and hurriedly sat next to him, squeezing him tightly. "Oh, it's so good to see you." She planted kisses on his cheeks. Markus smirked and squeezed her back. "Hungry?" She knew the answer before he replied.

"Starving! What shall we have?"

"French toast?" suggested Sylvie.

"With bacon and scrambled eggs. Maple syrup?" Markus squeezed his Mum and she laughed. Where did he put it all! He was the best distraction. Thank goodness he was here.

They both sat at the breakfast bar eating their huge feast that they had prepared together as Marcy fussed over them.

"So what do fancy doing today? I'm not going into work so we can spend the day together, if you like." Sylvie added, sometimes she forgot that her boys might actually want to do things without her tagging along.

"I need to get myself a new kite board for over the summer. My old one is wrecked. And then maybe lunch? I wanted to see Thea Miria too, so we could get her to come with us."

"Sounds like a plan. You can ring her and we can meet her down at the marina for lunch. Around one?"

Markus nodded as he carried on shovelling toast into his mouth. He must have been on his sixth slice!

Sylvie sipped her tea and shook her head. Her train of thought was interrupted by her phone. Her stomach contracted, knowing full well who it was. Well, there was no putting it off. She reached over for it and answered it.

"Morning, Julian." She tried to sound chirpy. She felt Marcy smile and start busying herself. Oh, she wished she wouldn't do that. She had really got the wrong end of the stick. She glared at her.

"Morning." He paused, and then added, "How are you?"

"I'm fine Julian, especially since Markus is here." Hopefully he would get the message that she couldn't discuss last night. "We're just making our plans for today."

"Oh I see, I just wanted to make sure… Well, we can talk later." She could hear him sigh, and she felt a pang of guilt again. This had been hard for him, and she wasn't making it easier. "So, what are you planning?" He changed his tone and tried to sound as upbeat as possible.

"We're going to get Markus a new kite board and then meet up with my aunt for lunch."

"Kite board? Nick sells those. You should pass by his shop, I know he's had a new shipment of them in time for the summer." Sylvie swallowed and forced a grin. Crap, now she'd have to pass by Nick's shop with Markus. She couldn't very well go to another shop after he'd suggested it.

"Oh, I didn't realise he sold that sort of thing too." Markus looked over to Sylvie realising that it was something to do with his impending purchase.

"Yes, he has all water sports equipment. I don't think he'll be there though this morning. He stayed over at Maggie's last night. But his manager will be, Christian. He's very good, knows his stuff."

She felt herself relax. Well, that wouldn't be so bad then.

"Okay, thanks for that; we'll definitely pass by. I'll speak to you later then."

"Sure, have a great day… Call me later if you can."

Oh no, he was back to being the vulnerable Julian.

"I will, bye." Sylvie put down her phone and looked up at Markus, who was watching her.

"So what was that about?" He sat back on his stool.

"Julian's son Nick has a shop that sells water sports stuff. He suggested we should go there."

"Cool. And the other thing?" Markus raised his eyebrows. Sylvie's eyes flitted away from his grinning face.

"Other thing?"

"Oh come on, Mum. He's got it bad. You tensed up when he spoke to you. He's always had a thing for you. Why would he ring you up and just ask how you are?"

Marcy crashed around in the sink behind them and Sylvie scowled.

"We work together and he's a friend Markus, that's all," she said adamantly.

"Yeah, yeah. Whatever. But he does like you, Mum, and that's okay, you know. Don't get all defensive. You should have someone in your life. You must get lonely. You and Dad did everything together and now, well, you just seem to work a lot and wait for me and Alex. I'm just saying… Well, I'd be okay with it."

Sylvie's face softened. He really was a good boy, so thoughtful.

"Thanks Markus." She hugged him.

"Not sure about Alex though," smirked Markus. Sylvie stiffened.

"What do you mean?"

"Well, he's a little less laid back than I am."

"How so?" Sylvie sat back down, waiting to hear this new revelation.

"Oh I know he's very calm and serious and that, but you know, Mum; he's a bit of a 'bad ass'."

Sylvie frowned in disbelief, surely not! Her sweet Alex, her gentle giant?

"Ask Marcy. A couple of years back we were out clubbing with Teresa and she was with this guy she knew. Alex got all defensive and nearly battered him."

"Alex nearly got into fight? I don't believe it." Sylvie shook her head.

"Honest Mum, he's really protective over people. Thank God Teresa explained that he was her boyfriend. He just sees red. Not so tolerant. But I think he likes Julian, so maybe he won't freak out."

Sylvie's heart sank. Well she'd have to deal with that when the time came.

"Anyway, enough about that. Go get yourself ready and ring Thea Miria. Marcy, can you get my suitcase out? I'm going to be packing it later on the evening."

"Of course."

JULIAN PUT DOWN HIS phone and sighed deeply; he wasn't going to get to speak to her before she left. He knew she would try to avoid him. He looked at the clock and then picked up his phone to call Nick. His phone was off, so he dialled up Maggie.

"Hi Julian." Her voice was relaxed and soothing, as always.

"Hi Mags, how are you?"

"Fine, just looking at the albums again. I didn't get to see them yesterday."

"Is Nick still at yours? His phone's off."

"Yes. I just heard him get up. He sat up 'til late with Vicki and had a bit to drink. To be honest, I think he's a little hung over."

"It's eleven. I take it he won't be going to the shop this morning?"

"I'm not sure. I have a feeling he's a little preoccupied these days."

"What do you mean, preoccupied?"

"He's got himself a girlfriend, and you know what he's like."

"A girlfriend? When did this happen?"

"Not sure, really. He seems pretty taken with her, though."

"You've met her?" Julian was a little put out.

"Oh no, I just guessed he was seeing someone and I asked him. He's keeping it very low profile, with us, I mean. Well, in the light of what happened before I can't blame him. But I think it's serious."

"Really? Can you get him to call me when he's up? I wanted to see him tonight before he leaves tomorrow."

"Of course. Hang on a minute, I think he's coming down the stairs." Julian held on the line. "Nick, Dad's on the line. He wants a word."

"Hi Dad," croaked Nick.

"Are you alright. You sound terrible."

"I'm fine. I think I overdid it a bit last night."

"Are you up for a visit from your old man tonight? I'd like to see you before you leave."

Nick ran his hands through his hair nervously. He wasn't sure he was up to it and he also didn't know what Sylvie's plans were.

"Unless you have other plans." Julian added.

"No that's fine, I'll be in. You don't mind coming to mine, though? I'll be packing."

"Great. Around seven then? Also, can you let Christian know that Sylvie will be down at your shop this morning? Her son Markus needs a new kite board so I told her to go to yours."

Nick took a split second to register what his father had just said. Firstly, how did he know? They'd obviously spoken. Secondly, it meant that he could also get to see her, even if it was with her son.

"Yes, sure Dad. I'll make sure she's looked after." His voice was strained. "When are they going?"

"I just spoke to her now, so soon."

"Okay I'll ring him now. Bye Dad."

Before Julian could reply he'd hung up. He sped up the stairs and jumped into the shower. He really hoped he'd catch her before she left. He hurriedly dressed and checked his phone. Crap! It was dead. He couldn't even ring her to tell her to hang on. He sprinted down the stairs as Maggie emerged from the kitchen. He kissed her goodbye and jumped into his Jeep. She stared after him in total shock. What on earth had got into him? Nick headed down to the marina trying desperately to keep within the speed limit.

CHAPTER 21

SHOPPING

T he marina was buzzing as Sylvie and Markus pulled into the car park. They made their way to Nick's shop and entered. Sylvie felt less anxious as she knew Nick wouldn't be there and he hadn't called her, so he was probably still at Maggie's. Christian was just finishing up with a customer as they closed the door behind them.

"Morning," he greeted them. It took him a second to register who she was then. "Oh, it's you, Mrs Sapphiris. How are you? What can I help you with?"

"Hi. Christian? That's right isn't it? Please, call me Sylvie." Christian nodded. "It's Markus actually, my son. He's looking for a new kite board." Sylvie spoke as though she was unsure of the correct terminology.

"Hi." Markus held out his hand and Christian shook it. "You've got some amazing boards here." Markus motioned to the selection on display.

"Yeah, Nick likes to have whatever's available stocked. We've got more in the back store. Do you want to have a look at them?" Markus turned to his Mum and she waved him on to go.

"I'll wait here, you go." She stood in the shop, looking round as she could hear them discussing style and weight. It was all totally alien to her, a different language. She moved around the shop to where the water skis and body boards were displayed.

She felt him come up behind her before he even spoke.

"Can I show you something?"

Nick's voice was laced with menacing humour, and made Sylvie catch her breath. He gently put his hand on her shoulder and Sylvie turned around to look at him. Nick's eyes were blazing red hot.

"I didn't think you were here." She held his gaze, trying to assess what was going through his mind. He was making her feel nervous and weak at the same time, her pulse raced especially as she knew Markus was only a few metres away.

"I just came now." His hand reached up to her cheek and before she could comment he pulled her close, holding her by the face and kissed her almost violently. Sylvie could only surrender as he pushed her deeper into the shop, around the back of the display where no one could see them.

His hand travelled down her body, and he grasped her behind and wrenched her up against him, all the while kissing her. Her hands grabbed his soft, untidy hair and she moaned. *Wow, he was always so intense.* He pulled away from her to catch his breath.

"Christ, Sylvie. I can't take this. I'm a wreck. I was so mad yesterday. I'm imagining the worst, Sylvie. You're being so evasive and I'm worried, worried that you're having second thoughts. You won't talk to me."

Sylvie took a second to catch her breath. "Nick, please," she pleaded. "I can't treat your father badly. He needs to understand how I feel and I want to let him down gently. I can't talk to you about this, it feels like I'm betraying his trust, and above everything else it's not fair on him or you. I need to be respectful of his feelings. He's my friend, remember that. I know this isn't ideal, but in twenty four hours we'll be together."

"Twenty four hours of hell, then heaven," he whispered into her ear. Sylvie heard Markus and Christian coming back through.

Nick bent down and kissed her quickly on the lips, then casually sauntered back around into the shop. How could he be so cool? Sylvie smoothed down her skirt and followed, hoping her mouth wasn't red from Nick's violent onslaught.

"Nick? I thought you weren't coming in." Christian looked at his boss in surprise.

Part Three – Spring

"I had a change of heart," he mused. "Hi. Markus right? Did you find what you were looking for?" He held out his hand and Markus shook it.

Sylvie slowly walked up to where they were standing and watched their exchange. But her flushed appearance didn't go unnoticed by Christian. His eyes passed between her and Nick.

"Yeah I picked one of the ones in the back. Your shop's sick! I've never seen so many designs. I'll be sure to get all my friends to come by. You've got the best selection I've ever seen." Markus was obviously impressed.

"Thanks. Which beach do you go to?"

"Down at Currium. The wind picks up there in the afternoon."

"Yes, it's one of my favourite spots down there too."

"You kite board, then?"

"Uh huh, I love all water sports."

Sylvie watched them as they carried on talking about their love of all things extreme. Her phone rang and it prompted them to stop their conversation.

"Hi Thea, you're already at Stathis's? Okay, order some wine and we'll be there in a minute... Stathis knows which one we like." She put away her phone. "Well, we'd better get going, Markus."

"Sure. I'll just settle up with Christian." He was clearly disappointed to break off his conversation.

"No!" Nick almost shouted, then checked himself and added, "Err... It's okay Markus. I'll sort it out with Sylvie. Don't take any money, Christian, and I'll get it delivered up to the house over the weekend. I don't think it'll fit in your Mum's car."

Sylvie was about to protest, but Nick put his hand up as a signal for her to stop. She didn't want to argue in front of Markus, so she let it go. Nick looked at the time. "Are you off to lunch?" He directed his question to Christian.

"Yes, in about ten minutes."

Nick nodded.

"Thanks Nick, really. You've been great. What are you up to now?" Markus inquired, wanting to carry on their conversation.

"Just some paperwork I need to catch up on."

"Oh, I was going to tell you to come with us for lunch, what do you say, Mum?"

Sylvie's eyes widened and she tried to look relaxed as she replied. "That would be lovely, but I'm sure Nick's probably very busy and we've already taken up too much of his time." She headed to the door, hoping her flushed face wasn't too obvious.

"Actually, I'd love to join you. I was going to grab a sandwich now anyway, if that's alright?"

Sylvie swallowed hard and smiled over to where Markus and Nick were standing. Christian stood, stock still and wide-eyed as he witnessed their exchange.

"Well, of course it is." Nick's eyes were mischievously glowing and she realised that he was enjoying seeing her squirm.

"Great. I'll meet you there in five minutes. I just need to sort out a few things here." He motioned to Christian, who was staring at Nick.

Markus grinned and joined his Mum as she headed out of the shop. Once he was sure they were out of earshot, he whispered, "You didn't mind Mum, did you? At least I'll have someone to talk sports with." He linked his arm into his Mum's.

"No, not at all." She hoped her voice didn't betray her as she tried desperately to sound nonchalant.

Nick watched them as they left, then turned to Christian who was still staring at him, almost open-mouthed.

"What?" Nick eyed Christian warily.

"You're kidding, right? I'm not an idiot. You've got the hots for your Dad's girlfriend?"

"She's just his friend," he replied, tight–lipped; emphasizing the word 'just'.

Christian looked at Nick as his face went through a myriad of emotions, and it began to dawn on him that he wasn't even close.

"Holy shit, Nick, you're seeing her? Jesus... this is... Oh my God! Does anyone know?"

Nick took a deep breath and shook his head.

"How long? What does it matter." He was talking to himself now. "Is it serious? What am I saying? Of course it's serious, it's you!" He stepped back and slumped in a chair, trying to absorb the information. Nick stood very still and watched as his friend started to evaluate the information.

"You know this is fucked up, don't you? Sorry, but it is. I hope you know what you're doing. Your Dad will flip."

Nick closed his eyes and tried hard to not to lash out in his defence. He knew Christian was only speaking the truth, he was only saying what everyone else would say, and it gave him an insight into the reaction he knew he was going to get.

"Just be careful, Nick. I really don't think I could go through what we all went through last time."

Nick clenched his teeth and reached for his first stick of chewing gum today. "This stays between you and me, right?" He knew that it wasn't necessary to ask, but he needed confirmation all the same.

"Of course man, not a word." Christian made a cross against his chest to confirm it.

Nick turned and stalked out of the shop and walked in the direction of Stathis's. As Nick approached the restaurant he could see Sylvie and Markus sitting with an older lady he recognised from the last time he'd bumped into Sylvie. They were talking animatedly and Nick enjoyed watching Sylvie, obviously relaxed, with her family. Her eye caught him and she waved to him. Within a few seconds he was by the table.

"Thea, you remember Nick?" Sylvie introduced Thea Miria to Nick, and they shook hands.

"Of course I remember Nick; I never forget a good looking man. How's that handsome father of yours? I haven't seen him for a while." Markus shook his head in disbelief and Sylvie squirmed.

"He's very well. I'll let him know you've been inquiring after him," Nick replied, taking a seat between Sylvie and Thea Miria.

"If I was twenty years younger, he wouldn't stand a chance!" Thea Miria mused.

Markus nearly choked on his beer and Sylvie patted his back.

"Thea!" chastised Sylvie.

"What? I'm in my sixties; I'm not dead, you know. Or maybe age doesn't matter to him."

"Oh my God, Thea! I can't believe you just said that." Her eyes focused onto Nick, who was laughing.

"I swear you're so uptight sometimes. Don't you watch 'E'; all the women are doing it. Demi Moore, Jennifer Aniston, Jennifer Lopez. They all have younger men, much younger men!"

"I'd do Jennifer Lopez any day!" Markus reflected as he took a swig from his beer. "What do you think, Nick?"

This time, Sylvie nearly choked.

"Jennifer Lopez?" he nodded, as though he would contemplate it, and let his eyes drift to Sylvie, who sat wide-eyed. "I think that age is a state of mind; I'm with you on this. My father seems to enjoy the company of young women though. However, he might be persuaded otherwise." Nick arched his eyebrows and laughed.

Sylvie shook her head in total disbelief.

"Well they keep saying that forty is the new thirty, and fifty is the new forty," Thea Miria said. "So by my reckoning that makes me about fifty five. So I'm not that far off, am I? Your father's in his early fifties, right? I wouldn't mind being a cougar." Thea Miria squinted and rubbed her lower lip.

"Can we please change the subject? I think we should have warned you about our topics of conversations. Thea Miria has an uncanny knack for touching on subjects with the delicacy of a sledgehammer." Sylvie smirked embarrassedly.

"I just don't like to pussyfoot around. When you get to my age, time is very precious."

Nick was resting back in his chair, revelling in the unusual dynamic he was witnessing. He loved their total honesty and how, even though they were of different generations, they were able to interact so comfortably.

"So you live on a yacht, if I remember correctly? Sylvie loves boats. You should take her out on it. My nephew hated them and she never got to go out on one."

Sylvie dropped her eyes and searched for her rings. *Oh God, she hoped Thea Miria hadn't clicked on!*

"Well, we'll have to see if we can get that organised." Nick smiled, as cool as anything, and looked over to Sylvie. His eyes rested a moment too long before he allowed his gaze to return to Thea Miria.

She returned his smile and nodded before she turned to Markus. "Markus, I've set up my Facebook account, but I really need you to show me how to put pictures on it. I've already got around fifty friends. It's truly an amazing invention. Some of my students who moved to China have got in touch. It's so addictive though. I never seem to get off it."

"I know, you can link it up to your mobile too, so you can check out stuff when you're out," Markus explained. "I'll show you next time I'm out. Alex will be back too, so he can show you if I'm not around.

"Hey Thea, what do Chinese people call Chinese food?"

Thea Miria frowned not understanding where this was going.

"They just call it food!" He laughed loudly as Sylvie giggled, and Thea Miria cringed.

"That was appalling, Markus." She shook her head in mock disgust. Nick chuckled, thoroughly enjoying their interaction.

"When's Alex home?" Thea Miria turned to Sylvie.

"Next Saturday. Then the house will feel full again."

"When do finish your national service, Markus?" Nick sat forward and picked up the menu as he asked.

"Next week, and then we get discharged. I really can't believe it's over."

"I know, I was lucky and only did six months."

Everyone looked over to him in shock.

"You did national service here? How's that? You're not a Cypriot, are you?"

Nick smiled. "I was born and brought up here. This is my home; I only thought it right for me to do it. It wasn't so bad. I got to shoot guns and drive tanks. That was fun. It also means I can have citizenship."

"Good for you." Thea Miria patted his arm.

Sylvie picked up her menu and scanned it in a feeble attempt not to continue staring at him. He was full of surprises. He looked stunning in his faded jeans and light blue t-shirt that made his eyes pop. She wasn't really that hungry.

"What are you going to order?" Thea Miria reached into her bag to retrieve her glasses.

"I think a salad. Seafood. You?"

"The same. It was lovely last time. Markus, what will you have?"

"I think I'll have the T-bone steak with a side order of stuffed squid."

Sylvie shook her head. Where did he put it?

"That sounds good. I think I'll have the same." Nick put down the menu and grinned.

They sat and enjoyed their meal, and spent the best part of the afternoon leisurely talking about a multitude of topics, Thea Miria being the catalyst.

She managed to find out that Nick not only loved to sail, but he could water ski, windsurf and hand glide. He enjoyed skiing in the winter months too as well as snowboarding.

Markus was totally fascinated; he'd always been a thrill junkie. Nick tentatively asked questions about them all in an attempt to learn all he could about the people who Sylvie so obviously adored. He built an excellent rapport with Markus, mainly due to their similar interests. He watched Markus periodically pick food out of Sylvie's plate. She didn't seem to mind. In fact, it looked like it was some kind of family ritual.

Thea Miria filled in a few blanks about Chris. He sensed that there was something unsaid even though she spoke of him fondly. Sylvie's expression changed when her aunt spoke of him. He couldn't quite tell if it was sadness or that she was feeling uneasy talking about her late husband. What Nick did find strange was that Sylvie fell silent when Chris was mentioned. She didn't seem to have anything to say.

Markus swiftly moved on to the subject of Alex and how he couldn't wait for him to be home, and Sylvie's eyes immediately lit back up at the mention of her eldest son. He sounded like a very kind, strong and protective man, and Nick hoped he would be able to get to know him before Sylvie and he came public with their relationship.

Before long it was time to go. Nick got up and approached the waiter, then reached into his back pocket and handed over his credit card. Sylvie immediately shot up ready to protest. Thea Miria took hold of her hand and shook her head.

"Don't. He obviously wants to pay. He's being gallant, a quality that seems to be lost these days, especially on the young." Sylvie sat back down slowly and smiled slightly at her aunt. Nick came back to the table to say his goodbyes. Markus thrust out his hand to shake Nick's and Nick took it.

"I might get to see more of you when I'm discharged. Down at Currium, maybe?" Markus couldn't hide his enthusiasm.

"I'd like that." He then turned to Thea Miria, who was still sitting. He held out his hand and she elegantly placed hers in his. "It was a real pleasure to see you again. I hope to see you again soon." He spoke softly to her and looked down at her through his lashes.

"I hope so, too. Thank you for lunch; that was very kind of you. Please give my regards to your father." She smiled wryly, and Nick gave her a knowing wink. He then straightened and walked over to where Sylvie was. Thea Miria hastily rose and grabbed Markus, ushering him towards the car park on some pretence that she needed him to look at the tires on her car. Nick stood a few inches away from Sylvie, invading her space like he always did.

"Thanks for lunch. You really shouldn't have." Nick shrugged, showing her that he wanted to and that it really wasn't a big deal. She rubbed her finger nervously. "Well I'd better get off. We'll talk later. Don't think I've forgotten about what went down at your shop." He looked at her, confused. "I need to pay you for the kite board."

He caught hold of her hands to stop her rubbing it and leaned into her to kiss her cheek. "I thought you meant the other thing that happened in my shop." His voice was smooth and sultry as he grazed her ear with his nose. Sylvie felt her whole body heat up. He pulled back, smiling seductively, and looked at his watch. "Twenty hours of hell… then heaven. I'll call you later."

Sylvie could only nod as she desperately tried to calm her racing heart. He turned away and walked off towards his shop.

Sylvie picked up her bag and quickly scanned the car park for Markus and Thea Miria. She hoped they hadn't seen her all flustered; Markus might be a little unaware, but her aunt wouldn't miss a trick. She saw them, Markus bent down looking at her rear tires and her aunt leaning on the open door of her car. She hastily walked up to them as Markus rose.

"They look fine to me, Thea." He clapped his hands together in an attempt to clean off the dust. "They'll need changing after the summer."

"Oh, here's your Mum. I'll be off then. When do you get back from Athens?" Thea Miria asked.

"Tuesday, late."

"Well, have a good time; you deserve it. You've started looking like your old self again." She hugged Sylvie and kissed her lovingly. "I had a lovely lunch with great company." Sylvie felt herself flush a little. "That Nick is something, eh? His eyes are unforgettable."

"Thea! He's old enough to be your grandson," cried Markus.

"Like I said, I'm in my sixties, I'm not dead! I can express my appreciation," she joked back, and then allowed her eyes to hold Sylvie's gaze. She patted her arm and got into her car and sped off like a woman twenty years younger than she was.

Markus went to get into the passenger side of Sylvie's car when Sylvie stopped him.

"You drive darling. You've never driven this car, and to be honest I've had too much wine to drive. You only had a beer."

Markus couldn't contain his glee. He slipped into the driver's seat and then put down the top. He expertly drove it out of the marina and onto the road that ran parallel to the beach. Sylvie sat back into her seat and allowed herself to daydream about Nick and how, in less than twenty-four hours, they'd finally be together.

Twenty hours of hell and counting!

NICK MADE HIS WAY back to the *Silver Lining*; he wanted to be packed before Julian came round. Thank goodness he'd called him. At least he'd seen Sylvie. He let his mind drift to their lunch as he hauled out his holdall and started folding various items of clothing. He really liked Markus, he reminded him of himself at that age. Full of enthusiasm, and open-hearted. He sometimes wished he was still like that. He'd become a lot harder over the last ten years' he knew that he was to blame for that. But circumstances had caused him to be more wary and cynical. He'd had his heart broken twice, and he was fearful of it happening again.

He felt that he had an ally in Thea Miria too. She was a perceptive woman and her comments and conversation direction did not go unnoticed by Nick. He was sure she was testing the water, trying to assess what was going on. He had a strong feeling that she suspected the truth.

It had been an eye-opener hearing them discuss Chris, too. Nick had always wanted to hear about him but couldn't very well ask anyone. The only people that knew him were his father, who he could definitely not ask, and of course Sylvie. He didn't think it was appropriate for him to quiz her on her recently deceased husband. Surely it was still a little raw. What did his father say? 'You couldn't compete with a dead man.' He really didn't realise how much gravity that phrase had. He saw how Sylvie reacted as they talked about him. In fact, she'd hardly said a word and she rubbed her finger as she always did when she was nervous.

Nick picked up the aqua halter top that she'd left there the day they went to the cove, carefully folded the freshly-laundered garment, and put it in his open case.

"Anybody home?" Nick's thoughts were interrupted with Julian making his way down the stairs.

"Hi Dad. I was miles away, just putting the last of my stuff in the case. Won't be long."

Julian popped his head in to Nick's bedroom and smiled.

"Shall I get you a beer?"

"Sure, Dad." A few minutes later he re-emerged holding two beers, offering one to Nick.

"Just put it on the side, Dad. I just need to get some stuff from the bathroom." Julian placed it on the bedside table as Nick went into the bathroom. Julian scanned the room as he took a drink of his beer.

His eyes came to rest on the open case where he spotted the silky halter top and his brow furrowed. Maybe Nick was going with his new, mystery girlfriend. Nick came out of the bathroom carrying a wash bag that seemed to be bursting with products. Julian smirked and Nick shrugged as a form of apology.

"So, this trip. Business or pleasure?"

Nick busied himself with his suitcase. "Business. I'm sourcing a yacht for a client." Nick discreetly covered Sylvie's top with a pair of trousers. The gesture was not lost on Julian. He averted his eyes understanding that Nick didn't want to tell him more.

"Did you sort out Sylvie's son out with a kite board?" Julian asked, changing the subject.

"Yes, he came by and Christian sorted him out. He's a good kid, loves his extreme sports."

"Oh, you were there then? I thought you weren't going down."

"Yes, I went down in the end. I had some work to finish off before I go off tomorrow." Nick started to feel himself get increasingly uneasy. He really had to get off this subject. "You hungry Dad, fancy some dinner?"

"Not really. I can't stay long, I just wanted to see you before you got off." There was an awkward silence, and Julian contemplated asking him about his girlfriend. Nick flipped the lid of the case shut and picked up his beer.

"Let's go on deck and I'll get some nuts or something."
Julian nodded in agreement and followed him into the lounge
area. Nick slipped behind the counter in the galley and pulled
out some nuts and olives.

"That's okay Nick, really. Don't bother. It was just a flying
visit. I'll finish this and let you get yourself together. Do you
need a lift to the airport?"

"No Dad, I'll be leaving my car at the airport. Thanks,
though." Nick grabbed a handful of nuts and wolfed them
down from sheer nervousness. Julian drained his beer and put
the empty bottle down on the counter.

"Well, I hope your trip is a success son. You seem to be a
little preoccupied. I'm sure everything will go well for you.
I'm very proud of you, you know that right?"

"Thanks, Dad." Nick felt terrible as he looked at his father,
whom he loved dearly. He might not be so proud of him if he
knew. Julian hugged Nick goodbye.

"If you ever need to talk things out, I'm here for you. Have
a safe trip, Nick."

Nick strained a smile and waited for him to leave. He
gripped the counter, allowing the feeling of utter despair
consume him, and in a swift movement sent the bowl of nuts
and olives flying across the galley.

SYLVIE STOOD IN HER dressing room, looking at her racks
of clothes in total despair. What was she going to pack? She
was useless at packing; she always took far too much with her.
It was always a sticking point with Chris whenever they went
away. He'd constantly grumble about the weight of her suitcase
and the volume of clothes, accessories and shoes that she
insisted she needed.

Sylvie huffed. Ah, yes. The shoes. Her eyes scanned the
racks of footwear to her left. Shaking her head, she tried hard
to rid herself of thoughts of the past. She looked back at her
clothes and pulled out her favourite cobalt blue jumpsuit and
smiled to herself. She hadn't worn it for ages. Hugging her
jumpsuit, she padded through to the bedroom where her

suitcase lay open on her bed. Sylvie carefully laid it on top of the few items she'd already packed.

Well, the past was the past, she thought to herself. It was time to focus on her future. That very thought made her giddy and she grinned.

She still couldn't believe she was going away for four whole days with Nick. It felt like a dream, as though she was living someone else's life. Her stomach clenched from both excitement and anxiety just thinking about him.

Tomorrow couldn't come fast enough. She knew this was a huge step for them; make or break. She took a deep breath.

One way or another, this weekend was going to change her life.

After this weekend, she needed to make life changing decisions. Decisions that would affect not only her, but also the people she loved in her life.

Tomorrow wasn't just about her and Nick; there was so much more at stake. She allowed herself to dream an impossible dream, just for a moment. That everything would fall into place and tomorrow could be the beginning of an unbelievable new future, a future she'd longed for with all her heart. A future she'd always been waiting for.

Glossary

Throughout *Waiting for Summer*, there are certain traditions and facts that are specific to Cyprus. These are listed below.

In Greek Orthodox weddings, the groom waits for his bride to arrive outside the church along with the rest of the guests. The groom gives his bride her bouquet before they go into the church.

Greek words used, and their translations
Thea – Auntie
Ya mas – Cheers, to our good health

Abbreviations
MILF – Mother I'd Like to Fuck

WAITING FOR SUMMER

BOOK TWO

"Moving, emotional and absorbing. An uplifting story that will make you believe the impossible is possible"

Excited yet apprehensive Sylvie embarks on her planned trip to Athens with Nick. A city which holds bittersweet memories. Can Sylvie shake off her past and move into a new future with this incredible man? This young man who made her feel so totally and completely loved. A new beginning she deserved.

While in their sanctuary, away from family and friends, Sylvie starts to believe that she and Nick can actually have a future together. A future she always dreamed of.

But once they return back home to Cyprus, it soon becomes clear that their love affair has too many obstacles, forcing Sylvie to make one of the hardest decisions of her life.

Sylvie's world is turned upside down again. Distraught and devastated she's left wondering if she'll ever find true love and happiness again. A love she once thought was possible. The love she'd always been waiting for.